CW00326408

WOUNDS OF WAR

COM	DIA	BRE	BAG	H/L	MAR
	2600				
BRE	BRI	EDG	HET	RED	WOO
ADS	BRA	CH	CHU	GAT	HEG
CL	CB	CR			SS

WOUNDS OF WAR

Margaret Thomson Davis

C

CENTURY

LONDON   SYDNEY   AUCKLAND   JOHANNESBURG

First published in 1989 by Century Hutchinson Ltd

This edition published in 1995 by Century Ltd,
Random House, 20 Vauxhall Bridge Road, London SW1V 2SA

Random House Australia (Pty) Limited
20 Alfred Street, Milsons Point, Sydney,
New South Wales 2061, Australia

Random House New Zealand Limited
18 Poland Road, Glenfield,
Auckland 10, New Zealand

Random House South Africa (Pty) Limited
PO Box 337, Bergvlei, South Africa

Random House UK Limited Reg. No. 954009

ISBN 0 7126 2586 0

Papers used by Random House UK Ltd are natural,
recyclable products made from wood grown in sustainable forests.
The manufacturing processes conform to the environmental
regulations of the country of origin.

Printed and bound in Great Britain by
Athenaeum Press Ltd, Gateshead, Tyne & Wear

This book is dedicated in admiration to my American friends, and all those courageous Americans, young and old, black and white, who each in their own way, have struggled to make freedom and justice a reality.

'Free at last. Free at last.
Thank God almighty, I am free at last.'

Words on the tomb of the Reverend Martin Luther King.

1

Over the years Jenny Thornton had become afraid of her husband. Watching for him, her grey eyes strained worriedly up from the window of the basement flat. All she could see was a forest of half-legs, trouser bottoms and skirts of raincoats flurrying in the wind. Puddles spurted shadows from car wheels to darken the musty gloom. It was impossible to make out anything else – except the ghost of her own reflection on the glass; the haunted look in the eyes, the wide sensuous mouth, the hair curling round the face like a soft cloud.

Had she thought about it she would have realized that although she was not conventionally beautiful there was a subtly erotic quality about her that was disturbing. She was uninterested in and oblivious to anything about herself, however, so obsessed was she with thoughts of Joe. He had become such a distorting shadow over her life.

The Glasgow flat where they'd lived since the first days of their marriage was at the corner of Victoria Road and Queens Drive and she hated it – especially when it was raining. On a hot summer's day its earthy smell, redolent with the perfume of a magnolia tree, had a soporific seduction. In winter it filled the nostrils with the cloying odour of decay. It was like being buried alive. Joe liked it. He even refused to cut down the overhanging trees on the Victoria Road side although they cast a black cloak over the sitting room and made it necessary, despite the colourful decor, to keep the light on all the time. At least the kitchen window on Queens Drive was not totally eclipsed. She turned back to the table with its red and white checked cover and blue willow-patterned dishes and began straightening the cutlery.

The children were late too. Their lateness gave a rawness to her anxiety that left every nerve end exposed. She thought she heard someone tap on the window and the noise made her jump with fright. But it was only a loose branch blowing in the wind.

Joe loved trees. She sometimes felt he thought more of trees and plants and everything to do with his job across the road in the park than he did of his wife and family. He even brought greenery into the house, its lush tendrils climbing, clinging, cleaving. It wasn't as if he was a country boy either. He had been brought up, like her, in a Glasgow tenement over the other side of the River Clyde in Anderston. She and Joe had grown up together. At 36 he was six years older than her. In those far-off days in Anderston that age difference then seemed enormous. She had adored him. He had been like a golden-haired god to her. She had been like the 'Lillibeth' in Richmal Crompton's *Just William* stories, always hanging about Joe and his pals. At 5 years of age she had already made up her mind that she was going to marry him. At 16, still with nut-brown Shirley Temple curls and round, eager eyes, still little more than a child, her wish had come true.

Instead of living happily ever after as she had expected, however, the dream turned into a nightmare. They had been married after Joe had returned from being a prisoner of war in Japan. Not right away because he had been in hospital for a time, then at a rehabilitation place. But they had got together as soon as they could. Everything was wonderful at first. At least, she'd thought it was. She had been so deliriously happy and excited she had hardly noticed any difference in him. He had always been thin and now there was a gaunt look about him. There was an aura of quietness, too. But he still had the same warm smile she remembered, his hair was still a deep golden colour, his eyes were the same startling blue. She wasn't a bit surprised to hear that he'd kept escaping from captivity during the war. So

2

many men never survived Changi Jail and work on what had become known as 'Death Railway'. Or lasted long in the jungle if they escaped. She knew her Joe – although tall and gangly, he had a wiry toughness.

On their honeymoon he had made love to her with such an urgency and desperation there was a kind of madness about it. He still did but it frightened her more than thrilled her now. He had always refused to talk about the nightmares, the shouting in his sleep, the malaria-like attacks which tests had proved were not malaria. Admittedly these distressing symptoms had decreased over the years and only happened very occasionally now. But there were other things that had become worse.

'Can I go to the pictures, Mum?' Rose flung her school bag on to one of the spar-backed chairs and flopped down on to another.

'You're hardly over the door,' Jenny said. 'And what about your homework?'

'There's all weekend, Mum.'

'It never gets done if it gets put off.'

'Oh, all right, I'll go to my room and do it now.'

'Where's Dode?'

'Across in the café with his pals, I think.'

'He'll ruin his appetite for his dinner.'

'*Can* I go to the pictures, Mum?'

Jenny hesitated, her eyes fixed helplessly on Rose's vulnerable young face. I looked just like her at twelve, she thought, only my hair was dark brown and curly not straight and black like hers.

'Oh, all right,' she capitulated. 'I suppose you'll be expecting me to fork out the money as well. I'm not made of it, you know.' She fumbled in her purse. Today it wouldn't do for Joe to see her. 'Don't tell your daddy, remember.'

'Of course not! Thanks, Mum.' Rose flung her arms round her neck before disappearing through to her room.

3

'Mrs Donovan let me bring home what was left of yesterday's baking,' Jenny called after her. But Rose's eager haste to avoid her father had first priority. This was Friday and they all knew what that could mean.

Jenny often thanked God for her own boltholes. She had two – one at Amelia Donovan's and another at Mrs Hazel Saunders'. She worked part time in both places – from 9 a.m. until 12 noon at Mrs Saunders' and from 12.30 till 3.30 at Amelia's. Amelia and her husband Douglas lived further along Queens Drive in Queens Gushet, a piece of land jutting out between where Langside Road began to run alongside the park and Queens Drive forked off to the left. 'Mary House' their place was called. The name Mary came from the fact that the area of the park was where Mary, Queen of Scots fought her last battle. Most of the streets and squares in the district had some association with the tragic Queen. Except of course Victoria Road.

Douglas's mother had bought 'Mary House' for her son and paid Jenny to do a bit of cooking and cleaning so that he wouldn't be neglected.

'It's not that my daughter-in-law means any harm, Jenny,' Rory Donovan told her when she first engaged her, 'but she lives in her make-believe world so much she's liable to forget her husband and son exist.'

Mrs Donovan was the owner of 'Rory's' department stores, two of the largest in Glasgow. She had acquired a big shop in Edinburgh as well and, although all the shops were managed by her brothers, Rory was still very much the boss as far as Jenny could make out. She couldn't help admiring her. A real spunky type with a great sense of humour and full of beans despite being on the wrong side of 50.

Jenny felt sorry for Amelia. She was about the same age as herself, a gentle, friendly soul whose health wasn't too robust. She suspected Amelia didn't have much of a life between the mother and the son. But maybe there was more to her than met the eye, judging by the steamy books she wrote.

'If only I could make more money with my books, Jenny,' she would say wistfully. 'If only I could write a bestseller!'

She suspected that if Amelia did make her fortune she would be off like a shot, despite her delicate constitution. Although what she would do about her son would be another question. She adored that boy.

She could not feel sorry for Mrs Saunders. Impatience was what she felt for her. All right, she had lost her husband at the very end of the war. He had obviously spoiled her, however, as her parents had done before him. Hazel Saunders was nearer 40 but well-preserved, with creamy blonde hair and a beautifully made-up face. She had a beauty treatment every week and a manicure and a hair-do sometimes twice a week. Jenny doubted if she'd ever done a hand's turn in her life. She was the type that expected everyone to dance attendance on her as if it was her right.

Jenny thought she heard Joe's key in the door. Automatically her stomach tightened and her shoulders hunched in an effort to protect herself. Sometimes Fridays and Saturdays could be perfectly normal, but one never could be sure. It all depended if Joe had been to the Queens Park Café. This was the oddly named pub in the next block only a few yards down Victoria Road. The actual ice cream café was called simply Queens Café and was across the other side of the same road.

It *was* Joe, and she was nauseated by the stench of whisky and beer the moment he entered the kitchen. His voice sickened her too. Normally it had a rich Scottish burr. Now it was slurred and sneering. 'Are they out again?'

'Rose is doing her homework and Dode won't be long.'

His tall figure tipped towards her. 'How do you know how long he's going to be?' Knowing that he was only interested in baiting her she ignored this question.

5

'I've made a nice steak pie.'

'Where is he?'

'I don't know.'

'You're lying.'

'Why should I lie? Joe, please sit down and have your dinner.'

'Yes, why should you lie, that's what I want to know.'

'I'm not lying.'

'The trouble is,' his mouth turned bitter, 'they know they can do whatever they like because you're never here to stop them.'

He couldn't endure her being out to work, that was the real problem. She lived in constant anxiety that he would do something to make her lose her jobs.

'Your precious jobs are more important to you than your family.'

'Don't be ridiculous,' she said. She always vowed to herself that next time she wouldn't rise to the bait. She would ignore him. She would keep perfectly calm. She would smile. She would humour him. She would do anything but allow herself to be drawn into the dark jungle of his head.

'You're worse than ridiculous,' he sneered, 'with your pathetic money-grubbing attitude to life.'

After the war his resentment had seethed against people in general. Everyone had changed. No one lived up to his standards. Then, when she'd decided to go out to work, his anger turned on her. Her rose-coloured spectacles had not allowed her to see anything wrong with him at first, certainly not during the first few idyllic days they had spent alone during their honeymoon. They hadn't gone anywhere. He had been away long enough, he said. They'd moved into the flat and never went over the door for nearly a week.

He felt so comfortable with her, he'd said. He would sit watching her all the time, never taking his eyes off her even while she was doing the most mundane jobs like raking out the dead ashes and setting the fire.

'I feel so happy,' he'd say. 'This is the happiest time of my life. I'll never forget it.'

How happy she had been, too. And how innocent. She had laughed at the eccentricities he had acquired while he had been a prisoner. She had not even worried about the war souvenirs he'd brought home, the Japanese sword he'd kept polished and hanging over the mantelpiece and the gun in the locker beside where he slept. He had no longer been able to sleep on a bed and, laughing, she'd lain on the floor alongside him. He had taken an aversion to carpets and every kind of luxury and so they'd only had bare boards. The boards were varnished, however, and didn't look too bad. She hadn't minded doing without any kind of luxury then. All she'd wanted or needed was him. But as time passed and the children began to arrive, and especially after her miscarriages, she'd longed for material comforts. She had been brought up in a poor district and, although she had been happy there, she still had dreams of other things, luxurious things.

Her ideas of luxury of course were relative. In the one-roomed flat in Anderston where she'd been born her camp-type bed had been covered by army blankets and a coat. Consequently, her idea of luxury in bed was – as well as proper sheets – proper blankets and a quilt. She'd had these things for years now but she still felt a thrill of appreciation every time she felt the soft, creamy blankets and satin-covered, feather-filled quilt. She had fought for them like everything else.

'There's absolutely no reason for you to be so mean,' she'd told Joe. Although it couldn't be said he was mean in other ways. He gave money generously to war veteran charities and he even visited the hospital for the war disabled with plants and other gifts. She still didn't see the necessity for being so mean about comforts and luxuries for his own home, though. There was no reason for his jealousy either, or his possessiveness. She had always been a faithful and loving wife.

7

She'd begun her struggle for normality even before Dode was born. At least the baby would have some comfort, she'd determined. She had also fought for the right to have friends to the house. Joe seemed to panic when he was in a room with more than three people. He couldn't bear noise either. She'd made no bones about it. 'You'll just have to get over this, Joe. You'll just have to pull yourself together.' She had been more than patient at the beginning, especially considering that she was so young. The time came however, when she had had to say 'Enough's enough!'

There were occasions when his passion was controlled with tenderness. He would stroke her hair and handle her body as if it were a piece of delicate Dresden china. Especially when he was suffering from remorse after a drinking bout. There were occasions when he could be so thoughtful and kind. He would bring her an early morning cup of tea in bed or order her to relax and put her feet up whilst he and the children washed the dishes.

To acquire any luxuries, however, she'd had to go out and work for the money to pay for them. Acquiring friends, at least having them to visit the house, had remained difficult for years. For one thing, Joe had clung to impossibly high standards. He had been so critical, there wasn't one person he hadn't picked to pieces.

'I view everything with fresh eyes now,' he used to say. 'And I can't bear what I see.'

He still detested people like Rory Donovan and her husband who had made so much money during the war, although it was only at times like this, when he was drunk, that his hatred showed. 'That woman,' he said, 'kept the black market thriving here during the war and her jail sentence doesn't change the kind of person she is. And her husband's not much better. He did nothing but sit around in London writing a lot of bullshit for propaganda films. Except when he was living it up with every woman he could get his hands on, of course.'

'Oh, for goodness sake, Joe! What's money-grubbing

about having a nice part-time job?' She struggled to keep her nerves from snapping. 'I enjoy it. You know I've always enjoyed cooking.'

'Especially for spoiled mummy's boys like Douglas Donovan.' Joe's eyes were such a beautiful blue, Jenny thought. He reminded her of the actor Peter O'Toole.

'He's quite a guy – your Douglas Donovan.'

'He's not *my* anything. Joe, your food's getting cold.'

'He doesn't care how his mother made her fortune. Just so long as she buys him his house and gives him plenty of cash to play around with.'

'Joe, it's none of our business what he has or does.'

'I, and millions like me, were supposed to be fighting and suffering for a better world for decent folk. Not for crooks and greedy grabbers like the Donovans.'

'Joe.' She gazed helplessly at him. She longed to reach through the steel wall of bitterness to the unhappy man beneath. She wanted to comfort him, to commune with him. They used to be so close.

'They're spreading like a fungus into my life.'

'Joe!'

'Now he's seeing you home.'

'It was lashing rain and blowing a gale.'

'It's only five minutes' walk. It's only just along the road.'

She heard the click of the outside door and prayed Dode would go straight through to his own room. He always tried to protect her but it only made matters worse.

'I'm going to have my meal,' she said loudly in a reckless attempt to drown the sound of her son's footsteps in the hall.

Her courage was all in her voice. Her legs felt as frail as autumn leaves. She had no choice but to sit down. She knew from past experience that there was nothing she could do except tense herself against what was to come.

'You're not having anything until you tell me what's been going on between you and that bastard.'

9

'You're mad,' she was shouting now, feeling as if she was going mad, too. 'I'm so sick of you going on about what people did or didn't do during the war. What does it matter now? It's been over for fifteen years. I don't care what they did.'

'Oh, I believe you. Your precious friends can do no wrong as far as you're concerned.'

'They're not my friends. I keep telling you, over and over again. I don't care about them.'

'Well, I care.' The madness in his eyes exploded into his fists. She flung her arms up in front of her face in an effort to protect herself. She hunched into herself, praying to keep from screaming in case the neighbours might hear.

Rose and Dode rushed into the room in a frantic bid to help her. What made her break down and weep was the anguished pleading in their eyes.

'Daddy, Daddy, please, no!'

They clung to him, desperately trying to hold him back from her. But he managed to give her one terrible blow that brought blood like wet cobwebs criss-crossing over her face. She had a sudden, terrifying premonition that he was going to kill her. She ran blindly from the room and from the house. Sobbing she clambered up the outside stairs on to the street and rushed across Queens Drive.

She didn't see the car until it was within touching distance. Staggering back, just in time, she lost her balance and fell. The next thing she knew the driver of the car was bending over her.

'Good God! I must have hit you. I could have sworn I braked in time.'

'It wasn't you.' With his help she struggled to her feet. 'Quick, please get me away from here.'

The man looked at her in surprise for only a couple of seconds before throwing open the car door and allowing her to clamber inside. He didn't speak until they were speeding away down Victoria Road towards the centre of the city.

10

'Your husband, was it?' he said eventually.

Jenny was trying to wipe the blood from her face. 'Yes.'

'Bloody coward!' His voice was full of disgust. 'I'll take you to the nearest police station. I hope they lock him up and throw away the key.'

'No, he's not a coward. And I'm not charging him. I've tried that before and it's no use.'

'What are you going to do?'

'I don't know. Keep away until he sobers up, I suppose. I'm terribly grateful to you. Just let me off anywhere now. I'll be all right.'

'You don't look all right. You can't wander about like that. I'll take you to a hospital.'

'No, I'm fine, honestly.'

'My hotel then. You can bathe your face there and have a drink to steady you up.'

For the first time she gazed round at him. He was a broad-shouldered man, probably in his late thirties, his raven-black hair and brows contrasting sharply with sea-green eyes.

'There's no need to look so apprehensive.' His voice was indignant as well as angry. 'What kind of rat do you take me for?'

'I'm sorry. Everything's happened so quickly, I hardly know what to think.'

'Relax!' he told her. But she found it impossible to wind down her aching body as she gazed out from the black Jaguar car at the crowded Glasgow streets.

11

2

The huge Central Hotel was attached to the Central Railway Station. A Victorian building, its ornate walls black with soot, it had an imposing entrance at the corner of Gordon Street and Hope Street. Jenny felt miserably self-conscious walking through the foyer with its luxurious carpets that muffled every sound and the giant chandeliers overhead richly glittering.

She imagined she must look a terrible sight with her blood-smeared face and the old brown skirt and Fair Isle sweater she was wearing. Especially when her companion looked so smart with his Savile Row suit and Crombie coat. He took a firm grip of her elbow and led her towards the lift. Once in his room he sat her down on the bed. The next thing she knew he had wrung out a cloth in cold water at the wash basin and was bathing her face.

'It doesn't look too bad,' he said. 'At least it's not a deep cut. But you're going to have quite a bruise there. I've got a tin of Elastoplast dressings. I'll stick one on.' He suddenly grinned at her. 'I used to be a Boy Scout. I'm always prepared for anything.'

There was something about his smile that immediately disturbed her. Despite the trauma of Joe's violence and the bewildering speed of recent events she was suddenly acutely aware of every detail of the hotel bedroom, and of him. All at once she became highly conscious of a feeling of intimacy between them. She saw his fingers close to her face, the straight-cut nails, the tanned skin. She felt the heat of his big hand against her cheek. She was conscious, too, of how close his face was to hers. She saw the hint of five o'clock shadow on the strong jaw. She thought she saw, through the cool veil of his eyes, the man inside. For a few seconds her heart thudded in panic.

'That's it.' He turned away from her and went over to wash his hands. He moved his large frame with an easy grace yet gave the impression of speed about to be unleashed. Her eyes clung to his broad back. Never in her life had she been so deeply affected by a man's presence. She had known Joe all her life and yet she had never experienced such a feeling of intimacy as she did with this stranger.

'I don't even know your name,' she said.

'Alaister Gregson. Most people just call me Al. What's yours?'

'Jenny Thornton.'

He grinned and winked at her. 'Hi, Jenny.'

'Thank you for being so kind.'

'Let's go along to the lounge and have a drink. You'll feel better once you've had a brandy inside you.'

'I feel much better already.' She wasn't sure if this was true. As she preceded him from the room all her senses heightened again. She even experienced the warm, musky smell of him. It caused her heart to race out of control and it took every last ounce of her energy to will it to slow down.

There were two women sitting at a table in the middle of the lounge. Both were wearing smart Chanel suits and fashionable 'blown-up' hairstyles.

'I feel awful in this old skirt,' Jenny whispered to Gregson. 'It's just what I wear for doing my housework.'

'Forget it! You look lovely.'

She attempted a laugh although her face hurt. 'You must be joking!'

'No,' he said, 'I've never been more serious.' But his eyes betrayed a glimmer of teasing laughter. 'With your sexy eyes and mouth why should you care about clothes?'

She sat down shakily but gratefully on one of the easy chairs in the corner of the room and Gregson ordered the

13

drinks. She seemed to have strayed into another world. She felt disorientated.

'So why are you living with a man who ill-treats you, Jenny Thornton?' Gregson asked, after the waiter set the glasses in front of them.

She didn't answer for a moment or two. 'Life's not that simple. He wasn't always like this. I've known Joe all my life. We were brought up together. Lived in the same street. Went to the same school.'

'That doesn't give him the right to ill-treat you. Nor does it mean that you have to put up with it.'

'Maybe not, but –'

'No "maybes" about it!'

There was an air of restlessness or impatience about Gregson. She saw it in the way he sometimes tapped his fingers on the table or suddenly stretched out his long legs or shifted about in his chair.

'You don't understand,' she said. 'You haven't met Joe.'

'Just as well. If I did he'd end up with a lot worse bruises than you.'

All at once she felt tired. She couldn't bear even the thought of any more violence. Her body as well as her face ached and she felt slightly sick. The brandy helped a little, but she longed just to creep into bed and try to find peace and comfort there. Yet unless Joe had sobered up, there would be no comfort at home. Even if he was sober, there could be no telling any more.

'You certainly don't look fit enough to deal with him,' Gregson added. 'Why don't I book you in here?'

'In the hotel?'

'Why not?'

She shook her head. 'I've nothing with me. Not even my handbag. No, I'll be all right if I can just sit and rest for a while.'

He shrugged. 'Take as long as you like.'

After a minute's silence she said, 'I don't understand.'

'What?'

14

'You're obviously a Glasgow man by your accent, yet you're living in a hotel.'

'I used to live in Springburn.'

'Really?'

'Born and brought up there. Glasgow wasn't big enough for me, though. So I went down south to make my fortune.'

She smiled. 'And did you?'

'I got by.'

'Doing what?'

'One thing and another. I'm an ideas man. I got the idea of coffee bars for the kids – somewhere where they could sit and talk and listen to the kind of music they liked. They caught on, the kids flocked to them. I've opened them all over the place.'

'Not in Glasgow. At least I don't know of any. Of course I'm not exactly a young thing any more.'

He winked at her again. 'You're gorgeous!'

She laughed and said, 'Ouch!' as her hand flew to her face. 'Don't make me laugh. It hurts too much. So you've come up to start coffee bars in Glasgow.'

'No. It's discos now.'

'Discos?'

'Short for discothèque. French.'

'What is it?'

'A dance hall where the music is provided by records selected and played by a disc jockey, instead of live groups.'

'Do you think that'll catch on? Won't people prefer live groups?'

'Most people can't get them. Oh, it'll catch on all right. I'm also into boutiques – that's actually what I'm working on at the moment. Small shops that specialize in the latest fashion in clothes. Again, mostly for young people. They are the ones who have the spending power now.'

'Yes, and they're more choosy, aren't they? Even about jobs.'

'I don't blame them. My mother was in service before she was married. Slave labour it was. Young people nowadays wouldn't put up with that and quite right too.'

'So was my mother. We came from Anderston.'

'I know it well!' he said, his eyes brimming with mischief. 'I wonder if a boutique would catch on there?'

'I don't think so somehow.'

'Oh, you never know. You'd be surprised at the places in London where they're cropping up. I'm thinking of them in big department stores, too.'

'That's certainly a novel idea.'

'I'm going to try "Rory's". They're the biggest and could easily accommodate what I have in mind.'

'I know her!'

'Who doesn't. She's quite a gal.'

'She came from Springburn, too, I think.'

'Yes, when my mother was alive she used to speak a lot about her. She used to boast she went to the same school. She told me that she saw her once in "Rory's" in Stockwell Street and spoke to her. Mother thought she was wonderful because she wasn't a bit standoffish. Took her for a cup of tea apparently and had a great talk about old times.'

'Yes, I can just imagine Rory doing that.'

'She's a tough cookie, though. I haven't managed to get anywhere with her so far.' His grin suddenly broke out again. 'In a business sense, I mean.'

'She's a very good business woman. I expect she'll know what will succeed and what won't.'

'Oh, that doesn't necessarily follow. She's of a different generation from the customers I'm aiming at. She may not be tuned in to their needs at all. There's quite a revolution going on. Kids don't want to go into a stuffy place with the clothes all behind glass and snooty ladies in black dresses and pearls swanning towards them asking what modom or sir wants.'

For a moment Jenny forgot her aches and pains and laughed again. 'Don't they?'

16

'No way! I haven't given up with Rory though. I've some business to attend to in London that'll keep me there for a few weeks but I'll be back.'

'I hope I'm not making you miss your train or anything?'

'No, I drove up.'

'Oh, I forgot about your car.'

'Anyway I've some other people to see tomorrow. And I've to go through to Edinburgh the day after. Nothing on tonight though – how about having dinner together?'

'Look at me!' Jenny cried out. 'Look at my face!'

'Yes, gorgeous?'

'You're crazy! I couldn't go into a restaurant like this.'

'You can do anything you fancy, honey. But if you'd prefer a bit of privacy I could have dinner sent up to my room.' The look in his eyes started her heart drumming out of control again.

'No, I'd better go home soon. To be honest, I don't feel fit enough to eat dinner tonight.'

'Do you feel fit enough to go home?'

'Yes. It'll be all right. He'll have calmed down by now. He'll be worried about me more than anything.'

'Oh, really?' Gregson raised sarcastic brows. 'How considerate of him.'

She sighed. 'I wish you'd known him before.'

'Not my type, love.'

'Sometimes I can hardly believe he's the same person.'

'Have another drink.'

She hesitated, longing to be home and collapse into bed, at the same time unable to prise herself away from Gregson's company. 'All right, thanks. But after that I must go.'

'I'll take you home.'

Her eyes strained wide with anxiety. 'Joe mustn't see me with you.'

'I'll drop you round the corner from your place – anywhere you like.'

17

'You're very kind.'

She lingered over the second drink and it was as if there were two different people in her head. Fears of Joe and worries about the children were there as usual. At the same time, other unfamiliar thoughts and feelings were running parallel with them. Strange, dreamlike sensations.

She sighed. Time to return to reality.

3

'You will have another, won't you, Mrs Donovan?' Hazel Saunders absently patted her blonde hair. 'Shall I ring for Jenny to pour? I'm never quite sure of the correct amount.'

'Don't worry, *I* am. I know a good belt of whisky when I see one.'

Hazel visibly winced. She was a doll of a woman with apple-shaped breasts, a tiny waist, shapely hips and baby-soft straight hair that curled elegantly in at the ends. She reminded Rory Donovan of Marilyn Monroe. She had the same helpless, fragile quality that men find so appealing.

'One shouldn't allow a guest to attend to herself.'

'No problem,' Rory assured her as she splashed a generous dram into the crystal glass. 'How about you?'

Hazel's mink-coloured eyes widened. 'Oh no, whisky is much too strong for my delicate digestion. But perhaps just a tiny drop of dry Martini?'

Rory gave her a refill, thinking wryly that the tiny drops had so far amounted to three full glasses.

Hazel Saunders, weak, vain and snobbish, was the type of person she despised, but as well as being a neighbour and not creating any fuss when she purloined Jenny for half of every working day, Hazel was her best customer at 'Rory's' in Sauchiehall Street. The chic Balmain dress in draped rose wool she was wearing at the moment had cost a small fortune.

'How's your daughter, Mrs Saunders?' she asked.

Hazel's face acquired a bewildered expression. 'In actual fact, Mrs Donovan, it's because of Rowan I invited you for a pre-lunch drink today. Well,' she gave Rory a faintly accusing smile, 'I *did* expect you for coffee but of course, when you were delayed at the shop. . . .'

Rory arched an enquiring brow, thinking, surely she's not going to ask me to give her daughter a job? Not as a shop assistant, that would be far too common.

'We live in terrible times, Mrs Donovan. I'm sure you'll agree.'

Rory didn't. 1960 was proving a good year for business. There was virtually no unemployment so there was plenty of money around. People – especially young people – were throwing it about like it was causing an unbearable itch in their pockets.

'Oh, I don't know,' she said, stuffing a cigarette into her long cigarette holder. She knew people thought holders like this were more reminiscent of the twenties than the sixties but she didn't care. She did what she liked and to hell with what people thought.

'But, my dear, you must surely admit, the world and the values we have always known are being turned upside down and thrown to the winds. It's frightening, I get so upset. I don't know what mummy would have thought if she had been alive – just look at the way young people dress!'

Ah, Rory thought, I get it, she wants me to kit Rowan out in clingy silk or wool day dresses and floaty organza for evening like mummy, instead of the jeans and sweaters Rowan wears all the time. She laughed. 'I can't keep up with the sale of jeans.'

Hazel shook her head. 'I'm surprised you encourage their sale, Mrs Donovan. It's doing nothing to raise standards.'

Rory shrugged. How was she supposed to transform Rowan Saunders when she couldn't do a thing with Amelia's boy? Harry was beginning to look like an eccentric tramp. The last she'd seen of him he was wearing a gold earring and an old khaki raincoat reaching practically down to his ankles. He'd bought it at a jumble sale for sixpence.

'But what I think most upsetting,' Hazel's voice betrayed a tremble, 'is the way they sneer and mock at everything our generation hold dear. Decency, self-discipline, respect for someone older than oneself, morals, good taste, breeding, the proper order of things. . . .' She took several grateful sips of her Martini. 'In my day,' she continued, 'young men were very respectful. And they looked so smart in suits and waistcoats and nicely polished shoes, just like their fathers. And girls had such pretty dresses. Mummy had all my dresses made in Paris. I'll never forget the day I was presented at court. Most of the debutantes were frightfully overdressed. Mummy said I looked like a beautiful shepherdess among them. That dress, simple though it looked, cost mummy and daddy a fortune, but they agreed it was worth every penny. It was as a result of my "coming out" that I met my darling Derek –'

'What about Rowan?' Rory hastily interrupted. She was in no mood for a tearful trip down Memory Lane with 'darling Derek'.

Hazel feathered her forehead with an elegantly manicured finger. 'I don't know, Mrs Donovan. I confess I'm depending on you to help. You're such a strong person.'

'Your daughter's 20 years of age, Mrs Saunders. I can't force her to do anything she doesn't want to – any more than you can.'

'She's such a pretty girl really and there are nice styles available for young people. She doesn't need to dress so scruffily. I like these wide-skirted dresses with lots of stiff petticoats underneath one sees quite a few girls wearing. So pretty and feminine. But apart from her appearance Rowan's mixing with the most dreadful people. You *must* have seen them. No one in the street could miss them. I'm so worried, Mrs Donovan, I feel quite ill.'

'I'm sorry. I don't see what I can do.'

'I wondered, if she had something interesting to occupy her time, something in which she could meet the right kind of people. Social work is all very well, my dear, but I couldn't *tell* you the awful places it takes her to. She

21

visits some of the worst slums in Glasgow and has to deal with people that live like animals. It can't be good for her.'

'You're not expecting me to give her a job in one of my shops?' Rory still couldn't believe it.

'Goodness, no!' Shock registered on Hazel's face. 'I would never dream of such a thing.'

'What are you suggesting, then?'

'Something. . . ,' Hazel vaguely fluttered her hands, 'something artistic perhaps. Your husband and your daughter-in-law are both writers. I'm sure if you spoke to them about Rowan and asked them to use their influence. . . .'

Rory gave a derisive burst of laughter. 'You think journalism would be a safe and respectable career? Something to put your daughter on the right track?'

Thinking of all Donovan's hard-drinking, hard-swearing, fornicating friends – not to mention Donovan himself – Rory shook her head. 'You've got to be joking.'

'But I thought –'

'You thought wrong – about journalism anyway.'

'But your husband is so charming and he has won such distinguished awards.'

'He's tough, he's had to be. To get these award-winning stories he's roughed it in all sorts of hellish places, including the Soviet Union. They're talking of sending him to Vietnam next.'

Hazel gazed round the room with its heavily up-holstered Victorian furniture, its rich brocade, its velvet and tasselled cushions, as if desperately seeking comfort.

'A very charming, talented man. And that fair-haired little girl, Amelia isn't it?'

'Little girl? She's 31.'

'So sweet and gentle. Everything a lady should be.'

'You obviously haven't read her books.'

'I'm sure they must be quite delightful. But they look so huge and unfortunately I don't get much time for reading. I have so many charity duties.' Oh yes, Rory thought, swanning through the wards of the local private nursing home with a book trolley, making cow's eyes at all the patients.

'I admit I do indulge myself with the occasional *tiny* book by that delightful Miss Cartland.'

'Oh, yes?'

'She writes such *nice* stories, doesn't she?'

'I wouldn't know.'

Hazel sighed. 'There's so much that isn't nice today. I seldom even look at newspapers now. They tell one of so many unpleasant things that are happening. People don't even seem to think nice things any more. Apart from these awful creatures she has to deal with in her work Rowan thinks and talks about nothing else but the Bomb. I know it's a dreadful thing but there are people who say it's very necessary that we retain it, not ban it. And I'm sure it doesn't help one way or the other to behave as she does. I'm sure your little daughter-in-law would be such a good influence.'

'Amelia's not all that younger than you. What are you? Late 30s, early 40s?'

'A lady should never speak about age.' Hazel's gaze contained a gentle reprimand.

'Well I'm 58,' Rory said, just to shock her, 'and I don't care who knows it.'

'If I spoke like that my nanny would say "Wash your mouth out, you naughty girl." '

Silly cow, Rory thought, then glancing at her watch began stubbing out her cigarette.

'It's time I was away.' She smoothed on her gloves. 'I'm meeting my husband for lunch in town.'

Hazel's eyes widened in panic. 'But what about Rowan? You will at least speak to Amelia won't you? I'm sure being a lady novelist would be a *nice* career.'

'Why don't you speak to her yourself?'

'We've never been properly introduced. I have only met her on one very brief occasion when she was in the nursing home having her operation. No, on two

23

occasions. Twice I came round with my little trolley while she was there.'

'Amelia wouldn't mind.'

'You think not?'

Rory delved into her handbag. 'Here's her address.' She scribbled on the back of one of her business cards and passed it across to Hazel. Hazel blinked down at it and Rory said 'Queens Gushet', knowing the woman could hardly see her tea cup in front of her, never mind the writing on the card. She was so vain she never wore her glasses in public.

'Queens Gushet,' Hazel echoed, her face lighting up. 'Oh yes, that's at the *better* end of Queens Drive from where Jenny lives. A delightful place.'

'I bought them a house there.'

'How very kind.'

'Phone her up.'

'No, I think a little note would be better in the circumstances.'

'Suit yourself,' Rory said, rising. 'But I've got to go.'

Hazel rose too but Rory knew from past experience that she would not accompany her to the door. That, apparently, was not 'the proper thing to do'. Instead she would ring for her maid, as she always referred to Jenny. She constantly bemoaned the fact that she couldn't get proper staff nowadays. Nobody, it seemed, wanted to be 'proper maids' any more. Jenny refused to wear uniform; she appeared looking neat and attractive in a russet brown wool dress that complemented her shapely figure and the brown of her short curly hair.

'Hello, Jenny,' Rory greeted her.

Jenny smiled. 'You're looking as glamorous as ever. I don't know how you do it.'

'Money, dear,' Rory said. 'I keep at least one Glasgow hairdresser and beauty parlour in business.'

Jenny laughed but was immediately silenced by Hazel's icy tones.

'Please escort Mrs Donovan to the door, Jenny.'

'We've done it again,' Rory said, after they were out in the hall with the sitting room door closed behind them. 'The trouble is, Jenny, we don't know our place. Are you all right, by the way?'

'Yes, fine.'

Jenny helped Rory on with her mink coat but Rory immediately turned on her again. 'What's wrong with your face?'

'Oh, I'm always banging into something.'

'For God's sake, wear your glasses. Don't be like Hazy Hazel.'

'I haven't got glasses.'

'Well, get some. How's my daughter-in-law behaving, by the way?'

'I like Amelia.'

'I never can understand how you manage to put up with either of them – Hazel or Amelia.'

'I like cooking.'

'If I had your talent,' Rory said, 'I'd be putting it to better use. I'd be making money at it.'

'I earn a decent wage, especially with what you pay me.'

'Peanuts!' Rory scoffed. 'You could make a fortune in business – a restaurant for instance.'

'A restaurant of my own?'

'Nobody makes a fortune working for anybody else.'

'I'll never have enough money to buy a restaurant.'

'Thank God for that,' Rory said, 'I want you to carry on cooking for my son. I've come to the conclusion that Amelia's lost some of her marbles. She'd certainly never remember to make any meals for Douglas or Harry.'

Jenny shook her head at her, but the older woman, unrepentant, gave her a wave before clipping away down the drive and sliding elegantly into the driving seat of her silver-grey Rolls-Royce.

As the car purred away it occurred to Rory that she could help Jenny get started in business. But then she thought, to hell, why should I? When I was clawing my way up from the slums of Springburn nobody helped me!

25

4

Rowan had been kept late at work. When she arrived home she was surprised to hear, coming from the direction of the sitting room, the deep rumble of a male voice mingling with her mother's giggly, inebriated tones.

Rowan was tired and couldn't be bothered thinking who Hazel's visitor might be. She nearly didn't go into the room. She was in no mood to cope with her mother's over-indulgence in alcohol or any of her snobby upper class friends. Not that Hazel had many friends of any kind nowadays. She could be such an embarrassment after a few drinks.

Hesitating tiredly in the hall, Rowan caught sight of herself in the heavy gold-framed mirror. She looked out of place in such luxurious surroundings. It was as if she still had clinging to her some of the atmosphere of the slum tenements. Her severely tied-back hair, her unmade-up face, her shabby belted raincoat had blended very well into the tiny rooms and kitchens and single apartments from which she'd just come. She'd had to deal with enough drunks for one day, or the results of drinking. Mostly men who'd spent all their wages in the pub and then come home to beat up their desperate and indignantly complaining wives. It was the women and children she had always to worry about and look after.

With a sigh she decided that on this occasion she should rescue her mother's guest. As soon as she opened the sitting room door she saw it was George Beattie, a young man she'd met the night before at Minna Flemming's 21st birthday party in the Plaza. She had a date with him for Saturday.

He rose apologetically. His face was red and he'd been sweating.

'You left your purse in my car. I happened to be passing. . . .'

'Wasn't it terribly kind of dear George?' Her mother got up with difficulty and swayed towards him. She was wearing high-heeled court shoes which did nothing to help her sense of balance. Before Rowan could reach her she had stumbled against the young man and was clinging, giggling, round his neck.

'Mother, I'll take you upstairs.'

'I'd rather dear George took me upstairs.'

Rowan's cheeks were burning now. 'Come now, Mother.' Desperately she caught hold of the older woman and struggled to prise her away from the wretchedly embarrassed young man.

'Go away,' Hazel pouted. 'You're just jealous. You're always trying to spoil my fun.'

'Perhaps you'd better go,' Rowan told George, who had managed at last to disentangle himself. 'I'm sorry about this. She's quite different when she's sober, she'll be horrified at herself tomorrow.' The truth was, of course, her mother wouldn't remember a thing about the incident. 'By the way,' she added miserably, 'I can't manage Saturday.'

She wasn't sure if he looked disappointed or relieved and was too tired to care. Still clutching at her mother's struggling figure, she said, 'Do you mind if you see yourself out?' He was already halfway towards the door.

'I can manage Saturday, George,' her mother called. 'I can manage any time, darling.'

It always unnerved Rowan how alcohol could change the normally prim and proper Hazel into a raging nympho. 'I'll help you upstairs to bed, Mother,' she said after George had disappeared. Her mother was pouting like a child again.

'I don't want to go to bed without George.'

'Don't be silly, Mother.' She dragged Hazel, still

27

struggling and protesting, out of the room and up the stairs. She knew from past experience that if she managed to get her mother on to the bed she would be unconscious in a matter of minutes.

She wasn't particularly upset about losing her date with George Beattie. He wasn't really her type, not at all socially aware, not even very intelligent. All he'd talked about that night at the party was Rangers and Celtic football matches and the latest Elvis Presley single. He never mentioned the Bomb. He was an exceptionally good dancer, though, she'd really enjoyed dancing with him.

What she was acutely distressed about was the humiliation of him finding out about her mother. She'd long ago stopped inviting her friends home; there had been far too many embarrassing incidents like tonight. It made her so sad for her mother's sake. Despite the fact that she detested everything Hazel stood for she still loved her mother and it was painful to see her keep making such a fool of herself at her age. Hazel had once been a debutante and been presented at Court; in her youth she had mixed with nothing but wealthy and often titled chinless wonders, judging by their photographs and the stories she'd told about them. Meeting Derek might have been the making of her, had he survived the war. Rowan was thankful that her father, although wealthy, had come from stronger Scottish stock. She liked to think that it was from him she'd inherited her own strengths, such as they were.

Somehow she managed to wrestle her mother out of her powder-blue dress, suspender belt and stockings, get her into her nightie and safely between the sheets. It always amazed her what a good figure and skin her mother had; she was, after all, in her late thirties and drank with reckless abandon. She must have been a stunning beauty in her debutante days. Beauty was the one thing she did wish she'd inherited from Hazel, but alas, with her father's strength of character had also come his freckles and sandy hair.

As she'd expected, her mother sank into immediate unconsciousness. Rowan hung the figure-hugging blue dress on a hanger, tucked it neatly into the wardrobe and then took the underwear along to the laundry basket in the bathroom. Her mother had not set the table or prepared any supper for her and as usual Rowan blessed Jenny Thornton when she found some homemade soup and a dish of Jenny's delicious Boeuf Bourguignon in the fridge. Alone in the spacious, high-ceilinged kitchen with a book propped in front of her Rowan ate the meal.

The book was based on the lectures of a futurologist, Herman Kahn, given at the Princeton Institute of Advanced Studies. He was advancing the thesis that thermo-nuclear war had to be made into a practical proposition because a totally disarmed world which renounced war was unbelievable. It was he who had introduced the concept of 'acceptable damage'. His suggested estimate of what was 'acceptable damage' in return for striking the first blow was 'somewhere between ten and sixty million dead'. His assurance that it was still possible to declare war and that 'we must have an alternative to peace' filled Rowan with horrified curiosity. What kind of man could this be who could talk so glibly of 'a limited war capability' that could mean the catastrophic deaths of millions?

His optimistic opinion had been much appreciated of course by 'the military-industrial complex' – the Pentagon, the RAND Corporation (for which Kahn's research was done) and the weapons industry. Deterrence always had one decisive advantage over disarmament as a policy: it made some people a fortune. No wonder British economic recovery was so poor by comparison with that of Germany and Japan. *They* were not spending their resources on obsolete weapons. A nuclear arms race was a good recipe for national bankruptcy but it was very profitable for those who designed and manufactured the weapons. And of course each escalation perpetuated the struggle by forcing the other side to match or overtake the enemy's latest threat. In their man-to-man talks at Camp David the previous year President Eisenhower and the Russian leader Khrushchev had, she read, admitted this to each other. She thought arms manufacturers must be *the* most wicked and irresponsible people in the world.

Once through in the sitting room with her coffee she abandoned the book, if somewhat guiltily, in favour of her mother's *Queen* magazine. She always found it a wonderfully escapist read when she was exhausted and overwhelmed by the harsh realities of life in the world in general, or at home. Eventually she trailed upstairs to have a long relaxing soak in a hot bath and then to bed.

In the morning before rushing off to work she took her mother her usual breakfast tray of coffee, orange juice and buttered toast. 'Come on, Mother,' she pleaded, as she tugged open the curtains, 'I don't want to be late again. Sit up and take your tray.'

Hazel groaned and shaded her eyes with her hand. 'I have one of my headaches, darling. Just you go on.'

'No, I don't want you still lying here when I get back. Sit up, Mother. You'll feel better after your coffee.'

Hazel sighed. 'Oh, very well.'

Rowan helped her into a sitting position and plumped up an extra pillow at her back before balancing the tray on Hazel's knees. Then she waited until her mother had taken a few sips of the coffee.

Hazel smiled gratefully at her. 'You're such a good girl, darling. What would I do without you?'

Rowan hardly dared think – although, more and more, she had been trying to face the fact that something would have to be done to force her mother to help herself. Neither of them could go on forever like this. Sometimes she felt her mother was like a leech, sucking from her not only her youth but her very life's blood. She was a continually worrying responsibility. Even when Rowan went out with her friends, anxiety about her mother remained niggling at the back of her mind. Often she wondered what she'd done to deserve such a fate. As if it wasn't bad enough that she came from a well-off background and had been educated at one of the best private schools in Scotland. The school prided itself on producing in its Scottish pupils upper class English accents; this had since become something to be ashamed of. A good solid working class accent was the thing. All her friends had lapsed into broad Glasgow vowels and Scottish burrs and it was particularly important that she should get down to basics in this way. Her job was hard enough without making it even more difficult for herself with an alienating accent. Sally and Betty who were also dedicated social workers felt the same. Hugh was a struggling novelist who at the age of 21 had been in almost as many jobs. 'A writer needs experience of different kinds of people and ways of life,' he'd explained. Tommy was having his own struggle to be an artist. His father kept trying to force him into the family hardware business, one of the biggest in Scotland. Instead of encouraging or praising Tommy's undeniable talent his father was forever crying out about what a disgrace he was. His mother was quietly ashamed of him.

All of them suffered in one way or another with their parents, although it was agreed that Rowan suffered more than most. Her mother could, admittedly, go for weeks at a time without a drink but this was only a futile attempt to convince herself, as well as her daughter, that she was perfectly all right and had no drink problem. It was a pathetic charade.

'Do you know,' Rowan had confided to her friends, 'I'm beginning to feel older than my mother. We're going through a role reversal. I worry about leaving her on her own, I quiz her about where she's been if she goes out, I lecture her like a Victorian parent. I'm telling you it's making me old before my time.' In fact, despite her earnest expression, Rowan didn't look more than her 20 years with her pony-tail, her freckled unmade-up face.

31

'We keep telling you,' Betty had said. 'It would be a kindness to your mother to leave her. You're just encouraging her.'

Rowan had felt really angry about that. 'Encouraging her?' she'd squealed incredulously, 'Don't be bloody ridiculous!'

'You know perfectly well what Betty means,' Sally'd insisted. 'By looking after your mother the way you do you're cushioning her from the real effects of her alcoholism. She'll never face reality until she has to face it alone.'

She knew in her heart this was true but couldn't bear to abandon her mother to all the horrors that would no doubt overtake her. She even knew that the day would come when she would allow her mother to sink into the pit but she kept pushing it to the back of her mind, unable to contemplate such a tragedy.

She kept thinking instead that she would find some way to force her mother to see sense.

5

Hazel didn't feel well. Getting up in the morning was becoming more and more of a physical ordeal as well as an emotional one. It reminded her, in a way, of how she'd felt all those years ago when she'd first heard that Derek had been killed. At first she had been dazed, unable to take in the enormity of what had happened, or the finality of it. Then she had become physically ill.

She admired people who had strong constitutions. Even as a child she had been 'delicate'. There wasn't a childish ailment she had not suffered acutely from; every draught gave her a cold, every emotional upset brought on a high temperature. Her nanny had been dismissed immediately when it was discovered that she had been telling fearsome bedtime stories that gave her nightmares from which she awoke screaming.

Her ever-vigilant parents had also found that she suffered from a 'murmur at her heart'. As a result, school gymnastics, swimming, tennis and all other sports were banned. Although they were happy about her marrying Derek, they had been worried on account of her 'weak heart' and especially because she would be living so far from them in her husband's native Scotland. They were most acutely concerned when she became pregnant. Pregnancy, like marriage however, had unexpectedly agreed with her; she had never felt better or happier.

Even so, the most energetic activity she had ever performed – apart from giving birth but she had been anaesthetized for that – was arranging flowers, playing bridge or reading stories to Rowan when her nanny brought her to the morning room and the drawing room for her twice-daily visits. She used to enjoy all of these activities but after Derek's death she lost interest in everything – including Rowan.

By the time she had recovered sufficiently to attempt to pick up the threads of her life again, it was only to discover that everything had changed. She was no longer welcome at bridge parties or indeed at any other gathering of her friends. They never said so of course, and she was sure that they did their best to be kind but she sensed that she was not wanted. Another single person had always to be found to partner her at bridge since regular husband and wife partnerships had long ago been firmly established. A single woman was an encumbrance in any of the social scenes she'd once moved in, and more than that – she was a threat, especially a woman as attractive to men as Hazel knew she was. Hadn't Derek told her often enough? And she'd seen the way some of the husbands looked at her.

After coffee mornings a large part of every conversation revolved around husbands – mostly of a boastful nature, how well they were doing in business, what a wonderful evening out they'd had at the Golf Club dinner dance, where they were going on holiday together.

Hazel felt increasingly isolated. She was nonplussed to find that she had so little in common with anyone any more. Perhaps if one of her friends had been widowed like herself everything might have been different but their husbands had, for one reason or another, escaped being called up, or else, as serving officers in the Forces, they had been fortunate enough to survive unharmed. After the war, in fact, they had settled back in their businesses and their old routines, almost as if nothing had happened to upset them.

The war had changed everything for her. Derek had been called up. Then, when Rowan's nanny had left to join the VADs, she'd been forced to take over full responsibility for the child. It had been a terrifying experience at first. But somehow she'd come to terms with it by thinking of Rowan and treating her as one of the lovely dolls she used to treasure when she was herself a child. She began to enjoy shopping for tasty treats for her to eat and lovely clothes to dress her in. A fluttering sense of achievement began to excite her; she was actually managing her child by herself. Too soon, however, her euphoria dwindled when she began to sense in the child a resistance, an embarrassed stiffening away when she kissed and cuddled and petted her. She came to realize that Rowan was a sturdy, undemonstrative girl, not a bit like her mother. It made her feel more isolated than ever.

The teenage years, as they were now called, were accepted as the difficult and rebellious phase of a young person's life but Rowan had developed a difficult, rebellious side to her nature long before that. Much as she loved her daughter, Hazel couldn't help thinking that fate had played her another cruel trick in making Rowan a tomboy. As a result she was denied even the pleasant diversion of dressing her daughter in the pretty, feminine clothes she herself appreciated so much.

At a very early age Rowan had a mulish determination about clothes as she had about everything else. On one occasion Hazel had been horrified to discover that Rowan had discarded her pink, frilly knickers and had been going about for the whole day without wearing any knickers at all. Rowan had also cast aside the lovely dolls her mother had so eagerly chosen for the nursery; instead she clung fiercely to an old, increasingly shabby teddy.

No matter what she did Hazel could not reach any rapport with the child. Sometimes she wondered if what she was really seeking was a substitute for Derek's love and Rowan sensed it. She missed the closeness she'd had with her husband so much.

In the years that followed she lost first her dearly loved father, and then the death of her mother brought complete desolation. Without the safety net of even her mother's love and support she began to flounder helplessly in self-doubt.

Had she ever fully appreciated her parents' devotion, or Derek's, when he had been alive? She began to see that in many ways she had taken Derek for granted. This thought in particular tormented her. If only she could tell him how sorry she felt now for all her thoughtless, selfish little ways. She struggled to comfort herself with the knowledge that Derek would have understood her minor faults, her peccadillos. Derek had loved her not despite her weaknesses but because of them. The thought only patched over the surface of her pain. Nothing waved the magic wand and banished the hurt except alcohol. She was pathetically grateful that she had found such an escape route from her anguish. It was like suddenly being administered an anaesthetic instead of having to face the terrors of the surgeon's knife fully conscious.

The relief, the peace of mind after a few drinks was incredible. It enabled her to find enough spiritual, mental and physical energy to keep going. So eager did she become to avoid the hopeless struggle with herself and trying to cope with her day-to-day existence she could not start a day without the little boost of optimism a drink gave her. Sometimes, so anxious was she to make sure of that first drink, she slept with a bottle hidden under the blankets.

It was all very well for tough and resilient people like Rory Donovan. Rowan, like Rory Donovan, had obviously been born a fighter. Regrettable as it might be, Hazel conceded, she was a weak person herself in every sense of the word. She was someone with little stamina who needed to lean on other people for strength. She had always needed to be looked after and protected from the harsh realities of life and she needed to be protected still. Alcohol was a poor substitute for a friendly shoulder but in the circumstances, where no other help was available, it was better than nothing. All the doctor had ever done for her was give her tranquillizers.

Rowan was seldom in the house now to do anything, what with her awful job and even more awful friends. But of course when she was at home she did what she could and she could always be depended on in an emergency. It was some comfort to know that, in her own way, Rowan did care for her and looked after her. It was the raft that Hazel clung to as she was tossed about in a bewildering sea.

Sometimes if Rowan was on holiday from work or it was a Sunday she would stay in to keep her company and Hazel would be childishly grateful. They'd have a quiet but companionable breakfast together in the large kitchen. They seldom used the dining room now but even in the kitchen Hazel felt lost and dwarfed among the towering cupboards and high-backed chairs if she were left on her own.

Rowan would kindly make her tea and toast. Not only that, she would use the silver toast rack and napkin rings and linen napkins – do everything the way she liked it. Afterwards Rowan would say, 'You go through to the drawing room, Mother, I'll wash up.'

'Thank you, darling,' she'd say with heartfelt gratitude, 'I did enjoy that. You set the table so beautifully. It makes such a difference, don't you think, to keep to decent, civilized standards?'

In the drawing room Hazel would switch on the electric imitation coal fire before settling down to leaf through the *Glasgow Herald*. She hated imitations of anything – just as she hated having to use the drawing room at this time of day when it should have been the morning room. It was a question of cutting down on housework, however. She kept advertising in the *Herald* for a cleaning woman and sometimes she had a few replies. None of the women had shown the slightest pleasure at the prospect of working in a big Victorian villa. One had been openly impertinent. 'You'd need an army of cleaners to keep this place decent. I don't know how that housekeeper of yours can stand it,' she'd said, meaning Jenny.

Normally Hazel would have immediately dismissed such a woman from her presence but desperation had forced her to point out, albeit coldly, 'Most of the rooms are not used now, there is only my daughter and myself. Mrs Thornton does not live in. You would not be required to clean the whole house.'

'Well,' said the woman grudgingly, 'I'll give it a try.' Hazel's mother would have turned in her grave if she'd heard such impertinence.

The woman had lasted three weeks before suddenly deciding to leave. Hazel had swallowed her pride and offered more money to help persuade her to stay. She'd turned out to be an excellent worker and had given the house a much-needed spring clean. She wouldn't be persuaded however.

'I'm a thorough type,' the woman explained, 'I have to do things thorough. I can't see a place half-done and this place is definitely too much for me, everything's such an old-fashioned clutter. It's like sinking back into Victorian times.' Ignorant, insolent creature!

Hazel was truly thankful for Jenny and Rowan. At least she could depend on them.

6

Jenny felt shocked and frightened. 'You shouldn't have come here.'

Gregson leaned a hand on the door lintel and looked down at her. 'Do you think I could have gone back to London without checking to see how you were?'

Again there was this powerful sense of intimacy. 'I'm sorry, I can't ask you in. Joe might come back at any minute, he's on early shift.'

'Come out with me, then.'

'It's no use.'

'What's no use?'

She flushed with embarrassment. 'There's nothing to talk about. I appreciate your concern, but everything's fine now.'

'I don't believe you.'

'Please, I'm so afraid he might come –'

'And you say everything's all right? I'll give you one minute to collect your handbag and coat.'

She saw by the look in his eyes, the firm set of his jaw and his aggressive stance that he had no intention of going away. Helplessly she turned back into the house, struggled into her camel coat, tied the belt tightly round her waist, grabbed her handbag and in a matter of minutes was sitting beside him in the sleek Jaguar.

'What's the point?' she asked as he pressed the starter button on the wood-panelled dashboard. The car purred into life and soon Gregson was carefully pulling into the flow of traffic.

'The point is, love, I don't give up that easily.'

'Look, Mr Gregson –'

'Al!'

'Al, how many times must I tell you? I'm married. I

have children. I'm up to here with worries and responsi-
bilities. I can't face any more complication in my life. I
appreciate your kindness but I told you not to contact
me again. You're not helping me by doing this.'

'You're not thinking straight, Jenny.'

'What do you mean?'

'It doesn't make sense to stay with a man who treats
you like this Joe does.'

'You don't understand.'

'You're right!'

She felt hustled, harassed, unable to cope. 'It doesn't
make sense either,' she said, 'for me to dash out of my
house instead of cooking a meal for my husband and
family to sit here talking to you.'

'Doesn't it?' He glanced round at her and their eyes
met. It was only for a couple of seconds but it was as if
they had made love. She closed her eyes and leaned her
head back against the seat. They drove in silence for a
time and then he said, 'I'm rushing you, aren't I?'

'Yes.'

'I've always been a bit of a hustler, always on the
move, too.'

'What does your wife feel about you dashing all over
the country so much?'

'I'm a widower, my wife died three years ago. In
childbirth. The baby was stillborn.'

'Oh, I am sorry.' Jenny gazed round at him but he
kept his eyes fixed on the road ahead.

'Ellen had a heart condition and was advised against
having a family. But she was desperate to have a baby
and kept pleading with me and insisting that she would
be perfectly all right. For a long time after her death I
blamed myself.' The fingers of both his hands
straightened and lifted slightly from the wheel. 'Eventually I had to come to terms with it.'

She touched his arm in sympathy and it was then he
glanced round and the impact of his eyes made her
immediately withdraw her hand and look away. As they

drove along in silence she kept asking herself what she was doing here with a complete stranger while at any moment her husband and family would be arriving home expecting their dinner. The odd thing was she didn't feel that Al Gregson was a stranger.

'Let's go in for a drink, then I'll drive you back.'

It was then she realized that he had taken her to the Central Hotel.

'Not in my room, don't worry,' he said reading her thoughts, 'in the public lounge in perfect respectability.' He grinned as he helped her out of the car. 'Although you're welcome in my bedroom any time.'

'This is ridiculous,' she said trying to prise her elbow free of his hand but his grip was too strong.

'Don't you ever get a kick out of doing spontaneous, crazy things?' he asked.

'No.'

'Well, it's time you learned. Tomorrow we'll climb the Campsie Hills and drink champagne at the summit.'

The sudden vision of herself attempting such a feat made her laugh helplessly.

'It's the middle of winter!'

'So?'

'You really are crazy.'

He brought gin and tonics clinking with ice from the bar and instead of sitting at the opposite side of the table he joined her on the two-seater settee against the wall. The heat from his body radiated out like energy and every now and again his knee brushed against hers burning it as if by an electric shock.

'Now Jenny Thornton,' he said, turning the full force of his attention towards her, 'tell me all about yourself.'

She cooled her palms against the cold moist sides of her glass and wished she could press it against her cheeks. Eventually she sighed and said, 'I'm the wife of Joe Thornton who works in the park across from where we live. And I'm the mother of two children, 12-year-old Rose and 14-year-old Dode.'

41

'That's not telling me anything about the real you.'

She stared at him in surprise. It was a long time since she'd thought of herself in any terms other than as a wife and a mother.

'Do you like travelling?' he persisted. 'What do you think of Mary Quant's geometric hairstyle, or *Lady Chatterley's Lover*? Or the war in Vietnam.'

'I don't have much time to think about myself and my opinions.'

'Well, it's time you did. Starting thinking of yourself right now.'

She smiled. 'I can see why you're so successful in business. You've obviously got great energy and enthusiasm.'

'Never mind about me,' he said, 'what about you?'

She couldn't begin to tell him about the private and exhausting world of fear in which she had been struggling to survive for most of her life. Somehow, in the luxurious surroundings of the Central Hotel lounge, in the company of this forceful man with his positive approach, her world seemed unreal.

'I've told you I'm just an ordinary suburban wife and mother.' For a moment she hesitated. 'I do enjoy cooking, I find everything about food and the pleasure it can give people deeply satisfying. People say I've quite a talent for it.'

'I'm not surprised.'

'Aren't you?'

'I bet you're good at sex as well.'

She flushed. 'What's sex got to do with it?'

'It's one of the pleasures of the flesh. Like good food and drink.'

'Trust a man to think like that!'

The twitch at her mouth betrayed her amusement but at the same time she couldn't free herself of tension. She said, 'I think you'd better take me home.'

'Relax!'

'How can I in the circumstances?'

'I'll call for you after lunch tomorrow and we can have the whole afternoon.'

'No, please don't. I've enough to worry me without clandestine meetings.'

'After tomorrow I'm off to London. Getting out of that underground prison of yours and up into the hills will do you good.'

'It's not an underground prison,' she protested, 'what an awful thing to say.' Yet there was a chilling ring of truth to it.

'I'll ask the hotel to supply a picnic tea.'

Helplessly she laughed. 'It could be thick with snow up on the Campsies.'

'Good! We can build a snowman. Or have a snowball fight.'

Still quietly laughing, she shook her head.

'You'll come?'

'I thought you were up here on business.'

'My business will be finished by lunchtime. Will you come?'

'Oh, all right – but just for an hour or two, I must be back in plenty of time to prepare the evening meal.'

As soon as she had agreed to meet him again she was harassed by a mixture of heady excitement and heart-thumping apprehension. She would have to take the afternoon off work. She would warn Amelia, of course, but she daren't think of what Joe would do if he ever found out. Resentment against Gregson flared up too; why couldn't he just leave her alone? It wasn't for her good that he was pursuing her like this. He must know how it only made things worse and put her in an even more dangerous situation. It was just typical male selfishness. Her resentment mushroomed until she couldn't trust herself to speak to him on the way back to Albert Avenue where he'd agreed to drop her.

Then just as she was about to ease herself out of the car she was taken aback by his hand gripping her shoulder, detaining her. Pulling her towards him he kissed her.

Brief though it was the kiss sent her into such turmoil she hardly knew where she was.

'Take care,' he said and gave her his characteristic wink before the car slid smoothly away to disappear among the stream of traffic.

She stood for a few minutes struggling to compose herself before approaching the house and facing Joe and the children. But it was a long time before she could once more regain some degree of concentration on what she was doing. Even Rose noticed there was something different about her.

'Mum, are you sure you're all right?' she asked worriedly.

'Yes, I'm fine, dear. Really.'

'Three times you didn't hear me when I spoke to you. You seemed so far away somehow, I was frightened.'

'I'm sorry, darling.' She pulled the child to her and hugged her close. 'I was just daydreaming, that was all.'

But she was frightened, too.

7

Jenny came prepared in a warm tweed skirt, canary yellow polo-neck sweater and quilted green anorak. A yellow woolly hat was pulled down over her curls and a matching scarf was slung around her neck. Gregson was wearing an anorak of dark glossy grey with a turned-up collar.

As the car spun through the countryside to the north of Glasgow a frosty sun was sparkling the fields with diamonds of light. In the distance the hills of Campsie were a dark shadowy blue against a pale sky. As they passed a village there was a little surge of noise which reminded Jenny of a couple of lines from a poem,

> The noisy geese go gabbling o'er the pool,
> The playful children just let loose from school.

Above, a flight of crows drifted negligently towards their rookery. Away from the village the car was soon enveloped in the deep silence of nature again.

'There won't be another soul up there today,' Jenny said.

'Good, we'll be able to celebrate in solitude.'

'Celebrate what?'

'Finding each other.'

She sighed. 'There's no use talking like that.'

'I've got the champagne in the boot. And caviare and smoked salmon and strawberries.'

'Strawberries?' She laughed incredulously.

'Marinated in vodka.'

'You're joking!'

'Everything for your delight.'

At a loss for words, she shook her head.

Now they were passing a river that murmured along

45

under the shelter of trees bent low over brown ripples and glittering foam. Soon they were on the road that snaked up to the brow of the hill. Gregson stopped the car.

'This isn't the place I have in mind for our picnic. But just look at that wonderful view!' They got out of the car and stood gazing at the wide vista spread out beneath them and beyond into the distance. Down in the valley, sheltered cosily by its ring of hills, lay the city of Glasgow with its roofs and spires and silver ribbon of river.

A cool breeze tugged at Jenny's scarf and whipped colour to her cheeks. For a few minutes, as she took deep breaths of the clean air, she felt a soothing of her troubled spirits. Until she became conscious of Gregson watching her.

'This is what you've needed,' he said, 'to get away from your problems, see them in perspective.'

'It doesn't make them disappear,' she replied sadly before returning to sit in the car. He joined her and the car shot forward, making her stiffen and hold on to the edge of her seat. The road was narrow and dangerous and kept climbing to greater and greater heights. There was no fence or barrier of any kind between them and the valley below.

'Must you go so fast?' she burst out eventually.

'It's exhilarating.'

'Not to me.'

'Come now,' he grinned without taking his attention off the road, 'admit it.'

She kept silent. There was a tremor of excitement lacing the anxiety she felt. She might have enjoyed the thrill of the ride in other circumstances but her nervous system had been under attack for so many years now she wasn't able to cope with anything beyond normal everyday existence. She was thankful when he stopped the car at a wider, flatter area where the only view was of heath and heather. Gregson produced a picnic basket and a tartan travelling rug from the boot.

46

'Aren't we going to eat in the car?' she said.

'Of course not. Come on, follow me.' And he was off across the road and down a path through prickly gorse and thistles. She scrambled after him, calling out, 'You're mad. It's bitterly cold.' She could see their breath freezing in misty clouds in front of them.

'So what?' he called back. 'It's –'

'Don't say it! I know, you think it's exhilarating.'

'Well, isn't it?'

They'd reached the bottom of the steep twisting path and she stopped in surprise to admire the unexpected sight of a stream dancing, tumbling, splashing merrily over silvery grey boulders and gurgling along over slabs of rock of the same sparkling colour.

'It's completely sheltered down here, quite a suntrap in fact.'

'How on earth did you find such a secluded spot?' she asked Gregson as he spread the travel rug over a grassy area nearby. 'It's lovely!'

'I'm full of surprises,' he said. 'Sit down!'

She did as she was told, still thumping her gloved hands together and shrinking into the woolly nest of scarf, despite the fact that what he had said was true. It wasn't nearly so cold now that they were safe from the teeth of the wind.

'It's hot tea we need, not champagne.'

'I have that too. We can have the tea first if you like.'

'Yes, please.'

He fished a large flask and a couple of mugs from the basket.

'Wonderful.' She warmed both hands round her steaming mug of tea and sipped at it in exquisite appreciation. Then came the dainty sandwiches of smoked salmon. 'Mmmm . . . delicious,' she murmured as she ate, 'the fresh air seems to have given me an appetite.' She closed her eyes in ecstasy over the caviare. 'This has got to be Russian Beluga.'

'Nothing but the best is good enough for you, love,' he

47

said gently. He was watching her again, his green eyes thoughtful.

'Why are you looking at me like that?' she asked.

'I'm thinking how alive you look, and how intensely you can appreciate the good things in life when you get the chance.'

She wondered in some apprehension if she'd appeared greedy, too enthusiastic about the food and drink. But she could not prevent herself from being equally intense about the champagne. After a couple of glasses she had recklessly decided to abandon all thoughts of the fearful problems in her life – at least for this short afternoon. How much did she have left of this glorious escape, this taste of freedom? One short hour – perhaps less? She would savour it, enjoying it to the full. After another glass of champagne she had abandoned herself in Gregson's arms, submitting to his kiss, with as much intense appreciation and enjoyment as she had the food.

Until soon a fever of passion overcame her and swept her along until it was a kind of madness. She had never experienced such an awakening before. Yet Gregson was gentle and slow in his lovemaking, continuing to relish everything about her. Eventually, when both their appetites were exhausted, he wrapped the travelling rug around her and held her cocooned in his arms.

It wasn't until much later on the way back to Glasgow in the car that she began to feel the guilt, the fear and the hopelessness again.

'I'm off to London first thing tomorrow,' Gregson said, 'but I'll write as soon as I can.'

'I'd rather you didn't. What's the point?'

'The point is we love each other, Jenny.'

'I hardly know you.'

He glanced round at her, his eyes narrow with sexual intimacy. 'I know every inch of you!'

She flushed and looked away. 'You know what I mean. I've known my husband all my life.'

'You can't love a man who abuses you. Look, I've still

48

to persuade Rory into this boutique idea. I've just a few loose ends to tie up in London over another deal and then I'll be back.'

There would be no stopping him. She could see that. He was as determined to have his own way in his personal life as he was in business. Realizing this made apprehension spread like a fungus along every nerve, until she felt sick at the thought of what might happen. He didn't understand the complicated relationship she and Joe were enmeshed in, how unpredictable and dangerous he could be, how vulnerable, how desperately loving.

Even before leaving the car at the corner of Albert Avenue she was distracted and absent-minded and only murmured a brief goodbye to Gregson. Already her afternoon of sensual indulgence had taken on an unreal quality. It couldn't have happened. It *mustn't* have happened.

'Where have you been?' Joe asked as soon as she entered the house.

'The dinner's all prepared, it's just got to be heated up.'

'I asked you a question.' Joe rose from his chair, his blue eyes unnaturally bright in a pale, tense face.

'I went for a walk,' Jenny gave him a tremulous smile. 'I'd one of my headaches and I thought it would do me good.' She realized too late that she ought to have phoned Amelia to find out if Joe had been checking up on her. Now she didn't know how much he knew. Avoiding his eyes she stripped off her gloves, scarf and hat wondering with thumping heart if there was any tell-tale grass on her coat. Her fingers shook as they fumbled with the buttons.

'You're lying,' Joe accused coming towards her.

'No,' she said, shaking her head. 'Oh, no,' she repeated piteously. She was shaking helplessly now and hanging on to the buttons of her coat as if somehow they'd support her.

8

Next afternoon Amelia came into her kitchen to find Jenny not, as she'd expected, beating up the eggs for the custard for the Donovans' evening meal, but standing staring into space, bowl and whisk motionless in her hands. 'No tea this afternoon, Jenny?'

'Oh! Good grief, I forgot all about it!'

'That's all right, I'll make it. I'll have mine here with you now that I've come through.'

'Oh, I am sorry.'

'It doesn't matter, I wanted to talk to you anyway.'

'The kettle was boiling.'

'Fine.'

Jenny finished switching the eggs, poured the mixture into a dish and placed it in the oven. Amelia made a pot of tea and sat down at the table.

'I've been worried about you for some time, Jenny.'

'Why?' Jenny said cheerfully. 'I'm sure there's no need.'

'I'm not blind. You keep turning up with cuts and bruises. And don't tell me you keep bumping into things, you never bump into things and hurt yourself here.'

Jenny sipped at her tea for a few minutes. Eventually she said, 'Strictly between you and me, Amelia – it's Joe. He goes berserk when he gets a drink, he doesn't know what he's doing.'

'Oh dear! I suspected as much. Have you tried to get help?'

'I've tried everything, believe me. Nothing works.'

Amelia's face twisted in sympathy. 'Jenny, what can I say?'

'Nothing.'

'If there's anything I can do, anything at all. . . .'

'Thanks.' She couldn't help smiling. 'But I think you've got enough problems of your own.'

Amelia rolled her eyes. 'You noticed!'

'If there's anything worse than a female nagger, it's a male one.'

'I know. Sometimes I think Douglas is trying to wear me away or drive me mad like a Chinese water torture. But at least he's never been physically violent. I couldn't stand that, I'm a terrible coward for pain. Or, to use the current jargon – I've a very low pain threshold!'

'As if that wasn't enough,' Jenny said absently, 'there's somebody else now.'

'What? You must be a real masochist!'

'I don't know how it happened. Well . . . , actually I do. At least, I know how we met.' And she told Amelia about their first meeting, then went on to say, 'He's got an awful nerve. He keeps arriving on my doorstep and each time I nearly die of fright in case Joe sees him.'

Amelia was intrigued. 'He sounds like one of my romantic heroes.'

'I know, but these aggressive types are all very well between the covers of a book, it's a different story when you've to cope with them in real life. I've had more than enough of aggressive men.'

'I can see your point. I've had enough of men – period! What are you going to do?'

Jenny shrugged. 'He's back in London, I don't know for how long but he says he'll write. Now I'm in agony in case Joe sees a letter from him.'

'If he writes, will you reply?'

'No. Maybe not answering his letters will put him off. Or he'll meet someone else. Or he'll be so caught up with new business challenges he'll forget about me.'

'You seem to have got some breathing space anyway. Meantime, what are you going to do about your husband? You surely can't go on forever allowing him to abuse you like this.'

'I wish I could work things out and make everything

51

better between Joe and me. I *have* tried but nothing does any good, at least not for long. It's really wearing me down, Amelia, I feel quite ill. I get so tired I just can't stand any more. I know I have no alternative but to get away. I've left him and gone back to my mother before of course and he's persuaded me to return. But not this time. I just can't take any more.'

She wondered if Gregson had been the catalyst in her final decision to leave but didn't think so. He was just an added complication in her life; having to cope with another man was the last thing she needed or wanted.

Jenny felt a bit better after confiding in Amelia. It was good to have somebody to talk to who understood, or at least partly understood. But as she left Mary House and walked along Queens Drive towards home she still felt worried and apprehensive.

How strange and mixed up life was. She'd never liked the basement flat but now that she'd decided to leave it she was only aware of its comfort and security as a home. She kept thinking wistfully of basic things like her cosy bed, her cushioned kitchen chair, all the cooking utensils and dishes she had gathered over the years, her boxed-in bath where she could have a luxurious soak in private, the hot bathroom air heady with the perfume of her bath oil.

Joe had gone quiet again. Whether it was because of feeling guilt and remorse or that he'd simply forgotten his latest attack on her, she neither knew nor cared. While she was waiting for the potatoes to boil she gazed at her face in the kitchen mirror. Now as well as the cut that Gregson had dressed there was an angry-looking weal on her forehead.

'Darling, I'm sorry.'

She hadn't noticed Joe coming into the kitchen. He had been in the sitting room reading the evening paper, the electric light glinting on the rich golden colour of his hair. He came over to her and tried to pull her into his arms.

'The potatoes should be ready now,' she said, turning away from him. She sensed the immediate tension in him and it triggered off terror. 'Darling, help me set the table, will you?' she said hastily. 'We can have a nice relaxing evening after dinner. All right?' She smiled and gave him a quick kiss on the cheek. But she was thinking, please God, let me get safely away from here, let me get safely away as soon as possible!

Joe set the table, quietly and methodically. Later, during the meal, he spoke in a pleasant and easy manner to the children and even, much to their delight, gave them five shillings each despite the fact that it wasn't pocket money day.

'Thanks, Daddy,' Rose hugged him enthusiastically. Dode's thin face lit up, 'Thanks, Dad!'

Jenny tried to smile but all the time she was anxiously wondering if there was a twisted reason behind Joe's behaviour. She was suspicious and apprehensive about him all the time now. She had begun to feel so locked in paranoia she doubted if she could ever be free of it – even if she managed to free herself from Joe. Could it be that he was making sure the children were out of the way this evening? And, if so – why?

After the meal Joe helped her with the dishes. She washed and he dried and as they were doing this Rose came in to the kitchen. She'd changed from her navy pleated skirt, white blouse and school tie. Ready for going out, she was cosily wrapped in a hooded duffel coat over denim trousers and fur-lined boots.

'Dode and I are away along for Harry,' she announced, her eyes round and sparkling with excitement.

'Amelia's boy?' Jenny asked in surprise, 'I didn't know you knew him.'

'We've known him for ages, he's in Dode's class.' Rose groaned at her mother's appalling ignorance.

After she'd gone, Joe said, 'Didn't that ring a bell?'

'What?' She eyed him cautiously, not knowing what he meant.

53

'Rose hanging about with her brother and his pal. That's what you used to do with me and my pals. I used to think you were a right little pest.'

She tried to laugh. 'Thanks very much.'

'Surely you must remember.'

'I hero-worshipped you. Yes, I remember.'

'I wish we could have those days back,' Joe said with a faraway, wistful look clouding his eyes, 'how lucky we were.' Suddenly his tone hardened and hatred iced over his face. 'The yellow bastards have all the luck now. They're doing all right. They're even over here enjoying themselves.'

Jenny hardly dared breathe. Any thought, any mention of anything Japanese immediately lit the fuse of Joe's madness. Nothing she could say in the circumstances would be the right thing although saying nothing could also prove a dangerous mistake. She was saved on this occasion by the telephone ringing but was glad her back was to Joe when she answered it. Otherwise he would have seen the blood drain from her face when she heard Gregson's voice.

'Darling,' he said, 'I'm going to miss you, I can't wait to be with you again.'

She hated him for thoughtlessly subjecting her to such terror.

'Who is it?' Joe asked and she replied without looking round, 'Amelia. She wants me to go in a bit later tomorrow. Something's turned up and she has to go out.' Then supposedly to Amelia she said brightly. 'Yes, of course. Whenever you like. Yes, that's fine with me.'

Gregson said, 'He's there, is he?'

'Yes.'

'Tell him what a wonderful time we had. Get your own back for all the rotten times he's given you.'

'Goodbye,' she said and put down the receiver. For a minute or two she couldn't turn round.

'Is there something wrong?' Joe asked.

'No, I'm just writing a reminder about the change of time. I've such a memory these days.'

'You don't need to remember to go along to skivvy for Amelia Donovan. I keep telling you to forget her and her job.'

'And I keep telling you that I like Amelia and I enjoy cooking.' The words burst from her before she could stop them but she immediately tumbled out others to save the situation. 'Please don't let's talk about it now. You were saying about how I used to follow you around – do you remember our first kiss?'

Some shadow of anger still clung to Joe's face but he said, 'The night I got my call-up papers?'

'No. Long before that.'

He shook his head. 'It was the night I got my call-up papers. I realized that I'd be separated from you; it was as if I was seeing you with new eyes. I remember the terrible urgency of the realization, I suddenly felt I'd wasted so much valuable time. Yet you were still only a child.'

'It was the night of Davie Gillespie's birthday party.'

'What was?'

'The first time we kissed. There was a game of postman's knock and I called your number. You were very ungentlemanly, I remember, and scornfully refused me but I insisted. You wouldn't kiss me but I kissed you.'

He laughed. 'You're right, fancy you remembering that.'

'I had to stand on a stool.'

'You chased me mercilessly. You realize that?'

'I've never denied it.'

His blue eyes held hers. 'Shameless hussy,' he said.

9

Amelia could sympathize with Jenny. If it hadn't been for her writing, she didn't know what she would have done, her own life was in such a mess. For a start she was married to Douglas Donovan but if she was in love with anyone it was still Andrew Summers although she hadn't seen him for years. Her boy, Harry, was the son of neither Douglas nor Andrew. Not that Harry knew that of course, he believed Douglas was his father. Douglas, his mother, and her own mother knew the truth, but she prayed to God that none of them would ever tell Harry.

She wondered if she could get away with denying it if the worst came to the worst; after all, she had been married to Douglas for nearly all of her pregnancy. Harry *could* have been Douglas's son – at least, from an outsider's point of view.

It wasn't as if she had purposely done anything wrong. She had just gone to watch the firework display on VJ night, celebrating the end of the Japanese war. She still remembered the horror of being caught up in the drunken rabble in George Square, then being dragged into a nearby lane and raped.

When Douglas had persuaded her to elope with him she hadn't known she was pregnant. It was hard to credit how innocent she had been. But the truth was, she hadn't a clue then how babies were made. Looking back, she realized that Douglas had assumed she was a virgin and put her on a pedestal. His oversized ego demanded that he should be the first with any girl. The wedding night had been traumatic. After a quick, vicious climax he had rolled off her to lie at her side, head jerked back against linked hands.

After a long silence in which she'd sunk into an abyss

of misery and bewilderment, she'd managed to ask, 'What's wrong?'

'Aw, shut up,' Douglas had snarled. 'You know damned well what's wrong.'

This was nothing of course to his treatment of her once he found out that she was pregnant. 'You sly little slut,' he'd almost wept with rage, 'you've tricked me into marrying you to give your bastard a name. You'll be sorry for this. Nobody takes me for a mug and gets away with it.'

He had certainly succeeded in making her suffer all during her pregnancy. Even after Harry was born his hatred still burned strong enough to try to make Harry suffer too. To protect Harry she'd left Douglas then and returned home, forgetting that home was even worse, albeit in a different way. She might have managed to survive in the digs she had eventually found, but her mother kept storming into the place and offending the eccentric, spinsterish landlady. Eventually the landlady had thrown her and Harry out.

Amelia sighed, remembering how relieved and ecstatically happy she'd been when she'd found work. Finding a job in which one could keep a baby was not easy; having a baby, as far as employers and landladies were concerned, was like having leprosy.

She remembered her bitterness too. To think how willingly and how hard she had worked. She was so grateful for what she'd believed was a safe roof over her and Harry's heads, she would have done anything for the invalid Mrs Robertson, her employer's wife. Mr Robertson of the fat belly and groping hands had been a different story, however. She'd had to draw the line at what he'd wanted her to do. Even now, she felt drained at the thought of the continual struggle life had been, fighting to survive while Harry had been a baby. It had been her and Harry against the world.

What had helped, at least for a time, was her love for Andrew Summers. It was he who had inspired her and

57

encouraged her and given her enough confidence to work at becoming a writer.

Douglas had no idea. She gazed across the living room at him. It was a dull winter's morning and rain was sweeping the streets on either side of the house and occasionally blowing in gusts against the windows. The trees and bushes surrounding the house and bordering the park across Langside Road seemed to have taken on a language of their own, whispering, hissing, creaking. Although it was still too early to leave for their lunch date at her mother's place in Balornock, the living room light was on. Douglas was hunched over a large pad of paper, intent on sketching Prince, the elderly collie who was stretched out sound asleep in front of the fire.

She was sorry for her husband now. Pity had not been the reason she had gone back to him, but it probably had some influence on her decision, she supposed. As a teenager at the Glasgow School of Art and for a few years after he had graduated he had shown great promise as an artist; there had been quite a fuss made of him. Perhaps it had all happened when he was too young. Maybe it had been like a youthful fling that had all too quickly settled down into middle-aged mediocrity. Yet he was still only 33, a couple of years older than herself.

Douglas had suffered a terrible blow to his pride because of his mother's black-market dealings and prison sentence. Rory had made a lot of money during the war and it did nothing to increase the family's popularity. Helena, Douglas's twin sister, had escaped most of the unpleasantness because she had married a Russian and settled in Leningrad. Helena and Amelia were friends and their friendship had gone some way to healing the breach between Douglas and herself.

Then there were the concerted efforts of Douglas's mother and her own mother who had been friends – off and on – since childhood. Rory had been furious at Amelia and Douglas's elopement and secret marriage at Gretna Green. But Douglas's mother and her own were old-fashioned enough to be even more shocked at the idea of divorce. Looking back Amelia also realized that Rory was worried about the fact that her son had lost direction, lost his magic touch in art, had begun to gamble to be the big man, to buy popularity by throwing money around, treating his friends to everything from drinks to expensive presents.

'Douglas needs to settle down,' she remembered Rory telling her mother, 'and so does Amelia. It's time they did, in my opinion. I admit I was against the marriage to begin with but I'm willing to do my best to help them get a fresh start.'

Even though the job as housekeeper at the Robertson house had turned out to be such a fiasco at least Amelia had not given in to her mother's pressure to come back to live with her. Immediately what would be best for Harry came into the argument, however – what would be best for Harry always won. Amelia would do anything for her son. From the wonderful moment of his birth he had been the most important factor in her life, her very reason for living. Many were the times she would have given up the battle for survival had it not been for her devotion to him. He was her miraculous accomplishment. She used to gaze at him as he slept when he was a baby and marvel at how she had produced something so perfect.

In every other area of her life her self-confidence was non-existent. Even in her writing she couldn't believe she had any talent; it was only another example of her grim determination to hang on and try to provide Harry with a home. She had persevered for years through dozens and dozens of rejections but despite her five published novels she had earned no more than a few hundred pounds a year. Far from being enough to buy a proper house for Harry and herself the earnings from her writing had proved barely sufficient to supplement her meagre wage at the Robertsons and to keep Harry and herself in clothes.

She'd often kept herself going with the hope that one day she would make enough money. She used to tell Harry that, long before he was old enough to understand. She could chat for hours about the lovely home of their own they'd have one day, all the toys and splendid things she'd be able to give him. Deep down, however, she did not believe she could ever perform such a miracle on her own.

She supposed, if she were honest, that Rory's offer of a house had been the deciding factor in her return to Douglas, more even than her mother's nagging. It was not just a tenement flat either, but a real house with a garden for Harry to play in. When Rory had found Mary House she had persuaded Amelia and Douglas to come and look round the place and then, being a clever woman, she'd switched her appeal to Harry.

'How would you like to live here, Harry?' she'd asked, 'and be able to play in the park and feed the ducks and go on the paddle boats every day?'

'Oh, Mummy, Mummy, can we?' Harry had begged.

He looked so happy and excited. She had never seen him looking so happy before. He had always been a quiet, serious child sitting in the Robertsons' silent house in Bearsden gazing at his picture books or patiently trying to create animal shapes with plasticine.

She couldn't resist his appeal. Had she done the right thing? For Harry's sake, she supposed so; at least now he had a good home where he could bring his friends. He lacked for nothing. Douglas wasn't perfect but then, what man was? Her own father, much as she'd loved him, had been far from perfect.

She thought she'd done the right thing. Or at least as right a thing as she was able to do at the time.

But things might have turned out so differently if she had not been so bitterly disillusioned with Andrew Summers. Admittedly they had never been lovers; at any rate, not in a sexual way. She had been too timid with men in those days, too afraid that she would be hurt again and even more afraid that she would be a disappointment to someone who in her eyes was so perfect.

She remembered the first time she had seen him; she'd gone to the Bearsden Town Hall to hear him speak about his writing. He and the chairman had to walk all the way down the passage between the seats, then climb the steps up to the platform. Andrew Summers's back was the first she had seen of him. He was a tall man with a self-conscious, shy hitch to his shoulders and a loping kind of gait. She had the strange feeling of immediately tuning into his character. When he turned she thought she had never in her life seen such an attractive face. There was compassion as well as a twinkle in his eyes, and a humorous quirk about the wide, generous mouth. The sight of him had melted her heart.

She had discovered that as well as being an up and coming poet and novelist, he was a teacher in the local school. She shook her head now at the memory of herself with baby Harry in tow, surreptitiously watching for glimpses of him coming from the school. She hadn't wanted him to see her. She wasn't capable of believing that he, of all people, would give her a second, or even a first glance for that matter. Why should he? She looked a right ragbag in her cast-off clothes bought for next to nothing at jumble sales. Poor Harry looked no better because she always bought his clothes a size too big in case she hadn't the money to buy him any others when he grew out of them.

But Andrew Summers had seen her at the shops one day and remembering how she had asked a question at his meeting in the Town Hall, he'd stopped to talk. That was how their strange love affair started. They kept meeting accidentally and talking for a few minutes about creative writing. And each word of his was a precious jewel in the counterfeit of her days. He had been gently encouraging and she had never known gentleness before. She had no experience of friendship with any man except the brief encounters with him. She had no reference point, no criteria for relationships with anyone, male or female, except rejection, betrayal and abuse. Getting to know Andrew Summers had been a revelation. It was like meeting God in the street every day.

He hadn't known at first that she was separated from her husband. Once he did, his attentions became more intimate. He began trying to persuade her to come to his flat.

'Amelia,' he said, 'we've snatched bits of conversation at street corners and beneath lamp posts and in rain, shine and force ten gales. Why don't you come to my flat one evening and we can talk at more length and in more comfortable surroundings?' He smiled. 'Will you?'

Was it then he had kissed her for the first time? She couldn't be sure. But she did remember that first warm meeting of lips as if the kiss was still fresh and sweet on her mouth. She remembered a blizzard of snow was swirling all round them as they kissed, white flakes powdering his hair and the turned-up collar of his anorak.

She wondered what would have happened had he not gone away on the Creative Writing Fellowship to York University. She supposed she would have got a divorce from Douglas and married him had it not been for the girl in York getting pregnant. She had suffered too much herself in being without love and support during such a time to wish the same on anyone else.

Summers had insisted he didn't love the girl; she was one of his students and had shamelessly pursued him, he said. He had resisted all her offers, he had assured Amelia, until one night after a party and a few drinks he'd returned to his room and found the girl in his bed. The thought of the girl, shameless or not, had brought back to Amelia all the loveless anguish of her own pregnancy. She could think of nothing else. All her unhappiness and insecurity returned to swamp her. She couldn't cope with it, the only way was to shut Andrew Summers out altogether. He had become only another problem in her life. He had married the girl eventually, and he was probably happily settled now in a home of his own. At least his child would have its real father.

What a confusion of emotion she had been in at the time, though. Was it any wonder she had succumbed to all the pressures put on her to settle down with Douglas again? The irony was that the home of her own she'd always dreamed of had turned out not to be *her* home at all – at least she'd never felt it was.

Rory had chosen it and paid for it and it was in Rory's name. Amelia and Douglas had had to go to one of Rory's department stores for all the furniture and Rory had been there all the time. It had been either Rory's choice or Douglas's that always won in the end; Douglas greatly admired his mother, which was understandable. 'You've got to give the old girl credit,' he'd often said. 'She came from one of the worst slums in Glasgow; she started with nothing and look what she's got now.'

Amelia sighed and Douglas glanced up from his sketch pad. 'What's wrong with you?'

She shrugged. 'Nothing.'

There was no point in trying to communicate with Douglas, she'd given up doing that. She'd told him long ago, for instance, that she felt depressed by the predominantly brown colouring of the furniture and furnishings of the house and that nothing was to her taste. 'The trouble with you,' Douglas had said, 'is you don't know anything about art.'

She recognized Art Deco when she saw it, it was just that she didn't particularly like its hard geometric lines. It felt unfeminine despite the group of nude bronze figures on the mantelpiece depicting female dancers, their erotic acrobatic poses reflected in the wall mirror, or the figure lamps dotted about the room. 'Nothing is *me*, I feel alienated in what's supposed to be my own home,' she'd told Douglas.

'You allow your imagination to run away with you,' Douglas had replied.

He blamed her imagination for everything. He had come to hate her ability to write and sell her writing, not that he ever admitted such a thing. It was obvious, however, in the way he kept trying to belittle her efforts and not only at writing; belittling her had become a habit. Sometimes he did it in quite a good-humoured, even an affectionate way. He had created such a convincing picture of her as a dumb blonde ditherer, incapable of doing anything on her own, that she had begun to believe it herself. After all, nothing had ever gone right in her life (except Harry, of course).

Now she didn't even have any sex in her marriage and was being made to feel that was all her fault as well. Douglas had become impotent; he said it was because she was not sufficiently sexually attractive. This had destroyed the last vestige of her self-esteem. She was now convinced that she could never be sexually attractive to any man.

Common sense told her that Douglas could not cope with his failure as an artist and her success as a writer and *that* was what caused his impotence. Deep down nothing could alter the way she felt, however. Nothing could change the conviction she had about her own lack of worth.

Yet, at the same time there was still so much loving locked inside her.

10

'Oh, come on,' Amelia sighed again. 'We might as well go now.'

'But Harry's not in yet! You know how your mother likes Harry to be there.' Douglas admired her mother almost as much as his own. The way he got on so well with Victoria annoyed Amelia intensely.

'So my mother will have one admirer less.'

'You're jealous of your own mother!' Douglas cried out incredulously. Although it wasn't the first time he'd made the accusation. It was, in fact, *the* one among her many faults that he most frequently enjoyed citing.

Before he had a chance really to get going and tell her she was a disgrace, he didn't know how her mother had ever put up with her and if she was half the woman her mother was she'd be fine, Harry appeared.

'Sorry I'm late, Mum,' he said, 'we met Dode's dad in the park and he was showing us some queer new foreign plants they've got in the greenhouse. Once he gets started on plants there's no stopping him.'

'We've just our coats to put on.' Amelia reached for hers lying over a chair alongside Douglas's sheepskin jacket. 'Is that anorak warm enough for you, son?'

Harry rolled his eyes. 'Yes, Mum.'

'Are you sure you don't need a scarf?' She knew her anxiety irritated him almost beyond endurance but it had become like an illness to her. She suffered unbearably with it herself.

'No, Mum,' Harry groaned.

She had to press her lips together to prevent herself from pleading with him to zip up the anorak and not leave it hanging open like that. The words ached in her head, bursting for release.

Douglas shrugged his broad shoulders into his sheep-skin jacket and buttoned it up. He wasn't as tall as Harry, who was an exceptionally well-built lad for his age, but he had a solid body.

'Every inch of me as hard as rock,' he was fond of boasting. He and Harry shared an interest in sport and keeping fit. Amelia was grateful for this. She tried to tell herself that Douglas had proved himself a good father to Harry by throwing him in at the deep end of the baths and teaching him to swim when he was little, and taking him to rough football matches and buying him boxing gloves.

Yet she couldn't help worrying and being anxious about his influence on Harry. Sometimes she feared he was purposely weaning Harry away from any interest in books and more studious occupations because he knew that's what she hoped he'd spend more time on. Could he be doing it just to worry and upset her? Even to come between her and Harry – to steal Harry's affection away from her? He'd tried every other method of hurting her over the years – although he always claimed that their relationship was completely innocent, denying most indignantly that he bore her any ill-will or had any intention of harming Harry or herself in the slightest way.

He reminded her of her mother who fought and continually nagged her husband all the time Amelia could remember. Yet since he'd died Victoria kept saying to everyone what a wonderful relationship she and Matthew had enjoyed. 'Never one cross word ever passed between us,' she was fond of saying. Her mother seemed actually to believe her own words. Did Douglas believe his? Amelia could never be sure; it was a constant source of anxiety to her.

In the car on the way to her mother's council flat in Balornock on the north side of the city Douglas and Harry argued loudly about the football match the previous afternoon. But it was a good-natured exchange

66

punctuated by guffaws of laughter from Harry and shouts of, 'Away you go, Dad. You must be needing glasses, that ball was nowhere near offside!'

Victoria was at the front room window watching for them as the car drew up in front of the close. She was a handsome-looking woman who could still hold herself like a queen although she'd put on a bit of weight and her hair was more grey than black. She waved and then eagerly hurried away. She was always either at her open front door or, if she could manage it in time, outside at the entrance to the close waiting to welcome them.

'Hello, dear,' she greeted Amelia, barely waiting for her daughter's kiss on her cheek before putting her arms out to give first Harry, then Douglas, an enthusiastic embrace. All it needed was her brother Jamie to arrive, Amelia thought, and her mother would no longer have any time for her at all.

As usual, they had Douglas and Harry's favourite lunch. 'You're the best steak-pie maker in Glasgow, Gran,' Harry said.

Victoria's head tipped up and her mouth primped with pleasure. 'I'm a good plain cook, son. None of your fancy foreign dishes for me like that Jenny woman makes.'

Douglas scraped his plate with equal satisfaction. 'I only wish Amelia had some of your talents.'

'Oh well,' her mother said magnanimously, 'it would be a dull world if we were all the same.' Then to Amelia, 'Don't just sit there dreaming. Clear away the dirty plates.'

Amelia did as she was told without a word. She always used to be rebelling but it had never done any good. Her mother used to accuse her of being moody and perverse 'just like your daddy.' Then she'd steam-rollered over her just like she'd always done with Matthew. He had put up a good fight but it had never done him any good either. Amelia believed the struggle had killed him in the end but she knew more about self-preservation. She

67

knew how to shut herself off, distance herself, keep quiet. Obediently she gathered the meat plates, carried them through to the kitchenette and placed them in the sink. She was standing gazing out of the window on to the back green when her mother bustled through carrying the empty vegetable tureen.

'Is that you at it again?' Victoria said. 'Honestly, Amelia, I don't know how that man puts up with you. I've said it before and I'll say it again. You've got a good man there. Not only that, you've even got a good mother-in-law. A bigger hearted, more generous woman than Rory Donovan would be hard to meet. It's time you pulled yourself together and realized how lucky you are. Bring the pudding plates through, they're up on the shelf.'

She brought the plates through.

'I was just telling Amelia,' Victoria said, 'what a lucky girl she is.'

'Hardly a girl, Mummy,' Amelia gave a wry smile.

'When you get to my age,' Victoria went on, 'and have to struggle along on your own, you realize only too well what it means to have a good man at your side. There's never a day goes by that I don't miss my Matthew.'

'Where're your lodgers today?' Amelia asked.

Victoria rested sadly accusing eyes on her daughter. 'Strangers are no substitute for my own flesh and blood.'

'Daddy wasn't your flesh and blood.' The words escaped before she realized and she immediately regretted them. There were times when she could keep quiet. And there were times when she couldn't.

'Don't pay any attention to her,' Douglas said, 'she's in one of her moods.'

'Oh, great!' Harry cried out, 'trifle!'

Victoria was diverted, mollified. 'I made it especially for you and your daddy, son. I know how you both enjoy my trifle.' She dished them large portions and pressed a jug of cream towards them while Amelia dished her own.

'What we need,' Douglas was saying now, 'is you over

68

at Mary House cooking for us. You'd be welcome to make your home with us any time, Mum. I mean it.'

Victoria gazed at him fondly. 'I know you do, son.'

Amelia could hardly believe her ears. How dare Douglas make such a suggestion without any warning or discussion with her? She felt sick with anger. She was also caving in with fear.

'But I couldn't put Aggie and her man out on the street.'

'Aggie and her man' were Victoria's lodgers. They were an elderly couple who, when they'd first arrived on Victoria's doorstep, had looked like a pair of tramps fresh from sleeping on a park bench and that's probably what they were. Victoria, however, had soon got them organized and cleaned up. They even went to church with her now. People marvelled at what a good Christian woman Victoria was.

'Well just remember what I've said.' Douglas licked his lips after scraping up the last of his trifle. 'There'll always be a bed waiting for you in Mary House.'

Amelia stared hard at the cropped head, the rugged face more like that of a boxer than an artist, the brown eyes apparently oblivious of having done the slightest thing out of place. Amelia stared and stared, concentrating on her husband as much silent hatred as she could muster.

11

The children didn't say anything at first. The misery they felt, though, was plain to see in their pinched white faces. They had left home with Jenny before to go and live in gran's room in Anderston and knew what it was like. Not that they had anything against gran. They loved her. But it was one thing visiting for a few hours, quite another having to crowd together in gran's 'single end' overnight, or worse, more than one night. They also loved their dad, despite his drinking bouts. He could be kind and good to them and to Jenny in lots of ways. Like her, they used to keep hoping that things would get better.

But not any more. Even Joe's treats of taking them all to the seaside and to the pictures or giving them presents could not make up for how he hurt their mother again and again. He never touched the children, although Jenny often wondered what would happen if he didn't have her to vent his frustration on, or whatever it was that made him behave as he did.

An added difficulty on this occasion, of course, was the fact that they were not on holiday from school like the last time they went to gran's. They would have to travel from Anderston until she could find digs. She had already put a card in a papershop near the school and been keeping her eye on the furnished rooms to let in the paper.

She was determined to avoid their lives being disrupted any more than was necessary by changing schools.

'I know it's too crowded at gran's,' she said. 'But I'll get a nice place of our own. I promise.'

'That's what you said last time, Mum,' Rose reminded her. 'And all the places were too dear. Or they didn't allow children. Or both.'

70

'I've got to try,' she said, 'what else can I do?'

'Dode and I could stay here,' Rose said, adding quickly, 'it's not that I don't want to be with you, Mummy, but it's so awful at gran's. I mean I know it's not gran's fault but it *is* awful.'

The sight of her daughter's eyes brimming with despair intensified Jenny's wretchedness. She tormented herself as she had done a million times before with the thought that perhaps she should just grit her teeth for the children's sake and go on putting up with Joe's behaviour. It was either that or leave. She'd tried everything else these past few years. She'd even sent for the police only to be treated like an embarrassment and told it was a domestic affair and none of their business. Next time, despite her distress, she'd ignored this cavalier attitude and insisted on bringing charges. This turned out to be a terrible ordeal for the whole family, herself included. Joe had been fined just a few pounds which she had to pay from the housekeeping money. The scandal in such a respectable neighbourhood had been the worst thing to bear. She'd overheard one woman say to another in a shop in Victoria Road, 'I don't know the wife, but a nicer, quieter, less violent man than Joe Thornton would be hard to meet. I always know my children are perfectly safe in the park when he's around. His wife must have provoked him beyond endurance. She probably deserved all she got.'

'We'd be all right here, Mum,' Dode said, 'unless you feel you *need* us to be with you.'

'No, it's not that, son,' she gazed helplessly at him, 'but with your dad being out at work there would be nobody to cook your meals and look after you.'

Rose said, 'I could cook.'

'Rose, you'd be at school most of the day. You wouldn't have time to do the cooking.'

'You're at work most of the day, Mummy, and you manage.'

'I've had more practice at managing than you,

71

darling. I'm 30 years of age. You're not 13 yet.'

'I could do it, Mummy, honestly.'

'No, it wouldn't be fair on you, Rose.'

Anger flashed in the child's eyes.

'I suppose you think it's fair to force me to sleep on the floor at gran's and have nowhere to put my clothes and things, and not even a bathroom to wash in and no toilet. It's disgusting!'

Dode's bony elbow nudged her into silence.

'Shut up will you! It's not mum's fault.'

Rose flushed and lowered her gaze. 'Well, it's not my fault either.'

Jenny gazed miserably at them for a minute before saying, 'Let's try it at gran's just for a day or two to see if anything else turns up.'

'Nothing ever does,' Rose muttered and her brother nudged her again. 'I told you to shut up.'

'We can't even see our friends.' Rose sounded near to tears.

'We'll see them at school,' Dode told her, 'what's the use of going on about it?'

For a wild moment Jenny nearly buried her head in the sand of self-deception as she had done so often in the past. She nearly assured herself everything would be all right if she stayed. She nearly believed everything was bound to be all right. She so desperately *wanted* them to be a normal, secure and happy family together. But the moment passed.

She packed as much as they could carry and as quickly as possible so that they could be safely away before Joe arrived home from work. She carried the case, and Dode and Rose struggled as best they could with cardboard boxes held together with string. It was an ordeal full of suspense waiting for the bus in Victoria Road in case Joe saw them. Even when stone cold sober now, his temper could unexpectedly flare up. She kept glancing over at the impressive entrance gates and the path beyond, which sloped up to the wide granite stairway and a magnificent terrace. From there she knew the view stretched back the whole length of Victoria Road and far across the Clyde beyond the city skyline to the Campsie Hills and Ben Lomond.

Standing out in the open so near the park she nursed her vulnerability like a pain. It was impossible even to begin to relax until she and the children were on the bus and speeding away towards the city centre.

The district of Anderston was situated along the riverside at the Broomielaw and its jungle of tenements had long since engulfed the main thoroughfare of Argyle Street. Argyle Street, in fact, at the Anderston end, had once been called Main Street when Anderston had been little more than a village and not part of the great metropolis of Glasgow.

Dode once remarked while studying the map of the city that the streets cutting off the Broomielaw – of which Cheapside Street where her mother lived was one – looked like a ladder lying alongside the river. Cheapside Street had a whisky bond that backed on to Warroch Street, the next street along. Beside this big whisky warehouse, and dwarfed by it, was the old tenement building where she had been born and brought up. It was black with soot and as she and the children climbed the turret stairway they had to go carefully because of the darkness and the crumbly stone stairs. Only one feeble gas jet lit each landing. The half-landing in between where the lavatory was situated had no light at all. Tenants had to take a torch or a candle when forced to obey a call of nature.

Jenny remembered how scared she used to be as a child racing up these stairs on her own, round and round past the lavatories with their ancient plumbing that made strange groans and grumblings whether anyone was using them or not, past silent doors in ghostly shadows from gas jets, before reaching the safe harbour of her mother's open door on the top flat. Her mother usually timed her return so that she would be at the door waiting to catch her recklessly flying figure and give her a reassuring cuddle.

Once inside the house with the door safely shut and bolted behind them nothing outside mattered. The dark turret stairs, the ugly bulkiness of the whisky warehouse, the old St Marks burial ground that also crushed into the short street, everything was forgotten. Inside the 'single end' the red glow from the fire brightened the black range making warm colours dance and flicker over its steel edges and the china dogs and glass face of the clock on the mantelpiece above. The occasional friendly crackle of the fire and the rhythmic creak of her mother's rocking chair added to the pleasant atmosphere. Sounds from outside, were far off. A dog barking or howling, the wind in the graveyard, a ship's hooter, the cries of other children in the tenement building, everything was remote and muted. Safe in their own small world of that single room, completely isolated, sealed in by dense fog from the river, her father and mother and herself had been perfectly happy.

She doubted if she would ever make her children understand that magic contentment.

'How *could* you be happy in a dump like that!' Rose always said. 'You're not remembering right, Mummy.'

But she remembered every happy hour. Her father's life of course had been ruined by becoming one of the army of men paid off in the shipyards. Now, looking back, she was saddened by the picture in her mind's eye of her father and other unemployed men huddled together for support in their misery at every street corner. They all wore thin suits and long white scarves knotted at their throats and flat tweed caps. Hands thrust deep into jacket pockets, from time to time their ill-shod feet shuffled from one street corner to another in an effort to protect themselves from the cold.

Her mother must have had an even harder time with trying to make ends meet. There had certainly been no money for new clothes or anything for the house. There

74

were times when they went hungry. Her mother and father could not have been happy then, and yet, to her, especially inside the house, they remained the same, the source of all the joy and security of her childhood.

'Come in, hen,' her mother's plump, aproned figure was waiting with the door open, 'I've a good fire going.' She gave them a kiss and cuddle. 'Take off your coats and get a heat.' She bustled about them. 'Goodness, they're soaked! Give them to me, I'll hang them up on the pulley.'

They crushed through the tiny windowless hall into the room. It amazed Jenny now to think that her mother had managed to cook and bake and wash and iron in such a confined space, not to mention bringing up a child. In this room which was smaller than her kitchen in Queens Park, she and her mother and father had somehow fed themselves and kept themselves and the place clean. But it was mostly her mother who had performed the daily miracles. For cooking and heating water she had only the open fire, the oven attached to it which was dependent on it for heat, and one gas ring on top.

The sink under the single window had a tap shaped like a swan's neck with only cold water. Pastry was rolled out on the wooden table that sat in the middle of the room and which you had to squeeze sideways to get past.

Her mother and father slept in the high recessed bed – or a 'hole-in-the-wall' bed as it was more commonly known. The bed was covered in a bedmat made of patchwork that had belonged to her mother's mother. Side curtains of cream cotton were looped back on either side of the bed and a cream vallance of matching material stretched across the front.

A 'truckle' bed had to be wheeled out from under the big bed for her every night. A chamber pot was also kept under the bed. It was needed during the night and first thing in the morning when a trip to the lavatory down on the half-landing could freeze you to death in the winter.

Any morning, summer or winter it was difficult to get in because of other neighbours getting there first.

Putting down her suitcase and allowing her mother to peel off her coat, Jenny said, 'I wish I didn't need to bother you like this, Mammy.'

Her mother gave the wet coat a shake, then did the same with the children's 'burberries'. 'How could you and the wains be a bother? I'll just shove these up on the pulley then I'll make a pot of tea.'

'I won't waste any time. I'll get a place as soon as I can, Mammy. I've got the *Citizen*. There's a couple that I'm going to see tonight.'

'You're welcome to stay here as long as you like, hen.'

One of the most wonderful things about her mother, and the thing Jenny appreciated most, was her un-questioning loyalty and support. She could always depend on her. It was wonderful to be so sure of this. And to have no need to explain or try to justify her actions in any way.

On similar occasions in the past, once the children were asleep and she and her mother were sipping a hot drink before going to bed, she had confided in her about the way Joe was. Her mother had sighed and said, 'The war has a lot to answer for. But you can't put up with him raising his hand to you, hen. You were quite right to leave. Maybe it'll bring him to his senses.'

But it never had. Crouched on the fender stool close to the fire Jenny sipped the tea her mother gave her. The room smelled of heat and the evaporating moisture from the coats dangling from the pulley overhead. The children had settled at the table and were playing a game of draughts.

Darkness had crept down making the window a black mirror that reflected the inside of the room. Her mother had lit the gas mantle above the fireplace and it was puttering and hissing. She had taken the biscuit tin down from its high perch beside the china dog ornaments to offer it around. The children delved their hands in and were now, to all appearances, munching quite happily as they played.

The room was cosy and comfortable, yet Jenny was no longer able to capture in it the contentment of her youth. It made her feel sad, and served to remind her of how a home could be but which was now lost to her. She was a piece of flotsam in a cold sea, belonging nowhere.

'You don't look well,' her mother said. 'Do you need to trail away out again tonight, hen?'

'It's their school, Mammy. I don't want their lessons to suffer. The quicker we get a place nearby the better. Then there's my work as well. Think of the bus fare for us all back and forward every day.'

'Whatever you think best, hen. Drink up your tea, that'll put a heat in you.'

'Are you not going to have a cup yourself?'

'After I take this coat back off the pulley. If you're going out tonight I'd be quicker to hold it in front of the fire.'

'It'll just get wet again.'

'No, the rain's stopped.' She hesitated. 'What if Joe comes, hen?'

'Do as I did the last time. Put the chain on the door and don't let him in.' She finished her tea then gave a big sigh. 'Well, no use putting it off. I'd better go.'

Her mother poked the fire into a cheery blaze. 'I'll keep it going until you get back and I've got extra milk for cocoa. Mind how you always used to love a hot cup of cocoa before going to your bed?'

'Sometimes it was an Oxo cube.'

'So it was! Well, I've got Oxo as well if you'd rather, hen. And there'll be enough water left in the kettle for you to have a good wash.'

Once again Jenny felt amazement at how her mother had always kept herself and the house so spotlessly clean without the convenience of hot running water. Even the draughty stairs outside and the ice box of a lavatory were religiously cleaned every week with hot water liberally

77

laced with Pine disinfectant. It could never have been easy, especially when some of the neighbours who had big families overcrowding the tiny apartments were too harassed to take their turn. Nobody could blame them for giving up in such a building where the very stones were crumbling away and the view from the kitchen window was of a claustrophobic back yard where the whisky bond blocked off the sun and where middens overflowed and heaved with rats.

Her mother gave her coat a last heat at the fire before helping her on with it. 'Button it up, hen. It gets that cold at night. I've got a scarf in the drawer you can have.'

'Thanks, Mammy.'

She looked around again as her mother went over to the chest of drawers. 'You know, you deserve a medal for the way you manage to keep this place, Mammy. It's always so nice.'

Pride and pleasure lit up her mother's face. 'Funny you should say that. Your daddy used to say the very same.'

'It's true.'

'Och, well, if there were any medals being given out I wouldn't be the only one. Have you seen Mrs McFarlane's wee room and kitchen? You could eat your dinner off that woman's floor.' She fussed the scarf around her daughter's neck, tied it at the front and gave it a pat. 'That'll help keep you cosy.'

It was just like her mother used to do when Jenny was a child. It reminded her so vividly of her schooldays that for a moment it was quite uncanny; she really felt a child again, setting off for school cosily wrapped up, her 'playpiece' of bread and jam parcelled in newspaper and tucked in her schoolbag along with her books.

Her mother saw her to the door just as she used to. 'Take care now, hen. And watch crossing the roads.'

Jenny laughed. 'I'm not a wee girl any more, Mammy.'

'You'll always be my wee girl,' her mother said.

78

Before she turned the corner of the stairs, Jenny glanced back. Her mother's small round body swathed in a floral wrap-around apron, her smiling face and neatly combed and 'Kirbyed' hair were still visible in the gaslight outside the door.

Jenny had never felt so unwilling to lose sight of her.

12

Rebecca Abercrombie had put her trust in God and she had been saved. She had been saved for a special purpose, of that she was certain. She had never confided this to anyone except of course to Alice, her closest friend. Everyone else knew that her mother had been killed in an air-raid and her house in Pollokshaws destroyed during the war. That was all.

Her mother had in fact been cut down while in the very act of breaking God's commandment with a lover; Rebecca had been horrified. She remembered arriving at the house and finding her mother and a Polish soldier in bed together. She remembered screaming abuse at her mother and also shouting brokenheartedly, 'How *could* you betray dad like this? When he's away fighting, putting his life on the line for us.'

Her mother had wept in distress but she hadn't believed her when she had said that her father was down in England having a good time with another woman. It wouldn't have mattered if she had believed her mother's desperate pleas of justification and self-defence, she was in too much of a state of shock to feel anything but revulsion and hatred. 'I hope you'll be punished for this,' she shouted before running blindly from the house, 'I hope you'll be made to suffer!'

As she'd wandered the streets she'd prayed that God would punish her mother. And he had, horribly: the house had received a direct hit. She still had flashes of memory of what she had seen among the rubble when she'd returned – like watching a horror movie. She had only allowed herself to catch brief glimpses of it between Venetian blinds of fingers.

Her father had come home to Glasgow on compassionate leave and as soon as the war was over he had sent for the woman from England and they had been married. They now lived in Christian Street in Pollokshaws. *Christian* Street of all places, and it not a stone's throw from where he'd lived with her mother! All her anger and bitterness had long since turned on him; too late, she'd believed her mother.

People often remarked that she was not like either her mother or her father. Her mother had been a mousy-haired woman with generous curves. Her father's hair was also mousy-brown and he had long since lost most of it. Like her mother, he was short in stature but over the years since her mother's death he'd acquired a beer belly which made him look worse.

She had photographs of her parents from happier days before the war, strolling arm-in-arm along the front at Dunoon. Her father sported grey flannel trousers that flapped wide against his thin legs; the trousers were topped with an open-necked shirt and a sleeveless Fair Isle pullover. Her mother's short, finger-waved hair was held in place with a childish-looking clasp. The breeze was frolicking with her floral print dress, its puff sleeves and sweetheart neckline looking inappropriately demure against her plump flesh. Other photos showed her mother in a cloche hat and earrings and a dark coat with a posy of artificial flowers on the shoulder. Her father was in coarse khaki uniform and clumsy boots.

Rebecca had a slim figure of regal height and bearing, topped with a luxurious crown of thick, black, frizzy hair. Her most unusual feature, however, was her glowing dark eyes. Her friend Alice used to say, 'What splendid dark eyes you have, Rebecca. You ought to be a hypnotist, not a social worker.'

In many ways she had enjoyed her job in the Social Work Department of Glasgow Corporation but she had become more and more frustrated at the restrictions on what she was able to do. On the one hand there was so much red tape, so much interference from other people in the Department who didn't agree with her methods. On the other hand there was her own growing anger at the sufferings of the innumerable women hidden away behind the closed doors of Glasgow tenements, women to whom for much of the time she was denied access by their monsters of husbands.

Rebecca felt that 'monsters' was not too strong a word for these men and indeed anger, born of bitterness against her father, had spread with the rapidity of an infectious disease to encompass all men. For women she felt enormous pity. Her mother was not the only victim of men's cruel and selfish behaviour. How else could the Polish soldier's actions be described? He had taken sexual advantage of a lonely and loving woman who had been betrayed by her husband. On her rounds as a social worker Rebecca had seen too many women taken advantage of, bullied, battered, dominated, emotionally blackmailed, raped, terrified literally out of their wits, tormented in a thousand cruel ways by men.

She'd struggled continually to cleanse herself of her hatred of the male sex but only because she knew hatred was a self-destructive emotion; hating men would be allowing them to destroy her. It was therefore partly for reasons of self-preservation that she'd begun experimenting in all sorts of methods of self-help and finding peace of mind and body. She'd started with yoga and was still an enthusiastic devotee. She'd become fascinated and enthusiastic about all sorts of therapies from hypnotism to spiritual healing.

Her boss at the Social Work Department had, among other things, accused her of being a 'dabbler'. He had been a man of rigid, old-fashioned and strictly conventional ideas. She had accused him of having a closed mind. She believed that the long knives had been sharpened to plunge into her back from that moment on. That short-sighted, bigoted, stupid man had persecuted her until she'd been forced to leave.

However, she had come to see that God meant it to be

that way. God was guiding her into paths where she could be of far better and more lasting help to women, who would be able to come to her in the privacy and safety of her own home. She could help them. She could build up their self-confidence so that they could deal successfully with the monsters who were making their lives such a misery. Real success to Rebecca was for the woman to free herself completely of male bondage and start a new and fulfilling life on her own.

Of all the many excellent methods she'd found – and was still finding – to help these women, hypnotherapy had proved the most useful. She'd studied the subject very conscientiously and even exercised her eyes night and morning before the bathroom mirror and bathed them with Optrex in her navy-blue eyebath. It had been Alice who had given her the idea of practising hypnotherapy although, as they'd both agreed later, it was obviously meant to be. God hadn't given her such eyes and such power in them for nothing.

Alice was 56, twenty years older than herself, squat in stature with wiry grey hair and pebble-thick horn-rimmed glasses. She suffered with bad legs which made walking difficult but nothing could crush her indomitable spirit. She had a real talent for telling fortunes with tea cups and tarot cards as well as with a crystal ball. That was Alice's God-given gift; she also made quite a good living at it.

Sometimes Rebecca visited Alice's home, a high-ceilinged, five-room-and-kitchen flat round the corner from Christian Street where – as Alice often said – she rolled around like a pea in an empty can. Alice had a wonderful sense of humour.

Sometimes they met in Battlefield House in Langside, where Rebecca had lived for the past seven years. It was a villa, the only remaining building from the time of Mary, Queen of Scots. It stood by itself on an island of land between Algie Street and Millbrae Road known as Battle Place. A neglected length of back garden with

83

knee-high grass was bounded by a brick wall in which was a door leading to a back lane; on the other side of the lane was an undertaker's parlour.

The front of the building had a splendid view of the monument to commemorate the battle of Langside. High on top of the tall obelisk was a lion squatting up on its haunches with one of its front paws resting on a cannon ball. The obelisk itself was decorated with carvings of thistles, roses and fleur de lis and was set on a square base on the corners of which perched an eagle with massive wings outstretched. The monument stood on top of the wide hilltop centre where Battlefield Road met Langside Road. Across from it was the south end of the park, lush with silver birches, butterfly bushes and the winter-perfumed, abundant escallonia.

Here it was on 13 May 1568 that the actual battle had been fought. It had raged over the site of Battlefield House, the Monument, Battlefield Road and right down the grassy hill of the park to the other side, to Queens Park district at Balvicar Street and Queens Drive.

Many people believed the area was haunted and, from time to time over the years, sightings had been reported of the ghostly figures of Mary Queen of Scots' highland troops in the park. Many hundreds of them had been buried there after the battle. Rebecca kept hoping that she would see something but so far she had not been lucky.

'You will, though,' Alice prophesied, 'you will. God did not direct you to Battlefield House for nothing.'

Both she and Alice believed that nothing happened without a purpose. Everything was part of God's plan and God had planned that she live in a place so rich in spiritual energy. Although Rebecca had once confessed to Alice that she did not much like to be on her own in the house. 'Not that I'm afraid or anything silly like that,' she assured her friend. 'It's just that I know every moment is precious and I have so much work to do. I'm just impatient to devote every waking hour to helping my "friends".'

'Friends' was the term she used rather than patients or clients to describe the people who came to her for help.

'I have an ever-open door to them,' she told Alice. 'They know they can phone or come to see me any time of the day or night and I will welcome them and do my best to comfort and help them. Isn't that what friendship should be all about, I tell them.'

'Yes,' Alice agreed, 'indeed more than that, my dear, sisterly love.'

'God's love, Alice.'

'Yes, indeed.'

Alice always professed admiration at Rebecca's patience and forbearance. Although she herself had regular clients call at her own home they were always by appointment only. She liked peace and quiet and would never put up with people wandering in and out and gathering for chats and unending cups of tea and impertinent raids on her biscuit tins.

Peace and quiet was never complete in a tenement, of course; footsteps reverberating up and down the stone stairs, distant music and English voices on wirelesses, children crying, couples quarrelling, make up a pot-pourri of sounds that seeped constantly through the walls. Alice didn't mind as long as they were distant and the source was not inside her house. She knew and was glad that fear kept most of her neighbours at a respectful distance. She encouraged this state of affairs as much as possible because it not only resulted in the privacy she wished, it was a source of great amusement to her.

'You're very naughty, Alice,' Rebecca accused her, but couldn't help laughing at Alice's antics to scare off the neighbours. She and Alice had many a good laugh together, although sometimes Rebecca lectured Alice about this aspect of her nature, especially if she had dropped in unexpectedly to see Alice and sensed the lack of a warm and welcoming atmosphere. Alice would politely insist that she was welcome at any time but Rebecca would fix her with a long dark stare and say meaningfully, 'I don't need a crystal ball to find out the truth about people, Alice.'

Alice would go even cooler then, go further into herself rather than become more outgoing. Despite this little difference in their natures, however, they got on exceptionally well. It helped perhaps that Alice dropped in to see her much more often than the other way round.

Rebecca actually preferred it this way; it was still an ordeal for her to visit Pollokshaws and the street so near where her mother had been killed. The quickest way to get to either Alice's home or her own father's was to pass the very spot. She usually managed to avoid seeing the gap in the street however. The house was still not rebuilt and weeds grew tall and thick over the rubble. If she happened to be with someone else or for some reason could not avoid passing the place she did her deep breathing to help control any feeling of panic. In through the nostrils, down into the throat, fill the upper then the lower chest and deeply into the abdomen. Then contract the abdominal muscles and slowly push the breath up and out again.

Despite the discipline of deep breathing the thought of her mother kept leaping to her mind, her poor mother.

Her mother had been a good-natured, generous-hearted woman who had been nothing but loving to her as a child. Rebecca would gladly have given her own life a thousand times over if it could have erased the cruel words of hatred and accusation she'd flung at the poor woman during the last precious moments she'd seen her alive.

Her distress was also reawakened every time she saw her father so fat and contented and pleased with himself now. She tried to avoid seeing him as much as possible. That was another reason why it was better if Alice came to Langside to visit her. If it was spring or summer they could eat a picnic lunch in the park.

Sometimes they sat on one of the wooden benches at the high part near the flagpole and admired the view. It always amazed them how many church spires there were in the area around the park; they agreed that it must be the most densely 'churched' area in Glasgow, if not in the whole of Scotland. There was even the majestic ruin of Langside Hill church across the side to the left of Battlefield House, looking from her window. It had been hit by an incendiary bomb during the last war and the destruction caused to its beautiful interior had been tragic. The church had originally been designed and built by Alexander Skirving who had been chief draughtsman to the brilliant Victorian architect, 'Greek' Thomson. The interior of the church had been lined with wood and covered with coloured stencilled decorations that had astonished everyone who saw it. The incendiary bomb had set ablaze the paint-impregnated woodwork and the resulting inferno had lit up the whole south side of the city.

Although Rebecca seldom attended church now, the fact of so many places of religion around her was a comfort; she felt she was on holy ground. In Pollokshaws, a densely populated crush of tenements further along from Langside where she had spent her youth, she had been a regular attender at Sunday school, then bible class then church.

Since those days however she had found her own path to God. Her shadowy Aladdin's Cave of a living room was crammed to overflowing with books on sacred rituals and chakras and auras and reincarnation, to mention but a few of the branches of knowledge that had caught her attention.

She had been reading a fascinating book on Kirlian photography that evening in March while sitting at her front room window, with the green plush curtains draped back, waiting for a 'friend' to arrive for treatment. The 'friend' was nervous of the dark and liked to see the guiding and comforting light from her window as she came along the quiet street. It was while she was sitting waiting that she noticed a red glow in the dark

87

sky. Then she thought she made out fingers of flame in the distance closing around the roofs of tenement buildings. So intent was she with this phenomenon that she hadn't noticed the 'friend' approaching along the street outside. It was the clamour of the doorbell that dragged her back to immediacy.

'Come in, my dear,' she greeted the timid little woman on the doorstep. 'Forgive me for keeping you waiting. I was at my front room window and I thought I saw flames over by the river.'

'Yes, oh, it's a terrible thing.'

'A big fire is it, dear?'

'Really terrible! Lots of people burned to death, I hear. I passed quite near it on my way to you.'

'How awful! No wonder you're upset, come on through to the kitchen and have a cup of my camomile tea. I thought I heard a bang earlier on, was there an explosion?'

'Terrible, really terrible! It was the whisky bond in Cheapside Street. Exploded suddenly like a bomb. They say the whole street is a raging inferno.'

'Oh, those poor people,' Rebecca's voice rocked with drama as she filled the kettle, 'those poor, poor people!'

13

Harry felt a marked man. Ever since the incident at the dance in Langside Hall he had been afraid this would happen.

It had been all right at first. The record player was blasting out 'Don't You Rock Me Daddy-O' and coloured lights flashed through the gloom, breaking up the sharpness of the walls and creating the illusion of being in a strange space and time. He had got up to dance with Jean Ferguson and had really enjoyed their energetic communion with the crazy lights and music. Back at the side of the hall he and Jean were sharing their experiences of mad Effie, the terror of the maths department at school, when he noticed the Gorbals Boys come in.

The Gorbals district of Glasgow was a thorn in the side of Queens Park. It lay halfway between the latter and the city centre. A jungle of black tenements and dusty streets, it was where dogs roamed loose and children played football with tin cans. It was where packs of youths armed themselves with razor blades and knives they called gibs, and warred with one another. Sometimes these youths made sorties into more respectable districts like Queens Park, where they shocked the residents with their rough appearance, playing noisy football in the park and shouting foul language that echoed through the quiet leafy streets. Even Scout dances needed bouncers because of this danger. It took a brave bouncer to face up to one of these marauding gangs, but they did their best.

Sometimes a few of the Gorbals Boys would appear in the café, swaggering and defiant, daring anyone by their very manner to challenge their right to sit at one of the tables and spoon ice cream or drink Iron Brew.

Harry, being a friendly type and with no territorial aggressiveness had often spoken to tnem in the café. They were all right on their own or even in twos. He'd shared his fags with them and had a good laugh. He'd even, on occasion, defended them in arguments with Queens Park types like Farquhar Forbes-Smith. Farquhar was a snobbish twit who never sat about in the café with the rest of the blokes. He just went to the counter to buy his ice cream and ginger and hurried straight out again as if afraid he'd be contaminated by the 'ignorant masses'.

Masses was the operative word, Harry had discovered. The very same Gorbals boys he had grown to like and thought he could number among his pals turned out to be disappointingly and dangerously different en masse.

They were en masse that night at the dance. He had experienced a shiver of apprehension when he saw the size of the crowd shouldering its way into the hall. He managed to quell his fears however, and give a friendly nod over to Frank and Jacko. Frank especially had become quite pally with him after discovering they shared the same enthusiasm for Queens Park Rangers football team. Frank gave a jerk of recognition that displayed bravado tinged with embarrassment.

Soon afterwards it became apparent that the Gorbals Boys had picked on Lindsay McDonald to be their sport for the night. Skinny, bespectacled Lindsay was a bit of a wimp and often Queens Park boys kidded him at school or in the café. It was one thing taking the micky in those circumstances. It was just harmless fun and not going to endanger life or limb. Being tormented by the Gorbals Boys had no such built-in assurance. Lindsay looked frightened. Sweat moistened the sickly putty colour of his skin. His glasses seemed to have grown enormous on a shrunken face.

Harry felt sorry for him. It became more and more difficult to concentrate on what Jean was saying or even

90

to listen to the music despite the fact the volume was turned up so high it was mind-blowing. At home his mum and dad complained when his record-player was only half as loud as this. His dad in fact went quite berserk, 'Turn that bloody racket down!' he'd bawl. His mum always said, 'I worry about your ears. You'll be deaf before you're grown up!'

Most of the dancers seemed oblivious of the knot of bodies tightening around Lindsay, and the guffawing and jeering. Eventually Harry said, 'I can't just sit here.' And before Jean could protest or before his nerve deserted him, he got up and pushed his way rapidly towards the crowd manhandling the terrified Lindsay.

'Give over!' He aimed his words at Jacko who, at that moment, had Lindsay by the tie and was making spasmodic attempts to choke him, much to the hilarity of the knot of onlookers. 'He's liable to have a heart attack!'

'Fuck off,' Jacko sneered.

'Look, everybody's having a good time listening to the records and dancing,' Harry made a desperate attempt to remain reasonable and friendly. 'Why don't you do the same. Leave the poor guy alone.'

'Leave the poor guy alone!' Jacko went into a mimicking act, exaggerating Harry's friendly appeal into an obsequious whine. It was at that point that Harry realized that all the mindless attention had turned on him. Lindsay was forgotten. He had become the new sport, the next victim. He could see the lust for blood in their eyes. His instinct for self-preservation warned him the situation had to be terminated immediately. Shooting out his fist he smashed it into Jacko's face. Jacko's leer was immediately drowned by a welter of blood from his nose. The blood-lust in the eyes of the other Gorbals Boys changed to fear.

Harry pushed his way back to Jean and asked her up to dance. It was while he was dancing that Frank – Frank of all people – came up behind him. He felt a sudden pain in his shoulder and thought Frank had punched him. He stopped dancing long enough to give Frank an angry punch in return. A real belter it was that knocked Frank staggering backwards among the dancers like a drunken man. Everyone stopped to look as Frank slithered to the ground at their feet. Then they gasped in disbelief as Harry continued to dance. He didn't realize why at the time, he imagined they must be feeing a bit awestruck at the force of his punch. Or perhaps even at his brass neck at standing up to one of the Gorbals Boys and risking retribution from the others lurking in the flickering shadows. Harry caught glimpses of their shabby figures and drooping jowls as the welter of emerald, ruby and purple lights kept zigzagging across the walls.

It wasn't until later when he went to the gents that he noticed the bloodstain spreading across his shirt. Only then did he realize he'd been stabbed. Everybody had thought he was being such a tough guy purposely ignoring it. He nearly fainted with fright. Sick at the sight of himself, now bleeding thick and fast, he was desperately stuffing a hanky against the wound when Dode Thornton sloped in.

'Look at my good shirt!' Harry stared tragically round at him, eyes black shadowed, cheeks white. 'It's all stained and torn, my mum'll have a fit!'

Dode's face creased in fellow feeling. His mother nagged at him about clothes as well.

'Maybe,' he said, 'if you come home to my place we could do something with it. My folks'll be in bed; nobody'll know. Rose would help; she's a good sewer, she won a prize for it at school.'

'You're a pal, I really appreciate this. You know what my mum's like.'

'No bother,' Dode said grandly. 'Come on, we'd better get out while the going's good.'

Harry prayed the Gorbals Boys wouldn't be waiting for him in the shadows of the hall doorway. In his weakened state he couldn't imagine now being so crazy as to face up to such a crowd. The mere thought of this madness made him feel weak at the knees.

Langside Hall was a large stone building like a church, half hidden by beech trees. It backed into the park grounds at the corner of Pollokshaws Road and Langside Avenue. In the darkness outside he and Dode trod warily, jerking at every creak and rustle and not even relaxing when they rounded on to Pollokshaws Road. They quickened their steps and by the time they reached the end of the tree-lined side of the park with moonflashes from the pond signalling through the branches they were racing like whippets.

The railings dog-legged through the shadows of Balvicar Street on to Queens Drive but they hugged the comparative safety of the lights and the traffic on Pollokshaws Road before reaching it.

Dode's home was a basement flat opposite the Victoria Road entrance of the park. The tall, wrought iron park gates were locked. Even if they had been able to cut through the park, however, they would never have dreamt of doing so in the dark; too many people had been ambushed that way in the past. Dode being with him would have been no help at all. Dode was tall for his age but skinny and gaunt-faced. A bit like his dad. Dode's dad battered his mum, but Dode was a nice bloke, the type that wouldn't hurt a fly.

'Your mum's lucky,' Dode said, 'your dad's great! Helping you get so fit and showing you how to defend yourself.' Harry agreed his dad wasn't bad – as dads go. He was all hard muscle too. And his mum was small and thin – his dad could've flattened his mum, but he'd never once raised a finger to her.

The basement of the tenement building had bottle-green storm doors that were shut and locked. 'Come on round to the lane,' Dode whispered, 'I've got keys for the back.' The lane was barely discernible even with the Victoria Road lights. Their feet crunched along its loose stones and Harry suddenly wondered if he was leaving a trail of blood.

'In here,' Dode said, opening a wooden door in the wall. The back court was in inky darkness except for the moon's grey flicker on black windows. Dode turned the key very gently in the door and shut it again with equal care. They didn't dare put on the hall light. Dode felt his way through to the kitchen with Harry clutching on to the back of his jacket. The hall was an upside down L shape with the bedrooms and bathroom first and then the sitting room on the corner of Victoria Road, the kitchen facing on to Queens Drive. Before shutting the kitchen door Dode switched on the light and they winced at the loudness of the click; it had exploded in the sleepy silence of the house like a firecracker. They stiffened into immobility for a few seconds, expecting the worst. But nothing happened.

'Don't make a sound,' Dode said, 'my mum and dad have ears like elephants. I'll go and waken Rose.'

Suddenly realizing how cold he was Harry shivered and stared miserably round the kitchen. Everything was painted red and white. Dode's mum had obviously tried to make up for the basement darkness by having colour schemes as vivid as possible. He went over to one of the chairs and lowered himself gingerly down on to its checked cushion. His shoulder hurt, it felt as if the blood had hardened over it like a stiff shell.

Dode seemed to be gone for an eternity but when he did reappear he was accompanied by his young sister. She was wearing a red woolly dressing gown over blue pyjamas. The tasselled cord of the dressing gown dangled loose and there was a teddy bear motif in gold on the pocket. Her eyes were bright with conspiratorial excitement.

'Look at my good shirt, Rosie.' The tragedy in Harry's whisper was reflected in his eyes. 'What'm I going to do?'

'Don't worry,' Rose said, 'I'll fix it, but first we'll have to get if off. Dode's brought a crêpe bandage from the bathroom cupboard and my facecloth.'

Harry tried not to look at the scarlet mess that was now his shoulder. Keeping his eyes averted, he allowed Rose and Dode to peel off his shirt. That shirt was his pride and joy; pale green with a buttoned-down collar and the same pearl buttons on the cuffs. It was in fact festooned with tiny pearl buttons and the last word in fashion. He thanked God he had taken off his suit jacket at the start of the dance and it had been saved any damage. It was a real snazzy suit, a glossy bronze-brown, lightweight and well cut. His mum worried about it being too lightweight for January. She'd said, 'You'll catch your death of cold.'

His mum was a regular prophet of doom, she worried about everything and spread anxiety like a plague. He had a terrible and continual fight to defend himself from being undermined and weakened by her. If she had her way he would be a soft-centred wimp like Lindsay McDonald, totally unable to defend himself. He was grateful to his dad for helping him in this respect. In fact in most respects his dad went to the opposite extreme from his mum; his mum's anxious love was suffocating. His dad had never shown him the slightest affection. A good job, too, because his mum had never stopped hugging and kissing him. She'd do the same even yet if he didn't keep fending her off. This need for constant watchfulness to make sure he never weakened made him feel resentment against her. That made him feel guilty and the annoyance at suffering guilt on top of all the other things he had to put up with increased his resentment.

What did his mum, or any other grown-up, know about the struggle for survival in the youth jungle of the Glasgow streets? One thing was certain, she would have a fit if she saw his good shirt ruined. That was his big worry of the night. Parents were always nagging on about things like scuffed shoes, stained school ties and lost jacket buttons. The mind boggled at the fuss there would be about a torn shirt.

Dode and Rose did their best to help him. Dode wiped the blood with the facecloth wrung out in ice-cold water. Then he put a pad of cloth, a clean, white tea-towel, against the wound and bound it tightly with the crêpe bandage.

Rose rinsed his shirt in cold water and then washed it and hung it in her mother's hot-air dryer with the heat up at 'full'. Then she sponged off some spots that had dripped on to his trousers. When his shirt was almost dry she took it out and sewed up the tear. She took a long time doing this so while they were waiting Dode, very stealthily, made a pot of tea. The tea made Harry feel better and he was reassured by the marvellous job Rose was making of the shirt. Only one more ordeal remained – for this night, at least – the journey from Dode's to his own home.

'How are you going to get home?' Dode asked, as if reading his mind. 'They could finish you off next time.'

'I'll go with him,' Rose volunteered. It was the accepted practice, the unwritten code, that no one, not even the Gorbals Boys, attacked you on the street if you were accompanied by a girl.

'I don't know. . . .' Harry hesitated uneasily. He was thinking of the fit Rose's mother would have if she found out.

'They won't know,' Rose said, with even more impressive telepathy than her brother, 'I'll slip through and put on my duffel. Won't be a minute.'

'I'll come too,' Dode said, after she'd left the kitchen.

'I won't forget this, Dode,' Harry fervently assured him.

Dode shrugged his thin shoulders. 'You'd do the same for me. We've got to stick together, it's the only way.'

It was true. Parents were no use, they had absolutely no understanding about anything – except that his dad had bought him a punch bag and a pair of boxing gloves and taught him how to fight. Nevertheless, Harry shuddered to think what life would be like without pals; it was a hard enough struggle as it was.

He finished his tea just as Rose reappeared with the hood of her navy blue duffel coat pulled over her short hair. For a few seconds Harry's nerves went taut with concern. What if the Gorbals Boys mistook her for a boy? But surely not with that fringe of hair hanging over her brow and that soft round look about her face and eyes.

The three of them set off with Rose trotting along in the middle. They didn't speak. It was one of those occasions when just surviving took up every vestige of energy and concentration. Even though they kept to the opposite side of the road, they could hear the park whispering as if it was inhabited by ghosts. The eerie sound of the elms and horse chestnut trees and the holly and rhododendron bushes made their eyes strain wide and their scalps tingle.

Queens Gushet was in the middle of where the road widened and split into two. Mary House was partly concealed by a dark mantle of trees.

'We'll wait until you get to the door,' Rose whispered.

'Thanks, Rosie, and you too, Dode.'

The gate in the iron-spiked fence creaked open and shut. His feet crunched along the path. Reaching the safety of the porch, he turned and stuck up a thumb then, in case his friends hadn't been able to see the signal, he ventured a throaty call of 'Okay!' Then he turned his key in the door and crept, his shoulder throbbing, upstairs to bed.

14

'You're a fine one to criticize me,' Rowan said.

Hazel fluttered her lashes in a way that had always melted her husband Derek's heart. 'I'm not criticizing you, darling, I'm just trying to help you.'

'You'd do better to concentrate on trying to help yourself.'

Hazel blinked again and gently fluffed out the deep soft frill at the neck of her frock. 'What do you mean, darling?'

'Mother, you drink!'

Hazel flushed; Rowan had such an unfortunate, brusque turn of speech. 'You enjoy a glass of wine, Rowan, it's a perfectly civilized habit.'

'Not the way you knock them back, Mother.'

'Rowan!' A tremble shook the older woman leaving her weak and exhausted. She doubted if she would have enough power left in her legs to stand up. 'How dare you talk to me like that. If your father was here now he wouldn't allow you to treat me in this manner.'

'Father wouldn't have allowed you to drink so much.'

'Rowan, you're upsetting me – I do *not* drink too much.'

'Mother, you do, I wish you would face the fact.'

'You're being ridiculous! Please leave the room at once.'

'I'm not a child any more, you can't just dismiss me. You drink too much, Mother.'

Tears rushed to Hazel's eyes and spilled down her cheeks. Blindly she groped around for a handkerchief. 'Will you please ring for Jenny, I feel quite faint. I don't know what's come over you, Rowan. You used to be such a nice, well-behaved little girl.' She could no longer see her daughter for the tears that had temporarily blurred the sight of Rowan's straight hair tied back in a ponytail, the faint brush of freckles over her nose and cheeks, her black polo-necked sweater and trousers.

'It's evening, Mother. Jenny comes in the forenoon. Anyway, what could she do for you that I couldn't or wouldn't? Bring you a drink? I'll bring you a drink of water or I'll make you a cup of tea before I go out. Or I'll stay with you if you want me to, I could phone my friends.'

Hazel shook her head, struggling to control her quivering lips. At last she managed to say, 'I'd rather have the evening to myself, thank you.'

'Please make an appointment with Doctor Bennett, Mother, or ask him to call tonight. That way you could have a quiet talk with him. You need help.'

'I'm perfectly all right, Rowan.'

Rowan sighed. 'Oh, hell, what's the use. Don't wait up, Mother, I'll be late.'

Hazel was too upset to ask where she was going and who she was going to be with. 'Very well,' she said with as much dignity as she could in the distressing circumstances, 'good night, Rowan.'

'Night.' And she was gone.

Hazel sat in the quiet, listening for her daughter's departure from the house. Footsteps were muffled by the thick carpet in the hall but she detected the faint tinkle of the crystal drops in the chandelier as the outside door opened and let in a cold blast of March wind. Then the door banged shut. The place was sealed in silence again.

She felt not only intimidated by the silence but dwarfed by everything in the drawing room, from the ornate black marble fireplace with its brass shovel, poker, tongs and long-handled brush propped inside the brass fender, to the huge gilt-framed mirror above the fireplace, reflecting the deep green carpet, the plump, buttoned chairs and sofa, the tapestry cushions, the writing desk, and the landscapes and seascapes in heavy gilt frames decorating the walls.

She was shaking so much, she had to hang on to the furniture for support on her way over to the drinks cabinet. She splashed a recklessly large amount of vodka into a glass and gulped it down. In a few minutes, during which time she poured herself another, it steadied her and she felt better. She took the bottle back to her seat and placed it on the table beside it, then sat nursing her glass.

She did *not* have a drink problem, she assured herself. She could take a drink or she could leave it. To test this she had never touched a drop for a whole month after New Year. Was it any wonder that she had resorted once more to the temporary comfort of the vodka bottle when she was so distracted with worry about her daughter?

Now the foolish girl was taking drugs. 'Pot' she called it and it was smoked in a cigarette. 'Pot's harmless, Mother,' Rowan had assured her, 'it's not nearly as strong or as harmful as the tranquillizing drugs you've been swallowing like sweets for years.'

It was heartbreaking to see her with one of those cigarettes between her lips and her eyes unnaturally vacant; all her friends had the same dreamlike appearance. It was unnerving, too. Hazel didn't know who to turn to for help any more. Mrs Donovan, a very hard woman really, had not proved at all sympathetic. Her daughter-in-law, Amelia, had phoned to say that if Rowan was genuinely interested in being a novelist she was welcome to come to Mary House to speak to her.

'I'll do my best to encourage her and help her in whatever way I can,' she promised.

But Rowan had pooh-poohed the idea as soon as she'd heard of it. 'Me a writer? Don't be silly, Mother. I haven't the slightest talent for writing books. But if I did have a go at a book it wouldn't be the kind of tripe Amelia Donovan writes.'

Hazel felt utterly helpless. She had never for a moment stopped missing her husband but she had never longed so much for his strength and loving support as she did now. He would have known what to do. He would have dealt with this problem of Rowan as calmly and efficiently as he had dealt with everything in their lives. He would have protected her against even the slightest worry. She had a sudden wave of angry resentment that he was gone. How could he have left her forever? She needed him.

Forgetting again that Jenny was not on duty she leaned over to press the bell. No one came. She rang again and again before tearfully remembering. She wanted Jenny to draw the curtains. It was very dark outside and the brightly lit room would be like a film set for any passer-by to stare at. She staggered and knocked over her glass; its contents splashed over the skirt of her dress, darkening its pattern of pink roses. Ignoring the stain she wended a zigzag path across to the window, bumping into furniture on the way. Reaching the gold embossed curtains she grabbed them and clung to them then staggering, drew them across to cover the bare glass. As she did so she thought she noticed, despite her haze of alcohol, a crimson splash of sunset staining the sky.

Rowan and a group of friends met in the Clydeside Bar to discuss the next 'Ban the Bomb' demonstration. Sally and Betty sat with Rowan on a bench against the wall. They all wore the shabby duffel coats their parents hated so much. Sandy, Hugh and Tommy sat on the stools grouped round the table. Sandy wore a gold earring in one ear, Hugh sported one of his dad's jumpers; his dad was huge and the jumper came down to Hugh's knees. He'd tied a piece of string round his middle which made old ladies think he was absolutely diabolical. Tommy had a wonderful bushy beard. They all wore long scarves and CND badges. The table top was crowded with beer glasses and rings; cigarette burns showed darkly through puddles of spilled liquid. Overflowing ashtrays were everywhere and a thick pall of smoke filled the poorly lit room. The people tightly packing the place, sitting or standing, were like hazy figures in a dream. The noise was far from dreamlike, however, having the power and substance of continual knock-out punches. Rowan and her friends, even though they were huddled close to one another, had to shout to make themselves heard.

Rowan felt that there was excitement in the air – not just in this Glasgow pub but in the whole country, in the whole world. She, even more than her friends, was aware that things were beginning to happen: new ideas, new trends, new people. She felt it most in London which she often visited. For instance, people like Jocelyn Stevens and Mark Boxer and Anthony Armstrong Jones had taken over *Queen* magazine and changed the appearance of it with exciting new layouts, irregular blocks of print dropped in the middle of large white spaces, and pictures that were the result of the new style of photography, the essence, the very image of the new decade with their grainy, pacy look like 'realistic dreams'.

The prose too had a new breathless, disconnected style describing affluence and youth in a new world. Everything was now for youth. Articles appeared under headings such as 'A Bad Year for Dodos' and said things like 'Judges and generals are the very stuff which dodos are made of'. Other headlines belted out at the reader: 'Facing the Crazy Sixties', 'The Sixties' Face', 'Keeping Pace with Pace', 'The Tense Present'.

Young new designers like Mary Quant and John Stephens were rivalling the older Norman Hartnell and Hardy Amies. New working-class photographers had appeared all over the place like David Bailey, Terence Donovan and Brian Duffy.

The general question now was 'What do you need to be in the sixties?', and the answer 'First, you should be under 30. Second, you should be in tune with the times. . .'.

Rowan had long ago decided that her mother was

definitely not 'with it'; she still lived in the nostalgic world of cinema romantics like Michael Wilding and Anna Neagle and the stiff-upper-lip wartime heroics of Kenneth More, Richard Attenborough, Jack Hawkins and John Mills. Or in the theatre of the fifties with the tinkling piano music and the period sentimentality of shows like *The Boyfriend* and *Salad Days* and *Separate Tables*.

They went regularly to London 'for the Season' as her mother quaintly put it. This now meant simply to shop and see some shows. Rowan had long since refused to accompany her mother, however, to the old-fashioned theatre of her choice. She horrified her by going instead to see films like *Rebel Without a Cause* starring the teenage hero, James Dean; going to see plays like *Look Back in Anger* and musicals like *Fings Ain't Wot They Used to Be*; buying books like *Room at the Top* and *Saturday Night and Sunday Morning*.

Her mother was a right old dodo, Rowan decided, unused to anything except complete dependence on a man, clinging to every outdated concept from class consciousness onwards. She would be laughable – if she wasn't so sad. She was so weak, so helpless, so bewildered by the winds of change she was using alcohol both as a protection and as an escape. Rowan had tried to help by locking the drinks cupboard or even emptying every bottle of booze down the kitchen sink, but it was no use. Her mother just bought more. She had bottles of vodka not only in the drinks cupboard now but hidden all over the place. In her regular searches Rowan had found bottles in wardrobes, under beds, at the back of broom cupboards, at the bottom of laundry baskets. Trying to stop her mother getting her hands on a bottle was a hopeless task. She'd even had a private word with her mother's doctor, only to be told that there was nothing he could do unless her mother came voluntarily to him for help. Before she was likely to do that, he said, she would have to admit to herself that she was an alcoholic.

That had been the first time that Rowan had truly faced the stark fact herself that her mother was an alcoholic – that she would do anything to get alcohol, and was capable of any kind of behaviour once under the influence. She'd once embarrassed Tommy by coming into the room where Rowan and her friends were listening to music and dancing. She'd hung on to Tommy and forced him to move round the floor with her while she ogled him and flirted with him. It was pathetic. Rowan had felt like weeping with sadness and anger.

Now they usually just met in a café or a pub. Her friends' parents weren't as bad as her mother but they were also upper-middle-class types. They too were 'squares' and 'dodos' and, it was generally agreed, 'enough to make anybody sick!'

Rowan and her friends, caught up in the excitement of the new age in which they felt they could really 'do' something about the world in which they lived, sat in the pub, setting everything and everybody to rights. A couple of years before they'd had the uplifting experience of the Aldermaston March. Then there had been other marches in different parts of England and Scotland. Now they planned their role in the next 'Ban the Bomb' march in Glasgow. They also discussed how they could support not only the Civil Rights Movement in Britain, but the terrifically exciting campaign and dramatic marches and demonstrations in America that were hitting the headlines.

As far as America was concerned, the problem would be how to get over there. Leaving their jobs was no problem – jobs were ten a penny, they could always get another when they returned to Britain. It was taken for granted, of course, that their parents would refuse to fund such an adventure despite the fact that they could, without exception, well afford it. Hitch-hiking was discussed but money would still be needed for food and for the journey by sea or air across the Atlantic. They had faith, however, that such an undertaking would be possible; anything was possible nowadays. People, especially young people, had power to change the world. It was a time of change and positive thought and action!

Heads close together round the table they planned the action that was necessary; the first priority was to bring about the end of the H-bomb. So intense was their discussion and so loud the noise around them that they did not even hear the sound of the fire engines outside.

15

The first place Jenny went to turned out to be an attractive terrace house within easy walking distance of the school. It wasn't expensive either. The rent had been stated in the advert and because it was such a reasonable sum she had taken it for granted that there must be something wrong with it. She felt a wild surge of hope when she saw by the light of a street lamp the warm, red sandstone building with the pretty pink curtains at the windows. It even had a bright orange doormat with 'Welcome' blazoned in yellow across it. A brass lantern with a crimson light bulb bathed the porch in a warm and welcoming light.

Jenny rang the bell, her heart singing along with its cheerful chime. A grey-haired woman with a kindly face opened the door. She reminded Jenny of her mother.

'I've come about the rooms to let,' Jenny said eagerly.

'I'm sorry,' the woman replied, 'they've just been taken.'

Jenny couldn't believe it. From the first moment she set eyes on the house she knew it to be the solution to all her problems.

'I'm sorry, dear,' the woman repeated.

'Oh . . . yes . . . I see.' Jenny made a brave attempt to swallow down her disappointment. 'Well, I suppose it can't be helped. Thanks, anyway.'

'I hope you find something else,' the woman said before gently closing the door.

Jenny remained standing, hugging her coat around her for a minute, struggling against her need to weep before turning back into the darkness. She tried to cheer herself with the thought that the next place might be equally good. She was tired, that was all, and her face and body still hurt from Joe's latest attack. Sometimes she ached for days afterwards; often she was subject to more abuse before the pain of the last time went away. It was becoming more and more exhausting, draining her spirits as well as her physical energy. She couldn't sleep for the pain. She would lie in bed beside Joe longing for him to comfort her yet knowing it was no use.

As she retraced her steps back along the street it occurred to her that the incredulous disappointment she'd felt at finding the rooms let was similar to how she always found it difficult after an attack to believe that Joe could have treated her as he did. She gave a big, shuddering sigh.

It was then she noticed, over in the direction of the river, that the sky had taken on a rich, golden glow. She wondered, without much interest, what it could be.

The next rooms she had seen advertised were almost a mile away and she felt so tired and dispirited she decided to go into the nearest café and have a reviving cup of tea before going to enquire about it.

It was while she was in the café that she heard a man at the next table say 'It must be the worst fire in Glasgow's history. I certainly don't remember one as bad.'

'I suppose it must have been caused by the build-up of whisky fumes,' said his woman companion. 'That's probably what caused the explosion.'

Jenny's mind went blank. It was as if she'd lost consciousness without moving. She sat like a corpse until she heard herself say in a bewildered voice, 'There's a fire?'

The woman turned towards her in surprise. 'Haven't you heard? Surely you must have seen it, if you haven't you're the only one in Glasgow.'

'Where?'

'Cheapside Street and Warroch Street. They're fighting just now to stop it spreading. . . .'

Consciousness, agonizingly acute, rushed back. Jenny

flew from the café knocking a chair over and punching people aside in her desperation to be away. Her mind kept screaming, My children! My children!

She thanked God for the taxi that came cruising past as she burst out of the café. Scrambling into it she babbled to the driver to please, please go as fast as he could. Her children and her mother were in Cheapside Street.

'It won't be easy getting there, hen,' the driver said, 'the whole area's crowded with sightseers. Streets near Anderston Cross are lined with cars nose to tail, even George V Bridge is packed with folk.'

'Oh please, please.'

'I'll do my best. If I tell the police you're worried about your weans they'll probably help.'

The journey was a nightmare descent into hell. Giant cinders were flying and hissing into the River Clyde. Firemen were keeping a continuous stream of water aimed at the roofs of the quayside engineering works. At Springfield Quay where the vessel *Yoma* was berthed red-hot embers showered over the ship and two tugs were desperately trying to remove her. At Terminus Quay the same urgent struggle was being made to get the ore carrier *Dunadd* to safety.

From a distance it seemed as if it was some ghastly Guy Fawkes night; showers of sparks like golden rain were arching hundreds of feet up into the air over the warehouses and storage sheds in the wharfs, then whirling in the sudden gusts of wind.

As they drew nearer, the scene was more reminiscent of air-raids with flames shooting up from jagged outlines of ruined buildings. The air shuddered with the thunderous crash of falling masonry. The flames at times had a curious blue colour and the air was heavy and sickly with whisky fumes.

Nearer still it became like daytime, so bright was the blaze. The surrounding warehouses stood out black and harsh against the unnatural light and in all the streets of the area the windows of buildings sparkled and gleamed as if in bright sunlight.

Jenny couldn't see any sign of the tenement building in Cheapside Street. She felt in a state of collapse and it was the taxi driver who had to give a coherent explanation to the police.

'Most of the people have been evacuated,' a policeman told her. 'Some have already made arrangements to stay with friends or relatives, others are still standing around.'

Frantically she ran up and down streets, crushing through tight blocks of people, crying out over and over again, 'Rose! Dode! Mammy!' There was no response. She was shaking so much her legs could hardly hold her up eventually. Then she heard someone call her name and somehow she found herself in Joe's arms.

'The children are all right; the children are all right,' Joe kept repeating. 'They're at home, they left your mother's place shortly after you. They were bored and decided to come over to Queens Park to see some pals. They've been there all the time.'

She wept against Joe's chest in relief before anxiety tightened its grip again.

'Mammy?'

Joe shook his head. 'I can't find her, Jenny. Unless she got out and was on her way to Queens Park when I was on my way here. We may have missed each other but I doubt it. Dode or somebody would have come back and let me know. Or your mother would have told the police.'

'What are you talking about?' she asked, as if he was stupid, 'she *must* be all right.' The alternative was too horrific to face.

Walls were falling now, leaving steel skeletons. Internal floors remained in place for a time, then one by one crumpled. Barrels of whisky kept exploding and bursting into flames adding to the rubble in the street.

'I'd better take you home,' Joe said, 'the children will

be waiting. They're far too worried and upset to sleep.'

'I can't leave here!'

'There's nothing you can do.'

'I must find mammy.'

'I'll come back if you like. Your place is at home with the children.'

Hysterical now, she began half-laughing, half-crying. 'I might have known you'd say that. That's all you ever say. "Your place is at home with the children. . . . Your place is at home with the children!" '

His hands hardened on her. 'Pull yourself together.'

'Leave me alone.' She kept seeing her mother's face, not his. The yearning for her mother was far worse than any pain her husband could inflict.

'You're coming home with me.'

Home. Where was home? What was home? A place of safety? A haven of peace? Somewhere she would be loved and cherished and looked after?

She had no home now.

16

'When will you two get it into your heads?' Harry groaned. 'I've been telling you for the past month now, it wasn't your fault. You've no need to feel guilty.'

'I can't help it,' Dode said. 'I keep thinking – maybe if I'd stayed with gran I could have got her out.'

'Oh aye, and you'd have rescued Rosie as well, I suppose.'

'We should have both helped,' Rosie said. 'We shouldn't have gone out and left her, we weren't supposed to go out.'

'So?' Harry shrugged. 'You didn't do what your mother told you? So what? It's not the first time that's happened and it won't be the last. The point is, if you'd stayed the both of you would have died along with the old lady. You just keep kidding yourself about being able to help her. You couldn't have. Her house was smack up against the whisky bond! It went up along with it. When will you get that into your thick heads? Nobody expected the explosion. The firemen had just arrived to investigate a trickle of smoke somebody thought they'd seen and there were nineteen of them killed. If trained firemen hadn't time to do anything, how could you?'

They were loafing at the Balvicar Street, Pollokshaws Road entrance to the park. All three of them wore jeans, jerseys and anoraks. Rose's anorak was bright red, a startling contrast to her dark hair. Harry's was navy blue and Dode's a greasy brown much the same colour as his hair. Dode kicked a tin can against the railings.

'I suppose you're right. It's just that I feel so awful about it.'

'We don't know what to do about mum, either,' Rose said.

111

'How do you mean?'

Rose shrugged. 'She seems to have given up. She doesn't go to her work. She hardly does anything in the house, sometimes there isn't any dinner made for us. Sometimes we come in from school and she's sitting by the fire staring into space. It's weird.'

Dode said, 'At least dad hasn't hit her since the fire.' He sounded worried and uncertain. 'At least, not while we've been in,' he added.

Things were getting a bit chaotic at Harry's own place since Jenny had stopped coming in. His mum still shut herself away in her writing room for most of the time and his dad either shut himself away in his studio at the top of the house or he disappeared out somewhere, probably to the casino in town. He enjoyed going there despite the fact that he seldom won anything. Harry couldn't understand the attraction – but then, he couldn't understand anything about grown-ups. As often as not he had to make his own tea when he got home from school and everyone else's as well. He was becoming quite a good cook with practice. He drew the line at housework though; housework was for girls.

His mother was always apologetic when she surfaced from her writing room and found him busy in the kitchen.

'Darling, I'm sorry!' she'd cry out, 'is that the time already?' Sometimes she'd go on to say, 'Do you know, Harry, you've the makings of a wonderful chef. You've a real flair for cooking. I never realized until now that Jenny's not here.'

'When's she coming back?' As usual he felt irritated. Cooking was all very well, he quite enjoyed it, but he had homework to do. And he needed some time to go out with his pals.

His mother always looked vague in reply. She could look quite eccentric when she emerged from her writing room, her fair hair escaped from her chignon and ruffled where she'd been rubbing her head, either in excitement

112

or perplexity while writing. 'Poor Jenny,' she said, 'it was a terrible shock losing her mother like that.'

His dad wasn't much better, although he never looked vague. More like a sergeant-major with his cropped head and straight-backed, almost military bearing. He would just shrug and say, 'Haven't a clue.' Although once he did add, 'Who needs her anyway? You produce better grub.' It was a rare compliment and one Harry secretly treasured. He couldn't recall any other way he'd ever pleased his dad – at least, if he had, his dad had never let him know about it.

As well as doing the cooking he found he had to see to his own clothes. He had to wash and iron his shirts and press his good suit if he was wearing it to a disco. He didn't mind too much because clothes were so important and he'd never had faith in his mother or Jenny looking after them properly.

The only thing that really worried him was whether it was another erosion his mother was making on his manhood. He felt furious if she complimented him on his ironing or even said what a good boy he was in helping her so much. At best he would go all moody and surly and act as if he hated the sight of her. Or he'd be downright cheeky or sarcastic. The worst of it was, she never cheeked back or lost her temper and shouted at him. Like all mums she nagged about his clothes and his general appearance. (His hair for instance.) Apart from that she usually just went all hurt and quiet. Once tears had come into her eyes and in matching distress he'd put his arms around her and said, 'Sorry, Mum. I didn't mean to be rotten.'

'You're not rotten,' she hugged him in return, with such gratitude it made him feel worse. 'You're the best son any mother could have and I love you more than anything else in the world.'

He could imagine her saying the same thing even if he committed murder. He supposed he ought to feel glad but he didn't, he felt terrible. Such an obsessive and total love was like a strait-jacket; it made him feel vulnerable as well as inhibited.

He always envied Dode and Rosie in this respect. Before Jenny's mother died and she went queer she used to row with them often. And she never said she was sorry. His mother was always apologizing for herself. His dad was surprisingly good-natured about that, it never seemed to irritate him. On the contrary, his mum and dad seemed to get on better together if his mum had got herself into a helpless mix-up about something. His dad was good at organizing her, it seemed to bring out the best in him. Sometimes they even had a good laugh about it.

'Honestly,' he told Dode, 'my mum and dad are a right pair. I don't know what to make of them at times.'

'I used to think you were lucky that your mum didn't have to go out to work,' Dode said, 'now I'm not so sure.'

'I suppose you could say my mum does work. She gets paid for her writing – although dad says it's just enough to cover her paper and postage and all her other expenses. She's obsessive about it, though.'

'How do you mean?' Dode asked.

'Och, she does everything to extremes. She'd sit at her desk from first thing in the morning till last thing at night if dad let her. You talk about *your* mum being weird, at times *my* mum goes right over the top.'

Rose's eyes widened. 'Off her head you mean?'

Harry shrugged. 'In a way I suppose. Sometimes she calls dad and me by wrong names. She gets mixed up between us and her characters.'

'That's weird,' Rose said.

'I know. The other day I found her sobbing and crying and I asked what the heck was wrong and she said "Davie's died" and I said "Who's Davie?" Turned out he was one of the characters in her book.'

'Really weird,' Rose repeated.

The weirdness of parents had drawn Harry and Dode and Rose closer together. Each of them had other friends

114

that they spent time with as well, of course. Harry sparred now and again with Big Sam McFarlane in the ring. Dode wasn't tough enough for that. He often palled up with Hector Brown; there was a putting green in the park and Hector and Dode shared a liking for the game. Rose had a friend called Betsy with whom she regularly went to the pictures.

There was an unspoken agreement however, that he and Dode were 'best friends'. Rose was okay but a bit of an embarrassment the way she hung about so much with Dode and him. Sometimes they had to resort to quite devious means to get rid of her or to avoid her company.

'We're going to the Ban the Bomb march,' Dode said.

Rose looked very intense. 'We're definitely against it. The Bomb, I mean.'

'So am I,' Harry agreed. The Bomb was *the* height of grown-up madness. They were actually making things that could destroy the whole world or at best, pollute it, poison the earth and the air beyond recovery. It didn't bear thinking about. No prowess at boxing, none of his keep-fit exercises or his weight-training programme would do him any good if somebody dropped an atomic or hydrogen bomb. Fear at the thought of the Bomb, hollowed him, secretly caved him in. Sometimes it seemed too mad to be true, sometimes he couldn't believe that anyone could be so crazy. And his disbelieving would bring temporary comfort and relief.

Rose said, 'Did you see the film about the bomb America dropped on Japan? Children with their clothes burned into their skin, some people melted completely away –'

'All right, all right,' Harry said hastily, 'you don't need to go over it again. We all saw it.'

'Are you going on the march then?'

Harry nodded. He was all for marches and demonstrations. He would willingly march from one end of the country to the other to help the Ban the Bomb campaign. The only thing was, apparently some beatnik types

115

belonging to it were freaking out and taking drugs – although he'd never seen anything happening like the press were trying to make out. Some marchers might look a bit weird but looks didn't do anybody any harm. Not like so-called respectable politicians and scientists who were acting stupid enough to kill everybody in the whole world. He kept thinking how incredible that was. Yet, it really *could* happen. Already there were enough bombs being stockpiled to kill everybody. He despised grown-ups for their blind stupidity.

Dode said, 'I've made a banner. Well, more of a placard. I've stuck a big bit of cardboard on a pole.'

'He painted on it in big letters, WE WANT TO LIVE NOT DIE.' Excitement widened Rose's eyes. 'It looks great!'

'There's going to be thousands,' Dode caught the spark of his sister's enthusiasm, 'they'll *have* to pay attention.'

'And it's not just happening here,' Harry's own enthusiasm was kindled, 'people all over the world are rising up in protest and taking to the streets.' He felt suddenly, happily optimistic. There was such a charge of hope in the air. He might live to be as old as his mum and dad after all.

'Let's go to the Queens Café for a Coke,' he said and they all set off, still talking enthusiastically about how they were going to save the human race.

17

Blythswood Square, just up from the main shopping thoroughfare of Sauchiehall Street was one of Glasgow's most elegant addresses. Its leafy central garden was still private, for the use of occupants of the surrounding buildings. Its handsome early Victorian houses of silvery grey now housed offices and clubs but they once had been the homes of wealthy, famous, and sometimes notorious Glaswegians. In Victorian times Madeleine Smith had lived here at No. 7. She had allegedly poisoned her lover, Pierre L'Angelier but had escaped the hangman's noose with the Scottish verdict of 'Not Proven'. This verdict, as every Glaswegian knew, meant 'We know you did it but we're letting you off with it this time. Go away and don't do it again!'

The March was to start in the square and make its way through the main streets of the city until it reached Glasgow Green. Harry nearly hadn't come. He'd been so angry and embarrassed when he learned that his mother was planning to be there. No doubt she felt compelled to go in order to keep an eye on him – he could just imagine her shaming him in front of his pals. He cringed at the thought of her saying things like 'Are you warm enough, son?' or, 'You'll get rheumatics if you get wet, take my umbrella,' or, 'I was worried in case you got hungry so I've brought you some sandwiches and a flask of cocoa.'

She insisted of course, that she was going because she, too, was anxious to ban the Bomb.

'Well,' he told her, 'I'm not marching with you!'

'Don't worry.' She gave a nonchalant hitch of her shoulders and a scornful laugh. 'I've no intention of tagging along with you and your friends, I have my own plans.'

117

Despite her attempt at merry unconcern she was obviously hurt; she always was. She never failed to make him feel terrible. It didn't help either when he arrived at the Square with Dode and Rose and saw her wandering about on her own, looking, as she so often did, worried and anxious but with her eager-to-please look at the ready. He was forever thankful that it was his dad he resembled. He had his dad's positive aggressive look.

Although it was quite a bright spring day she was wearing a plastic mac over her bulky coat, a large blue woollen scarf wound round her neck and she had matching woollen mittens and hat. The shopping bag over her arm no doubt contained sandwiches and hot drinks and medicines. Or at least a First Aid pack and a tube of glucose tablets. She was a terrible hypochondriac. He and his dad often shook their heads and groaned at her about the times she pestered the doctor or the money she wasted on vitamin pills and potions. She was a sucker for any new wonder health aid.

And of course, she ate tranquillizers like sweeties. It was enough to put anyone off drugs.

Dode said incredulously, 'Is that your mother over there?'

'Just ignore her,' Harry pleaded.

Rose sighed. 'I wouldn't have minded if my mum had been able to come.'

'Not along with us though,' Dode said.

Rose seemed to shrink with misery inside her duffel coat. 'I just wish she'd get better, that's all.'

It was Harry's turn to sigh. 'Parents are a terrible worry aren't they?' He tugged back his broad shoulders. (His dedicated weight-training was beginning to pay off.) 'But there's nothing we can do about them just now so come on, let's get ourselves organized.'

People were beginning to bunch together under large coloured banners that displayed their allegiance to the different branches of the Scottish Labour Party or Co-op Societies or trade unions. But there were banners of

118

other political parties, too, and of a variety of Churches. Indeed every aspect of society seemed to be represented from Women's Guilds to Karate Clubs.

The banners billowed in the breeze like a crimson, blue, emerald, white and gold crush of sailing ships. A jungle of placards jostled together underneath them. The square was becoming crammed with people and the air quivered and buzzed with anticipation.

Harry was astonished at how many policemen were appearing from all the side streets. Policemen on large prancing horses as well as foot patrols.

'Would you look at them?' he nudged Dode, 'you'd think we were criminals or something.'

'Don't stare at them like that, Harry,' Rose pleaded. 'They're liable to arrest you just because your hair's long.' It was true. The police had a grudge against anyone young and especially with long hair.

Dode suffered even worse because, especially lately, he'd begun to look a bit weird. Jenny wasn't looking after him now. Unlike Harry, however, Dode wasn't much good at taking over and doing things for himself. He looked a real grubby-looking drop-out in that brown anorak. It was all frayed and stained and should have been thrown in the bin long ago. Rose was also being hard put to it looking after herself. Her hair wasn't nearly as glossy or as neat as it used to be and her face looked paler and thinner. The doctor had been talking of putting Jenny into a hospital for electric treatment on her head or something horrible like that. But so far she was still sitting at home doing nothing.

The march was now snaking out of the square led by the rousing strains of the Clydeside Miners' Brass Band. Jangling, jumbling in with the trumpeting miners came the Dixieland Stompers from Auchenshuggle and the Jazz ensemble from Townhead. Working hard to compete with this riotous sound but not quite making it – at least not at any great distance – were various skiffle groups and beat groups and single guys twanging at

119

guitars and singing at the pitch of their voices. Soon everyone was enjoying a sing-song. Some older groups were belting out old songs like 'Ten Green Bottles' and daft songs like 'Mares eat oats and does eat oats and little lambs eat ivy . . . .'

The crowd Harry, Dode and Rose were marching with were singing 'We shall overcome, We shall overcome, We shall overcome some day.' They were all from the south side of the City as their banners proclaimed; Queens Park Youth Club; Pollokshaws Debating Group; Langside Bowling Club; Pollokshields Harriers; Langside CND and many more crowded together and shuffled along. There was even the Queens Park Pipe Band, in full tartan rigout with a kilt-swinging drum-major built like a prize bull, beating the hell out of his big drum.

'I'm starving,' Dode said eventually. 'Anybody got anything to eat?'

Harry produced a Mars Bar but nobody had a knife with which to cut it so he and Dode and Rose took bites in turn.

By the time they reached Glasgow Green and everyone was pouring in, filling every corner of the park, and loudspeakers were being set up on platforms, Rose was complaining about being tired and having pains in her stomach. Harry had noticed earlier that her pace was slowing and she was hugging herself inside her duffel. A couple of times she'd gazed up at him with round bewildered eyes as if appealing to him for help. Her black hair had lost its glossy cleanness and her fringe instead of cutting a straight neat line across her brow had grown too long and now straggled across her line of vision.

He'd thought at first that her stomach pains must be the result of the recent neglect of her meals. Perhaps she'd not had any lunch and then the Mars Bar had proved a bit sickly on an empty stomach. But then another thought crept into his mind, embarrassing him.

120

They were all getting older. He was almost 16, Dode 15 and Rose must be 13 now. He'd read in a book his mum had given him about the facts of life that girls took monthly bleedings. He'd been embarrassed at his mother pressing that particular book on him; if anyone should have given it to him it should have been his dad.

The more he thought of it however, and the more his increasingly awkward glances down at Rose registered the unusual dark shadows under her eyes, the more he was convinced that this was what was happening to her. For the first time in all the years he'd known her he felt shy. It was as if she had suddenly become a stranger.

All the same, he said to Dode, who hadn't seemed to notice, 'Dode, Rosie isn't feeling so good.'

'What's wrong with you?' Dode asked.

Rose gazed up at him through her fringe. 'I've got awful pains in my stomach.'

'I knew you shouldn't have come with us,' Dode said. 'I told you, didn't I? But you will insist on always following us around.'

'I was all right earlier on.'

'No you weren't,' Dode insisted, 'you were griping about pains this morning. You're a right nuisance. You're always the same, always spoiling things for us.' He lit up one of the cigarettes he called 'joints'. Harry had seen him rolling them. Two cigarette papers were placed one slightly overlapping the other filled with a mixture of marijuana and tobacco and rolled into a long thick cigarette. The marijuana had first been 'cooked' in foil over a lighter flame. Dode took a deep puff, exhaled very slowly and then offered the joint to Harry who refused.

'You'd better beat it home,' Dode said to Rose.

'Are you coming with me?'

'What?' he shouted, 'do you think I'm daft? It's all just starting here. Why should I come with you? You know your own way home.'

Glasgow Green was right beside the river, so she

121

wouldn't have all that far to go to reach home. Nevertheless Harry didn't like the idea of her trailing away on her own looking so miserable. There was nothing he could do about it though. A few months ago he might have said, 'I'll chum you home, Rosie,' and walked alongside her and chatted with her without thinking about it. But suddenly he was so self-conscious he couldn't bring himself to do anything.

Suddenly two policemen appeared at Dode's elbow.

'What do you think you're doing?' one of them asked.

Dode's pale face turned an even sicklier hue. The cigarette stuck from his mouth like a white tree trunk. His eyes acquired a hunted look and he didn't move a muscle or say a word.

'What does it look as if he's doing?' Harry said, ignoring Rose's frantic nudges.

'You watch it!' the other policeman warned him. 'Just watch it, son.'

Rose intervened in a sweet childish voice that already had the wiles of a grown woman about it. 'I'm sorry, officer. You've just taken us aback, that's all. Could you tell us what my brother's done wrong, please?'

The first policeman spoke to Dode again but in a quieter more reasonable tone this time. 'What age are you?'

'He's 15,' Rose volunteered for the still apparently paralysed Dode.

'Hand it over,' the policeman sighed.

Dode peeled the cigarette from his lips and held it out. The policeman broke it open to reveal the black specks of marijuana.

'How about you?' he asked Harry.

'What is it?'

'Pull the other one,' the policeman said.

'If it's some sort of dope,' Harry said, 'you can count me out. I'm into physical fitness, weight-training, all that kind of jazz. I look after myself.'

Dode found his voice at last. 'He's telling the truth. He didn't know anything about it.'

'Well, I think you'd better come back with us to the station.' Then to Harry, 'You and your sister come as well. Then we'll send for your mother and father. I don't suppose they've any idea what you lot have been up to.'

'I'm not her brother!' Harry didn't mean the words to sound so indignant – as if being Rosie's brother was the last thing on earth he'd want to be – they somehow just came out that way. He felt suddenly angry and resentful and unbearably miserable.

'Well, whoever you are,' the policeman said. 'You'd still better come along with us.'

He supposed he could have argued, refused to go, insisted on his rights. But what rights did anyone of his age have? None that he knew. They would just get him for obstruction or breach of the peace or some trumped up charge. Anyway, he didn't want to desert Dode and Rosie.

He sat jammed between them on a bench in the police station and could feel them trembling on either side of him as if they'd both been seized by a bout of malaria. He began to wonder if their dad battered them as well as their mum, although they'd always insisted he never laid a finger on them.

'Why are you getting into such a panic?' he asked them eventually.

'Oh, Harry,' Rose whispered, 'we're afraid for our mum.'

18

'If you were looking after the children properly,' Joe said, staring at Jenny with cold expressionless eyes, 'this never would have happened.'

'It wasn't mum's fault,' Dode said, 'it's the latest craze, Dad. Everybody's smoking hash.'

'If you didn't just sit there feeling sorry for yourself all the time,' Joe continued, ignoring Dode, 'you would have seen he was getting into trouble. I can't cope with everything. I've to work long hours day and night across there.'

'He never smoked in the house, did you, Dode?' Jenny appealed to her son who eagerly agreed.

'No, never, Dad. Honestly. How was mum to know? No way was she able to know anything about it.'

'But what do you care,' Joe went on, 'about making anybody suffer.'

'No, Dad. It was me!' Dode raised his voice in alarm. 'Oh, please leave mum alone. She can't help it, she isn't well.'

Rose joined in. 'Please Dad! Oh please don't hurt mum.' She began to sob. 'Oh please, please.'

But it was no use. They knew it was no use. And Jenny knew it was no use. More than that, Jenny sensed how the atmosphere in the police station had triggered off memories of his own incarceration. She had never seen Joe look so quietly demented.

He began repeating, over and over, in a low tone, 'Don't you dare do that to me! Don't you dare do that to me!' He didn't seem to be seeing her as he hit her. He had a blind, almost confused look that made her weep for him as much as for herself. Then she couldn't weep any more, couldn't even breathe before slipping backwards and downwards into darkness.

Jenny awoke cautiously in hospital. Before daring to open her eyes she kept very still and listened. There were strange voices and the trundling of trolleys. Then she detected a pungent antiseptic smell. Slowly she allowed her eyes to open. She was propped up in a sitting position in a small but bright and pleasant-looking ward. Five other women were sitting up in bed drinking tea.

'Nurse!' one of them shouted, 'she's come to.'

A plump-bosomed nurse came bustling immediately towards her.

'How do you feel, dear?'

'What happened?' Jenny asked and immediately caught her breath with the excruciating pain in her chest.

'Just relax and try not to worry. You've a few cracked ribs, a torn ligament and extensive bruising — but if your son hadn't managed to get the ambulance so quickly you might have been worse.'

She didn't want to remember. She closed her eyes again and prayed for complete oblivion.

'I'll bring you a nice cup of tea, dear,' the nurse soothed, 'that'll cheer you up.' The tea did help a little. So did the conversation of the other women patients.

'Men!' One of the women with a face like an old map spat out the word in disgust. 'I wouldn't have another one even if they paid me a million pounds.'

A patient in the bed opposite laughed. 'Well, I'd maybe suffer an old man with a bad cough for a million pounds, Mrs McKay.'

'Not me,' Mrs McKay assured her, 'not after all I suffered with that rotten bastard I was married to. See when he died? I used my last penny to bury him and then I went to the Social Security to get a refund. They told me I couldn't get any money for the funeral because I'd already paid for it.' She looked around the ward. 'As if they couldn't have told me that beforehand! I just said to them, "Well, if I'd known that I would have stuffed him in a plastic bag and tossed him into the Clyde!"'

Jenny was shocked and yet a helpless giggle escaped.

'Battered me stupid for thirty years,' Mrs McKay went on. 'Made my life an absolute hell, that man did.'

A dainty looking woman in a pink crocheted bedjacket in the end bed murmured, 'You poor thing, why didn't you leave him?'

'Easier said than done, hen. I was battered stupid as I say. Then there were the weans. Seven of them I had, I couldn't leave them. And who would have taken eight of us in? Anyway, I hadn't any money.'

'Yes,' agreed another woman, 'it always comes down to money in the end. Economic freedom's the only freedom there is for a woman – for anybody, I suppose.'

'See when that man died?' Mrs McKay was obviously enjoying her spell of reminiscing. 'It was the happiest day of my life, that was *my* freedom, hen.'

Jenny suddenly felt sad. Sad for Mrs McKay's wasted life. Sad even for Mr McKay; surely he couldn't have been happy either. Joe wasn't happy.

Poor Joe, she thought. Then suddenly her heart gave such a lurch it pounded against her rib cage making her cry out. She had remembered about Gregson's letters.

'What's wrong, dear?' The nurse came hurrying to her side.

'I must go home right away!' What if a letter came while she was in hospital and Joe opened it? Nobody would be able to stop Joe then. No matter where she was or who was with her – he would kill her. And he would seek Gregson out and kill him too. Sick with panic she tried to push back the blankets and struggle out of bed.

'Don't be silly, Mrs Thornton,' the nurse's voice took on a stern admonitory note, 'you're not fit to go home yet.'

Jenny was in agony, physical as well as mental, as she persisted in her efforts to move.

126

'Mrs Thornton,' the nurse's anger was becoming indignant. 'Get back into bed at once.'

Jenny made a desperate appeal to the other women in the ward. 'Please help me, it's urgent I get home. I've just remembered something.'

'Don't worry, hen,' Mrs McKay said, 'I'll have your clothes on in a jiffy and then I'll phone you a taxi.'

'Oh, thank you.'

'Get back into bed at once, Mrs McKay!' The nurse sounded outraged now; there was mutiny in her ward and it was her duty to quell it. Mrs McKay, however, after suffering Mr McKay for thirty years was not going to be intimidated by anybody else.

'Away and boil your head, nurse,' she told the younger woman in quite a casual, good-humoured tone as she brushed her aside and began rummaging in the locker beside Jenny's bed.

'You're lucky your young lad didn't take your clothes away, hen. I expect he'd be bringing a case for them today. Just you sit there on the edge of the bed. I'll have you dressed in a jiffy.'

The nurse's stiff apron crackled over beside the two women. 'Doctor will not allow you to go home today, Mrs Thornton.'

'Don't listen to her, hen.' Mrs McKay struggled breathlessly with Jenny's tights. 'You can sign yourself out. I've had to do it many a time while my man was still alive.' Suddenly she let out a hoot of laughter. 'Thank God he can't sign himself out of where he is!' The nurse swept away speechless with fury.

'You'll be okay, hen,' Mrs McKay comforted Jenny. 'There's no bones broken, cracked isn't as bad.'

'It's so important, so terribly urgent I get home,' Jenny said, huge-eyed and trembling. 'Something I must do, you see . . . .' She felt she needed to repay Mrs McKay's kindness by some sort of explanation. 'To prevent my husband finding something.'

'Listen, hen,' Mrs McKay had won her fight with the

127

tights and was now easing off the short open-backed hospital gown that Jenny was wearing. 'You don't need to tell *me* anything about men, or what you've to do to survive being lumbered with one of the rotten bastards. Do you think you could manage to move your arms just a wee bit, hen, so that I can slip on your bra?'

Gently Mrs McKay managed to dress Jenny ready for leaving.

'I'll hang your handbag over your arm, hen, and just take your time now. You'll get there okay. While you're doing your soft-shoe shuffle down the corridor to the front door I'll phone for your taxi.'

Jenny gazed in speechless gratitude at the older woman.

'Away you go, hen,' Mrs McKay said, 'you'd have done the same for me, I'm sure.'

Jenny tried desperately to hurry away but only her mind kept racing forward. Her body just managed to move with excruciating slowness, shoulders hunched protectively forward, shuffling feet not able to lift from the ground for fear of jarring her body.

'Poor wee cow!' she heard Mrs McKay address the ward behind her, 'I know exactly how she feels!'

19

Gregson's letters came once a week or every ten days. They were a constant torment to Jenny. It was her one and only stimulus of the day: getting to the post before Joe. Otherwise she had no energy – nor did she care about Gregson or his letters or indeed anything else. Her only emotion was fear in case Joe found out.

She could recognize Gregson's writing at a glance now. Every time a letter arrived she would snatch it up with trembling hands and furtively stuff it into the pocket of her dressing gown or skirt. Later, while Joe was at work she would read the letter, but lethargically and without interest. Then she'd burn it.

Sometimes a sense of longing would tug at her when she remembered the gentleness of his lovemaking. Sometimes the loving terms of his letters would make her ache to be with him. But she was so emotionally and physically debilitated by the treatment she was having from Joe and the ambience of fear she was living in that these sweet longings were soon drained away.

She wrote to him once and tried to explain that although she returned his feelings she was in an impossible position and dared not see him again. She pleaded with him to stop writing. It was pointless to write, she told him, because she wasn't able to reply.

After completing his business in London he had had to dash over to America instead of returning to Glasgow as he'd previously planned. She prayed that he would never return to Glasgow. She felt so debilitated by fear and depression she believed she would simply give up and die rather than face the trauma of Gregson appearing on the doorstep again and Joe finding out. Joe made a big enough issue of Amelia coming to see her, so much so that she prayed that Amelia wouldn't return again either. It had, in fact, become a secret terror if anyone came to the door. It only took a ring at the doorbell or a knock on the door to make her feel faint.

Her whole existence now was encompassed by her fear of Joe and her inability to do anything to protect herself. She had no longer any stamina. Every last vestige of energy had gone. What was the use of doing anything, anyway?

Joe was still ill from what he'd suffered during the war. Every now and again his nightmares would return and he'd wake up crying out in terrible anguish. She wondered exactly what it was that he had suffered. Once she'd met one of his Army mates who'd told her in confidence that for years Joe had been tortured by his Japanese captors. He hadn't said exactly how. All he'd said was, 'They seemed to pick on Joe. Maybe because he was such a tall, good-looking bloke, I don't know. It's a bloody miracle he survived what they put him through. . . . They didn't even seem to break his spirit – although, by God, they tried hard enough.'

Thinking of Joe made her feel sad as well as frightened. She seemed caught with him in a situation of helpless inevitability. Often she wondered if her plight was her own fault. Perhaps she should have years ago, at the beginning of their marriage, insisted that Joe saw a doctor or a psychiatrist; instead she had told him to pull himself together. Perhaps she should have stayed at home right from the beginning and gone along with his revulsion against any normal standard of comforts or luxuries. Instead she had gone out to work so that she could buy all the comforts she felt she needed. Well, what use was her comfortable flat to her now? She couldn't care less about it.

Amelia had tried to help. She had come and collected her and taken her along to Mary House to watch Princess Margaret's wedding on television. (A television was one luxury Jenny hadn't managed to get.) But watching the wedding had only made her weep. She'd become so distressed in fact, Amelia had had to switch off the television and half carry her through to the kitchen where she'd made her a cup of coffee and put a stiff brandy in it.

Another time Amelia had taken her into town in the hope that a visit to the shops and a cup of tea in a restaurant would help cheer her up. They'd met Rory in her Sauchiehall Street department store and she'd been very kind and treated them to their tea. Because both women were trying so hard to help her she'd tried equally hard to smile and appear brighter. The brightness had been only on the surface, however. It was far away from the darkness inside and did nothing to lighten it. Rory had given them a lift home in her car and as they had passed the Central Hotel Jenny'd been reminded again of Al Gregson.

Thoughts of Gregson made her feel apprehensive. At any time now he could return to Glasgow and come to her door. Yet surely not; he must know that the door could be answered by Joe, what could he say? Surely he would just pretend he was a salesman or something and give Joe an excuse to shut the door without any harm being done? But would a man of his forceful temperament be able to do that?

So apprehensive was she about Gregson's reappearance she even primed the children that if a man of Gregson's description came to the door asking for her they were to say she'd gone away and they didn't have her address. She suspected they thought she was going a bit mad. But she didn't care, maybe she was mad. What did it matter?

Sometimes Joe was gentle with her. Sometimes in bed in the darkness of their room he held her in his arms and wept. She just stroked his hair and didn't say anything. There was nothing to be said.

Hazel missed the delicious meals that Jenny used to

131

make for her and Rowan as well as the way she also found time to tidy up the house. Without Jenny her life was not only less pleasant but increasingly confusing. She kept forgetting to buy in enough food and then there would be nothing with which to make a meal. Jenny had always brought in whatever food was needed, given her a bill and she had written a cheque. Any shopping she had done in the past, she realized now, had been almost like a game. She'd played at trying on clothes and shoes and sometimes she'd see other things that took her fancy – a tin of tea or biscuits with a pretty picture on the lid, an attractively wrapped box of crystallized fruits, a tin of toffees for Rowan. But never anything so prosaic as chops or bread or potatoes. She had never thought of such things, as if they somehow appeared on her plate by magic. Now she had to try to think of them for Rowan's sake although, as often as not, Rowan had to go out to the shops for the essentials that she had forgotten. Occasionally Rowan had a bout of cleaning the house too, or at least, the kitchen. She did it with a bad grace however; Rowan could be very bad-tempered at times. This was strange because neither Derek nor herself had ever had these faults.

'This place is an absolute disgrace, Mother,' Rowan would fume. 'If you can't cope with keeping it decent you should sell it and buy something smaller – you'd be better in a room and kitchen in a tenement than here. You'll never get anyone else to work for you, you know, not with the size of this place and the way you carry on.'

To please Rowan she'd found a feather duster in one of the kitchen cupboards and had floated round the drawing room and the dining room, with a drink in one hand and the duster in the other, flicking at the furniture and ornaments and making dust motes dance in the air. She'd even thought of buying herself a pretty apron – one of those Dutch ones with a frill round it and a pocket the shape of a heart.

Rowan had come in while she'd been dusting. 'For

132

God's sake, Mother!' she'd groaned, 'can't you do anything without a drink in your hand?'

'Darling, it's noon,' she'd told her daughter, 'a perfectly proper time to have a little aperitif.'

Rowan went out a lot; Hazel supposed it was to be expected with young people. Despite the long hours of loneliness it subjected her to she wouldn't have minded if Rowan had behaved more as a young lady should and had had proper gentlemen escorts. It wasn't that she was straight-laced. She wouldn't have minded Rowan being with high-spirited young men friends who knew how to enjoy themselves.

She remembered all the debs' coming-out parties she'd gone to and the high jinks all the bright young things had got up to. At one party the police had arrived after cushions had been hurled into Park Lane and waiters who had gone to retrieve them were pelted with champagne, the glasses crashing on the pavement and the champagne flowing in the gutters below the first floor balcony. Plates of kidney had also been thrown. At another jamboree whisky, champagne and gin had been flung on the passers-by below and boxes of cigarettes had been emptied on a tramp. At the same party food and drink had been used as missiles against the ladies who walked Park Lane at night. Of course it had been the fault of one of these street ladies who had provoked the attack by shouting a taunt of 'filthy rich'. And as Sir Bertie Buchanan, one of the guests, had said the showering of the people below with champagne and cigarettes was simply a spontaneous gesture to the poor. But what fun it had all been, what a glamorous and glittering era.

What fun did Rowan enjoy? What parties did she go to? What balls had she attended? When Hazel had been young she had reported to her mother all the excitement of every occasion she'd attended – even the one where the Honourable Charles Foxwell swung on the chandelier at Claridges.

Rowan was so frightfully serious, so political; her whole life seemed devoted to causes. All she seemed interested in was things like the Bomb, Women's Lib, or the Civil Rights Movement. It was all so frightfully worrying and depressing. Hazel couldn't imagine what kind of families her friends came from. They looked and acted like a disgraceful bunch of hooligans, shouting slogans and causing obstructions and having to be literally carried off by the police. It really was quite shameful.

She didn't know what the world was coming to. There was no sense of decency. Young people just didn't know how to behave any more.

20

It was Amelia who saw Rebecca's advert and thought she might be able to help Jenny. The advert said:

Pendulum diagnosis, Aura Healing, Hypnotherapy. Gentle and loving guidance in conscious, connected breathing and creative thought, as well as related purification and relaxation techniques to influence positively your entire life. If you are troubled, confused, lacking in energy and are desperate for help, phone Rebecca for an appointment or a friendly chat.

Because Amelia lived not far along the road from Jenny she had been able to call in to the basement flat to see her several times. She would have gone more often but Jenny's husband did not make her feel welcome. He was never rude but he did make it plain that Jenny was not returning to work for Amelia or for anyone else and so there was no need for her to go to the trouble of calling. She did not seem able to convince him that she had no ulterior motive in coming to enquire about Jenny. She missed her help in the house admittedly and she would certainly be glad if Jenny returned but she was genuinely worried and disturbed by Jenny's condition.

It was understandable to suffer from shock after the tragic circumstance of her mother's death. It was not surprising that she suffered the trauma of grief and even depression. But that the depression should last so long was disturbing; after all, quite a few months had passed now since the tragedy.

If something wasn't done Jenny was going to end up tragically herself. She had been such a spunky, cheerful type of person. She was still struggling to function normally but it was pathetic to see how hopeless and tired she looked and how she was failing to hold together any semblance of normality. For years Jenny had appeared at her house every afternoon except Saturdays and Sundays; regular as clockwork, always neatly dressed and always a smile on her face. Now anyone just needed to glance at her to make tears overflow down her cheeks. She was dressed in old trousers, a grubby sweater and slippers all the time. Sometimes she just sat around in her dressing gown all day.

The advert, Amelia decided, was worth a try – it gave a local phone number. She plucked up courage eventually and dialled the number and a soft, low pitched voice answered. Amelia liked it immediately. It was so soothing, it made her feel happy; it had an opium-like effect. She felt mesmerized by it. Soon she was thinking this might be the very person to help her as well as Jenny. This could be the answer to a prayer.

She hadn't been in as depressed a state as Jenny although it was only her writing that had saved her – that and her constant and determined efforts to prevent herself from becoming like Jenny. She took Valium and Librium for calmness and codeine for the headaches that seemed to come when the calming effect began to wear off. She took vitamin pills and potions and did exercises to keep her spirits from sagging. She studied books on every aspect of positive thought and how to improve her self-image. The tranquillizers however failed to soothe away her acute anxiety. The codeine never completely cured her headaches. Despite the vitamins she swallowed by the mouthful she still had a constant struggle with depressing thoughts and her self-image was as abysmally low as it had always been.

She couldn't wait to tell Jenny about the advert and subsequent phone conversation. She couldn't wait to meet Rebecca.

Jenny was apathetic. Her shoulders drooped; her head sagged forward; helpless tears filled her eyes. 'You don't understand, Amelia. I know you mean well, but it's no use.'

'You feel that way just now.' Amelia was determined that she would get Jenny to Battlefield House even if she had to drag her there. 'But you're just needing the right kind of help, that's all. The right person to help you get better and I've a feeling this Rebecca is the right person. Oh, Jenny I just know she is!'

Jenny shook her head. 'You always feel everything in extremes, Amelia. I've heard you say something or someone is this marvellous before, remember.'

'It was her voice,' Amelia said, 'it sounded so calm it did me good just to hear it. I had a really long chat with her. I told her all about you, Jenny, and I promised we'd both go along to meet her. Her house is that old villa standing by itself at the other side of the park in Battle Place, just facing the monument.'

She hoped Jenny wouldn't remember – or care – about the funeral parlour situated at the back of Battlefield House. Anyway, there was a long stretch of back garden and a wall in between and why should it matter anyway? Except that, with Jenny feeling so depressed. . . .

Jenny sighed. 'I really haven't enough energy to go anywhere, I'm sorry.'

'I've ordered a taxi. It'll be here any minute.' She hated forcing Jenny like this but desperate straits needed desperate measures.

'Oh, Amelia . . .' The tears flowed faster. 'You don't understand, nothing's any use.'

'I refuse to believe that.' Amelia went to fetch Jenny's camel-hair coat, bustled her into it and tied the coat belt as if Jenny was an awkward child. 'There's no harm in trying anyway. Come on, Jenny, you must try, you *must*!' Hurriedly she struggled into her own warm coat of soft moss green. It was very seldom either she or Jenny ever felt warm enough to go out without a coat; being depressed seemed to affect the circulation and make the blood perpetually chilly.

137

Amelia could hear the taxi hooting impatiently outside and she was near to tears herself by the time she managed to win the struggle, both mental and physical, to get Jenny out of the basement flat and up into the bright summer's day. The flat was dark enough to depress anybody. At least Mary House let in plenty of light and she didn't mind looking out at the trees in the garden or in the park. The few trees in the garden didn't block her view either of Queens Drive or the busy Langside Road. And in the summer especially, the park was alive with people and ablaze with summer dresses as well as flowers.

The taxi took less than ten minutes to reach Battlefield House. As Amelia paid the driver, then helped Jenny out, she suddenly felt apprehensive, her courage and her enthusiasm deserting her. She could just imagine Douglas if he found out – and she had never been good at hiding anything – groaning and shaking his head and saying, 'Will you never learn? Will you never stop getting yourself mixed up with weirdos and charlatans and hangers-on that you've got to be rescued from? You think you know about people but in fact you're anybody's mug. A child could pull the wool over your eyes and take advantage of you. You're a danger to yourself as well as to other people.' She still felt nervous when the door of Battlefield House opened and she saw the tall, striking-looking woman with the thick frizz of blue-black hair and proud firm features.

'My dear friends,' the woman sounded genuinely pleased to see them, 'welcome to Battlefield House. Do come in and make yourself at home. I'm Rebecca Abercrombie and you,' she smiled at Amelia, 'must be Amelia Donovan. Not the Donovans of the famous "Rorys" department stores, I take it?'

'Rory is my mother-in-law,' Amelia admitted.

'Really!' Rebecca looked impressed. 'Well, well!'

'This is my friend Jenny Thornton.' Amelia put her arm around Jenny's shoulders.

'Of course, of course.' Rebecca suddenly flung her arms round both of them and hugged them to her with surprising stength. 'We are all, from this moment on,' she announced, 'loving friends and sisters.'

Amelia felt taken aback and slightly embarrassed, uncomfortable too. The hairpins securing her straw-coloured chignon were working loose from her hair and piercing the skin of her neck instead.

'Come through to the kitchen and I'll make you a cup of my camomile tea,' Rebecca said, releasing them.

As they followed her they could hear her singing to herself or rather chanting some strange-sounding repetitive phrases. Amelia couldn't be certain if the words were English or foreign but there was an undertone of happy satisfaction in the voice that was delivering them. Douglas would definitely have said, 'You've found a right nutter this time!'

The kitchen had an old-fashioned clutter of furniture. A Welsh dresser bulged with dishes of various patterns and piles of letters and papers and books and potted plants. A solid oak table and spar-backed chairs filled the centre of the floor. There was a high stone mantelshelf over a fairly modern-looking Raeburn stove and cooker. A front-loading washing machine stuck out from underneath a wooden work surface that was cluttered with bread bins, biscuit tins and cake tins. Above twin sinks a double window was covered with a cream net curtain and topped by a rolled-up blind. And above everything there were two ceiling pulleys from which a variety of garments dangled. The place had a cosy lived-in look.

Rebecca waved a hand in the direction of the biscuit and cake tins. 'My home is your home. Help yourself to whatever you want.' Jenny sank down on to one of the chairs.

'I can give you ordinary tea if you'd rather,' Rebecca told her.

'It doesn't matter,' Jenny said.

139

'Yes, it does,' Rebecca said, 'everything matters. You matter. You are a child of the Universe, no less than the trees and the stars. You have a *right* to be here.'

It was her eyes that fascinated Amelia most; they were truly beautiful, large and lustrous but calm. Those eyes revealed Rebecca to be a caring person, Amelia felt sure. She might have her little idiosyncrasies but a person with eyes like that must surely be sincere and compassionate. Amelia experienced a sudden rush of hope.

'Could I be a patient, too?' she burst out recklessly.

'Friend, dear. *Friend*!'

'Could I?'

'Of course. Of course.'

Jenny roused herself enough to say, 'I can't afford treatment, I have very little money of my own. A few pounds in my Post Office savings book, that's all.'

'And your husband won't help you, dear. I know. I know.'

'He helps as much as he can.'

'Money isn't the prime consideration with me,' Rebecca said. 'Granted I have to live but I have faith that God will always provide. If you can't give me anything, somebody else will give me a little more. Have a digestive biscuit, dear, and don't worry, it's amazing how these things work out. The important consideration is you're needing help and I'm going to help you.' She turned her dark eyes on Amelia.

'And you too, of course, my dear.'

The soft, compassionate depths of Rebecca's eyes had such a soothing effect on Amelia she could have slithered off the chair she felt so relaxed and relieved.

Rebecca Abercrombie, she decided, was *the* most wonderful person she'd ever met in her life.

21

The silver-grey Rolls-Royce skimmed quietly along the
leafy Pollokshields Street. Large villas lay back from
well-kept lawns on either side. Some of the grassy
frontages behind brick walls sloped steeply upwards and
driveways like mountain paths snaked around to reach
dignified front doors. The car began to slow down.

'What's up?' Douglas Donovan asked, 'why are you
stopping here?'

'Isn't that Hazel Saunders?' Rory said.

'Who?'

'You know, the woman who lives in the next house to
me. I've told you about her. And you met her at the last
New Year's Party I gave. Remember? A few of the
neighbours came in.'

'The snobby Southern Belle type? I was surprised she
was a friend of yours, she doesn't seem your kind of
person, Mother. I thought she was a pain in the arse.'

'So she is. And she's not a friend.'

Douglas gave a burst of laughter. 'She looks pissed out
of her mind. She got a bit under the weather at the party,
didn't she? Didn't dad have to escort her home?'

'You'd better do the needful this time, Douglas.'

Douglas stopped grinning immediately. 'She's not our
responsibility. Come on, Mother, I haven't all day.
Hauling me up here to visit Winnie is bad enough. I was
in the middle of a portrait commission.'

'You were only working from photos, don't be a selfish
sod,' Rory said. 'Winnie looked after you more than I did
when you were a kid. The least you can do is give her a
bit of attention now she's on the way out.'

'Okay, okay, I'm going to give the old girl a bit of

attention. But I'm not having anything to do with that lush.'

'For God's sake, Douglas. Look! She's fallen flat on her face now, we can't just leave her there.'

'Yes, we can. Serves her right, silly cow!'

Rory stopped the car. 'Maybe you can but I can't.'

'Mother!' Douglas groaned before reluctantly following her on to the pavement.

'Help me to get her to her feet.' Rory began tugging at one of Hazel's arms. The prostrate woman moaned and mumbled something incomprehensible.

'We're going to take you home, Mrs Saunders. Come on now!'

Douglas hoisted her up from the other side awkwardly, so that her sky-blue dress became hitched up.

'This is ridiculous, Mother.'

'Oh, stop complaining, Douglas, just shove her into the back of the car.'

'Well, if she spews all over the seat, it serves you right.'

'It won't take me a minute to drive her up to her house. Look – one of her shoes has dropped off.'

Douglas made a grab for the pink high-heeled sandal. 'Then what?'

'She's got a daughter, she can take over.'

'And if the daughter's not in, we leave her with a servant, okay?'

'Don't be daft! Servants are scarcer than gold these days. Jenny used to work part time for her as well as Amelia. As far as I know she hasn't had any more luck than Amelia in finding a replacement.'

As they heaved Hazel's floppy rag-doll's body and her shoe unceremoniously into the car, Douglas said, 'Well, we dump her on the doorstep if no one's there to take her in.'

'Just be quiet and get into the car,' his mother snapped.

Hazel was making swaying efforts to sit up straight.

142

'Those pavements . . .' she managed, 'are in a shocking state of disrepair. I shall complain most forcibly to the Council.'

'Is Rowan at home?' Rory asked as she drove up the Saunders' drive.

'Rowan?' Hazel repeated in a daze. 'I think so, yes, I think so.'

'Might be a good idea for me to have a word.'

'Mother,' Douglas warned.

'Be quiet, Douglas! You wait in the car, I won't be long.'

She got out and rang the doorbell, then returned and opened the back door of the car.

'Come on, Mrs Saunders. Here, let me put on your sandal, then I'll give you a hand out.'

'You are kind,' Hazel said, 'it was such an unfortunate accident – I feel quite shaken. But I shall complain most forcibly to the –'

'Yes, yes,' Rory interrupted impatiently, 'can you stand up? Here, hang on to my arm.' She half-carried, half-dragged the teetering Hazel towards the door which opened just as they reached it and revealed an ashen-faced Rowan. Without a word Rowan supported Hazel at the other side and between her and Rory they steered the dishevelled woman into the sitting room and sat her down.

'A little accident,' Hazel smiled, 'but I'm fine, darling, there's no bones broken. I'm naturally somewhat shaken though. Perhaps a tiny brandy . . . ?'

'You'll be well aware by now of your mother's problem, of course,' Rory said, at which Rowan nodded. 'You'll have to do something about it, love, she was flat on her face when I found her today.'

'I've tried everything,' Rowan said miserably, 'it's ruining my life.'

'Oh, you mustn't let it do that,' Rory said, 'you've a duty to yourself. You've got to survive.'

'My poor, darling Derek didn't survive,' Hazel

143

became suddenly tearful. 'He said he'd come back to me and everything would be just as it was before.' She fumbled ineffectually for a handkerchief.

'Nothing's been the same for any of us since the war,' Rory said. 'It doesn't do any good to keep living in the past. Your husband's been dead and gone years ago, Mrs Saunders, it's time you faced that and built a new life on your own.'

'I'm not strong like you, Mrs Donovan. I need someone to look after me.'

'You've no right to keep expecting your daughter to do that. Maybe if she left you and you were really on your own you'd *have* to pull yourself together.'

Hazel's eyes widened in alarm. 'Rowan wouldn't leave me, would you, darling? I'll be all right in a few minutes, I promise. It was the shocking state of that road, it could have happened to anyone. I was just coming back from doing my nice little charity job when I tripped on an uneven paving stone. I shall complain most forcibly to the Council.'

'Mother, you didn't turn up at the hospital today, I phoned them.' She glanced back at Rory. 'God knows where she'll have been.'

'Of course I was there, darling. They've made a mistake. They are a tiny bit inefficient.'

'Mrs Saunders, stop lying to the girl,' Rory said, 'can't you see, she's sick to death of the whole sordid business?'

Hazel gripped the arms of her chair and struggled to regain some semblance of dignity. 'I really don't know what you are talking about, Mrs Donovan. I appreciate your assistance after my accident but I'd prefer if you left now.'

'You were so pissed you couldn't stand up,' Rory said.

'How dare you speak to me like that!' The floods of tears returned. 'How can you be so cruel?'

'It's no use,' Rowan said, 'I've tried plain speaking as well. Nothing helps, she just keeps getting worse. For years it was so gradual I never noticed – or maybe she was more clever about hiding it then. Eventually I began to notice her swings of mood. It got that I never knew where I was. She could be so sweet and gentle then suddenly she'd become nasty and sarcastic and hurtful to me, for no apparent reason. I thought those days were bad enough, but now this. . . .' She shrugged helplessly.

'Darling, I've never been sarcastic or hurtful to you, I love you too much. How could I hurt you?'

'You never remember, Mother. It's all a complete blank to you afterwards.'

'What do you mean you couldn't hurt her, woman?' Rory said, 'what do you think you're doing now? Having neighbours picking you up drunk in the street and bringing you home to her looking like something the cat dragged in. And you've had the gall to talk about how *she* looks!'

'Accidents can happen to anyone, I shall complain most forcibly to –'

'Oh, be quiet, Mother!'

'I'd better go,' Rory said. 'My son's waiting outside in the car.'

'More and more,' Rowan confided, when they reached the hall, 'I just give up and go out with my friends and try to forget her. I don't know what else to do any more.'

'Quite right,' Rory said, 'there's no point in wasting your life. They say that alcoholics have to hit rock bottom before they feel the need to do anything about themselves. Maybe if you got right away for a while she'd be forced to face facts and seek help for herself.'

At the door Rory put a hand on the girl's arm. 'Whatever you do, you mustn't feel guilty. You're young, you've your whole life in front of you. Make the most of it. Grab it with both hands.'

Rowan hesitated. 'Actually, for some time now I've been thinking about a trip to America. There's so many exciting and worthwhile things happening there just now that I'd like to be part of. But I've kept putting it off because, well – I do feel guilty about going away so far. It's one thing going out for an evening but. . . .'

'You deserve a decent break, of course you must go. I take it you can afford it?'

'Yes, I've managed to save quite a few pounds.'

'Good for you. Have a wonderful time in good old US of A.'

'Oh, I still don't know if I should.'

'She'll destroy you if you don't get away now, while you can. Take my advice. Get the next flight out of here.'

Rowan smiled. 'I doubt if I could manage it as quick as that, but thank you – you've helped me to make up my mind.'

22

She was suspended in the kind of inertia that dully floats between waking and sleeping. Her eyes were closed, her body felt heavy but she could still hear the soft, soporific voice. It was telling her that it was making her relax. Jenny thought how useless this was. For months she had been in this heavy-limbed trance-like condition but with her eyes open. She could open her eyes now if she wanted to, only she couldn't be bothered.

'You are feeling the tension flowing out of your forehead and scalp,' the voice was crooning, 'your scalp is relaxing. Your Third Eye – that special area in the centre of your forehead, above and between your eyes – is relaxing. . . .'

Her Third Eye . . . it was so stupid, yet at the same time she was thinking – was that the eye that kept looking back?

'Your eyes are relaxing and all the muscles round your eyes are relaxing and your eyes are sinking deep into your head. . . .'

She could see Cheapside Street and the other familiar streets hugging the riverside. The complete world of her youth. No other place existed.

'Your cheeks and your lips are relaxing. Your jaw is becoming heavy and relaxing. Your teeth are separating. The very base of your tongue is relaxing. . . .'

She could hear the rag-man blowing his horn to announce his arrival. This had been the spur to send the children rushing up tenement stairs to plead with their mothers to search out rags they could exchange for a shiny blue or crimson or yellow balloon. The rag-man's cart that he managed to heave along despite being so small he could barely reach its handles was always piled with a mountain of rags and festooned with bouncing balloons. He was known as 'Wee Willie' and he was one of the many Glaswegians whose growth had been stunted in childhood before the war by rickets and whose legs had gone bandy.

'Your throat and the back of your neck is relaxing . . . your shoulders and your arms are relaxing. . . .'

There was the delicious smell of her mother's Scotch broth as she skipped up the stairs. Tears beaded her eyes then zig-zagged down to her chin. Why was she lying here on this woman's settee listening to her monotonous voice? It was pointless. She wanted to stop the charade by telling her so, only she couldn't be bothered.

'Take a deep, deep breath . . . in through your nostrils and slowly, slowly out through your mouth. Now your chest is relaxing. . . .'

All the girls used to play skipping games in the street after school. They'd chant in time to the monotonously whirring ropes:

Vote, vote, vote for Jeannie Smith,
Here comes Helen at the door.
Helen is the one that we all love the best
So we don't want Jeannie any more.

Diddle, diddle, dumpling, my son John,
Went to bed with his trousers on,
One shoe off and one shoe on,
Diddle, diddle dumpling, my son John. . . .

Queen Mary, Queen Mary, my age is sixteen,
My father's a farmer on yonder green,
He's plenty of money to dress me in silk
But no bonny laddie will take me awa'.

Sometimes she and her friends would sit on the pavement and concentrate on the serious business of exchanging transfers or scraps as they called them;

148

cherubs and angels were favourites. She had a book full of all sorts of beautiful coloured scraps.

Sometimes she'd been allowed to play rounders with Joe and his friends. She remembered running with the ball until she was choking and breathless in her efforts to please Joe.

Sometimes they all took part in a back-court concert for charity. All the neighbours leaned their folded arms on the sills of open kitchen windows and watched with good-natured appreciation. A short sketch might be performed with the wash house acting as dressing room. Then someone would do a tap-dance, someone else would recite a poem. Her mother used to call down. 'Sing "The Old Rugged Cross", hen.' It was one of her favourites.

'Your breathing is nice and easy now. . . .'

But it wasn't. Her chest was heaving in panic with the crushing weight of grief.

'Your heart is relaxing . . . your lungs are relaxing. . . .'

Stupid, stupid woman. She wanted to tell her so but what was the use? She allowed the voice to drone on.

'You are one with all of life. . . . You are not lonely or abandoned but one with the very power that created you. . . .'

She wished the woman would stop. She wished she was in her own bed, she wanted to sleep in peace, she wanted the unconsciousness of sleep that completely blacked everything out. But even in sleep there were sights and sounds and voices. Joe's voice, telling her to snap out of it. 'Maybe if you washed your hair and had a bath you'd feel better. I'd feel better as well – how do you think I feel coming home every day to see you sitting there in that state? Can you blame me for wanting to knock some life back into you?' She didn't even cry now when he hit her or shook her about like a rag doll.

Eventually she heard the woman say 'I'm going to count to three and on the count of three I'll snap my

149

fingers and you'll wake up feeling calm and refreshed and happy. One . . . two . . . three.'

As soon as Jenny heard the click she opened her eyes. She stared helplessly at Rebecca. She might be experiencing what could be interpreted as a certain calm but she was anything but refreshed or happy.

'How do you feel, my dear?' Rebecca asked.

Jenny shrugged. Foolish tears returned. She had known it wasn't going to work yet she felt bitterly disappointed. Rebecca linked arms with her as they went through to the kitchen where Amelia was waiting.

'It'll take a little time,' Rebecca explained, 'but you're going to be all right! You're going to be full to overflowing with optimism and joy. I'm going to enter into your mind-field and shift your thinking. I'm going to expand your mind-field and open up your thinking patterns into new ways of seeing and being. Did you make a pot of tea like I said, Amelia, dear?'

'Yes, I hope it's all right. Douglas always says I never make it strong enough.'

'Douglas is your husband?'

'Yes.'

'The next time he says that, dear, you tell him it is as you want it to be. Sit down, Jenny, love and enjoy a nice cup of tea and one of my home-made biscuits.'

'You bake as well?' Amelia laughed.

'I can bake when I want to but these were brought by one of my "friends". My "friends" are very kind.'

'No doubt they appreciate how much you help them.'

'They do, dear, they do. Now, while Jenny sits there and has her tea and biscuits and enjoys a look at some of these magazines and books you can come through to the sitting room.'

Magazines and books were piled higgledy-piggledy on chairs and work surfaces along with tins and corn dollies and potted plants. Among the titles were *Towards Enlightenment by Tarot, Reincarnation and the Working of Destiny* and *Ceremonial Energies and the Power of Sacred Ritual.*

150

Amelia gazed uncertainly at her friend. 'Will you be all right?'

'Of course she'll be all right,' Rebecca said. 'Follow me, dear.'

Rebecca's tall, queenly figure was dressed in a loose caftan in an oriental pattern of green and gold. The material floated out and shimmered through the inadequate light of the hall.

The sitting room was even more cluttered than the kitchen. Large silk shawls, fringed and unfringed of oriental and Paisley patterns were draped on the walls along with grotesque African masks, paintings of animals and seascapes and splashes of colour that seemed to have no shape at all – although one of them might have represented the torturous flames of hell. There were framed poems and a picture of a faceless, seated figure, knees splayed in yoga pose, with wheels of colour from head to groin. More shawls were draped over chairs, and ashtrays were full of crystals and semi-precious stones. Joss sticks burning on the mantelpiece were crushed up against fat brass Buddhas, fat black Buddhas and skinny ivory men with long beards and a forgotten cup of camomile tea. On a table beside the settee was a picture in blue pastel in which could barely be discerned a ghostly face with closed eyes and a blur of light shining from its forehead.

'Just make yourself at home,' Rebecca said.

Heart beginning to patter with apprehension, Amelia sat down on the edge of the settee.

'Lie back, put your feet up and I'll cover you with a rug. It's important that you're nice and cosy.'

A gas fire hissed barely a yard away from her feet and Amelia began to realize that the room wasn't just cosy, it was stifling. It was as hot as hell. She began struggling out of her cardigan.

'Try to relax, dear,' Rebecca soothed, 'it's important that you abandon all movement. Let it go. Just lie there – perfectly still and quiet and calm.'

They'd been chatting earlier in the kitchen and Amelia had confided to Rebecca some of her fears and feelings of inadequacy. Now her confessed weakness made her feel vulnerable and frightened; she wished she hadn't been so open. This was another of her faults – Douglas said she talked too much and he was absolutely right.

'First I'm going to make you relax more deeply and beautifully than you've ever relaxed before.' Rebecca's voice lowered in tone, became like a purr. 'Then I'm going to put some positive suggestions into your sub-conscious mind that will help you to become more self-confident. They will help you to grow into a radiantly happy and fulfilled human being. . . .'

Amelia felt herself stiffen away from where Rebecca was squatting on a low stool beside the settee. She was thinking, I'm mad, why do I keep getting myself into these awful situations? I need locking up for my own protection. Oh, please God, just let me get out of here and I'll never do anything like this again.

She closed her eyes and lay half-listening to Rebecca's voice, half-thinking of all the idiotic things she'd done in her life and how she would never learn. She felt like weeping at her own foolishness. She was 31 years of age, for God's sake! It was high time she had more sense. If she hadn't grown up by 31 when would she, how could she grow up? Then, something Rebecca was saying caught her attention.

'Deep at the centre of everyone is a child who has a joy in life, a child who has a loving spirit, and so in adult life it is our duty and responsibility to look after that loving child and in any situation in which we, as adults, feel worried, tense or anxious or less than confident, we should remember just that part of us is the child within us who has perhaps been hurt by someone. . . .'

Amelia found this unexpectedly intriguing. It was a novel switch of viewpoint. Thinking of herself in this way was as if she was suddenly looking at a stranger. No, not

152

a stranger. How could any child be called a stranger? Her love for Harry had given her a tender compassion for all young people. Suddenly, in her mind's eye she saw herself as a little girl, helpless and alone, frightened and unloved.

She saw the small shoulders hunched in futile attempt at self-protection. She saw the large bewildered eyes, averted as if ready to ward off expected blows. Her mother and father were shouting at each other. Her mother was leaving her father yet again. She was taking her brother Jamie with her but as usual did not want to take Amelia.

'Well, she's not staying here!' her father bawled, losing his temper completely in his harassment. 'You can do what you like with her but you're not leaving her here.'

'*You* can do what you like with her,' her mother flung his words back at him, 'it's high time you took your turn of the responsibility. You take care of her!'

And hadn't he just, Amelia thought bitterly. Hadn't he just!

She had been too shocked and afraid to make a sound then but she could hear herself weeping brokenheartedly now.

'And on the count of three,' Rebecca was saying, 'I'll snap my fingers and you'll wake up. . . .'

She opened her eyes. The image of the abandoned child had gone but cobwebs of grief for it still hazed her consciousness. She felt so shaken she doubted if she would be able to rise from the settee. She lay clutching the rug up to her mouth, gazing silently round at Rebecca.

'You must have faith in God and me,' Rebecca said, 'the faith that surpasses all understanding.'

Amelia allowed herself to be helped into a sitting position and then to stand up. For a few seconds she cautiously tested her feet as if she wasn't sure if they would be able to support her. Rebecca kept an arm around her shoulders as they returned to the kitchen. She was a sorry sight with her mascara clownishly streaking her cheeks, her fair hair matted with sweat and hanging in tendrils over her eyes.

After a cup of tea Amelia began to feel better. She even washed up the dishes for Rebecca, who said she was expecting another friend any minute, but added reassuringly, 'But don't worry, my dears, my home is your home. Stay as long as you like. This is your refuge and your strength.' Amelia thought that was a truly wonderful thing to say.

Later, walking home through the park, Jenny agreed. She added, 'I don't think she managed to hypnotize me though. I'm sure I could have opened my eyes if I'd wanted to. I wasn't in a trance or anything.'

'No, I don't think I was either,' Amelia said, 'all the same, I found what she said very interesting. Some of the things have given me food for thought. And she is a fascinating character, isn't she? I love different kinds of people, don't you?'

Jenny shrugged.

Then suddenly Amelia laughed. 'I've never been hugged so much for years, have you? I thought she was going to crush us to bits at her front door before we left. I don't know how she managed to get her arms round us both at the one time like that and hug us with such strength. She's so much bigger than me, my nose was being flattened against her bosom, my hairpins were puncturing the back of my neck.'

A giggle erupted unexpectedly from Jenny's sad face. 'What on earth must we have looked like? I must be mad to allow you to drag me into your idiotic schemes.'

'Oh Jenny,' Amelia linked arms with her, 'she's going to help you, she is! I know she is.'

She felt with secret sadness, however, that there was no hope for herself.

23

'This Abercrombie woman could be dangerous,' Joe insisted. 'Jenny is in a bad enough state without some charlatan tampering with her mind.'

'I've told her.' Douglas spread out his hands in a gesture of hopelessness. 'But that's Amelia, she not only gets herself into all sorts of trouble, she involves other people as well.'

'Thank you for your usual loyal support, Douglas,' Amelia said, surprised at the bitterness she felt. At least Joe Thornton had the guts to stick his neck out, coming to Mary House to fight for what he thought was right for his wife. At least he had loyalty. She could imagine that no one would dare criticize Jenny in his presence. Anyone could say anything to Douglas about his wife. He enjoyed the chance to make a fool of her or belittle her in any way he could.

'I believe Rebecca Abercrombie is helping Jenny,' she said.

Douglas rolled his eyes. 'What do you know? You know nothing about anything, except making a mess of everybody's lives.'

'I see no sign of improvement in Jenny, Amelia,' Joe said quietly. 'I care too much about my wife to have her brainwashed and put at further risk.'

Amelia longed to say, some way to care for your wife, bashing her about all over the place, but she decided not to risk it in case Joe punished Jenny for having told her about his behaviour. 'It's not brainwashing,' she told him instead. 'Rebecca says hypnotherapy isn't a matter of her having power over us. All she's doing is bringing out the real person buried inside us by all sorts of inhibitions. She's just trying to get rid of our inhibitions.'

'My God!' Douglas said, 'the mind boggles!' He turned to Joe. 'She says she's not being brainwashed but it's Rebecca this and Rebecca that from morning till night. I'm bored out of my mind hearing about Rebecca bloody Abercrombie. I bet she's a right nutter. Have you met her?'

'I believe I've seen her in the park doing T'ai Chi.' A note of bitterness crept into Joe's voice. 'One of the new devotees of everything Eastern.'

'What the hell's T'ai Chi?' Douglas asked.

Amelia said, 'It's a balance between Yin and Yang. Rebecca says that these are the two elemental forces of life.'

'It looks like a rather foolish slow-motion dance,' Joe said. 'It would be laughable – that woman would be laughable – if she wasn't so dangerous.'

Amelia shook her head. 'Honestly, she's not like that at all. She's so kind, she tries every way she knows to help people. T'ai Chi is just one of the Eastern philosophies and methods she uses because she believes the East has so much to offer. We can learn such a lot from them.'

The words had hardly escaped from her mouth when she realized she shouldn't have said them. Not to Joe Thornton.

'You must forgive me,' Joe's blue eyes were like ice-picks, 'if I fail to share your admiration.'

'Oh dear,' Amelia reddened with embarrassment, 'I'm sorry, I forgot you'd been a prisoner.'

'That's just like her,' Douglas cried out, 'she keeps opening her big mouth and putting her foot in it.'

'I do not wish my wife to have anything to do with Rebecca Abercrombie,' Joe said in a quiet smooth voice that didn't match the expression in his eyes.

'It's up to Jenny, surely. It's what she wants to do.'

'Jenny's not herself just now. She's not capable of deciding what's best. As her husband it is my responsibility to look after her interests. Not yours,' he added pointedly.

156

When Jenny received a phone call from Amelia and heard that Joe had gone to Mary House, some of her old fire sparked back into life. How dare he try to spoil her friendship not only with Rebecca but with Amelia! She still shrank from any confrontation with Joe however. Fear of his temper and the pain he could cause made her excessively cautious. Too much of her courage and energy had been depleted to risk even contradicting him. She felt secretly angry and resentful however.

He wanted to keep her a prisoner in the house all day with him as jailor allowing no one else near her. He certainly did not deny himself access, she thought bitterly. He had sex as often, if not more often, than ever. It was true what Rebecca said – this wasn't love, just selfish possessiveness. Well, let him think he possessed her. She'd keep going to Battlefield House and she'd keep seeing Amelia without him knowing about it.

Instead of Amelia calling for her at the flat they could meet in the park and walk across to Rebecca's together. The park covered 148 acres and so the chances of bumping into Joe were remote. Or they could meet at Battlefield House. She had to go this week anyway because it was Rebecca's day-course on relaxation; she'd promised to bake some cakes and biscuits for the fourteen or fifteen people who were coming. She hadn't baked or even cooked anything for – she didn't know how long – but Rebecca had been so good to her she'd felt spurred to do something in return.

'God alone knows what my oven's like,' Rebecca had laughed, 'but Amelia tells me you're magic in the kitchen so I'm sure you'll be able to do something with it.'

At first she hadn't known how she would be able to cope, with the crushing weight on her shoulders that kept exhausting and depressing her, but Rebecca had been adamant.

'Come on now, I know you're not going to let me down. You're going to come over here early on the day and you're going to do battle with my oven. I'll have all the ingredients ready. Amelia can be your kitchenmaid and grease the baking tins and wash everything up afterwards. Won't you Amelia?'

Amelia had readily agreed without any apparent concern about the reversal of roles. After all, it had been Jenny who had worked for Amelia in the past. It was Amelia's friendliness and total lack of snobbishness that had always endeared her to Jenny.

Tears of fatigue and frustration had come to Jenny's eyes. 'I'd like to, Rebecca, but I just don't feel able.'

'It's all in the mind,' Rebecca assured her, 'all you need to do is keep telling yourself that you *are* able, and you *will* be. "Every day in every way", keep telling yourself, "I am feeling better and better"!'

She had tried but in actual fact it was her anger at Joe that had spurred her into action.

When Amelia had phoned her to tell her about Joe's visit to Mary House she'd promised to phone again on the day of Rebecca's relaxation course to find out what Jenny had decided to do. When she did phone Jenny told her they could meet as they walked across the park on their way to Rebecca's.

As soon as she emerged from the basement she was taken aback by a loud banging of drums and the impertinent tooting of 'penny whistles'. Mixing in with these sounds came the trumpets and the raucous skirl of the bagpipes. Damn it, she though, it's the Orange Walk – she'd forgotten it was the day for this annual event.

Dressed in blue with coloured sashes draped across their shoulders, the men marched in memory of the Battle of the Boyne and the defeat of Catholic King James by William of Orange – although she doubted if many of the marchers knew or cared much about the reason for the march, or about religion for that matter, despite the bible carried on a velvet cushion at the head of the procession. It was common knowledge that the marchers took delight, however, in strutting provocatively past every Catholic church they could find en route, and banging their drums as loudly as possible as they did so.

Standing on the kerb waiting for the procession to pass so that she could get across she felt so weary again she nearly turned back into the house. Only she couldn't be bothered, it was easier just to stand and do nothing. And to think that first thing this morning she'd felt so much better. She'd enjoyed a leisurely bath and put on a pretty, full-skirted, floral dress. She'd actually looked in the mirror – something she'd not done for ages – and taken some interest in flicking a comb through her curls. She had even used some mascara and a slight dusting of eye shadow to give depth and definition to her grey eyes. She'd experienced a shiver of excitement as she'd taken from its hiding place at the back of her underwear the money she'd been secretly saving to pay for the relaxation day-course.

The march took an age to file into the park where they would fill it to overflowing, not only with themselves but with a sea of litter. At least they would keep Joe busy trying to protect his precious flowers and plants. She remained standing for a minute or two after the road was clear still uncertain of what to do. Again it was angry thoughts of Joe that spurred her on.

Rebecca had said, 'You have lost one refuge at your mother's, Jenny, but you have found another. I am your refuge and your strength now.' She couldn't afford that to be taken away from her.

Amelia was already in Battlefield House when she eventually arrived but it was Rebecca who flung open the door looking more regal than ever wearing a royal blue scarf plaited round her thick frizz of hair like a crown. A matching caftan edged with gold reached her gold-sandalled feet.

'Welcome, my dear, everything's ready and waiting for you.' She gave Jenny one of her enthusiastic hugs.

In the kitchen Amelia had an apron tied round her

coffee-coloured slacks and the sleeves of her cream blouse were rolled up. Her fair hair was pinned back in a neat chignon. 'I'm making the salads,' she told Jenny. 'What do you think so far?' she asked, indicating a couple of bowls.

'All right,' Jenny said tying an apron round her own waist, 'but is that all there is? Lettuce, cucumber, hard boiled eggs and tomato?'

'What should we have dear?' asked Rebecca. 'Just tell me and I'll get it.'

'Rice. We could do different things with a rice base.'

'Yes, I've got that.'

'Raisins, nuts, mandarins, cottage cheese, cabbage, carrots, olives, peppers –'

'Hang on,' Rebecca laughed, 'there's only going to be fifteen of us, not a hundred and fifteen. But I think I've got most of these. Anything I haven't got I can send Milly out to the shops for. She's through in the sitting room Hoovering just now.'

'Is she your daily?' Jenny asked.

'No, no, dear,' Rebecca said, 'just a "friend" like yourself. I'll call her to come for a cup of tea before you start. You must have had a struggle getting through the park today – or did you take the long way round?'

'No, I managed. It was pretty awful right enough.'

'You came though with flying colours. Good for you!' She opened the kitchen door and shouted. 'Milly, dear. Tea's up!'

Milly turned out to be a tiny bespectacled lady who looked far too well-brought up and also too frail ever to have put hand to Hoover. She was expensively dressed in jet stud earrings and a silver-grey wool jersey suit that tied in a neat bow at the neck.

'Milly's been such a help,' Rebecca said after introductions had been completed. 'She's cleaned every carpet in the place. Sit down for a minute dear.' She whisked away a pile of papers from the chair, then plumped up the loose cushion.

'Milly usually enjoys my rocking chair best but it's filled with shopping, dear, and I've nowhere else to put it at the moment. You'll just have to make do with this.'

'Thank you,' Milly murmured. She looked so stiff with embarrassment (or was it fear?) Jenny wouldn't have been surprised if, when Milly lifted her tea cup, her arm had cracked and fallen off. Everything about her looked tight to cracking point, her shoulders, the expression on her face, the way her hair was screwed up. When she did lift her tea cup her hand revealed a tremor that made the tea splash about. She was forced to grab the cup tightly with both hands in an effort to control it.

'I'm sure you're all looking forward to this afternoon's meeting as much as I am,' Rebecca said, swooping down on to another chair. Then she stretched luxuriously, throwing her head back and pushing her hands up and out in a dramatic gesture. Relaxing back down again she enjoyed a long drink of tea. 'As well as relaxation tuition I'm going to teach you metamorphic massage. It'll do you all the world of good.'

'What's metamorphic massage?' Amelia queried uneasily.

'Ah!' Rebecca looked mysterious, 'wait and see! At about four o'clock we'll break for afternoon tea and some of Jenny's delicious cakes and biscuits.'

'I hope they'll be all right,' Jenny murmured, 'I'm a bit out of practice.'

'Of course they'll be all right dear. But before that, at about one o'clock we'll have a buffet lunch of salad and crusty bread and butter. How about throwing in a couple of apple tarts while you're at it, dear, and we could have that for pudding?'

'Well, I suppose. . . .'

'Wonderful, wonderful! Oh, that'll be Dorothy at the door, she volunteered to come early and give the bathroom a little clean. Everyone is so loving and kind.'

She rose in one smooth flowing movement and floated

161

serenely from the room leaving behind her the tight little group sitting in worried silence.

At least Dorothy looked fit and strong enough to attack the bathroom. A ruddy-faced woman, more muscular than flabby, Amelia could imagine that if she accidentally bumped into Dorothy she'd bounce off that ample but resilient-looking flesh.

'Well, what are you lot lazing about here for?' Dorothy gave an earsplitting laugh. 'Lots to do. No time to waste. No, it's not tea I want, it's water with plenty of disinfectant in it. I'm a great believer in disinfectant, especially for bathrooms.' Another roar of laughter convinced Amelia that Dorothy was more in need of relaxation treatment than any of them. 'I've got a thing about germs. Can't stand them!'

'Yes, Dorothy dear,' Rebecca's voice acquired a low, slow hypnotizing quality, 'you're going to make a very nice job of the bathroom. And it's going to be beautiful and pure and clean, I'm sure.'

Dorothy seemed to wind down a little despite herself. She looked a little sheepish. 'Got to get started. Excuse me, folks, don't like to waste any time. Everything necessary in the bathroom, Rebecca?'

'I believe so dear, just shout if you need anything.'

Dorothy waved to everyone round the room before leaving as if she was off on some venture that would take her to far flung Empires rather than the bathroom across the hall.

Amelia told Jenny later that she'd felt embarrassed for her and had begun to wonder if it was such a good idea to gather all Rebecca's 'friends' together like that. At the same time she couldn't help feeling lucky to be meeting such interesting characters. 'I wish I'd brought my notebook,' she said.

'I think I'd better get started, too,' Jenny told Rebecca now.

'I'll wash up the cups, then I'll grease the tins,' Amelia said and began clearing the table.

162

Milly snapped to her feet. 'I've to Hoover the hall.'

'And I,' Rebecca announced, 'must go through to the quietness of my study and lie down on the floor.'

'Lie on the floor?' Amelia giggled.

'Of course,' Rebecca eyed her severely. 'The fact is it's the best place to relax every muscle. And I must first relax down to Theta for a time before I can give of my best to my friends. Theta,' she added, 'is the stage of brainwave that is found in the deep trance states of Yogis.'

'Oh,' Amelia appeared suitably subdued and impressed, 'I didn't know that.'

'There's a great deal you don't know, Amelia,' Rebecca said with overtones of mystery in her voice.

Somehow Jenny managed to get the baking done. The rows of golden scones and sponge cakes and dark treacle biscuits cooling on racks on the kitchen table filled the room with a rich spicy aroma and gave her a deep sense of satisfaction and pleasure. She sat down and just stared at them for a while.

'Are you all right?' Amelia asked.

'I'll put jam and cream in one of the sponges and icing sugar on the others,' Jenny murmured absently. With another effort she rose and soon she had everything ready and set out on the hall table as Rebecca wanted.

She felt tired afterwards but her glow of achievement lasted all day. The relaxation course helped, too. She had almost felt happy strolling back through the park arm-in-arm with Amelia, listening to her laugh and chatter about some of the fascinating and amusing events of the day.

Once Amelia had gone, though, it was different. At Jenny's request Amelia had cut across towards the smaller exit along past Mary House. 'I'd rather not risk Joe seeing you coming out the main Victoria Road gates with me,' Jenny'd explained. For Joe would be home now or perhaps coming from the Queens Park Café in Victoria Road. The full realization of what Joe being

163

home meant snatched the ground from under Jenny. She had to cling to the park railings after Amelia left. She had originally intended to be back before Joe but everything at Rebecca's had gone on longer than expected.

He would ask where she had been. Even if he was sober he might question her. She wondered if she dared lie, tell him she had just been out for a walk. Her mind once more confused with fear, uncertainty and guilt, her shoulders hunched down and she gave a shuddering sigh as a wave of helplessness engulfed her.

24

'Mother, I want to talk to you!'

Hazel put down her *Herald*, folded away her reading glasses and gazed encouragingly across at her daughter who had settled in a chair opposite.

'Yes, darling?'

'I don't think you appreciate the important and exciting times we are living in, Mother.'

Hazel smiled ruefully. 'I realize only too well how society is changing, Rowan. Exciting however, is not the word I would choose to describe it.'

'People are doing things to change the world.'

Hazel sighed. 'Yes, that is true.'

'People have power!'

'Yes, dear.'

'Young people especially.'

Hazel sighed again. Rowan was wearing blue jeans and a checked open-necked shirt. With her slim figure and freckles and tightly tied-back hair she could be mistaken for a boy. Yet there were pretty dresses around – wide-skirted dresses with lots of frou-frou petticoats. If Rowan would wear one of those and use make-up to hide her freckles and have her hair cleverly styled . . .

'In my day –'

'It was different, I know, Mother. It must have been frightfully dull and repressive. Now there is a new freedom and even the poorest or most ordinary young person can get somewhere by doing something he enjoys. Jenny's son, Dode for instance, has got himself a set of drums and he's formed a group. They were playing at a party I was at the other night. They weren't all that good but at least they were *doing* something. And it was fun.'

'Yes, dear.'

'And people *care*.'

'About what, darling?'

'Everything. The Bomb; Vietnam; Women's Liberation; Civil Rights. People are in a ferment, Mother, people are on the move.'

'It sounds awfully exhausting, darling.'

'Especially in America.'

'America?'

'Mother, you read the papers. You must know the courageous struggle going on there for Civil Rights.'

'I get so easily upset, Rowan. I confess I try to avoid even thinking about conflict and violence.'

'I want to be part of it.'

'Part of what, darling?'

'My friends feel the same. There's a call for help gone out from the American Civil Rights Movement in the Deep South. They're asking for every freedom-loving person to go to their aid.'

Hazel didn't understand. Her mind had retreated to that bleak no-man's-land from which only a drink could rescue her.

'Yes, dear,' she said.

'So I'm going.'

'Going?'

'To America.' There was a long silence that Rowan eventually broke with a desperate repetition of what she'd said before. 'I'm going to America.'

'But you can't,' her mother managed to say.

'Why not?'

Hazel had never felt so frightened for years. 'Please don't tease mummy, dear.'

'I'm not teasing, Mother.'

'You can't leave me here alone.'

'You're a grown woman, it's time you learned to take responsibility for yourself.'

'You couldn't be so cruel.'

'It's not a case of being cruel. I'm a grown woman too

and I'm perfectly entitled to go on a trip to America or anywhere else. It's you who are being cruel trying to keep me tied to your apron strings.'

Hazel gazed in helpless bewilderment at her daughter. 'But I've no one else to look after me.'

'It's time you learned to look after yourself. There's no reason why you shouldn't be as capable as any one else. You've just never tried.'

'Rowan, you don't understand.' She stared in mounting panic at her daughter. 'Oh Rowan, please don't do this to me. You don't *really* mean it, do you?'

But despite her desperate efforts to hide from the truth, it had kept leaping out at her unexpectedly, scaring her into recognition. She had pleaded, she had become ill, the doctor had been in attendance, all to no avail. Rowan had eventually deserted her.

At first Rowan had postponed her trip. Then her friends had gone on without her, arranging to meet her somewhere abroad. They were actually hitch-hiking across Europe en route to America. After Rowan's friends left, Hazel had felt a little better, a little reassured; Rowan would not go now. But she had. One day she had disappeared without even a goodbye, just a brief note.

The loneliness was too much to bear. It even outweighed her worries about the trouble and danger Rowan might get into. The house stretched silently around her, bleak as a graveyard, a terrifying reflection of her inner self. Never before had she been so grateful for a drink. After a few vodkas she didn't care too much about anything – she even forgot to eat. After a few days there was nothing in the house anyway and she didn't feel confident enough to go out to the shops. The pavements were so treacherous. Nothing was the same any more. She didn't know what the world was coming to when ladies needed to carry groceries. She remembered the times when shops were only too pleased to deliver anything one wanted. Not any more. She detested these new 'supermarkets' that were springing up all over the place. They confused her with their aisles of shelves like a maze of streets in which one could so easily get lost. No one cared. Gone was the kindly personal and respectful interest of the family grocer, the small shops with mahogany counters and a white marble shelf for cutting cheese and patting butter. And the cheerful 'message boy' on the bike with the basket fixed to the front.

All gone.

Occasionally a salesman would come to the door. Normally she would never have allowed any of these people over her threshold whether to chatter on about encyclopaedias or demonstrate a new kind of carpet cleaner. Jenny had strict orders about that.

Now Jenny was gone too.

The day the man came with a new kind of floor mop she had been feeling so frighteningly lonely she had consumed reckless amounts of vodka to blot out the pain. When she'd heard the loud ringing of the doorbell she had in fact reached a high point of elation. She'd been giggling to herself and imagining she was floating around the drawing room in her negligée, a pink froth of organza edged with white ermine. Sometimes her pink and white cloud bumped into furniture and walls, making it whirl about. It was hilariously funny!

At first she'd thought she'd heard heavenly bells ringing and giggled all the more. She'd doubled up with giggles in fact and had to hold on to a chair for steadiness.

Then she told herself not to be a silly girl – it was her front doorbell. Somehow she found herself at the door and there to her surprise and delight was the loveliest man she'd ever seen. The sun was shining on his corn-coloured hair and the eyes that met hers were as clear and blue as the summer sky. The fair hair and blue eyes made a startling contrast to the rich tan of his skin. And he was so tall compared with her. An Adonis of a man.

168

She gazed up at him in the helpless, dewy-eyed, yet flirtatious way that Derek loved so much. But she had to hold on to the doorway because her legs were wobbling.

He asked, very politely, if he could come in. It wasn't often that one met such charming manners. He was selling a new kind of floor mop, he said. Something she would enjoy using – it was so easy and efficient. One didn't even need to get one's hands wet, he said. He could see she was a lady, he said, and wasn't accustomed to such menial tasks but what could one do these days? Staff was impossible to find; the next best thing, he assured her, was a good, labour-saving gadget.

Such an understanding, such a clever young man. And so very good-looking.

She couldn't remember if she had actually invited him in to the house but she supposed she must have done. She stumbled a little going across the hall and again while making her way down the corridor towards the kitchen. The second time the man supported her with an arm around her waist.

How long was it since she'd felt a strong, supportive arm around her? Far too many cruel, empty years; she'd forgotten how wonderful it felt. How wonderful to melt against a man's strength, to give oneself up to his love and protection. To be wanted and treasured and respected. She was in a dream of delight where reality lost its edge and became confused with her inner imaginings. She had no memory at all of what happened after she reached the kitchen. If she ever reached the kitchen at all.

She woke up in bed still wearing her gauzy pink negligée with the white ermine trimming. As usual she couldn't move her head for a minute or two. It was packed with knives that threatened to pierce through her brain. Her mouth felt parched. She had to concentrate with exquisite care on peeling her tongue from where it had withered against the roof of her mouth. She needed a drink and automatically began feeling around for the

169

bottle that she always had ready in the bed. Then she nearly fainted. There was a sleeping man lying beside her. She struggled up and stumbled, whimpering, out of the room and along the corridor towards the bathroom. There was another bottle hidden under the dirty linen in the linen basket. With hands shaking so much it took her some agonizing minutes before she managed to open the lid of the bottle. Then she drank deeply from it.

She tried to remember what had happened the night before but it was a complete blank. She tried to think who the man could be but had absolutely no idea. Never before in her life had she been so frightened. She became conscious of her near-nakedness and longed to get back into the bedroom for some clothes, but was too afraid to move. Another deep draught from the bottle gave her enough courage and she quietly and cautiously made her way back to her bedroom. The clothes she'd last worn lay scattered about. Not daring to risk the creak of the wardrobe door she decided against seeking a different outfit. Retrieving the discarded skirt and blouse she hastily pulled them on.

The man's long hair was dyed a brassy yellow and he was wearing a gold earring. His skin was a dirty brown colour and a dark stubble was growing round his jaw and upper lip. He had an obscene-looking tattoo on the arm that was flung over her pink satin quilt, defiling it. She could see the bushy black hair under his armpit; the air was thick with the musky smell of male sweat. She felt sick but at the same time the alcohol was scattering her fear and bringing reckless anger in its place.

How *dare* this man be in her bed. She wished him out of there. Immediately.

'Get out!' she heard herself say. 'Whoever you are get out of my bed and out of my house!'

He opened his eyes, nasty, impudent eyes and stretched leisurably. 'Mornin' darlin',' he said.

'Did you hear me? Get out of here at once.'

'What's changed your tune? You couldn't get enough of me last night.'

She was shaking so much she had to lean against the dressing-table for support. 'There's been a terrible mistake. Please go away and leave me alone.'

'Naw, I couldn't be so cruel,' he said, stretching again. 'What's for breakfast darlin'?'

'Don't call me that.'

'Okay.'

She averted her eyes as he flung back the blankets and swung his legs from the bed. She could hear him whistling as he dressed.

'You'll need a bit of company now that your daughter's gone.'

'How did you know about my daughter? Are you one of her friends?'

'I read her note. I had a look through your handbag as well darlin' and borrowed a few pounds. I knew you wouldn't mind.'

'Just go. Just go away. Please!'

'I like it here. It's quite a place! A regular Aladdin's cave. I'm going to enjoy myself today having a good old poke around.' He laughed. 'If you'll pardon the expression. You'll have to wait for yours until later.'

He had obviously no intention of leaving. It was like some nightmare film that she was taking part in.

'But first, what's to eat? My belly thinks my throat's cut.'

'There isn't anything,' she said her voice sounding plaintive like a child's, 'I was going to go to the shops.' Her thoughts were now seeking any means of deliverance and escape; she felt totally incapable of dealing with the situation.

'Get me some fags when you're at it,' he said. 'What are you going to use for money? Have you some more stashed away in the house?'

'I always use my cheque book when I'm shopping.'

'OK, but you'd better not take too long. I've been nice

171

to you so far, darlin' but you'd be surprised at how nasty I can be if I get annoyed. Just you do as you're told and we'll get on fine.'

Willing herself not to faint she somehow reached the wardrobe and took out her coat. It happened to be her mink – she had forgotten to put her furs in cold storage this summer. She was glad of its lightness and warmth, however, so violently was she shivering.

'Christ, that must be worth a bob or two,' the man said. 'Yes, darlin', we're going to get on fine and dandy.'

She clutched the coat around her and took a few tentative steps towards the door.

'What do you think you're doing?' the man asked and she gazed round at him, eyes strained huge with apprehension.

'You said –'

'Your handbag. Your cheque book.'

'Oh yes.' She picked it up. 'I'm so upset.'

'No need, darlin'.' His hand patted and squeezed her bottom as she passed. 'I'm going to give you a real good time. You enjoyed it last night and you'll enjoy it again. Just relax and trust me.'

He went whistling cheerfully along to the upstairs bathroom. She carried on down the carpeted stairs holding on tightly to the dark polished wood of the banister. Her one thought was to get as far as possible away from the house. But once outside in the street she didn't know where to go. She felt dazed and ill. She hadn't eaten for she couldn't remember how long and lack of food had weakened her and made her feel dizzy. Her hair hadn't been combed and straggled over her face, once pink cheeked and doll-like, now grey and drawn. Her eyes had lost their dewy sparkle.

She thought at first of turning up Rory Donovan's driveway and seeking refuge in the Donovan house. She was far too afraid however that the man might see her and drag her back before she reached the front door. Anyway the house was usually empty during the day.

172

Then she thought of Jenny. Jenny would help her and know what to do. But on the way to Jenny's place in Queens Drive not only the awfulness of her situation but the shame of it kept tormenting her. What could she say to Jenny or to anyone? She had slept with the man. She must have invited him into her home, into her bed. He had not broken into the house. He had not raped her — she could have gone to the police if he had. Although, even then, shame and humiliation might have prevented her.

In Queens Drive she walked past Jenny's basement flat several times, feverishly rehearsing what she should say once she gathered up enough courage to approach Jenny's door. But no courage came.

25

Hypnosis started a film rolling in Amelia's mind. Scenes from the past came to vivid life.

'Mummy, teacher says tomorrow is a school medical examination day.'

Victoria's face changed. She had been relaxing by the fire reading a book by Ethel M. Dell and happily munching at a chocolate biscuit. Her saucerless cup of tea sat at her feet on the red tiles of the fireplace.

Amelia stood before her in the odd assortment of clothes in which she had struggled to dress herself that morning. The long brown woollen stockings, the cotton summer dress over which she'd pulled the navy woollen jersey with the scratchy collar. She stood with hands behind her back waiting for she never knew what. She was always waiting hopefully around her mother when she was small, a habit that she had eventually come to realize irritated Victoria intensely.

This occasion was no exception. Indeed it was very much worse than usual. Immediately after Amelia's announcement about the school medical examination her mother's expression retreated inwards, cutting the child off. The mouth twisted, the whole face tightened and tipped up in that strange dignity of disgust her daughter had seen so often and which always had such a devastating effect on her.

Amelia waited in silent incomprehension. Then her mother said, 'Get away from me!'

Amelia went to sit on the edge of her bed and stared blindly at the floor. She could hear children playing outside. They were from a far-away different world. Inside the house the silent air was charged with the urgency of tension. She could hear bath water running.

Her mother sharply called her name. In the bathroom Victoria was waiting with sleeves rolled up and a tight, stiff face.

Before Amelia had time to realize what was happening her mother had set upon her, rapidly tugging off the navy jersey, the cotton dress, the woollen stockings, the navy knickers, the liberty bodice and vest. Then she had been literally flung into the hot water. A panicking heartbeat had been visible in the child's narrow chest as she'd slithered helplessly about under the brush Victoria was roughly scrubbing her with. Her frightened eyes could see how dark grey the skin of her body was compared with the smooth pink of her hands. She stared at the gritty, grey skin, her distaste now equal to, indeed surpassing Victoria's. For Victoria could only be contaminated by touch; Amelia was trapped forever inside the disgusting shell.

The film rolled on. She was a teenager. She had gone to her mother in total innocence and terror. Never having been told anything about monthly periods, thinking she had developed some terrible disease, she'd appealed for help. Her mother again shrank back in revulsion and disgust. 'Get away from me!' she'd said.

Those words, that look would never go away.

It was no use telling herself, Amelia had long ago decided, that it was her mother's problem, not hers. She had always suffered from her mother's attitude towards her and she suffered still.

Rebecca said, 'You must learn not only to like yourself, Amelia, but to *love* yourself. Love and forgiveness cure all ills. Love and forgive yourself, love and forgive your mother.'

But there she was on the screen, living in her mother's house when Harry was a baby. Victoria was bathing him, feeding him, crooning over him, not only ignoring her daughter's pleas that she wanted to attend to her own child but pushing her aside when she attempted to do anything for the baby. Her mother was trying to take

175

Harry from her. She could see the anger burning in the young Amelia's eyes, the murderous emotion.

An older Amelia appeared next; an Amelia who had suffered much in her attempts to survive with Harry on her own. Her mother was saying, 'Those whom God has joined together, let no man put asunder! You married Douglas Donovan of your own free will. It was your own wicked fault that the marriage broke up. The least you can do is go back to him now that he's giving you a second chance. You've dragged poor Harry around for long enough. It's time he had a proper settled home. He can stay with me. . . .'

The murderous look narrowed Amelia's eyes again. Never. Not for any reason would she allow her mother or anyone to take Harry away from her.

'Poor Harry!' Victoria kept saying, eventually taking another tack, 'poor *fatherless* Harry!'

It disturbed Amelia to think that she was almost beginning to wish that Douglas was dead now. Or that he'd somehow disappear – run away with another woman, rob a bank and have to flee the country, anything to be free of his continually belittling tongue.

'What's stopping you from freeing yourself?' Rebecca asked.

She'd asked herself this a thousand times. Usually she told herself it was because of Harry. She had gone back to Douglas to find Harry a secure and happy home where he would lack for nothing. She'd stayed so as not to disrupt Harry's primary school years. Then his move to secondary school was surely disruptive enough without the shattering experience of his home and family breaking up. Then there had been the strain of his 'O' levels. Soon there would be his 'Highers'. Harry must come first.

Rebecca said this was wrong. 'Your first duty is to yourself,' she insisted. 'If you're miserable and unfulfilled how can you give happiness to anyone else?'

Amelia kept laughing this off. 'I wouldn't go so far as

to say I'm miserable and unfulfilled. I'm very lucky really. Douglas has his good points as well as his bad and I really am a trial to him at times. I don't conform to normal wifely standards, shutting myself away in my writing room for most of each day, scribbling away like mad. . . .'

'He shuts himself away in his studio to do his painting, doesn't he?'

'But that's different.'

'How is it different?' Rebecca wanted to know.

'Well, he does earn enough to keep us with the commissions he gets and the paintings he manages to sell in his mother's shops.'

'Have you ever counted up how much you've contributed to the household expenses over the years?'

'Oh well, Douglas says –'

'Never mind what Douglas says. What do you say?'

'Actually I spend quite a bit on myself these days.'

'Money isn't important in self-development,' Rebecca airily assured her.

Amelia could not be convinced that money wasn't important. She had suffered too much insecurity and humiliation when she had been without any. Indeed money, or the ambition to acquire a great deal of it, was the strongest pivot on which her life revolved. She had come to believe that money was her only protection, the only proof of self-worth that there was ever any chance of her achieving, the only key to independence. Money was freedom. Yet she was becoming more and more extravagant with it. Douglas said she was crazy. She had this obsessive urge to spend money as soon as she got it. It was a lemming-like characteristic that made her exasperated with herself, but over which she seemed to have no control. Rebecca said she was afraid to be on her own again. That was the root of the trouble. It was courage she needed, not money.

26

The relaxation course had been a great success. Every time Rebecca thought of the fourteen passive bodies stretched out on her sitting room floor she felt a glow of satisfaction. They'd first of all pushed the furniture and chairs back against the walls. It was a large room and they'd had plenty of floor space to stretch out on. She'd sat in a corner on a low stool, centring herself down to Beta, then slowly and quietly she'd guided the others in relaxing the skin of their scalps, then right through every part of their bodies, skin, flesh and bones, down to the soles of their feet. Her voice, smooth as syrup, had flowed over every corner of the silent room. There'd been no movement, no other sound except the sleepy whisper of breathing. Gradually she had led their minds through an imaginary country lane into a beautiful garden, describing everything on the way in minute detail, the warm grass underfoot, the silky leaves brushing against fingers and cheeks, subtle scents floating into nostrils. She'd guided them down steps into a deeper part of the garden where it was warm and sheltered and still.

She'd not only hypnotized the whole group but she'd initiated them into the secrets of hypnotizing themselves. She thought it doubtful however that many, if any of them, would reach a high degree of success in this; certainly not in one session. They did not have her gift, her psychic powers.

The day-course had been a huge success all the same, and had done all her friends a great deal of good. They'd been enthusiastic in their praise and their appreciation of her had been most touching. But even without this much repeated thanks for so many precious hours of therapy and fellowship, she'd been able to sense their feelings. A great wave of love, gratitude and admiration had kept surfing towards her. It had showed in their eyes when they looked at her, in the way they touched her when she passed, it had vibrated in the air, electrifying it.

After the general relaxation session she'd demonstrated metamorphic massage and had them all squatting on the floor massaging each other's feet.

As she'd confided to Alice afterwards it had looked amusing enough to see stiff, dignified little souls like Milly and mountains of flesh like Dorothy, stretched out on the floor. (Dorothy had looked like a grounded whale!) The sight of the crowd of them squatting down awkwardly, each shoeless and stockingless, with one leg cocked up in the air having her foot massaged was absolutely hilarious. They had all, Milly and Dorothy included, enjoyed a good laugh at that – an excellent method of relaxing tensions. 'Laughter,' she had told them, 'is a wonderful tonic.'

Afterwards, she and Alice had laughed until the tears ran down their cheeks and they'd had to indulge in the steadying influence of a glass of sherry. A sense of humour was another God-given gift and both of them were most fortunate in having been so amply blessed.

Rebecca's only disappointment of the day had been the fact that Elvira Fortescue-Brown had not turned up for the Relaxation Course. Rebecca felt it a feather in her cap that a woman from such a distinguished family should have sought her out. It had indicated to her that God was widening her sphere of influence, singling her out to be different from other hypnotists. Of course she had never been like other hypnotists. She had always studied and practised a wide variety of therapies; she'd kept an open mind to every avenue that might lead to helping people. She was proud of the fact too that she made no difference between any of her 'friends'. High or low born, rich or poor, they were all given the same welcome and the same loving care. Not that she'd had

179

any high-born friends until Elvira had appeared on the scene. Of course the secret thrill she had experienced when Elvira had come into her orbit was only because it meant her reputation was spreading far beyond social, economic and geographical barriers. Elvira lived in a country area some miles from Glasgow. It couldn't be distance, however, that had kept her from attending the course – Elvira had a fast car and thought nothing of distances. And Rebecca had told her, 'I have several spare bedrooms, my dear, you must stay here overnight. I'll invite my friend Alice for supper and she will read our tea cups or our cards.'

But despite this enticement, Elvira had not appeared.

'Husband trouble,' Alice prophesied, 'you mark my words!'

'Yes,' Rebecca said, experiencing a sudden lifting of spirits, 'I have that feeling myself. It's not that she didn't want to come. Men are men, Alice, no matter to what social stratum they belong. I must tune into her chakra. I must commune with her spirit and give it courage. I must guide her towards me again.'

After Alice had gone she had put out all the lights and with only the flame of a single candle she had concentrated on Elvira.

Elvira's non-appearance had been unexpectedly disturbing. Enlisting the aristocratic and wealthy had been the next obvious step in the worldly recognition of Rebecca's work and divine purpose in life. It was part of God's plan that those with influence should use it on her behalf. Rebecca felt indignation and sorrow at Elvira's blindness. Underneath those lofty feelings, however, lurked the dangerous weakness of self-questioning. Only by Elvira's return to the proper scheme of things could the shadows of her own self-doubt be totally dispelled.

The candle flickered feebly through the darkness but Rebecca's great glowing eyes clung tenaciously to it. At the end of her period of concentration she went to bed content in the knowledge that soon Elvira would come.

The next day she was proved right. It had been arranged that some of her friends would meet her in the park and share a half-hour or so of the health exercise, T'ai Chi. An area had been chosen that was considered the most private because of the shyness of the women and the danger of some ignorant Glasgow youths using the T'ai Chi circle as a target for jeering laughter.

Rebecca had just pulled on a pair of green slacks and a loose green top (green had healing vibrations) when she heard the doorbell ring. Before going to answer it, she fluffed up her hair in the mirror and checked that her face was serene. Healing work demanded that anyone entering one's house must see that one's face and bearing was supremely calm and confident, and one's heart perfectly clean.

Elvira was standing on the doorstep looking as delightfully aristocratic as ever in her casual Jaeger clothes and jewellery that was in quiet good taste but undeniably expensive.

'Welcome, my dear.' Rebecca stretched out her arms and although Elvira looked at the ready to use her dignity to ward off an embrace, Rebecca was too quick for her. Grasping Elvira to her bosom with great enthusiasm Rebecca cried out, 'I knew you would come today,' then whirled the startled Elvira into the hall, ignoring her muffled protests.

'I don't see how –'

'I'm psychic. It's something I've developed over the years. I've concentrated on this ability, I've nurtured it and fed it in every way I could. As a result it has grown stronger and stronger. Oh yes, I knew you were coming all right.'

'In actual fact –'

'You don't need to make any excuses about yesterday, dear, I know you would have come if you could. Never mind, there will be plenty of courses. That one was so successful I've decided to make it a regular occurrence. Meantime you can join us in T'ai Chi.'

Elvira's eyes betrayed anxiety despite her reserved, superior face. She was not a bad-looking woman in the slightly long-faced, long-nosed, horsy way that was typical of her class. 'T'ai Chi?' she echoed in what sounded like distaste. She had a habit of tipping back her head and looking down her nose in this coolly questioning manner at whoever she happened to be talking to.

Rebecca gave her another hug. Barriers had to be broken down. 'You'll enjoy it and it's in a very sheltered private part of the park. You must open yourself to new and enriching experiences, my dear. Take off your stockings. It's important your bare feet are in touch with the earth.'

'I hardly think. . . .'

'You shouldn't be wearing stockings on a lovely sunny day like this. Always let the air circulate around your skin as much as possible. Take them off in the bathroom if you're shy.'

Elvira hesitated as if wrestling with the perplexing question of whether it was more undignified to argue with Rebecca, or denude herself of her stockings.

'While you get yourself ready,' Rebecca said, 'I'll go and fetch my door key and then we'll be off. Our other "friends" will be waiting but it won't take us a minute. It's only across the road. Isn't it lucky that I live so near the park? The quietest part too.'

Elvira discreetly slid off her stockings and tucked them into her handbag.

'You can leave that here,' Rebecca said, 'we don't want to be distracted by worldly possessions. We want to commune with nature. We want to tune into the basic relationship in the universe inherent within and between everything that exists in nature. Come on, dear, that's us ready.'

In the park there were six of her 'friends' waiting. Amelia, Jenny, Milly, Dorothy, Theresa and Sadie. Theresa, in her twenties, was the youngest of the group, pale-faced and pimply, her hair shedding dandruff wherever she went. Sadie was the eldest, with grey wiry hair kept in place with a brown hairnet. Undersized, with legs bowed as a result of the rickets she'd suffered as a child, she always wore her dresses extra long to try to hide their deformity. Rebecca made the necessary introductions, before arranging the women in a wide circle, then instructed them to kick off their shoes.

She kicked off her own shoes with great panache then took big dramatic breaths with bushy head flung back and arms outstretched. She had a violet scarf knotted round her forehead with the ends dangling down over one ear. Violet was the colour of the sixth chakra she told them, and this vital force centre had been regarded in the East since antiquity as the seat of the arts, music, poetry, dance, drama, and literature. Then she explained how there were channels known as meridians which conducted the flow of energy through their bodies and T'ai Chi was one of the methods to keep these channels open and unobstructed.

'In maintaining an upright yet relaxed and fluid stance in living we will ensure the maximum release, not only of our potential, my dears, but also the full flourishing of all the living systems of the world and so bring about an earth on which heaven is made visible.'

Then, after a startling flourish as if she was going to attack them with a two handed Karate chop, she led them into the slow, still, positioning of their bodies and limbs. It was while they were balancing with one leg on one side slightly bent, foot communing with the earth, the arm on that side hanging down but also slightly bent, and at the same time the other leg and arm bent high up, that Jenny broke the silent concentration needed for such an awkward pose.

'Look over there!'

'Jenny,' Rebecca reprimanded, 'we don't want to lose our stillness, dear.'

'But I think I know who that is. I can't be sure the way she's huddling down on the seat and I can't imagine why

183

she should be here of all places and at this time of day. . . .'

'It isn't like you to chatter, dear, but I suppose, in your condition it's a good sign.'

'Even at this distance she has a look of hopelessness about her, hasn't she? I certainly recognize that, I mean I know how it feels.'

Resignedly Rebecca dropped her raised arm and leg, then instructed the others to do the same – an order they complied with in obvious relief. She said, 'So you think she's a friend in need, dear?'

'Well, I don't know if you could call her a friend. At least not of mine – in the normal sense I mean. If it's who I think it is, she was my employer. A Mrs Hazel Saunders. She lives in one of those huge villas in Pollokshields.'

'Really?' Rebecca's interest was now actively engaged. 'Go and bring her over, dear. If she's in need of help that's why she's here. She will have been guided into my orbit.'

'I'll go and see what she says.'

'Never mind what she says, dear, just you bring her to me.'

The others, Rebecca could see, were interested too. It wasn't much use trying to concentrate on communicating with the universe for the time being. So they all just stood watching Jenny's progression to the seat half-hidden by bushes on which a figure hunched like a baby bear in a brown fur coat.

In a few minutes Jenny returned with the woman who appeared as if she'd just got out of bed. Her creamy blonde hair was matted and tangled and her face looked unmade up and unwashed. She was also stockingless which made an odd combination with a mink coat.

'Hazel, my dear!' Rebecca greeted her. 'What's wrong?'

Hazel gazed up at Rebecca's tall imposing figure like a petrified child. 'I can't go home.'

184

'You can't go home? Why can't you go home?'

'There's a man there. And he won't go away.'

'A man? A man?' Rebecca's voice grew indignantly louder. 'Who is this man?'

'I don't know,' Hazel quavered, 'I think he came to the door selling something yesterday. Now he won't go away.'

'Won't go away?' An unexpected explosion of anger completely shattered Rebecca's Yin and Yang. 'Won't go away? We'll soon see about that!'

27

Wasn't it just like life? Harry thought. There he was, coming through the park after a really good gig, happy as a lark, not a care in the world. Or so he had temporarily kidded himself. His mother had bought him a guitar for his birthday, he'd felt so grateful he'd given her a spontaneous kiss and hug. 'Thanks Mum, that's really fab!

Her face had mirrored his delight. 'I could pay for lessons as well, son.'

'Oh! Fab, Mum!'

Dode had a paper-run and a milk-run. He kept falling asleep at school but now it was the school holidays that problem wasn't a worry any more. At least for the time being. Dode had persuaded his mother to take out a 'club' in her name at a local music shop. Thanks to the 'club' Dode was now the proud owner of and was paying up on a basic set of drums. His father had blown a fuse when he'd found out but after being convinced that Dode was working hard to meet the payments he'd simmered down and actually agreed to contribute something every week to help him.

Harry's own dad had showed quite an interest in his guitar and often tried his hand at a bit of strumming; Harry had already shown him a few chords. In fact it had become, surprisingly, a point of contact between them. After each guitar lesson his dad would say, 'Okay, let's see what you got today then.' And they'd sit together with the guitar and he'd show his dad what he'd learned.

It was surprising considering how his dad had always shouted at him before when he'd tried to play music on his record player. Of course he couldn't play his guitar as loud as his record player. Anyway, there he was walking cheerfully through the park one night – Dode and Rose having left a bit earlier because Rose had always to be in before midnight, her father's orders, not her mother's. Her mother was still away with the fairies and neither knew nor cared where Rose was or what she was doing. His own mother was away in a dream most of the time as well, but in a different way, at least she got paid for it. Rose was a fab singer and when she put on a bit of make-up – white lipstick, thick black eyeliner and spiky lashes – her op-art earrings, and her ankle-length white boots, she could look at least 16. Her fringe was now fashionable and she used lacquer to give her hair a blown-up look. She had a shift dress she'd made herself out of upholstery fabric – that, with her wide hipster belt, looked really fab.

He never walked through the park after dark as a rule. But the euphoria he was in had made him careless. They had been paid handsomely for the gig, the first time they'd made any real money. Not only that, they'd been given another booking. He was going to buy a new pair of trousers and a shirt with his share. Dode was going to pay off the rest of what he owed on his drums and Rose was going to buy more material and make herself another two dresses.

He was within sight of the Victoria Road gates when he was stopped in his tracks. A crowd of Gorbals Boys had suddenly emerged from the bushes in front of him yelling 'Young Team Ya Bass.' His first thought was to run but from the corner of his eye he caught the movement of others behind him. He was well and truly surrounded, he had no choice but to make a fight of it. He managed to land a few hard punches but was almost immediately knocked to the ground from behind by a blow on the head with what felt like an iron bar. Once down, all he could do was curl up into a ball with his arms over his head in an effort to protect himself. He tried not to cry out but the viciousness of boots thumping

187

into his body soon made him scream in agony. It was the saving of him as it turned out because Mr Thornton had been passing nearby on his way to lock the gates and heard him.

'What the hell's going on?' he roared as he came racing towards the crowd who were kicking Harry around like a football.

Dode's dad was a tall man and the bomber jacket he was wearing made him look broader and heavier than he actually was. He was also carrying a torch the size of a truncheon that obviously could be used as a weapon. The Gorbals Boys melted away into the darkness.

'My God, it's you, Harry,' Mr Thornton said. 'Here, let me help you up. It's a good job I came along. They looked as if they were hell bent on killing you.'

Harry groaned but with Mr Thornton's help managed to struggle to his feet. He had no sooner done so when he staggered over into the bushes and vomited.

'I'd better get you to a doctor,' Mr Thornton said. 'My car's across the road, I'll run you down to the Victoria.'

Harry was in no condition to argue. Within minutes he was in the Victoria Infirmary having emergency treatment and very thankful for it. The treatment made him feel better, especially after the pain-killers began to work. Mr Thornton waited for him and then ran him home. Dode had always insisted his dad had his good points despite the way he treated his mum. Now Harry believed him.

'Do you want me to come in and explain to your mother and father what's happened?' Mr Thornton asked.

'Oh, no! No, thanks,' Harry answered hastily. (His mother would have had a fit!) 'They'll be sound asleep. I'll be okay. I'll just go straight to bed and I'll tell them in the morning. Thanks a lot Mr Thornton, you saved my life!'

'I wouldn't walk through the park as late as that again, Harry.'

'Don't worry, I won't!'

It was fortunate that his face hadn't been damaged. That way his mother need never know, he would never have heard the end of it if she had. She did notice him wincing in pain a couple of times, however. He'd made a casual reference to a fall that had bruised his ribs and her worried nagging about that had been hard enough to bear.

'Were they badly bruised? Could they be cracked or broken? How had it happened? Shouldn't he go to a doctor? Was he *sure* he was all right . . . ?'

He had lost his temper and shouted. 'I *told* you I was all right, didn't I?' and the shout had just about killed him. He had to get out of the room hastily so that he could have a good groan in peace.

Dode knew the truth of what had happened and somewhat to Harry's consternation he passed the word around all the boys in Queens Park, Langside and Shawlands. There was a mass meeting in the park and it was agreed that no way were the Gorbals Boys going to be allowed to get away with the attack on Harry.

Harry appreciated the loyalty and true friendship of such a number but he did not yet feel fit enough for the sortie into the enemy territory and the battle that they were planning. He still ached and throbbed from the attack he'd suffered and his nerves were a bit shattered as well. He had no intention of acting chicken, however. Readily he agreed to go along with the crowd, search out the guilty parties on their home ground and 'make mincemeat of them'.

The date of the battle was set for the next day and, try as he did, he couldn't sleep the whole night. This did nothing to make him feel any fitter.

'You're looking awfully pale, son,' his mother said worriedly, 'are you sure you're all right?'

'I'm fine, Mum,' he groaned. 'Away you go! You'll be late for your T'ai Chi or whatever it is you're into now.' It was lucky for him that she was in a hurry, otherwise she would have gone on and on.

189

He had a bit of practice on his punchball after she'd left. It was absolute agony but with masochistic determination he persevered. It was his fists he'd have to depend on and they were better than most! He had in fact one hell of a punch. Or so he'd often been told. Somehow he couldn't see himself putting the boot in, it wasn't his style. He would have much preferred to have 'a square go'. He realized however that to venture into the Gorbals on his own with the honourable intention of having 'a square go' would be the height of folly. It would, in fact, be committing suicide – he had no illusions about that. It had to be a gang fight or nothing. Doing nothing might encourage the Gorbals Boys to have another go at him, his pals were quite right. He still didn't look forward to the event though.

'You keep to the back,' Dode said, 'you're still suffering wounds from the last time.' The rest of the lads agreed.

'No way,' Harry said, 'I'm not hiding behind anybody for any reason. I'm up front. But thanks all the same.' He really had fab pals. He especially admired the guts that Dode was showing. After all, poor Dode looked such a weed with his long, lank hair, gaunt face and skinny body. Dode was no fighter, never had been. He definitely had guts though. Rose, womanlike, was terrified of the whole idea. She was creating such a dramatic fuss and being such a prophet of doom she had them all in danger of losing their nerve.

'Will you shut up, Rosie,' Harry shouted at her in exasperation. 'We don't need you trying to undermine us before we start.'

'I don't want you to get hurt again, Harry,' she wailed.

'Just shut up,' he shouted. 'I'm sick of listening to you!'

At least that had got rid of her. She'd trailed off, sobbing noisily, her eye make-up streaking clownlike down her face.

Thirty of his pals and himself set off in grim silence for the Gorbals, knowing that long before they got there word would have flashed along the grapevine and the Gorbals Boys would be massing together. The Gorbals Team would be ready and waiting for them.

28

'I'm perfectly able, you know, to go with Hazel on my own,' Rebecca assured Jenny. 'Indeed I could go and deal with this man without Hazel. Except of course she needs to be there to prove I have the authority to enter her house. She is my credentials, so to speak. Without her, I could be another stranger trying to break in.'

Jenny shrugged. 'I just thought I might save you a bit of time by showing you where the house is. By the look of Hazel she's in no state to find her way home.'

'Very well, dear. You come along.'

'If Jenny goes, I go too.' Amelia's voice did not reflect the courage of her words; it was high pitched with nervous anxiety. 'I feel so guilty I can't bear to just sit here. It was me who persuaded Jenny to come today. If she hadn't come she wouldn't have seen Hazel and she –'

'Wouldn't have been able,' Rebecca interrupted calmly, 'to have brought her to me and poor Hazel would have been denied my help and support. All right, my dear, you may come too. But you must thank God for having the opportunity to help a friend and you must come rejoicing and with good heart. The rest of you wait quietly here in the peaceful atmosphere of my home until we return. Practise your T'ai Chi, meditate!'

The rest of the women were much too excited, however, to sit quietly meditating. They had returned with Hazel to Rebecca's kitchen where Rebecca had dispensed cups of tea plus the glass of brandy Hazel had begged for. Before Rebecca, Jenny, Amelia and Hazel left for their confrontation with the male intruder, the others were already abuzz with talk. Even Elvira had been swept up in the drama of the occasion and was

192

disagreeing with Sadie who was insisting they should call the police.

'I can imagine how Hazel must feel,' she said, 'one has to consider adverse publicity. Newspapers can twist the truth. People who haven't met her might not believe her. Think of the scandal!'

'The police wouldn't believe her,' Teresa said. 'The police are men. And nobody's safe with any man. What difference does a uniform make? Bastards! Dirty bastards, all of them.'

Teresa had been raped. The man responsible had got off scot-free. The judge had more or less suggested she'd 'asked for it'. Between what she'd suffered from the rape, what she'd suffered in the police station from the ruthless questioning followed by the rough and humiliating examination by the police doctor – all men – she was left not only a nervous wreck but a very embittered woman.

Dorothy boomed out, 'Safety in numbers. We should all have trooped along with Rebecca. Safety in numbers, that's what I say! Shoulder to shoulder! Shoulder to shoulder!'

'I'm quite sure,' Elvira's voice acquired its cutting edge of coolness and successfully chopped off Dorothy's over-excitability, 'that Rebecca will be more than capable of dealing with the situation on her own.'

'She'll have to be,' Sadie said, 'I can't see how Jenny and Amelia will be of any help.'

Amelia was thinking the same thing as they made their way along the quiet street where Jenny said Hazel lived. As Jenny had predicted, Hazel was no use. They were having to half-carry her, half drag her along – or at least, she and Jenny were struggling to do this, one on either side of the shivering woman. Hazel wasn't just trembling, she was violently shivering with fear. They were all apprehensive to say the least – all, that is, except Rebecca, who was floating serenely along in front of them to all appearances as if she hadn't a care in the world. If anything, she looked as if she was enjoying herself.

'The keys, dear,' she said, putting out a hand towards Hazel when they reached Hazel's front door.

'I didn't bring them,' Hazel wailed, 'I was in such a state. I just wanted to get away from him.'

'What'll we do now?' Amelia whispered, as if the man had his ear to the other side of the door.

'We ring the bell,' Rebecca said loud and clear and they all (except Rebecca) jumped like startled deer, not only at the ringing of the bell but at the clanging noise of the door knocker as Rebecca attacked it as well.

In a matter of seconds the door was flung open. A tall man with blond hair and a gold earring bawled, 'What the hell?'

Rebecca pushed past him and they crowded nervously after her, keeping as close as possible for safety. 'Now, young man,' she said, 'it's time you left and went about your legitimate business.'

'I was invited in here, I'm a guest,' the man protested indignantly.

'No, you are not.'

'I was asked to stay as long as I liked.'

'No, you were not,' said Rebecca.

'Who the hell do you think you are? It's her house,' jerking a thumb towards Hazel, 'and her and I have a thing going, know what I mean?'

'Is that your case over there?' Rebecca pointed to a long case on which was written, 'Milligan's Magic Mop'.

'Mind your own business,' the man sneered.

'Take that case,' Rebecca commanded, 'and leave this house at once! At once, do you hear? If you do not, I will phone for the police to come and remove you.'

'The police know her kind,' the man sneered. 'She needed a bit of rough. She practically dragged me in.'

'No, she did not and it'll be your word against not only the ladies you see before you but several others waiting in my home to testify against you and the terrible state of fear to which you'd reduced this poor woman. Women

194

living alone must be protected against men like you who will go to any lengths to take cruel advantage of them. I shall not only point that out to the police but I shall tell your employers. I will also inform them that I intend reporting the matter to the newspapers. The public must be warned against a firm that employs dangerous men like yourself to go around terrifying defenceless women. I will leave no stone unturned, believe me!'

The man obviously did. Although mouthing obscenities and calling both Hazel and Rebecca names that none of them, including Rebecca, could bring themselves to repeat later, he left. Rebecca went to the door and called after him, 'And remember, don't you ever dare come near this place or contact this woman in any way, ever again.'

Hazel went straight to the drinks cabinet in the drawing room and, to the astonishment of the other women, grabbed a bottle of vodka and tipped it straight into her mouth. Before Rebecca managed to prise it from her, she'd downed a startling amount.

'Have we another little problem, dear?' Rebecca asked.

'I was in such a state,' Hazel explained, 'I needed a drink to steady my nerves.'

'Nobody needs that amount of alcohol, dear.'

'I'll be perfectly all right in a minute.' Hazel fluttered her eyelashes up at Rebecca. 'Thank you for looking after me, I'm so very grateful.' She smiled weakly. 'I feel better already. You've all been so kind.'

'Are you sure you're all right?' Rebecca said.

'Yes, really!'

'Battlefield House in Battle Square, remember,' Rebecca said, her great dark eyes peering close to Hazel. 'I'll be there if you need me.'

After they were back out on the street Rebecca shook her head. 'Poor woman!'

'Alcoholic, do you think?' Amelia asked.

'Undoubtedly.'

'Now that I come to think of it,' Jenny said, 'she did used to drink quite a lot, but people like that often do, don't they? There's never any shortage of money to buy the stuff, that's the trouble.'

'She'll be so frightened on her own now,' Rebecca said, 'she'll come scurrying back down to Battlefield House at our heels. Wait till you see!'

'Maybe we shouldn't have left her there alone,' Amelia said.

Rebecca eyed her pityingly as if she were a likeable imbecile.

'I know what I'm doing. And by the way, I allowed Jenny to come with me because I knew that all this excitement would do her a power of good. And I was right. She's been so concerned about Hazel she's forgotten about her own troubles. You look bright and cheerful, dear,' she smiled at Jenny, 'speaking comparatively, of course.'

'I hardly think,' Jenny sighed, 'it's right of me to feel cheerful in the circumstances.'

'You're doing fine, dear,' Rebecca assured her. 'Keep up the good work. "Every day, in every way", remember, "I am getting better and better". You're still repeating that cheerfully to yourself every morning, I hope.'

'Well. . . .'

'Good.'

Amelia and Jenny lapsed into silence for the rest of the way. They were forced to do this in order to save their breath to help them keep up with Rebecca's long, purposeful strides. As soon as they reached her kitchen, however, they burst into vivid detail about the recent drama at Hazel's house. Rebecca's part was painted in such heroic terms that everyone was left gasping in admiration.

'I told you,' Elvira said, 'how capable she was.'

'Could you beat it,' Sadie gasped, 'the pluck of the woman. You're the bravest person I've ever come across, hen,' she told Rebecca.

196

'I'd love to have seen his face,' Teresa said, trembling with pleasure. 'Oh, I wish I could have been there when you demolished him, Rebecca.'

'Jolly good show, Rebecca,' Dorothy roared at the top of her voice. 'Jolly good show!'

'Yes, dear,' Rebecca soothed, 'have another digestive biscuit.'

'I don't know how you had the nerve,' Milly murmured, 'I really don't. You deserve a medal.'

'It's not a question of nerve,' Rebecca explained, 'it's a question of faith in oneself. I knew I was in the right. Now I must go and change into something more comfortable. Pour me another cup of tea Jenny, I'll be back in a minute.'

Admiration of Rebecca continued to be the enthusiastic topic of conversation among the women crowded round the kitchen table. By the time Rebecca had returned, her tall, straight-backed figure dramatically clothed in a flowing white caftan, they were quite carried away.

Her halo of black hair and her large, lustrous dark eyes were in startling contrast to the vivid white of her robe. She was an awesome sight. They were all aware of it. And it suddenly occurred to Amelia that Rebecca was aware of it, too.

29

Long ago there had been a leper hospital in the Gorbals. It gave Harry the creeps to think of those deformed creatures, hunched inside their hooded cloaks, wandering about with the sound of the clappers they carried warning people of their approach to beg for alms. So keyed up was Harry's imagination he could almost see them now creeping about the dark warren of streets. Dark was the operative word here. In Queens Park the buildings in his street were made of red sandstone and had a warm, welcoming appearance.

There was nothing warm or welcoming here. It was a blackness only relieved by graffiti. The initials 'GYT' for Gorbals Young Team was scrawled in big letters over every surface. 'Young Team Ya Bass' was even emblazoned across the side of a parked van. The buildings were black with grime and soot. The streets were so neglected that it was an ordeal to walk along them. Pavements were potholed and could twist the ankle of the unwary. Litter attached itself to shoes; puddles suddenly splashed up, engulfing the legs.

Harry and his pals were in strange territory. In silence they drifted in dribs and drabs down through the wan pools of light from street lamps. Shadows splashed fitfully over damp tarmac. Then, all at once, Harry's eyes caught the movement of their enemies coalescing out of the greater darkness. The air was rent with yells of 'Young Team Ya Bass!' and in a surge the Gorbals Team clattered towards them, the metallic sound of the segs on their shoes like the clicking of so many lobster claws. The sounds rang loudly between the canyon walls of the tenements.

'Into them!' screamed Dode and the Queens Park

Boys met the head-on rush. To Harry, everything seemed speeded up and yet at the same time slowed down. Images of cardboard silhouettes jerking in spastic convulsion flickered before his eyes like a strobe nightmare. Leering faces sprang into focus only to be smashed aside. A blow found its target on the side of his head. It went numb, it didn't affect him. Nothing could hurt him. He aimed a left jab to the nearest face, right cross, then left hook to the ribs. *He's* down, he told himself. Shuffle forward. Another one. Like skittles, they were. All mouth, all show but nothing to back it up. Even the completely unfit and weedy Dode was trouncing the Gorbals Team, until he was felled by somebody wielding a hammer. Another attacker was about to change the shape of Dode's face with a tackitty boot when, just in time, Harry caught him a right hook to the chin that sent him up in the air, arms flapping out like a ballet dancer. The majority of the Gorbals Boys were obviously so unfit Harry was sure they'd never seen the inside of a gym in their lives. They fought like wild animals but it was obvious that only their hatred was keeping them going. One by one they hit the ground and lay like piles of crumpled rags. Harry felt sorry for them. He would far rather have been friends. He knew better than admit to this weakness, however. Later, as they all swaggered home after the remaining Gorbals Team had turned tail and were swallowed back into the black caverns of closes, he roared with laughter, proudly boasted and took part in the verbal replay of the fight with as much relish as the rest.

His mother and father were in the middle of a fight when he returned home. They never used fists, of course, only bitter, hate-filled tongues. He slunk off to bed and tried his best to ignore them. Nevertheless their fight upset him far more than the one with the Gorbals Boys. His dad was furious about his mum getting mixed up with some woman who lived across the other side of the park. The woman apparently was getting his mum involved in a lot of trouble and his mum in turn was getting Dode's mum involved in a lot of trouble. It all seemed very complicated. He gathered the woman was a hypnotist, although she seemed to dabble in all sorts of other queer things as well.

That figured! Trust his mum to ferret out somebody weird or unusual, she had an absolute talent for it. For a while it had been lame ducks. One Christmas they'd had a disgusting old woman of 90 to Christmas dinner. ('She lives alone and hasn't a soul in the world,' his mum had explained.) The woman dribbled soup down her chin and onto her chest. She dropped bits of turkey and potato off her fork and sent Brussels sprouts rolling about the carpet. She ponged of urine but – even worse than that – she kept moving her false teeth about in her mouth. It made his dad and him feel really sick. As well as the old woman (as if she wasn't enough) his mum had invited a girl from a local orphanage. She'd met her somewhere and got talking. (His mum talked to *everybody*, his dad was always getting on to her about it.) The girl, real ugly and spec-y she was, gobbled everything in sight as if she'd never before seen food in her life and would never see it again. She was enough to make anybody sick.

He wished his mum and dad would stop. Life was difficult and scarey enough outside without it being the same or worse in what was supposed to be the safety of home. He didn't know how to handle situations like this.

He wished his mum would act normal like other mums. Well, maybe not like Dode's mum, but the mothers of every other of his pals were perfectly normal. They went to church, attended the Women's Guild, had coffee mornings, did their own housework and baked cakes and scones every week.

All at once, to add to his distress, the agony of his recent injuries returned with the force of a sledgehammer. He'd temporarily forgotten the pain in the heat of the fight and during the heady euphoria that followed it.

It was too much for him. He pulled the blankets over his head to hide his shameful tears. All it needed now to make his day was for his mum to come in to his room and see them. It helped to concentrate on hating her.

The more Amelia thought of it, the more she realized it was true what Rebecca had said. She had been referring to the way Douglas kept trying to bully her and belittle her.

'Some people need to stand next to a dwarf to make them feel big and if they can't find a dwarf they make one.'

Douglas was really a weak man. He could shout at her and act tough. With his sturdy build he could look tough, but he was spineless. He blamed everything and everybody, but especially her, for his failures from gambling losses to business ventures and he always depended on his mother to bail him out. He'd once opened a gallery but even that hadn't worked. She'd told him at the time he hadn't given it a chance. But because people had not immediately flocked to the place he'd become self-defensive and embittered about them. 'Suburban yokels who didn't know art from arses,' he'd sneered.

She'd thought from the start that he'd chosen a risky place for the gallery, so far from the centre of town, but having chosen it she thought he ought to have stuck with it. He should have held on until, by sheer determination, he had proved himself and won acceptance for himself. As she had with her writing.

As usual, he had just blamed her; everything was always her fault. She had been the one who had suggested the site of the gallery, he insisted. He said this so often and so bitterly she began to believe it herself. Being so constantly criticized drove her to blind hysteria.

Rebecca said it wasn't a bad thing to scream at him – the bad thing was to bottle up emotions. All the same, any time Amelia had been driven to such lengths she had seen the gleam of triumph in Douglas's eyes and she'd ended up frightened as well as exhausted. He'd nagged about her involvement with Rebecca and Hazel until she hated her own weakness for having, in her excitement, blurted out the story to him. Why oh why, she kept asking herself, could she not hold her tongue? Especially in Douglas's presence.

As usual he had made everything sound different. It was no longer an exciting adventure in which she'd helped to rescue a fellow human being in distress. Rebecca was no longer the female St George. It was all, in Douglas's eyes, stupid, dangerous, disgusting and just like her! 'Now you're mixing with drunks and nymphos as well as nutters!' he accused. 'You're a nutter yourself. I should have you committed to a mental hospital!'

She experienced stomach-turning fear at this threat but struggled not to let it show. More than once in the past when they'd quarrelled she'd threatened to leave. He'd hooted with laughter and asked, 'Where would you go? Suddenly got enough cash to buy a house, have you? You never have two pennies to rub together.'

Or he'd make a fool of her for being a hypochondriac. It frightened her more than anything when he shared his jokes and jibes about this with Harry. She became desperately worried about Douglas undermining Harry's love for her. She was so frightened and so unsure of what to do for the best when Douglas made a fool of her in front of Harry, she just laughed along with them for safety.

Rebecca said it was obvious she was being emotionally abused. As for the sex in her marriage – or rather the lack of it – that was his problem, not hers. He was impotent. That was the plain fact of the matter. And no, it was *not* her fault, Rebecca insisted. 'You have perfectly natural sexual desires, haven't you?'

'Well, yes but the thing is –'

'The thing is,' Rebecca interrupted, 'you are being

202

emotionally and psychologically abused. As a result you're experiencing negative feeling of worthlessness, shame, degradation, helplessness, humiliation, fear and guilt. Jenny is being physically abused. But it all comes to the same thing. Both Jenny's husband and yours are using various methods to make you both feel as you do. They're sapping your wills, trying to control your lives.'

'I don't think Douglas is quite the monster you make him sound. He can be kind in his own way. Harry's very fond of him.'

Rebecca gave her a reproving stare. 'The truth of the matter is that denying abuse is easier than facing up to it. Facing up to it involves taking responsibility for changing your situation. You obviously have a personality weakness there, Amelia, but don't worry, I can help you. And I am big enough to overlook your little ingratitudes and disloyalties.'

Amelia felt somewhat irked by this. Apart from anything else she had changed her situation too often in the past, that was partly what worried her. Over the years since her youth she'd left home to get married, left Douglas to return home, left home again to go into digs, left the digs to work as housekeeper in the Robertson house, left there to return to Douglas and Live in 'Mary House'. She didn't want to uproot herself. She didn't believe she could cope any more being at the mercy of everybody and anybody in the outside world. She just wanted to be safely and happily settled in her own home with a husband who loved her. Douglas had loved her once. Before her marriage he had thought that she was absolute perfection and when they were courting he had often told her so. There were still times when she wistfully remembered how joyously happy she'd felt then. If only they could somehow go back to those days.

Rebecca shook her head. 'You're not being realistic, you're just too afraid to face the facts. Denial protects you from feeling the pain that comes from knowing that your partner is no use to you and never will be.'

203

A new worry came to niggle at the back of Amelia's mind. Rebecca hated men. More and more Amelia's instinct was picking up the signs. It made her wonder sometimes if Rebecca's advice was always a hundred per cent dependable. Could her anti-man prejudice be affecting her judgement? It might be. Or again, it might not.

Probably Rebecca knew best. The chances were what she had begun to suspect was just another figment of her imagination. Douglas always said her imagination would be the death of her yet!

30

Joe was on early shift so it was safe for Amelia to come along for a cup of coffee and a chat.

'You would be welcome to come to Mary House,' Amelia said, 'but you know what it's like there. Douglas is at home most of every day. We wouldn't get much peace to talk.'

They had discovered that having people to talk to who understood and genuinely sympathized was a wonderful therapy. Being part of the group that now met regularly at Rebecca's was of vital importance to both women.

As Jenny said, 'I feel a tremendous release at being able to talk to other women. I feel as if I've been a sealed parcel all the time and suddenly the strings have been untied. I don't feel so isolated now,' she added, once they'd settled down with a cup of coffee and one of Jenny's homebaked scones – the first she'd made in her own oven for many months. 'I used to feel that nobody would believe me, not how it really was. Joe can be so nice, especially to outsiders. He can be nice to me too. Then I say something or do something that doesn't please him and suddenly he's different. Each time I can hardly believe it myself. I suppose I must still love him. Or maybe I just love the man I thought he was or want him to be, I'm not sure. Sometimes I feel so confused.'

'That's perfectly understandable,' Amelia said, 'if one minute he's being nice to you and the next he's knocking you about. I couldn't stand that. I can't stand physical pain. If Douglas hit me, I think I'd go berserk, I'd kill him!'

Jenny sighed. 'I didn't used to believe I'd put up with such a thing. But you never think it's going to happen again – they swear it won't, you see. And before you know where you are you're so run down you're not able to think straight, far less do anything about it. I'm not able to do anything, not with Joe. I feel so nervous and jumpy when he's in. I never know when he's going to lose his temper and start shouting at me. Even the sound of his key in the front door makes me feel jittery. I know this irritates him and makes things worse, but I can't help it.'

She sighed again. 'Then, what with one thing and another, especially my mother's death, it all became too much. I just kind of gave up I suppose.'

'At least you're able to recognize what the problem is now.'

'What to do about it, though? That's the thing.'

'Well, you know what Rebecca says and I must admit I agree with her. I couldn't stay with a man who battered me, I just couldn't.'

'But Rebecca says you're suffering as much as I am, only it's your personality your husband is abusing. Yet you're still living with Douglas.'

'Well, of course, I've Harry to consider. . . .'

'I've Dode and Rose. Although, poor souls, they haven't had much consideration for a long time, I haven't felt fit enough to bother about them. Oh, Amelia, sometimes I wonder if it's all my own fault.'

'Of course it's not your fault.'

'If he could just give up these bouts of drinking.'

'Nothing excuses a man knocking a woman about. Anyway, you've told me he's hit you when he's not been drinking.'

Jenny took a deep breath. 'I suppose leaving him is the only sensible thing to do. But, oh . . .' Tears gushed to her eyes. 'When I think of all the dreams and hopes I had at the beginning. When I think of how it could have been. . . .'

'Take some more deep breaths like Rebecca taught us,' Amelia pleaded. 'Please try, Jenny. It won't help you to get all upset. I'll do it along with you. In through the nostrils over the throat, down into the upper chest, further down into the diaphragm. . . .'

Suddenly in the middle of their desperate concentration on filling their bodies with air, they burst out laughing. Jenny wiped away what was left of her tears.

'You look ridiculous puffing yourself out like that, Amelia.'

'So do you. But not so funny as Rebecca's last class. Did you ever see anything so hilarious as the crowd of us doing those grotesque exercises that were supposed to release tension in our facial muscles? Did you see Dorothy? I thought she was going to explode or her eyes were going to pop right out of her head.'

'I know. It's all ridiculous in a way, yet it's such a comfort to be there.'

'Yes, it's having so much in common with each other, I suppose, at least as far as problems are concerned. And meeting like that on common ground.'

'And feeling safe. Did I ever thank you for taking me to Rebecca's, Amelia?'

'You didn't need to thank me. If I hadn't been trying to help you I wouldn't have found help for myself. Although I'm luckier than you, I've always been able to escape into my writing. Rebecca doesn't think that's healthy but I'd go mad without it. Rebecca says it's as much an escape and a dependency for me as alcohol is for Hazel. But I'm not convinced about that. Hazel doesn't enjoy the taste of alcohol, she's admitted that. I enjoy everything about writing. By the way, isn't it wonderful of Rebecca to take Hazel in like that?'

'Yes, that's probably saved Hazel's life. I told Rebecca that and she agreed. She said Hazel was in a terrible state when she arrived on her doorstep. She's having an awful struggle with her, did she tell you?'

'The last I heard, Rebecca was locking her in one of the upstairs rooms to prevent her getting out to buy a bottle.'

'When I was over for my last hypnotherapy session I

could hear faint thumps and cries coming from some-where upstairs.'

Amelia's face winced as if in pain. 'Poor Hazel. It seems a bit drastic.'

'Rebecca says once she dries out she'll be okay. As long as she never takes another drink. Alcoholics Anonymous say that too, don't they? It's that first drink they must avoid like the plague.'

'It's just occurred to me,' Amelia said. 'They need the support of each other too. That's how AA works, isn't it? And we need each other because we've lost confidence in ourselves. If I ever had any in the first place!'

'It seems so strange you saying that, Amelia. Don't get me wrong, I believe you – but I can see how other people wouldn't, just like they don't believe me. You've a sexy-looking husband. A wealthy mother-in-law. You've succeeded in a career for yourself. You've got looks. To all appearances you've got everything.'

Amelia sighed and Jenny hastily repeated, 'But I believe you and I believe Rebecca. You're just as much abused as I am.'

'I can't believe that, although I admit Douglas does frighten me at times. Fear's an awful thing, isn't it? It begins to feed on itself.'

'When I was in deepest depression,' Jenny said, 'it didn't bother me so much, I didn't care about any-thing. All my emotion was drained. I felt my body throbbing and aching after Joe hit me but the heavy lethargy I was suffering from dulled the physical pain. I just didn't have enough energy to feel anything acutely.' Her voice trembled. 'But now that I do have a bit more energy the prospect of Joe hitting me terrifies me – my bones turn to jelly at the thought. Last time he kicked me in the stomach after he'd knocked me down. It was agony.'

'Jenny, he must be mad! He'll end up murdering you. There's going to be a terrible murder – I just know it!'

Jenny managed a faint smile. 'You and your dramatic

imagination.' Then suddenly she jerked forward in her chair, eyes huge.

'What's wrong?' Amelia's voice reflected her friend's anxiety.

'Oh, Amelia, I think I heard Joe come in.' She began to shiver. 'Oh, Amelia!'

'Keep calm,' Amelia said, 'it's all right.'

'No, it isn't,' Jenny's voice dropped to a desperate whisper. 'He doesn't want me to be friends with you. He's forbidden me to have anything to do with you. Oh, Amelia, help me! I can't stand any more.'

The sitting room door opened and Joe's tall, rangy body filled the doorway. He stood perfectly still. His vivid blue eyes fixed unblinkingly on the two women.

Suddenly Amelia jerked to her feet pulling Jenny along with her.

'We were just going. We've to be at a friend's for coffee, we got chatting and nearly forgot. Come on, Jenny, we're late enough as it is.'

Still Joe didn't say anything but he stepped aside and allowed them to pass. Amelia hustled Jenny straight along the hall only stopping briefly to grab coats and handbags from the hall stand.

Outside on the street Jenny whimpered, 'I can't stand any more.'

'Come on,' Amelia said, 'if Rebecca was happy to take Hazel in I'm sure she won't turn you away. She told us right from the beginning her place was a refuge, didn't she? Let's get over there as quick as we can.'

Still clutching on to each other, fear sparking between like an electric current, they began to run, every now and again glancing furtively back as if they expected Joe to appear suddenly behind them.

'It's all right,' Amelia kept repeating, in an effort to comfort her distraught friend. 'You're going to be all right.'

'He'll come after me,' Jenny was still whispering, 'he always did when I went to my mother's. It'll be worse at Rebecca's. He hates Rebecca.'

'It's all right. She won't allow him to come near you.'

Once in the park they had no eyes for the colourful ribbons of plants in beds arranged in areas of finely kept lawns, nor the terraced gardens at the top of the steps. Their gaze was straining impatiently for the first sight of Battlefield House, sitting like a black crow on the brow of the hill behind the lofty grey monument.

They couldn't talk to Rebecca for a few minutes after she'd opened the door to them. It wasn't until they had safely reached her kitchen that they began to calm down and get their breath back. They were helped by Rebecca who posed majestically before them, commanding them to concentrate on breathing slowly and deeply and demonstrating with fingers on her own diaphragm as she took huge breaths. Eventually Amelia explained what had happened.

'Of course you can stay,' Rebecca told Jenny, 'and believe me my dear, this is the best, the most sensible decision you've made in your life. From this moment on you are free of that violent criminal.'

Jenny worriedly bit her lip. 'I can't exactly see Joe as a violent criminal. I can't see that I'm free of him either.'

'Oh, he'll try and get you back under his control,' Rebecca laughed humourlessly, 'but he will have me to deal with from now on. And he won't intimidate *me*.'

Jenny was twisting her handkerchief tightly between her fingers. 'I don't know. I feel I've been on a treadmill of problems for so long there just isn't any solution. How can I pay you for my keep, for instance?'

'There's the Department of Social Security. We'll contact them. You'll be entitled to payments, we'll soon sort that out.'

'And what'll I do about my children?'

'I'll contact them by phone. They're old enough to look after themselves and they can visit you here as often as they like.'

'It's terribly kind of you, Rebecca, but it doesn't seem right that I burden you with all my problems like this. . . .'

'Jenny, I'm very happy to have you stay here.'

Indeed Rebecca did look happy. There seemed a strange joyous radiance about her. 'I know now what my real mission in life is,' she said. 'It is to create a refuge for women. Not just some place where they can come for an hour's therapy or a few hours on a course, but a real refuge. A refuge in every sense of the word.'

31

It had been a huge relief to Rowan when she'd heard that her mother had given up drinking. Only then did she feel she could enjoy her travels with a clear conscience. Not that everything had been plain sailing; for a start she had been late in arriving in Amsterdam and missed her friends. They had met up eventually, however, despite the fact she'd missed seeing them at the prearranged time. They told her they knew she'd turn up sooner or later so they'd just come to Dam Square every day at the appointed time.

Amsterdam was packed with young people, not only from Europe but from the whole world, who seemed suddenly to have decided to converge on the place. They milled about and sat about and lay about the Square or hung about the Alexandria Club or some other club or café where there was music, drink and drugs. Dope was easy to get in Amsterdam. There was plenty to choose from, Black Gold and Sunflower Orange to name but two. Everybody was getting a buzz from marijuana. As a result everybody looked dreamy and happy and relaxed. Too relaxed and happy – that was the problem.

'Look,' Rowan kept reminding her friends, 'the whole idea is for us to get involved in something worthwhile and as far as I'm concerned that doesn't mean wasting time mooning about here stoned out of our minds.'

'The trouble with you,' they kept telling her, 'is that you can't relax. You're far too uptight and earnest. Let's face it Rowan, you're a born social worker and nothing else. You've never learned how to enjoy yourself.'

They all giggled together over that. They giggled a lot now. No matter how much she tried she could neither persuade nor bully them back into their original sense of duty and urgency. 'America and the Civil Rights Movement will still be there in a few months' time. What's the rush?' they told her.

More and more she was forced into the role of a spoil-sport – even 'an old square'. She began to feel isolated and alone even though she was among vast crowds of young people every moment of the day and night. She felt very tempted at times to accept the comfort and escape that marijuana afforded. As a result she began to have a more sympathetic understanding of her mother's addiction to alcohol. She thought a lot about her mother now with a mixture of love, pity and increasing admiration.

She was glad to learn that her mother had made some new friends. She hadn't mentioned in her letter where she'd met Rebecca and Milly but they sounded kind and supportive.

Which was more than could be said for Rowan's friends now, if they could be called friends at all. Already they'd paired off with some Norwegians and were talking about hitch-hiking to Spain. They'd said there was no reason why she shouldn't come along – which was ridiculous. She hadn't left a caring, worthwhile career in Glasgow just to have an extended European holiday. She had thought (although admittedly she'd never said so to anyone) that any experience she might gain in trying to help in the struggle for Civil Rights in the USA would deepen her understanding and profes-sional commitment. She would learn of different aspects of social problems in America and how to cope with them. Then she would be able to bring this new expertise to bear on the difficult problems she met with in Glasgow.

Her friends left without her and she tagged on to a group of Americans for a while; they were more like herself in being serious minded. They discussed Vietnam, for instance, and how President Eisenhower was now pouring American money and weapons into that country. Next, Rowan's American friends prophesied, it would be troops.

'But I won't be one of them,' Earl Lewis assured her, 'I'll come back here to Europe and I'll stay here rather than have any part in the lousy war.'

They all agreed that all wars were stupid, futile and absolutely wicked, wicked beyond belief, beyond words. This was brought home to them with horrifying vividness by a young Japanese who joined them, whose name was Tomita. He told them, 'Every building in my home town of Hiroshima was crushed to the ground and belched out flames. People were everywhere and shrieking, the skin burning off their bodies. The skin was peeling off in red strips and the shrieking sounded as if they were going to die at any minute – as if they were shrieking for death to come quickly and put them out of their agony. Burning people and dead people were lying about everywhere. I will never forget – never as long as I live, the burning people who died shrieking. I saw my mother die. I ask your pardon. I cannot speak of Hiroshima any more.'

To think that afterwards people like Admiral Leahy, one of President Truman's advisers, had said:

. . . the use of this barbarous weapon at Hiroshima and Nagasaki was of no material assistance to our war against Japan. The Japanese were already defeated and ready to surrender because of the effective sea blockade and the successful bombing with conventional weaons.

They all agreed it was enough to make anybody sick and none of them could understand how a so-called Christian country could do such a thing.

Like most of the others, Rowan did odd jobs to make some money. At night she dossed down in her sleeping bag wherever she could. The men were lucky. Lots of them were taken home to share a bed with obliging

214

Dutch girls. Rowan considered it a bit risky to go off she knew not where with a Dutchman. Although she didn't mind sharing a sleeping bag with Tomita and giving him a bit of comfort.

She became good friends with Mary Beth, an American girl from Nashville, Tennessee who said Rowan could come home with her if she didn't mind doing a bit of a detour before they went down South. Mary Beth had to visit relatives in Indianapolis first.

'You want to know what it's like for coloured folks in the Southern States, honey?' Mary Beth said. 'Well, ah'll tell you. If they'd really wanted to punish Hitlah all they needed to do was paint him black and send him ovah theah!'

'But surely there's lots of white people in the struggle for Civil Rights in America?'

'There shore is. My mamma for one. She's really somethin'. A fighta, that's what mamma is, a fighta!'

Mary Beth didn't look as if she took after her mamma. She was the same height as Rowan but plump and baby-faced, with corn-coloured lashes and long fair hair caught up in a haphazard heap on top of her head. Her voice had a lovely soft drawl. Rowan's hair was still swept back and secured in a pony-tail with an elastic band and her earnest look made her appear older than the innocent-eyed Mary Beth although, in fact, Rowan was the younger of the two.

It seemed such a good chance to go to the States with Mary Beth who could show her the ropes and give her an introduction into the Civil Rights struggle. And no doubt it would prove equally helpful to do a bit of travelling in America while she was over there.

Mary Beth, despite her baby softness, had already bummed about Spain and France and could tell of quite a few adventures. Her money had long since run out and, as she admitted, it was lucky she had her flight ticket to Indianapolis: 'My Aunt Abbie is goin' to meet me, she's quite somethin'. She'll drive us to cousin Ed's farm. It's

215

on the Wabash River in Indiana. Then from there we'll go to Decatur, Illinois to call on cousin Adeline. We'll just stay a couple of nights befoah goin' on down to Nashville. From theah we could go furthah South – dependin' on where the action is. But there's to be sit-ins at lunch counters in Nashville.'

'What's that?' Rowan asked.

'Y'all got to see it to believe it, honey. I went to non-violence workshops in Nashville before comin' on this trip. And ah'm tellin' you you'd better go to these classes before you do anythin' else.'

'How can they teach you non-violence? I mean, I *am* non-violent.'

'Honey, y'all have no idea the shit you get in the non-violent movement ovah theah. You gotta be tough, honey. You gotta be prepared. These classes try to help. They rôle play. Some students sit quietly while othah students act out the role of segregationalists. They jeah and poke and spit at you if you're the ones who are sittin' quiet.'

'Charming!' Rowan didn't like the sound of this. She'd never thought of anything quite so uncomfortable.

'We practised things like how to protect your head from a beatin' and how to protect each othah. If one person was takin' a serious beatin' we practised othah people puttin' their bodies in between that person and the violence so that the violence might be more evenly distributed and hopefully no one would get seriously injured.'

'I see,' Rowan said worriedly. This side of things had never entered the – she realized now – very idealistic discussions she'd had with her friends back home. It occurred to her that up till now she had led a very sheltered life. She wondered if she had the kind of courage needed for the sort of thing Mary Beth was talking about. Shame prevented her from voicing any doubts or fears, however.

It was with some trepidation now that she set off with

Mary Beth for America. It was a tiring journey with two diversions which meant touching down at Boston and Detroit. The first thing Rowan saw when she arrived in Boston was President Eisenhower's photo in the airport with a big sign above it saying 'Welcome to America'. Perhaps it was the tiredness but she had a sudden feeling of being very, very far from home. It was a sensation of being on another planet and never, ever being able to see home again. The feeling was banished from her mind almost immediately by her interest in her surroundings. It was the same in Detroit. Indeed she wished she could have had more time there to look at the restaurants, food bars and shops. She'd never seen so much food and in such variety. She was suddenly conscious of being in an affluent society and it occurred to her for the first time how very different the people in America must be as they had never suffered the terrible shortages and deprivations endured for so long in Britain – not to mention the bombing.

Perhaps the good food explained the number of good-looking men. She'd never noticed so many back home, certainly not with beards and Mexican type moustaches. And it looked as if every second man was wearing a baseball cap. The surfeit of food must certainly explain the hugely fat, short-trousered boy who sat with feet up on the chairs opposite her in one of the airport lounges. She had never seen any child so oozing with self-confidence and self-importance.

Another thing she became conscious of was the number of black people. She'd never known any black people in her life. She'd only remembered seeing one or perhaps two and that was in London.

The time difference meant she was even more exhausted on eventually reaching Indianapolis. There they were met by Mary Beth's Aunt Abbie, who turned out to be a tiny elderly lady with a stoop. She walked jerkily with a cane and Rowan learned later that she'd broken her leg and it was still pretty stiff and sore. Abbie, who she also learned was much tougher than she looked, greeted them with affectionate hugs and led them outside to the car park and a big grey Buick. Abbie was so tiny she could barely reach to see out the car window. She seemed short sighted, too, by the way she kept peering over and sometimes through the steering wheel, close to the glass. Not to mention being absentminded. Before starting the car she removed a white cotton bag, or mitten as she called it from over the hand brake. She said it was to remind her to release the brake because she so often forgot.

The drive was to be a very long one and what with one thing and another, Rowan's heart sank. She had a premonition that all was not going to be well.

32

'That's Jenny's money organized,' Rebecca announced with satisfaction. 'Now Hazel, I want you to understand it's each according to her needs and each according to what she can afford in the refuge. You've obviously never needed to think about money.'

'Oh, how awful of me.' Fluttering with embarrassment Hazel fingered a wisp of hair back from her brow. 'I should be paying you something, shouldn't I?'

'Yes, dear.'

'Oh, how can you forgive me!'

'Quite easily, as long as you pay up.'

'I'll give you whatever you say, of course,' Hazel's cheeks glowed bright pink against her blonde hair. Her hair was looking smooth and shiny and in better condition than it had been for years. It was newly dyed and she felt so much cheered after her visit to the hairdresser. She'd also been to the beauty salon where she'd had a facial and a manicure. Rebecca had accompanied her and sat patiently waiting for her on each occasion, eyes closed in yoga meditation. Hazel felt supremely grateful; she clung to Rebecca like a helpless child. She could look back now in horror at the state to which drinking had reduced her and she was terrified at ever sinking into such degradation again.

Admittedly, it had been extremely difficult at Rebecca's at the beginning. Indeed she'd thought she was going to die more than once. But she'd come through the dark tunnel and emerged safely into the light, as Rebecca put it. Now she was only too glad to do whatever Rebecca told her.

Sometimes she couldn't help smiling to herself, though. If Rowan could just see her at Rebecca's sometimes – washing the dishes and setting the table and sweeping up the kitchen floor! She'd even Hoovered all the carpets. Jenny did the cooking. Milly and Rebecca did the shopping. Milly was the latest arrival and already Hazel had developed a friendship with her. They were both 'ladies' and had come from good backgrounds. They had therefore a great deal in common, except that poor Milly's problem was her dreadful husband. Hazel could hardly believe that anyone like Milly's husband existed. She had never heard of such behaviour in her life. Her life was now full of shocking yet fascinating revelations.

Rebecca encouraged everyone to talk about their problems and when they couldn't talk – as poor Milly couldn't at the beginning – Rebecca talked for her and then they all discussed the problem.

Milly's husband was a very respectable lawyer in town. They had a bungalow in Bearsden, *the* most respectable place to live on the outskirts of Glasgow. He went to his office every day immaculately attired in pristine white shirt, pin-striped trousers, smart black jacket and bowler hat. Who would ever have imagined the sexual perversion to which he had subjected poor Milly? Rebecca said it was simply another way that a man used to humiliate and intimidate a woman.

He had forced Milly to have sex whenever the whim took him. He forced her to have anal sex and oral sex. Often she woke up during the night with him trying to force objects up her vagina. Other practices were so disgusting that Hazel felt sick at the thought of them. Milly had once tried to commit suicide which didn't in the least surprise Hazel or any of the other women at the refuge. 'It was all so shameful,' Milly said, 'I couldn't possibly tell a soul. And of course who would have believed it of Henry?'

Rebecca could talk openly about anything and she encouraged everyone else to do the same. She was shocking and amusing and absolutely amazing. Hazel had never met such a person in her life. Rebecca did a lot of meditating when she sat in lotus position on the floor, hands hanging limply on splayed out knees and eyes either closed or fixed on the flame of a candle. She had a regular stream of hypnotherapy patients coming and going, she was always organizing some kind of course or other, and there always seemed to be a crowd of women in her kitchen, drinking tea and talking. Hazel was kept very busy washing dishes.

Now that Rebecca had brought up the subject of money it occurred to Hazel for the first time that tea and biscuits as well as all the other items of food had to be bought. Rebecca was right; she had never needed to think about money before. Certainly one never *talked* about it. One had long ago been taught that it was not 'the done thing'. She had begun to see, especially in her present situation, that attitudes like that were not only impracticable but rather silly. She began to see, too, that *she* had been rather silly – quite apart from her drinking. Her foolish attitude to money had no doubt been the reason for Derek's will. He had left half of his money to Rowan in trust until she was 25. The rest, not a fortune but a comfortable enough sum, was to be paid into his wife's bank account in monthly instalments. Derek, she could see now, was trying to protect her against herself even beyond the grave. When Rebecca brought it to her attention that she should be paying money into the refuge she would gladly and immediately have handed over to Rebecca every penny of her capital. She told Rebecca this but then had to explain why she could not do so.

'Never mind,' Rebecca said, 'what you get every month is a princely sum compared, for instance, to what Jenny gets and I'm sure you will be wonderfully generous with that.'

And she had been, gladly. As Rebecca said, God's work was being done at the refuge and no money could be put to a better cause.

Rebecca had also helped her to arrange for phone calls and her mail to be redirected to the refuge and so, much to her relief, she'd heard that Rowan had arrived safely in America. She had also received a box number to which to send letters to Rowan. She was able to tell her daughter that she had stopped drinking and also to express her regret about all the worry and trouble she must have caused the poor girl in the past. She didn't mention the refuge. Rebecca thought it would be better not to in the circumstances. She had received such a lovely letter from Rowan in return. Rowan was so glad that she had at long last faced her problem and was now tackling it so successfully. Rowan was proud of her. She treasured that letter containing, as it did, the first compliment her daughter had ever given her. She kept it in a special silk purse in her handbag to protect it from getting damaged.

Other letters followed in which Rowan brought to life for her the journey to Amsterdam and then to the United States. So vivid were the descriptions of places and people she'd met on her travels that Hazel began to feel as if she was sharing every experience with her daughter, albeit in the safety of Rebecca's refuge. From the letters grew a feeling of closeness with Rowan that she had never had before. The letters were very matter-of-fact but for Hazel they built up a moving impression of a great tide of courageous and adventurous young people spreading out all over the world, getting to know each other, accepting each other. She began to admire their resourcefulness and independent spirit.

Although she did not approve of everything they were getting up to. Indeed she had been horrified when Rowan wrote that there were drug 'pushers' everywhere, but especially in Amsterdam. Rowan said her friends had already got into the drug scene before she met up with them in Amsterdam. She wrote of her surprise the first time she'd seen Sally go up to a man and ask if he was 'dealing' and the man had responded with the question 'A pound or a five pound deal?'

Rowan said she'd thought about drugs a lot recently and the effects people sought from them. She'd come to realize and to understand more fully what Hazel had got from alcohol. It was an escape from anxiety, it was soothing, it was a comfort. But in the end life had to be confronted. To seek escape was to take the path of weakness and constantly undermine one's ability to cope. Her mother's success in giving up alcohol had made Rowan turn away from drugs.

Hazel was deeply grateful for this and felt wonderfully enriched in spirit not only to learn that she had been of real help to her daughter, but that Rowan had acquired a genuine respect for her.

For the most part, however, the frankness in her daughter's letters shocked Hazel. They revealed a startlingly different world from any she'd ever dreamed existed. To give her time to recover from the shock of each vivid account of Rowan's experiences she delayed any reply. In this way she could more or less forget the disturbing epistles, or at least most of the trauma of reading some of their more shocking contents. When she did write to Rowan it was only about what was going on in Glasgow. She repeated titbits of news from the local papers, like how Daisy at the hairdressers' had run away with Mrs Elcho's husband, (a man old enough to be her father!). Mrs Elcho had been a regular customer there for years and her husband had always called for her.

In time Hazel acquired a degree of immunity to Rowan's worrying revelations. This gradual getting used to reading about what was, to Hazel, quite shocking happenings was to stand her in good stead for what was still to come, when Rowan reached the deep South of America and became actively involved in the struggle for Civil Rights.

Hazel found that last thing at night, just before going to bed was practically the only quiet time she could think about Rowan. There were always so many people milling about and so much happening during the day. Often very distressing things like when Milly's husband came and ordered Milly to return home with him. Milly would have obeyed like an obedient little dog. Hazel understood this; Milly had been well brought up and one didn't create scenes and make an exhibition of oneself in public. (That was one of the reasons Hazel looked back on her own behaviour with such horror.) Rebecca had calmly instructed herself, Jenny and Amelia, who happened to be there at the time, to take Milly into the kitchen and give her a cup of camomile tea, 'while I have a word with this man!'

Milly sat stiff as a statue at the kitchen table, unable even to move her mouth. Soon, however, Rebecca appeared, to announced triumphantly, 'He's gone and he won't be back. You can relax, Milly, that man will never bother you again.'

Milly still couldn't move a muscle. She just kept staring at Rebecca as if needing proof beyond all reasonable doubt.

'I told him that I, that we *all*, knew the whole sordid story and that I'd make sure that the whole of Glasgow, the whole of Britain knew before I'd finished with him. "It's the kind of thing that certain newspapers would revel in," I told him, "Think of the disgrace," I said. "Your reputation would be in ruins," I said. "Everyone in the land would know what a disgusting animal you are. I've had her examined by a doctor," I said. "I have plenty of evidence to back up what I'll take great pleasure in shouting from the rooftops." '

'Oh dear,' Hazel gasped. Although it had nothing whatsoever to do with her, she was so shaken by the whole incident she had to sit down.

'He was horrified,' Rebecca told them with grim satisfaction. 'Shocked and terrified to the core.' (Hazel wasn't a bit surprised.) 'He couldn't get away quick enough,' Rebecca patted Milly's rigid shoulders. 'You've nothing to worry about any more, Milly, believe me.' Nevertheless it took Milly quite a time to unstiffen. She'd never completely relaxed at the best of times.

'What Milly needs now,' Rebecca announced, after she'd enjoyed a cup of tea and a cream doughnut – Rebecca had become rather fond of cream cakes and it amazed everyone how she never seemed to put on any weight – 'is plenty of reassuring hugs.'

So they'd all given Milly's stiff body a hug, separately and all together, all crowding round her and laughing until she'd had to laugh too.

That night Rebecca's friend Alice was coming. Rebecca said Alice was, like herself, wonderfully psychic. She could tell fortunes by tea-cup, crystal ball, tarot cards and black mirror. Rebecca was keen to have as many people as possible lined up and waiting for Alice's services. Jenny and Amelia, however, thought it would just upset them to have their fortunes told and didn't want anything to do with it despite the fact that all the other women were greatly looking forward to this event.

Rebecca was very displeased at their lack of support. She quoted a poem at them in a loud, dramatic voice:

If thought can reach to Heaven
On Heaven let it dwell
For fear, like power, is given to thought
To reach to Hell.
For fear the desolation and darkness of thy mind,
Perplex and vex a dwelling which thou has left behind.

Rebecca said that Jenny and Amelia were both so full of fear they were frightened of their own shadows.

'There's nothing to fear from Alice,' Rebecca told everyone, 'she's just a woman trying to make a living like anyone else. She's just using the gifts that God gave her as best she can.' Rebecca had got Milly and four of her other friends organized to attend and so the numbers were made up despite Jenny and Amelia's 'regrettable ingratitude and lack of cooperation', as Rebecca put it. 'It's not as if Alice charges all that much for her services,' she said, 'she's not a greedy person.'

Hazel had expected someone imposing and dramatic like Rebecca but Alice was quite common looking really. She was much smaller than Rebecca, squat and shapeless with short wiry grey hair that looked as if she'd cut it herself. She had a few hairs on her face, too, one or two growing from an ugly brown mole on her left cheek. Her thick glasses, small and round and unfashionable did nothing to improve her appearance. She had also thick legs, a stumpy, ungainly way of walking and she was carrying a shopping bag. Still, it had turned out a most enjoyable evening.

Alice had told her that her daughter was returning in the not too far distant future and that this would mean great happiness for her. She described Rowan to a tee, it was quite uncanny. Hazel was terribly impressed. Next day she felt quite annoyed at Amelia who tried to spoil her enjoyment of the evening by saying, 'Hazel, you've spoken so much to Rebecca about Rowan you must have told her all these things and Alice could have found out from her.'

She didn't dare, of course, repeat to Rebecca what Amelia said. Rebecca was still displeased with her for avoiding Alice's visit. Rebecca also suspected Amelia of influencing Jenny.

'I'll have to have a serious talk with Amelia,' she said. 'She's a timid, anxious little soul who needs a lot of comfort and reassurance! But still . . .' Rebecca closed her eyes and put a finger to the 'Third Eye' in the middle of her brow.

'I can also detect a perverse, stubborn streak in her. Something I think that's been caused in her childhood. Something that needs to be rooted out and exposed to the light.'

She opened her eyes and smiled. 'God will show me the way, Hazel. Of that I am perfectly certain.'

226

33

It soon became obvious that Aunt Abbie had forgotten
the way to the farm. She *thought* she had taken the right
turn-off, she *thought* she was on the right road, but she
wasn't altogether sure. This was perhaps forgivable
considering Aunt Abbie was in her seventies. Rowan
thought, however, when covering what to her seemed
vast distances, Abbie's forgetfulness could have serious
repercussions. Unlike her own hilly Scotland the land
here was flat; there was nothing but totally flat earth
stretching out as far as the eye could see on every side.
The towns they passed seemed even stranger. Each
street could plainly be seen from one end to the other
spreading out on either side of the road with wooden
houses, or 'frame' houses as Rowan learned they were
called. Even the shops looked like wooden houses with
verandahs. Rowan had never experienced anything so
odd as being able to see a whole town at once like that.

It got dark and Mary Beth nodded off to sleep. Rowan
was afraid to stop talking to Abbie in case she nodded off
at the wheel. Although Abbie didn't look in the least
sleepy, gripping the wheel, her nose almost touching it as
she strained to peer through its spokes. Sometimes by
stretching her neck and moving her head from side to
side she managed a few glimpses over the top of the
wheel. She was really far too tiny to be driving such a big
car.

Eventually Abbie said she'd have to find a phone and
call cousin Ed to ask him to remind her again about the
directions. Rowan kept a look-out for some sign of life or
light in the pitch blackness outside but it was a long time
before she saw what looked like a café or restaurant.
After some uncertainty and false starts they found the

entrance to the restaurant and Aunt Abbie swerved the Buick off the road towards it.

'It's all for the best,' Aunt Abbie assured the girls, as they all got out of the car. 'A cup of coffee is just what we needed.'

Once in the restaurant, silently, sleepily Rowan and Mary Beth drank cups of coffee while Aunt Abbie, sprightly despite her stiff leg and walking stick, stumped across to the wall phone to make the necessary call. She returned, her pixie face looking cheered. 'I've remembered now,' she said, 'there's plenty of landmarks but the main thing to look out for is an illuminated elevator with a flag on top. We turn off the main highway there.'

Rowan couldn't begin to imagine what on earth an illuminated elevator could be, especially one with a flag on top, but she was too exhausted to ask. Back in the car, she gazed wide-eyed into the darkness, expecting at any moment to see the strange vision of a disembodied lift from Rory's department store, lights blazing, as it slowly floated up in the Indianapolis air, an American flag fluttering on top. It occurred to her that perhaps she was going off her head until Abbie cried triumphantly, 'There it is!'

An illuminated elevator was, it transpired, some sort of enormous machine that lifted up wheat.

Nevertheless, by this time, Rowan was not at all sure of Abbie's eyesight and she felt far from confident as the Buick suddenly lurched to one side and plunged into the blackness of what felt like a very bumpy country road. Mary Beth had collapsed into sleep again and even as they jarred and juddered along, she didn't wake up.

'Look out for a mail box,' Abbie said, peering closer to the wheel, 'there's a mail box at the end of cousin Ed's driveway.

'Is that one?' Rowan asked eventually and nearly had a heart attack as the car swerved across the road and in between two gateposts. Halfway up the rough drive a wooden house came into view.

'That's not it,' Abbie decided, 'but they'll know about cousin Ed's place.'

Rowan watched, heart in mouth, as Abbie's small figure lurched about in the dark across the grass frontage – she'd stumbled off the driveway – towards the house. As she waited after ringing the doorbell, the porch was suddenly flooded with light, the door opened and a huge, muscular man, naked to the waist, leaned against the lintel. Abbie barely reached his waist and had to tip back and strain her chin up to speak to him.

Rowan was too far away to hear what was said but she saw the man stretch out a long arm to point further along the road. Then the door shut. There was darkness again and Abbie came tottering and bouncing back to the car. 'No problem,' she chirpily assured Rowan. 'It's the next turning along.' She began backing the car fast on to the road which seemed, and indeed proved, a dangerous manoeuvre because she banged it into one of the gateposts. That woke Mary Beth up.

'What y'all doin'?' she cried out.

'It's all right,' Aunt Abbie assured her, 'I'm not worried.' With clouds of smoke belching out of the back of the car Abbie decided to go out frontways after all. She made a hair-raising turn which unfortunately took her slithering over the man's lawn. Then the car narrowly missed tipping into a ditch before finally reaching the main road again. Soon she was swerving between trees and bumping along a winding track until another wooden bungalow-like house suddenly leapt into the headlights.

'There we are!' said Abbie, as if it had been no trouble at all.

Rowan wasn't so sure. 'It looks exactly the same as the other one to me.'

'Not at all,' Abbie scoffed. 'Anyway, there's Charlie.'

Charlie was a very fat dog who lay flopped out on the porch. He opened one eye to watch them getting out of the car but didn't move anything else. Then the porch light snapped on and a plump woman and another muscular man came out at a leisurely pace, arms folded over chest. Abbie had told her earlier that natives of Indianapolis were known as 'Hoosies' and somehow it suited cousin Ed and his wife.

It was only once she'd safely arrived that Rowan relaxed and began to notice interesting differences from what she was used to – for instance here, despite being late evening, it was hot. In Glasgow, even in the height of summer, the nights were cool, even downright cold.

In the days that followed she became aware that eating and drinking habits were unfamiliar, too. At home she'd never seen such a thing as iced water served at meals – here there were big jugs packed with ice all the time and tall glasses clinking with ice were consumed at every meal. For breakfast they were served boiled eggs in bowls; she watched intrigued as the others scooped the egg into the bowl and mashed it up with a fork before eating it, along with what they called 'blueberry muffins'. To Rowan these looked and tasted like hot sponge cakes with fruit in them. Muffins were something quite different in Scotland and were eaten at tea-time, never for breakfast.

Another surprise was what she was given when she asked if she could have tea instead of coffee. Instead of her usual morning cup of strong, steaming hot tea she was presented with a tall glass half full of a pale amber liquid and half full of ice. She gazed at it in stupefied silence for a second or two.

'Something wrong, honey?' her hostess asked.

'No, no,' Rowan quickly assured her, 'it's lovely!' Privately, it seemed a sacrilege – she thought she'd never get over having to drink cold tea.

They were up early on the day they left and with jerks and starts set off for their next stop at Decatur, Illinois. Cousin Ed's wife was also driving off to a craft festival for which she'd made beautiful corn dollies and framed pictures made of homely things like lentils and herbs.

230

The craft festival was a hundred or more miles away and this was something else that amazed Rowan. The people here obviously thought nothing of driving long distances; distance didn't seem to matter at all.

It certainly didn't to Abbie who set off eagerly for their next port of call. Abbie, Rowan discovered, was an inveterate traveller. She'd been not only all over the USA but all over Europe and even the Soviet Union and Japan. In most places, too, she'd hired and driven cars. It didn't bear thinking about!

'Can't you just imagine, Rowan,' Abbie was saying now, 'how the Indians used to ride across these prairies – this was all Indian land once. The poor Indians! We haven't treated them well, you know. Can't you just imagine them?'

Indeed Rowan could. And again she had the slightly scary feeling of being far, far from home and on a different planet. It was very odd because she never used to think of America like this. America and Americans had always seemed perfectly familiar before, she'd seen the place and the people so often in films. Although she had never before seen the endless miles of sun-bleached, shoulder-high corn that grew on either side of the roads that she was seeing now. Nor had she had any idea of how long and straight roads could be. The long, straight road, fortunately empty of traffic, went on and on. They eventually came to a stretch where signs and hoardings stood on high stilts and crowded alongside slender telegraph poles. It felt like driving through a crazy Alice-in-Wonderland jungle. Then a town of wooden bungalows and wooden shops came into view, well spaced out on either side of the road and all with verandahs and porches. Another long empty stretch of road followed until a sign told her they were approaching 'Decatur, the Pride of the Prairies.'

'Haven't seen cousin Adeline for . . . don't know *how* long,' Abbie said. Then, stopping at an intersection she peered along the main highway at the hordes of large vehicles coming thundering along. 'I wonder if I could nip in before these big fellas?'

'No!' Rowan and Mary Beth cried out in unison.

'I could have if I'd been nippy.' Abbie sounded disappointed.

Cousin Adeline's street was lush with overhanging trees. Her house seemed very dark at first. The canopy of the porch kept the front rooms shady and that, Rowan discovered, was a blessing. So was the fine wire netting door that could be kept shut when the wood door was open. The netting kept out the crickets and other insects but let in the air. She discovered too having lots of iced water to drink was not only a blessing but a necessity. She felt continually hot and thirsty.

'This isn't hot!' cousin Adeline laughed. 'Wait till you get down South. You're not going to know what's hit you. Different altogether down South. Different climate, different folks, different life altogether.'

'Why is it,' Rowan asked, 'that you and Aunt Abbie don't have Mary Beth's southern drawl? I thought your whole family originally came from Tennessee.'

'No, no,' Cousin Adeline gave another of her hearty laughs. 'Aunt Abbie and my mother and Mary Beth's mother are all Yankees born and bred.'

'Bessie, that's my young sister and Mary Beth's mamma,' Abbie explained, 'she married a southern fella. I went down there a few years ago to settle, rented a nice house. I guess I never have picked up the accent though.'

'Don't think you've settled much either, Aunt Abbie,' laughed cousin Adeline. 'Can't see you ever settling.'

'I have to keep an eye on Bessie,' Abbie said. 'Your mamma,' she added to Mary Beth, 'is getting into all sorts of trouble down there.'

Cousin Adeline nearly fell over with hilarity.

'Who's going to keep an eye on you, Aunt Abbie?' Then to Rowan. 'She's worse than anybody I'm telling you, you just don't know what you're getting into down in old Tennessee!'

232

34

After Amelia's latest hypnotherapy session she had persuaded Jenny to go home with her to Mary House for a few hours so that she would not be involved in the fortune-telling evening at Rebecca's. Jenny didn't feel like sitting alone in the flat, but she did not particularly look forward to an evening at Amelia's either because of Amelia's husband. He was another aggressive man and she had no desire whatsoever to be in his company for any length of time. Douglas was outspoken, to say the least, and was likely to say, albeit in a joking tone, things like 'Have you not come to your senses yet and gone back to your husband?' To which Amelia would reply, 'Don't pay any attention to him.'

She supposed, for Amelia's sake, she could put up with Douglas for one night. Although she only agreed with some reluctance when Amelia added that his insensitive remarks were preferable to being worried sick by Alice.

It was Amelia, not Jenny who was afraid of Alice telling them something bad that would upset them. Amelia suffered from acute anxiety.

'I told him to mind his own business and leave you alone,' Amelia said.

Jenny couldn't help smiling at her friend's show of bravado. 'I can't imagine it, Amelia. He's always nagging on at you and as far as I can see you take it like a lamb.'

'Sometimes I find it best to avoid confrontation. When I do fight with him I get palpitations and headaches and stomach upsets and all sorts of things. It makes me feel really ill. I can't even write when I feel so upset.'

'I'm not criticizing you, I know how it is. Living with Joe was like walking on eggs. I got that I was afraid to say one word to him. And talk about feeling ill? When Joe came to Rebecca's that first time I nearly collapsed. Thank God it was Rebecca who opened the door to him.'

Amelia shook her head. 'You've got to admire that woman. She'd gladly take on an army of men and demolish them. Although she can get upset like the rest of us. I noticed she had to shut herself away in the sitting room to calm down after the confrontation with Joe.'

'She said she was having a quiet time of prayer.'

'Praying for Joe to drop dead, I bet! I think she would have felt all right if he'd shouted or even physically attacked her. But to miscall her and make those awful accusations in such a quiet, controlled voice was unnerving, to say the least. It just shows, though, as Rebecca said – he can control himself when he wants to. He must have wanted to hit her. I saw the hatred in his eyes, didn't you?'

'Poor Joe,' Jenny said.

'What do you mean – poor Joe? You were in physical danger with him, Jenny. You're the one to be sorry for, not him.'

Jenny sighed. 'You weren't there when I bumped into him in the grocers in Pollokshaws Road. He was doing the shopping, he looked so pathetic somehow.'

'Not as pathetic, I'll bet, as you did when you first went to Rebecca's. You were a nervous wreck.'

'I know. But he looked so desperately unhappy. His eyes haunted me for days afterwards.'

'It's a sad situation, right enough. I just don't want you to get hurt again, that's all. You've improved so much recently.'

Certainly Jenny was taking an interest in her appearance again. Rebecca had long since gone to the flat while Joe was at work, packed a couple of cases with her belongings and brought them back to Battlefield House. As a result she was now able to wear her navy suit, blue and white candy-striped blouse and navy sling-back, peep-toe shoes. She had shampooed her hair and brightened her face with a dusting of rouge and a touch of coloured eye shadow. She perhaps was no raving beauty, she told herself, but her features were still firm and unlined except for a few tiny creases around her eyes. Her eyes were grey and clear and frank and all the other women envied her naturally curly hair.

Even her posture had improved. For a time her shoulders had tended to droop but now, encouraged by Rebecca she had straightened up. 'Come on now, Jenny, shoulders back, head up. Fill yourself with the breath of life.' Sometimes Rebecca sounded like a sergeant-major.

Not that she felt completely recovered. She still felt depressed about her marriage and wished things could have worked out differently for her and Joe. She began thinking more of the good memories than the bad. She kept remembering Joe when they'd both been children together in Anderston. His parents had been even poorer than hers; at one time Joe'd had to suffer parish clothes, jaggy jerseys with woollen collars that scraped the neck as if they were made of thorns, and trousers that chafed the backs of his knees. She could still see in her mind's eye the angry red weals on his thin neck and legs.

He'd been so proud one year when he had received a football for Christmas; he'd never known to this day how his parents had managed it. For weeks it was as if that football had been stuck to the toe of his boot – he was continually dribbling it about the streets.

She remembered their sexual awakening, their first physical awareness of each other. It was a wonderful bonus to her. She had hero-worshipped Joe since she was at primary school. Joe had been the only boy in her life. She had been the only girl in his. The magic of love was just beginning to open up for them when he'd been snatched away to the war. It seemed incredible now when she realized that she had married Joe when she was not much older than Rose was now. Yet it had seemed the most natural thing in the world. Even her mother and father hadn't been too worried. After all, they'd known Joe since he was born.

'Well, hen,' her mother had said, 'I'd hoped you'd enjoy your freedom a bit longer, you're still just a wee lassie. But Joe's a nice lad. You'll be all right with him.'

Later her mother had blamed the war. 'The war has a lot to answer for,' she often repeated sadly. 'Women left widows without ever seeing their men again. Others getting their men back crippled in mind as well as body and feeling they've lost them just the same.'

Her mother was right, that's how she felt. Joe was lost to her just as tragically as if he'd been killed. Sometimes she felt overwhelmed by sadness thinking about him. She missed her children too; they came to see her occasionally but not nearly as often as she'd have liked. She didn't blame them, Rebecca's house wasn't a congenial place for young people. Rose and Dode hated it. They'd told her in furtive undertones, in case Rebecca would hear, 'You'd be better at home than here, Mum.'

They'd also told her, much to her consternation, that a man she'd once described to them had come asking for her. Her heart had immediately raced with a mixture of excitement and alarm. 'What did you say? Did you tell him I was here?'

'No, of course not,' Rose assured her, 'I did as you told me and said you'd gone away and I didn't have an address.'

It was the best thing to have done in the circumstances. No way could she cope with another man, another complication in her life. Gregson was an attractive, sexy man – but he was still a man and in the small, all-female world of the refuge she'd come to believe that any man meant trouble. Yet Jenny couldn't help feeling so disappointed she could have burst into tears. With an effort she put aside such foolishness and felt nothing but relief eventually. She thanked God that it hadn't been Joe who had answered the door. She forced herself to concentrate on her immediate difficulties.

It couldn't be denied that Rebecca's house wasn't a very comfortable place with so many people to-ing and fro-ing – especially now that she had to share the dormitory-like attic bedroom with Sadie, who had joined the residents. Not to mention piles of junk and trunks and fusty old books. Hazel and Milly had a bedroom each downstairs. This was because they paid more which she supposed was only fair. She had not forgotten how glad she was of the refuge when Rebecca had first taken her in; but it wasn't home. Apart from anything else, although she could understand Rebecca's argument about not accepting children to stay she couldn't in her heart agree with it.

Rebecca said her sole concern and care was with a woman in need. 'A woman for *herself*,' Rebecca insisted, 'not as a wife or a mother. But absolutely for herself. There are other agencies to care for children. They must be contacted when necessary to take over that responsibility, at least until the woman finds herself again and has strength to cope with her life.'

That was all very well but it was obvious that Rebecca had never known what it felt like to be a mother. Oh, how she missed her children.

She missed the flat, too, despite its disadvantage of being a basement; she could keep the lights on if she wanted. She could sit quietly and read if she wanted. She could arrange the furniture how she wanted. Everything in the flat had been to her taste. There was her nice satin quilt and matching curtains in her bedroom and the pretty patchwork cushions and the bright scarlet curtains in the sitting room. The blue and white willow-pattern dishes in the kitchen and the checked table covers and scarlet chair cushions. And everything so neat and tidy.

Every room in Rebecca's house was a clutter. Jenny had never been used to such careless confusion. Her mother had had to be terribly organized in the single-end in Anderston; everything had always been orderly and immaculate. Her own home in Queens Drive had been the same or at least until she had become ill. Now that she was so much better she longed to be back tidying it and cleaning it and putting it to rights. She shuddered to think what Dode's room and Rose's room would be like.

She missed telling them what to do and what not to do. She missed cooking nice meals for them and seeing them scraping their plates with enjoyment. She had had a *place* in life as a wife and mother.

Granted there was a bond of friendship and sympathy with the other women at the refuge: they had suffering in common and they all knew what fear was. She had no doubt, however, especially as they grew stronger they would experience the same longings that she did. Once a woman was married and had a home of her own she no longer felt the same even about the home of her parents, far less that of a comparative stranger like Rebecca.

Amelia said the answer was to have enough money to buy a place of your own, *really* of your own. Perhaps Amelia would manage that one day if one of her books became the bestseller she dreamed about. How could Jenny Thornton ever have that kind of money, though?

At the moment all the money (a mere pittance) that she received from the DHSS went to Rebecca for her keep. The few pounds she'd managed to save over the years was fast dwindling on little luxuries like haircuts and make-up for herself and presents for the children. She would have to find work soon.

Hazel was still very dependent on Rebecca and showed no signs of wanting to go home so there was no immediate hope of a job there. She no longer felt happy about returning to work at Mary House in her present circumstances. Douglas would be nagging at her as much as Amelia before she was finished. She wondered if Rory could help with a job. Either a job in her house or with one of her wealthy friends. She wasn't sure what Amelia would think of this idea; Amelia and her mother-in-law had never been close. However that was Amelia's problem.

Walking with Amelia along Queens Drive towards Mary House in order to avoid being present at Alice's fortune-telling session, Jenny resolved to get in touch with Rory the very next day. As it turned out she didn't even need to wait that long because when they arrived at the house the first thing they saw was Rory's silver Rolls-Royce parked outside.

'Oh dear,' Amelia groaned, 'she'll be checking up on me again. I wonder what I've done this time or rather, *not* done. What did I make for lunch and dinner today? Oh dear! I was so busy getting my quota of words done I left the cooking to Harry. He's much better at it than I am and I give him extra pocket-money to make up for it. I wish my mother-in-law would mind her own business!'

Jenny's eyes glimmered with laughter. 'I bet you're going to tell her off as well!'

'Don't be sarcastic!' Amelia gave Jenny a friendly dig in the ribs with her elbow. 'It's well seen you're getting more like your old perky self!'

Mary House was furnished mostly in Art Deco style. The front entrance wasn't large but it was impressive with its oak panelling, oriental rugs, tall grandfather clock, table and carved chairs in dark, rich wood. A lobby off the entrance hall had a tiled floor of brown and fawn, a brown painted wrought-iron umbrella stand fitted into one corner and a barometer hung on one wall. The other had hooks that bulged with coats and jackets and scarves. Amelia flung her coat over the rest, then said, 'I suppose they'll be in the living room. Come on!'

Douglas and his mother were lounging back on the easy chairs on either side of the honey-coloured tiled fireplace into which was built an electric fire. A fringed standard lamp behind Rory's chair picked out the spiral of smoke from the cigarette in her long black holder. As

239

usual she looked both expensive and glamorous. Jenny was not sure if her red hair was dyed but it was certainly as strikingly vivid as it had ever been and the slim figure in the lime-green Hardy Amies dress had obviously put on very little weight in the years Jenny had known her. Rory made Jenny feel quite homely and plump in her thick Arran sweater and kilted skirt.

'Hallo, Jenny,' the older woman greeted her, 'you're looking better.'

Douglas cast a long-suffering look in Amelia's direction. 'What's it been this time? Hypnotism? Pendulums, making a fool of yourself cavorting about in the park, or what?'

'How are you, Rory?' Amelia asked, ignoring him. 'Sit here beside me, Jenny,' she added, patting the seat beside her on the brown leather settee. Jenny imagined the three piece suite covered in real leather must have been expensive, but it was cold to the touch and not very comfortable. The parquet floor couldn't have been cheap either, not to mention the hand-knotted art rug in zigzag brown and black design in front of the fireplace.

'I would have thought, Amelia,' Rory said, 'that you didn't need to be hypnotized. You're in a trance half the time already.'

'It's more teaching you how to relax,' Amelia explained. 'I get very tense and anxious at times.'

'What have you got to be tense and anxious about?'

Jenny thought Amelia should have blurted out the truth in no uncertain terms, told her mother-in-law exactly how she felt and what she had to put up with. Amelia however, just shrugged and gave a little half-laugh. Admittedly Rory Donovan was an intimidating woman, super successful, self-confident, hard as nails.

Rory turned her attention back to Jenny. 'When are you getting back to work?'

Douglas said, 'When's she getting back to her husband, more like.'

'Douglas, that's none of your business,' Amelia said,

glaring at him from under lowered brows. Jenny was surprised at her set mouth and resentful eyes. Rebecca was obviously right in thinking there was a stubborn, perverse streak in Amelia.

'God! Look who's talking about minding your own business,' Douglas howled with derision. 'She's got half the female population of the south side at this Abercrombie woman's house. There's husbands coming here begging her to mind her own business and leave their wives alone.'

'A slight exaggeration, Douglas,' Amelia said sarcastically. 'It was only Jenny's husband.'

Rory said, 'He's got a point though, Amelia. What about Hazel Saunders? Her house has been shut up for ages. She's the talk of Pollokshields.'

Jenny decided to get a word in. 'She was the talk of Pollokshields long before she met Rebecca. Rebecca has been the saving of her, she's managed to stop Hazel drinking.'

'Anyway, it doesn't look as if she's ready to take you back,' Rory said, 'but you could start work here any time.'

'No,' Jenny managed. 'Things have changed too much. Amelia and I have become friends, I feel it would be too awkward and embarrassing to work here now. Anyway, I feel I need to branch out, challenge myself a bit.'

Rory shrugged. 'I'm sorry you feel that way – for Douglas and Harry's sake. At least I was always sure they were getting decent meals when you were around. But if it's a challenge you want, I'm planning to have a small dinner party for some important people. People like Sir Ian and Lady Russell. I was going to hire an outside caterer but I can't imagine anyone having your flair for cooking. Do you fancy tackling the dinner? I'll pay you well, of course, and I'll send a couple of kitchen maids from one of the staff canteens at "Rory's" to help you.'

After only a moment's worried hesitation Jenny said, 'Yes.'

35

Aunt Abbie had lost her walking stick. 'I won't worry,' she said, 'it'll be at cousin Ed's. He'll send it on.' She staggered about at high speed in the most alarming way but she refused to rest or be left out of anything. Rowan decided Aunt Abbie must be the stuff of which the old pioneers were made.

They all went to a downtown hairdressers and had their hair done. The hairdressers and all the other customers were thoroughly intrigued with Rowan's Scottish accent. One enormously fat woman kept loudly calling out, 'Say something else, doll. Aw go on!' and 'Ain't she a sweetie?'

Rowan decided that Americans must be the friendliest and least self-conscious people on earth, if somewhat embarrassing. She also decided that a great many of them ate too much. Just walking along one street she saw several people not just fat but *grotesque*! One quite young man with a fringe of beard was so fat his arms stuck out at either side like tiny wings unable to hang down. One woman's thighs took up half the width of the pavement. Her stomach hung over and made a fold as if she had a double groin, one on top of the other. Everything about her was heavy and bouncing about. To make things worse she was wearing a tight shirt and blue jeans which horribly accentuated every bulge and fold. There was a massive black woman as well. She was wearing a dress and looked like a moving bell-tent.

Everyone, fat or otherwise, seemed to have a confident, aggressive swagger – even black men and women, which surprised Rowan. She had been expecting them to look cowed and unhappy. She began to wonder if she'd been imagining what she'd been reading about Civil

Rights and Human Rights in America. Newspapers often did exaggerate things.

They had lunch out. Everyone obviously ate in restaurants much more here than in Britain – they even went out for breakfast. At seven o'clock one morning the restaurant was packed. The food was over-plentiful and had a sameness about it. It was proving too much for Rowan; she began to feel, that if she never saw fried chicken, potato crisps, french fries or hamburgers again for the rest of her life she would die content.

Aunt Abbie had a surprisingly good appetite for one so small. She enjoyed everything, whether it was food or hair-dos or driving or visiting friends and relatives. Her eyes were always as bright as a bird's except they weren't sharp like a bird's. They were round and soft and kept lighting up with childlike wonder. She never took offence at anything, not even back-seat drivers.

When Abbie was driving to the hairdressers', in between chatting to her, cousin Adeline kept saying things like 'You're going the wrong way, dear,' or 'Straight on, honey,' or 'Turn left at Broadway, dear.'

Rowan was getting worried about the heat. She couldn't imagine how it could possibly be hotter anywhere else. She lay sweating in her bed every night with only a sheet as covering and the window wide open, despite cousin Adeline's warning about prowlers. During the day, even first thing on a dull, cloudy morning it was hot. The ceiling fan was a necessity, never a luxury. She didn't like the insects that seemed to flourish in the heat. A huge beetle-like creature scuttled across cousin Adeline's sitting room carpet and made Rowan scream. Abbie said, 'It'll just be a cricket,' and stamped on it. Rowan had to look away.

The night before they set off for Nashville one of Abbie's friends took Abbie, Mary Beth and Rowan to dinner at a restaurant on the side of Lake Decatur.

Virginia and her husband Homer called for them in a long-bonneted black car, luxuriously upholstered inside.

Virginia was a high-powered businesswoman with blue eye shadow, stylishly cut hair and a nasal voice. Her baggy silk trouser suit was in different shades of blue and her flat Roman sandals revealed toes painted the same vivid scarlet as her finger-nails. She was also sporting more rings with bigger diamonds than Rowan had ever seen. Homer was equally startling in his salmon pink jacket and tie and white shirt and trousers. Rowan was shocked to discover he carried a gun.

'Maybe I don't need one so much in Decatur,' he admitted. 'Unless you're on foot of course. I always have one on me if Ginny and I go for a walk around here.'

The place didn't look menacing. They relaxed out on the softly lit verandah gazing at the dark shimmering water and sipping drinks made of ice cream and peppermint, called grasshoppers.

Homer said, 'Down South now – that's different.'

'Why?' Rowan asked.

'There's a kind of rage, a desire to kill down there. It gets to you.'

'It's true,' Virginia agreed. 'Underneath that sleepy, Southern hospitality, underneath all the love and kisses, there's a violent passion.' Rowan didn't like the sound of it.

'Willard gave his gun away,' Abbie announced. Then, for Rowan's benefit, 'That's Mary Beth's daddy.'

'Why'd he do that?' Homer asked.

'He was afraid if he'd an available pistol he'd kill somebody. Even Willard, who's one of the mildest men you ever could meet, says he's got this rage inside him, this wanting to kill somebody.'

'Maybe it's the heat,' Rowan ventured and everybody laughed although she hadn't meant to be funny. Although she couldn't help laughing herself when Homer told her about the 'red-necks' down South. His favourite description of them he said was that they were size 48 in jackets and size 3 in hats.

Next day they took a 'plane to Nashville. Abbie's grey

244

Buick had been hired and she had to leave it at the local hire office.

'I won't worry,' she told Rowan, 'I've a Buick of my own in Nashville. I'll drive you all over the place.'

'I'm not going for a good time or for sight-seeing,' Rowan said hastily. 'I want to get involved with the Civil Rights Movement.'

'You're going to the right place. With Bessie, I mean. She'll have you plum in the middle of the action. They won't let me. Bessie and Willard say I'm too old. I showed 'em!' Abbie chuckled. 'I've got a newspaper photo I'll let you see. It's me being dragged off by two big fellas, policemen. I'm laying about them with my umbrella. That was before I broke my leg.' She chuckled again. 'Now I'll be able to use my cane.'

'You'll do no such thing,' Mary Beth scolded. 'Mama's right. You just leave this fight to us youngah folk, you heah?'

'I've never been a quitter in my life,' Abbie said, 'and I sure ain't going to start now!'

They had a good flight, touching down at Louisville on the way. Rowan felt excited. She had put her worries about the heat out of her mind, believing Abbie who said, 'No need to worry about the heat, it's always cooler in Nashville at this time of year.'

As soon as she stepped off the plane at Nashville, however, it was like suddenly walking into a red-hot oven. Rowan felt beads of sweat immediately begin to trickle down her face and chest.

'Hi y'all!' A tall, well-made woman in a cotton print dress greeted them.

Abbie said, 'That's Amy Lou, one of Willard's sisters.'

'Willard and Bessie aren't back from a meetin',' Amy Lou explained with a lazy smile. She looked a very relaxed person altogether. 'So it's jes little ole me. Nevah mind. Y'all see them latah.'

They piled into Amy Lou's car and Rowan discovered that she was almost as hair-raising a driver as Abbie but in a different way. She lay back with one hand on the wheel and one arm along the back of Abbie's seat. (Abbie sat next to her in the front.) She kept looking back as she leisurely chatted.

'Rowan? That's a pretty name. This the first time you've been in the good ol' US of A?' Rowan was keeping an anxious eye on the traffic. Amy Lou however wasn't bothering about a thing. 'My, my! Y'all look jes' fine. How've you been Mary Beth? Had a good trip, honey?'

Mary Beth told her of some of the countries she'd visited and Amy Lou was suitably impressed. 'You don't mean it? Did you evah?'

Mary Beth's home was a two-storied 'frame' house standing in quite a large area of somewhat unkept grass. A wide rough-stone path led up to a side door. Rowan noticed a round gazebo with three white wrought-iron-work tables and matching chairs. One table had a dirty glass and an open book on it.

'Keep clear of the grass when you get out,' Mary Beth warned.

Abbie said, 'It's the chiggahs.'

'What's chiggers?' Rowan asked.

'Little red devils that bite you and burrow under your skin.' Rowan didn't like the sound of that either. She stepped quickly from the car on to the wooden porch.

'Theahs Willard's car,' Amy Lou said, 'your mothah and fathah must be home, Mary Beth. They'll give y'all a Suthan welcome.'

Sure enough both Willard and Bessie came to the door and warmly embraced Mary Beth and Abbie and Rowan. Then after they were shown their bedrooms and allowed to freshen up they returned downstairs for a long cooling drink.

In the sitting room they were introduced to a friend of Willard and Bessie who'd also been at the meeting. He was called Steve Jackson. A tall slim man in blue jeans and blue open-necked shirt, he rose to greet them.

Rowan knew, although nothing was said except the normal words of introduction, that from the moment their hands touched and she looked into his eyes, her entire life, for better or for worse, had changed.

36

Jenny became totally absorbed in preparation for the dinner party. First of all she asked to visit the Donovan household a couple of days before the event, in order to familiarize herself with the layout of the place and where everything was kept. Rory gave her a key and told her to wander about all day if she wished. She found, as she suspected, that because it was a large Victorian villa like Hazel's the layout was very similar.

The huge kitchen was situated downstairs at the back of the house and there were several smaller rooms leading off it, including a scullery with its own shallow stone sink, draining board and wooden draining racks. There was also a walk-in butler's pantry and a housekeeper's parlour. In Victorian times, when staff was plentiful and easy to come by, the running of a large house like this would be strictly regimented. For a start the male and female servants would be kept apart. The male indoor servants would be under the command of the butler whose duties included the care of the silver and the responsibility for the wine cellar. The kitchenmaids would take their orders from the cook and the housemaids from the housekeeper. The housekeeper's room was always placed, as this one was, within sight of the kitchen entrance and the back door of the house to enable her to supervise the work and the behaviour of the girls for whom she was responsible. Here were situated the housekeeper's spacious cupboards in which were kept special luxury items of food, a variety of spices, jars of preserves, and bottles of homemade wine. The keys to the cupboards would hang on the steel châtelaine the housekeeper wore round her waist. Those days, of course, were long gone and Jenny found none of the cupboards locked.

She decided, after admiring several dinner services, that on the day of the party she would set the table with the Wedgwood 'pearlware'; this was an improved version of creamware and had a delicate leafy border enclosed in a gold rim. She looked out the silver cruets, napkin rings and cutlery and worried about whether to use one of the beautiful white tablecovers or to have place settings on mats. She thought out an original design for a central floral arrangement. She drew plans and took notes until Rory said airily, 'Don't worry about it. No need for anything fancy. A couple of the guests happen to have titles but that doesn't mean they can't enjoy good plain food. And of course you know Al.'

'Alaister Gregson?' Jenny had to feel for a chair and sit down. 'He's going to be there?'

'Yes, and John MacFarlane and his wife. You'll have seen John on television.'

Jenny shook her head.

'Don't tell me that place you're in still hasn't got a television set?'

'Rebecca believes it takes up too much of people's time,' she said absently.

'She believes in relaxation, doesn't she? What better way is there to relax after a hard day's graft?'

Jenny shrugged. 'That's not the kind of relaxation she means.'

'She sees it as competition to her and the daft schemes she gets all of you involved in.'

Jenny was hardly listening to her. The thought of Gregson being at the dinner deeply disturbed her. Automatically she tugged up and tightly closed the drawbridge to her emotions. She had had as much as she could stand from men. What she must do now was learn how to protect herself against them. That's what Rebecca had said and Rebecca was right. To help banish Gregson from her mind she forced herself to concentrate on the preparation for the dinner. She made up and scrapped several menus before finally deciding on:

Asparagus and Orange Soup
Fresh Salmon en Croûte
Drambuie Syllabub
Homemade Petits-fours
Coffee

All her attention from then on was firmly focused on her cooking. Only the occasional ripple of excitement managed to crack the surface of her emotional control.

The women at the refuge were interested in the proceedings and looked forward to hearing a blow-by-blow report of what each guest looked like, what they talked about ('Listen at the dining-room door', Jenny was urged), and if they enjoyed the food. Donovan, Rory's husband, was away on an assignment so the party was just to be made up of Rory and her guests.

To Jenny's surprise Rebecca was more carried away than any of them. 'Sir Ian Russell is on the Board of Directors of several firms,' she enthused, 'and he's well-known for the money he's given to charity. Get talking to him. Interest him in the refuge and he might help us financially.'

'I won't get a chance to talk to any of the guests,' Jenny told her, 'I'll be far too busy.'

'Anyway,' Hazel had pointed out, 'it wouldn't be the done thing, Rebecca. Jenny will be there as a servant, don't forget.'

Rebecca had then turned her attention on Amelia. At the next meeting of the 'How to Find Your Personal Power Spots' class she'd tackled her. 'Speak to your mother-in-law. Tell her you'd like to be invited to this dinner party.'

Amelia was horrified. 'I couldn't do that!'

'Why not?'

'She wouldn't want me to be there. Why do *you* want me to be there?' she added, suddenly curious.

'You could talk to Sir Ian. Interest him into donating some money. We need cash, not only to improve the

250

present running of the place but to build an extension so that we can accommodate more people.'

'Oh, I couldn't do that!' Amelia repeated.

Rebecca's passionate eyes began to smoulder with annoyance.

'You're forgetting your positive thinking again, Amelia. All my patient devotion to your welfare is once more being cast aside and thoughtlessly thrown to the winds.'

Amelia looked as if she was willing herself to disappear.

'No, it's not that. I mean . . .'

'Go on! Tell me what you mean!' Rebecca demanded. 'Stand erect, Amelia. Look me straight in the eye.'

Pinned under Rebecca's stare, Amelia squirmed. 'He's a complete stranger to me. I couldn't ask him for money, I just couldn't. Anyway, as I said, Rory wouldn't want me there.'

'Nonsense!' Rebecca brushed Amelia's words aside. 'You've been at your mother-in-law's house hundreds of times. Anyway she couldn't refuse her son, could she?'

'Well, no but . . .'

'If you tell her Douglas wants to be there, you would be included in the invitation.'

'But Douglas *wouldn't* want to be there. He's not interested in his mother's business associates. We never go to her dinner parties because they're always given for business reasons. Our visits to Rory are more informal – just family occasions.'

'Do you believe in the urgent necessity of this refuge, Amelia?'

'Oh, yes. . . .'

'Do you believe that I do my best for every woman who comes to me for help?'

'Yes, of course. . . .'

'Have I done my best to help you?'

'Oh yes, I'm most grateful to you Rebecca. Your encouragement and emotional support is terribly important to me.'

251

'Then now is your chance to show your gratitude, Amelia. Now is your chance to return that support.'

Amelia did not say any more. She looked as if she had retreated far away to another world where she could just concentrate on worrying and being anxious. Afterwards she said to Jenny, 'I'd like to help Rebecca, but I don't see how I can – especially about money. I feel bad enough when I'm forced to ask Douglas for money. I've to act all silly and butter him up and keep apologizing for myself. It's so humiliating, I feel I die a little each time.'

Jenny didn't really want her attention diverted or diffused by Amelia's worries at that moment, she had enough worries of her own. But she managed in a slightly harassed voice, 'I don't suppose Rebecca meant to go cap in hand and ask Sir Ian outright for money. She said to interest him in the refuge. Tell him about all the good work etcetera and what a struggle Rebecca has at times to make ends meet. But if you and Douglas are going to be at this dinner I'll have to know about it as soon as possible, Amelia. I'm planning for six at the moment, not eight.'

She had decided on a damask linen tablecover. Its starched surface had a rich shine and would be a beautiful accompaniment to sparkling crystal and ornate silver. The centrepiece would be a low round bowl filled with roses and foliage. She had cooked at the refuge every day and it had stimulated her interest and roused her to try her best to produce cheap but enjoyable meals. Here, however, money was no object; only the challenge of catering for people with sophisticated tastes, people no doubt with experience in eating at first-class restaurants. At the back of her mind, however, the truth was she needed to impress Al Gregson. She kept flashing warning signals at herself. She kept telling herself she mustn't allow herself to be vulnerable. She daren't. Nevertheless she knew this was what was motivating her more than anything.

'The menu I've chosen,' she had explained to Rory, 'is

comparatively simple. What I'm depending on is the *quality* of the cooking, the actual taste of each dish.'

'Relax!' Rory laughed. 'It's not a cooking exam, love, only a small dinner party. If they don't like it they can lump it!' But Jenny couldn't relax.

When the great day dawned she awakened on a wave of excitement. She felt she had so much energy she couldn't stay still. Although it was far too early and no one else had stirred she had to get up. She dressed quietly in order not to disturb Sadie who was lying on her back, grey as a corpse but snoring in short spasmodic bursts. Picking her way over between chairs and trunks and abandoned lampshades she reached the attic window and sat gazing from it for a few minutes. A mist was shrouding the park and reaching out grey fingers to caress the monument.

Jenny's excitement suddenly evaporated at the thought of her family, Joe, Dode and Rose, asleep at the other side of the park. So near and yet so far away. She experienced such painful loneliness and confusion it frightened her. She felt sad too. What has happened to us all? she thought. With an effort she turned her attention away from the window and crept downstairs through the silent house to make herself a cup of tea.

The number expected at the dinner party was still six. Amelia had not attempted to be included among the guests for dinner but she had managed to persuade Douglas that they should drop in afterwards for a drink.

'Even that wasn't easy,' she'd explained to Jenny. 'There was something on TV he wanted to watch. It was an absolute torment to persuade him to go out instead – I had to humiliate myself, coaxing and wheedling and fawning around. Douglas enjoys me doing that, you know, he practically had me going down on my knees.' She had trembled at the memory of herself. 'I hate him when he makes me act like that, I really hate him!'

Jenny was sitting in the kitchen sipping a cup of tea when Rebecca appeared fresh from her invigorating cold dip in the bath. She had tried to persuade the other women to copy this drastic method of whipping up the circulation and purifying the blood, so far without success.

'Aren't you eating anything?' Rebecca asked.

'I'm so nervous. I hope everything's going to be all right.'

'Of course it will, dear. Why shouldn't it?'

Jenny hesitated. 'It's not the cooking. There's a man . . . one of the guests . . .'

'Yes, dear?'

'I've met him two or three times before and he's written to me while he's been abroad. He's a very persistent type. Rose told me he'd been at the house asking for me, although I warned him never to come to the door again. He did that before you see. I nearly died of fright.'

'Oh dear,' Rebecca sighed. 'Poor Jenny! Some people are just born victims.'

'Please don't say that.'

'It's true.'

'It's just I find him attractive.'

'Like you found Joe attractive?'

'Oh, but he's different from Joe.'

'Is he? In what way, dear?'

'He's heavier built than Joe and he has very dark hair and green eyes.'

'Now, now Jenny. You know what I mean, dear.'

Jenny bit her lip. 'All right. He's aggressive.'

'Poor Jenny!'

'Rebecca!'

'I can't help worrying about you, dear.'

'I know. I'm sorry.'

'You've not yet recovered from what Joe's made you suffer all these years. . . . Well, have you?'

Jenny shook her head. 'No. Oh no.'

'Well, then . . . I'll make some toast and you'll have a slice along with me.'

'I'll make it, Rebecca.'

'Sit down,' Rebecca commanded, 'you must conserve your strength.'

One of the reasons Jenny had suggested that she should attend to the toast was that she wouldn't make so much noise as Rebecca, who was likely to waken everyone else in the house. She did everything in grand dramatic gestures which in this case meant the reckless rattling of the bread bin and battering the toasting pan into the cooker.

'You'll be all right,' Rebecca said. 'I'll pray for you to be protected against this new threat, this new danger. While you're at the dinner I'll light a candle here and I'll sit on the floor in front of it and concentrate on you.' Rebecca settled down at the table and began enthusiastically buttering the toast. 'All I ask of you is that you keep your eye on Amelia. Don't let her wriggle out of keeping her promise.'

'Now she's going,' Jenny said, 'I'm sure she'll try her best to bring up the subject of the refuge.'

'Well, I hope so dear. This is our big chance, the more I think of it, the happier I feel. There's plenty of room at the back for a good sized extension – a two-tiered one could give us several extra rooms. With enough money I could also renovate and convert the existing building.'

'But . . .' Jenny hesitated.

'But what dear?'

'Even if Amelia does manage to broach the subject to Sir Ian there's surely no guarantee that he'll be interested.'

'It's up to Amelia to make sure he's not only interested but fascinated. Not only fascinated but eager to help. He has plenty of money to throw about. Why shouldn't he throw some in our direction? What better cause could he find than this? And who better than a professional storyteller to successfully tell the story of the place?'

'I'm sure Amelia will try her best,' Jenny repeated. She found it disturbing to see this new side of Rebecca.

There was a vulnerability about her happy enthusiasm. Her dreams of what she was going to do with money she hadn't got, and in Jenny's opinion hadn't the remotest chance of getting, were impracticable to the point of naïvety. For the first time, she felt sorry for Rebecca.

37

Harry, Dode and Rose jostled among the dense, dusty crowd at Paddy's Market. Dode and Rose were looking for second hand clothes. Their dad never seemed to think they needed any. Their mum couldn't afford to buy them clothes. Apparently their dad wasn't giving their mum any money.

'It's not that I want your mum to suffer,' he'd said. 'But anything I sent her would just go to that monstrous Abercrombie woman. I'd rather go to jail first.'

He nearly had because the Department of Health and Social Security had ordered him to pay up and warned him that if he didn't he would go to jail. In the end Dode's mum had pretended he was giving her the money rather than see him be shut up in prison. His dad liked open spaces – that's why he worked in the park. Dode's mum had confided in Dode that she was doing the occasional catering job to help keep herself. Dode said she looked much better and was beginning to talk about looking for a place of her own again. Dode and Rose lived in hope of that happening but at the same time they weren't optimistic. Harry felt sorry for Dode especially. His dad had begun to knock him about now. Rose was all right, she always escaped to a girl friend's house, often to stay overnight at weekends. Dode had nowhere to go. Harry would have liked (indeed had tried) to take Dode home to Mary House on Fridays and Saturdays when Mr Thornton got drunk but his own dad wouldn't have it.

'You're not bringing that dirty looking tramp in here!' he bawled. 'And that's that!'

He always angrily defended Dode but it only made his dad worse. Admittedly Dode did look a bit of a mess with his long greasy hair and grey unwashed face and odd ragbag of clothes. Dode always looked cold as well which explained his excitement and delight at finding the heavy ex-RAF coat in the market. Two unnatural blotches of colour fevered his cheeks as he tried it on.

'This is fab, man,' he told Harry. 'It's like being inside an electric fire.' He was short of sixpence to buy it and Harry managed to scrape it up in coppers. Dode wore the coat right away. It was far too long for him, reaching right down to his ankles. It was a bit on the wide side, as well, but Dode looked happy in it, that was the main thing.

Rose, who also looked pinched and cold, was success-ful in finding a red woollen scarf and gloves. She wound the scarf several times round her neck and smiled up at him.

'Think it suits me, Harry?'

It always embarrassed him the way she gazed up at him like a stray puppy dog hoping for a pat on the head.

'Oh sure, sure,' he said.

He thought the market must be jumping with fleas. He was beginning to itch all over. He'd heard that fleas preferred clean people and now he believed it. He'd had a shower earlier after his Karate class and his face, shining like a polished apple, reflected his pristine state. Since he'd found Karate he'd been attending classes three times a week. He was even more enthusiastic about Karate than he'd been about boxing or weight-training. He'd gone with his dad initially to a demonstration in the Langside Hall. He'd simply been curious to see what it was like. His dad was doing sketches of the different movements. Harry found the whole thing unexpectedly fascinating. He hadn't been prepared for the fastness of the movements or the flexibility and fitness of the exponents of the art. That's what it was – an art; a martial art.

He'd been enormously impressed with the steady rhythmic beat and the deep guttural sounds of the counting in Japanese: 'Eech, Nee, Son, Chi, Go. . . .'

258

His dad had been quite enthusiastic when he'd announced he fancied joining the Karate club. His dad had even bought him his Gi – the white, loose wrap-over top and baggy cotton trousers held up with a drawstring.

The more he heard about Dode's dad the more he felt he was lucky with his own. Of course, like most of the older generation he was a 'square' and definitely not 'with it'. Nevertheless he wasn't so bad. And despite being an artist, he was tough. Harry admired that. His grandfather Donovan was ancient (he must be at least 64) but he was even tougher. It felt good to come from a line of strong men. Sometimes he suspected that his dad encouraged him to be a hard man just to annoy his mum, but that was beside the point. The point was you daren't be a softie in Glasgow. There mustn't be any risk of him being like his mum – helpless and hopeless, utterly dependent, sometimes almost childlike. His dad said she'd get into even more trouble if she hadn't him to keep nagging at her. She was a worry in both their lives. His dad said she'd always been like that as far back as he could remember – getting herself into bad company and doing daft things.

At least since she'd been seeing the crank in Battlefield House she'd managed to kick the tranquillizers. Admittedly she now swallowed loads of herbal potions and pills instead, but as far as he knew they were harmless.

'This is my lucky day!' Dode said for the sixth or seventh time. He was so chuffed with his RAF coat. They were on their way to the local Cinema where a film called *Rock Around the Clock* starring Bill Haley and the Comets had at last reached the south side. Films from America always came to big London cinemas first, then after running there for an age, they moved to the small London cinemas before reaching the big cinemas in Central Glasgow.

Eventually (after another age) they reached the smaller halls. Harry and Dode could only afford the local cinemas but although they'd had a long wait to see *Rock Around the Clock* they'd heard plenty about it. They'd long ago read in newspapers how it caused cinema audiences to riot and rip out cinema seats and once outside on the street take part in orgies of vandalism. This knowledge added to their excited anticipation. Harry had been meaning to go to a Karate display with Danny Polson. The display was in Edinburgh and Danny's mum and dad were going to give Danny and Harry a lift. They originally belonged to Edinburgh and were meaning to visit relatives there. Unfortunately the Polsons developed 'flu and couldn't go. He couldn't afford to go on the train. So he'd just palled up with Dode instead. He didn't see so much of Dode and Rose these days. What with studying for his exams and also the keep-fit programme which now included Karate, he had very little free time. Anyway, he didn't have very much in common with Dode and Rose any more. They were more into music and smoking pot. Harry had more or less dropped out of the group, although he still joined up with them if the gig insisted on a threesome. Playing regularly in the group meant too many late nights. Nobody could keep in condition living like that. For most of the time now it was just Rose singing and Dode playing the guitar, which was a pity, of course, because Dode still preferred the drums.

They arrived at the picture house and joined the queue to get in. It was all young people making an impatient, restless buzz. At last they were past the paybox and plunging into the darkness of the hall. Then suddenly, the magic thing happened. As soon as the film started, the audience with one accord leapt to its feet and started bopping about like crazy to the music. Harry joyously joined in. He had never seen nor felt anything like it. It was the very breath of freedom. His youthful spirit soared up to the heavens along with everyone else's in the hall. With everyone else he laughed and shouted and sang as he wildly jerked and danced about.

260

One-two-three o'clock, four o'clock rock!
Five-six-seven o'clock, eight o'clock rock!
Nine-ten-eleven o'clock, twelve o'clock rock!
We're gonna rock around the clock tonight!

The words were yelled to a deafening, pistol-cracking
beat. It was a crude sound. It was a young sound. It
vibrated with highly-charged adolescent sexual energy.

Afterwards he and Dode and Rose continued the
joyous singing and wild gyrations all the way home. It
was a revelation. It was a releasing. It was how life could
be like. They had never felt so happy. They were so
happy and uninhibited they embraced each other when
they said goodnight at Dode's house. First he and Dode
hugged each other and then still laughing he swung Rose
high into his arms. It was when her slim body was sliding
down against his much more solid one that the surprising, embarrassing thing happened. He had an erection.
She must have felt it through her thin skirt. He had a
panicky struggle to get control of himself. He almost
threw her aside and with a hasty shout of ' 'Night you
guys,' he hurried off along the dark Queens Drive
towards Mary House. He felt deeply shaken and
ashamed of himself. Rose was only a kid. Anyway it was
surely a sign of weakness to show such lack of control.
Karate was very much into control, self-discipline and
body conditioning. There were the Katas, the sequence
of defensive movements that he practised with fast,
robotic efficiency. There was the Yaku Zuki, the special
kind of disciplined close-quarters punch where you
stood still, using hip action to punch instead of forward
movement. In body conditioning you actually used your
body as a target. You stood still, tensed yourself, focused
on your muscles while your partner hit you with different
techniques. He hit you as hard as you could possibly
bear so that gradually you could stand more pain.

He tried to discipline himself as he hurried along but
his body and his mind had been thrown into confusion.

It was terrible. Yet there was a shivering pleasure and excitement about it, too. In his imagination all sorts of forbidden thoughts and secret indulgences were born. They took on a lusty life of their own.

That night in bed he had a wet dream.

38

Rebecca stood, a proud, erect figure beside the flagpole at the highest point in the park.

The breeze whipped at her long skirts and made them ripple and crack and flounce about like the flag that fluttered high above her. Her world, Glasgow and the hills beyond, spread out at her feet. She felt light-headed with exhilaration and very close to God. He had opened her eyes and showed her the way ahead. She was destined to follow the path of service to her sister women, but on a much bigger and more important scale than she had ever done before. It was unfortunate that in this world worldly, material things were needed. As a result she must work courageously to gather in enough money and people of influence to make her destiny come to proper fruition.

Elvira was abroad on holiday at the moment but Rebecca had every faith that, once she returned to Scotland, she would be willing to lend her well-known and respected name to the cause. It would look very impressive on headed notepaper for instance. Rebecca could see it in her mind's eye: 'The Rebecca Abercrombie Refuge For Abused Women' (or, 'Women in Need' perhaps?) 'Patrons, Elvira Fortescue-Brown and Sir Ian Russell.' Well, why not? she asked herself. Why shouldn't people of this calibre agree to give their patronage to such a good cause? And why shouldn't Sir Ian give money? She was willing to devote her life and give everything she possessed.

Suddenly she experienced a crack in the positive euphoria she had been enjoying. For no apparent reason she remembered her mother. Her plump mother. 'No, not plump, Rebecca – generously moulded,' her mother used to say as, hands on hips, she'd proudly admired her curvaceous figure in the wardrobe mirror. Her mother had worn pink, boned corsets and lace-edged drawers and garters. She'd liked floral print dresses with low necklines and pretty earrings and hair clasps and cloche hats – and she'd liked buying her daughter pretty things too. Rebecca suspected, looking back, that her mother often spent more than she could afford buying pretty trinkets and clothes for her.

'I don't know where you came from Rebecca,' she used to laugh. 'You're not a bit like either your dad or me with that mop of black hair and those great dark eyes, but I'm real proud of you.'

Her mother used to take her everywhere with her and never tired of showing her off or of boasting about what a good, clever girl she was and later when she became a teenager, 'the best daughter a mother ever had.'

Suddenly Rebecca remembered why her mother must have come into her mind. They used to go to Pollok Park because it was nearer to where they lived in Pollokshaws. One day however, her mother had some reason to come to the Queens Park area and she said, 'Let's explore this park for a change.'

What a day it had been. They'd had a turn on the paddle boats on the pond – how they'd both squealed with laughter and splashed water on each other. Afterwards they'd strolled through the pleasant walled garden with fragrant plants rainbowing all around them and flowering cherry trees and azaleas that had never looked so lovely. Then they'd climbed up to the summit of the park, first admiring the circle of stones near the flagpole. The stones were the remnants of a military encampment of the sixteenth century.

'This park's dedicated to Mary, Queen of Scots,' her mother had told her. 'And this is where the battle raged.' Then she'd laughed. 'Come to think of it, you're more like her – you're going to be real tall when you grow up. The Queen was nearly 6 foot tall and black-headed. I've read that in a book and seen her picture. You're my wee Queenie.' She'd given Rebecca an enthusiastic hug. 'Isn't this great?' They'd stood beside the flagpole exactly where she was standing now. Her mother had kept her arm around her and added, 'Just you and me, Rebecca. We don't need anyone else, do we?'

They had been such good friends. Rebecca closed her eyes. Dear God, she thought, poor mother. Oh, my poor mother!

It was always the same when she was alone; the past would unexpectedly catch up on her. She couldn't bear it. If only she hadn't uttered those last cruel words to her mother. But no amount of wishing would ever take them back.

She strode away from the flagpole, out of the park and across the road to Battlefield House, head up, eyes shining with unshed tears. She struggled to comfort herself by remembering that Alice had assured her that her mother knew she hadn't meant what she'd said, that her mother had understood that she had just been upset. Her mother had contacted Alice several times in order to reassure her. 'Tell my Queenie not to worry,' she'd said. 'She's still my good, clever girl. The best daughter a mother ever had.' Alice said her mother had understood her work, too, and was very proud that God had chosen her for this purpose.

As Rebecca let herself into the house she took comfort from this and from the fact that Sadie and Hazel and Milly were in. Hazel and Milly had become close friends and were at the moment in the sitting room playing a game of two-handed bridge. Rebecca felt her confident, positive self again as she observed with satisfaction how both women had improved under her care. Hazel had recovered all her looks – and she was a very good looking, in fact rather a glamorous, woman. Milly was still a bit stiff and prim and proper but she was very much more relaxed than she used to be.

Sadie was trying to chat to them and unwittingly spoiling their game.

'Sadie, dear,' Rebecca said, 'why don't you and I go through to the kitchen and make a nice cup of tea.' She shepherded the old woman out of the room and through the hall.

Poor, undersized Sadie with her one and only frock – a shabby black that she always kept protected in the house with a cotton wrap-around apron. Both dress and apron were long to cover as much as possible of her legs that were bent to the shape of a full moon as a result of rickets suffered in childhood. Her husband was always throwing her out on to the streets; she'd often slept rough on one of the benches in the park. She kept insisting it wasn't the drink and most of the time he was as nice as ninepence. If it wasn't drunken rages that made him behave as he did however, he must be mentally deranged, Rebecca decided. Anyway, as Sadie said herself, 'I'm too old for park benches now, Rebecca. It was going to be the death of me if you hadn't taken me in.'

While they were waiting for the kettle to boil Rebecca said, 'You'll enjoy having lots more people here won't you, dear?'

'How? What have you been up to now, Rebecca?'

'What an odd thing to say, Sadie, I haven't been up to anything. But I'm planning to expand these premises so that I can accommodate many more residents. I told you.'

'Probably you did, Rebecca, I've a mind like a sieve these days. The funny thing is I can't remember what happened yesterday but I can mind everything about years back. I can remember as if it was yesterday getting married and moving into my nice wee room and kitchen. I was right proud of that place. Little did I think then that one day Rab Gourley would be living there on his own and I'd be in an institution.'

Rebecca was shocked. 'This isn't an institution! What a terrible thing to say.'

266

'Well, you know what I mean, Rebecca.'

'No, I do not, Sadie. I always try my very best to make all my friends feel absolutely at home here. And if any of them don't like the refuge they're absolutely free to leave at any time.'

'Och, I know, I know. You're a real gem,' Sadie looked suddenly anxious, 'and I'm just a daft old woman. My tongue runs away with me at times. I don't know what I'd do without you and this place.'

'It *was* the drink wasn't it?' Rebecca had always been annoyed by Sadie's refusal to say a word against her husband. She'd managed to keep her tongue from running away with her about him all right!

Sadie hesitated unhappily.

'Well?' Rebecca demanded – after all, she was open and honest with her friends, it was the least they could do in return.

'No.' Sadie sighed. 'It was other women. Not that I blame him. I've never blamed him.'

'Why on earth not?'

'Och, look at me, Rebecca. A bandy-legged, wee bachle. I never knew what he saw in me in the first place. He's a fine looking big man, my Rab.' She sighed again. 'I was always prepared for him to turn to other women but not for him bringing them into the house.'

Rebecca rolled her eyes. 'Sadie, I'm going to fit you in my appointments diary for a hypnotherapy session. We'll see if we can change your self-image.'

Sadie laughed then. 'It would take a lot more than hypnotherapy to change the way I look, Rebecca. Anyway you know fine I've only got my old age pension and I hand over all of that to you for my keep.'

'It's little enough to keep you, Sadie,' Rebecca said stiffly, 'and I give you back pocket money, don't forget.'

'I'm not complaining, Rebecca.' The anxiety strained at Sadie's face again. 'No, never. God forbid that I should be so ungrateful. All I meant was I couldn't pay you for your hypnotherapy.'

Rebecca gave a careless flick of her hand. 'If I can help you to feel happier and more content that's enough reward for me.'

'You're a real gem,' Sadie repeated fervently. 'A real gem, so you are!'

'And so say all of us!' Hazel laughed as she came strolling into the kitchen with Milly.

'I only do my best to fulfill the purpose God created me for,' Rebecca said modestly.

But her cheerful spirits had totally returned and she hummed a happy tune as she swept across the room to help herself to a cream cake from the fridge.

39

'The table looks a treat,' Rory said. 'How did you manage to make such shapes with the napkins? They're a work of art.'

Jenny flushed with pleasure. 'I enjoy doing it.'

'I can see you're enjoying yourself. Your eyes are sparkling, you've really come to life again.'

'I'm feeling much better, thanks.'

'How do I look?' Rory asked, flicking out her long dress. 'It's a Balenciaga model. Like it?'

Jenny gazed with admiration at the black lace top with the off-the-shoulder neckline and heavy cream silk skirt.

'It's stunning!'

Rory lit up a cigarette. 'You look very nice yourself, Jenny. I'd forgotten how pretty you were.'

'Pretty?' Jenny laughed. 'Me? You must be joking!'

'Of course I'm not joking – you have pretty hair, clear skin and sexy eyes.'

Joe had often said this about her eyes in their earlier and happier days and the memory caused her pain. She turned away from Rory to survey the room with its solid mahogany furniture, wood-panelled walls and Turkey carpet laid on the polished boards. The long table stood in the centre of the room and she had to admit to herself that it looked absolutely superb. It smelled nice too; the delicate fragrance of roses and fresh crisp linen blended sweetly with the other more pungent aroma of wax floor polish.

In the kitchen everything was equally well organized, all ready and waiting. She had changed from her working skirt and blouse into a slim-fitting turquoise dress and a single strand of pearls that had once belonged to her granny McBride. Instinctively she had discarded any idea of wearing black or anything that would, at an occasion like this, suggest a uniform. Although she was going to be serving the meal she would have refused to wear a cap and apron even if Rory had asked her to do so. Not that she had any snobbish ideas – on the contrary, she often used to think that if by some miracle she ever did have a restaurant of her own she would not allow anyone in her employ to wear caps and aprons. She believed in giving a sense of dignity and individuality to the job.

Rory had no snobbish ideas either and when the doorbell rang she blithely went to answer it herself, despite the fact that she had engaged a new housekeeper since Winnie, her old housekeeper of many years, had died. The new housekeeper was called Kath, a plump, good-natured woman who had been busy during the day making sure the house was looking its best but was now quite happy to keep out of the way. 'I'll be in my parlour if you need me,' she'd told Jenny.

Jenny, however, had everything well organized by the time Rory rang the bell for the soup to be served. She was somewhat taken aback though when Rory cheerfully introduced her to the guests.

'This is Jenny, folks, she's doing me a real favour tonight helping me out. She cooks like a dream. You've met already, of course, Al.'

'Yes. How are you, Jenny?'

'I'm fine, thanks.' Jenny gave him a brief smile and continued to dish the steaming soup, then before quitting the room said to everyone, 'Enjoy your meal.'

Gregson's sea-green eyes never left her until she shut the door. She found his attention disturbing. Back in the kitchen her mind kept wandering back to him instead of fixing her full concentration on what she was doing.

Mary and Bella, the kitchenmaids from 'Rory's' canteen, had washed up the cooking utensils and were now leaning with their backs against the sink, arms folded, waiting for the dirty soup plates. They were laughing and chattering. Jenny had thought earlier that they were an unnecessary distraction that she could have well done without. Now, however, she barely heard them. Her cheeks still tingled at the probing stare that Gregson had subjected her to.

She had forgotten his air of easy confidence and the sensuous glimmer in his eyes. Every time he looked at her he seemed to be thinking about the intimacies of their lovemaking. A very expensive-looking gold watch glittered against the tanned skin of his wrist and when he raised his wine glass Jenny noticed the hard-looking muscles of his arm and remembered the thrill of being held by him.

Each time Gregson's eyes met hers she had the same chemical reaction. Other men round the table, Sir Ian Russell and John MacFarlane were also very presentable men and they too looked at her with interest and admiration. Under their gaze, however, she felt nothing.

She had to force herself to go back to top up the wine glasses, not because she didn't want to – she was enjoying the evening and was keen to make sure everything went smoothly and well. It was just she hadn't expected to have to cope with a fluttering pulse and burning cheeks and general oversensitivity to Gregson. She'd never wanted to be at the mercy of any other man as long as she lived. She still felt she'd had more than enough of men. All she wanted was to find herself, explore her capabilities, do her own thing.

Back in the kitchen after serving the salmon en croûte and accompanying vegetables she tried taking the deep, calming breaths that Rebecca always advised. Only they failed on this occasion to bring the slightest calmness.

Damn! Damn! Damn! she thought.

Later, as she poured the coffee and passed Gregson a cup his hand touched hers and immediately sent her nervous system into chaos. The guests were enthusiastic in their praise of the meal.

271

'You're an artist, my dear,' Lady Russell smiled. 'I have never tasted such a light and delicious pastry or such a smooth and delicately flavoured syllabub.'

'And those petits-fours!' John MacFarlane rolled his eyes in appreciation.

'Why don't you start a restaurant?' Mrs MacFarlane asked.

'I told her she could make a fortune,' Rory said.

Jenny thanked them and said she was glad they enjoyed the meal. Then she escaped back to the kitchen. She had originally planned to relax and have something to eat herself there; perhaps even wait until the guests had gone and enjoy a chat with Rory about how successful everything had been. Now she just wanted to get away as quickly as possible. Leaving Mary and Bella to clear up she hurried through the moonlit streets hardly aware of what direction she was taking.

It wasn't until she was nearly at Battlefield House that she remembered Amelia and Douglas were going to drop in to Rory's for drinks after dinner. She'd promised Rebecca she'd stay and keep a discreet eye on Amelia and remind her to bring up the subject of the refuge to Sir Ian. It had gone completely out of her head. Her feet slowed as she approached the house. She had been looking forward to recounting to Rebecca and the other women every detail of the evening. Now she no longer wanted to share it with anyone.

She decided not to go through to the kitchen but slip straight upstairs to bed. Rebecca must have been listening for her key in the door, however. She pounced on her in the hall.

'Did Amelia speak to him? Come on through to the kitchen and tell us all about it.'

In the kitchen Milly and Sadie and Hazel were eagerly waiting round the table.

'I've made a jug of Horlicks,' Milly said. 'I find it helps me to relax. Shall I pour you some, Jenny?'

Jenny nodded.

'Is there something wrong?' Rebecca asked. 'Surely everything went well. I cannot imagine you producing a bad meal, dear – I simply refuse to believe that there was anything wrong with the meal.'

'No, no.' Jenny made a desperate attempt to pull herself together. 'They all enjoyed it. Lady Russell said she'd never tasted anything like it.'

'I knew it!' Rebecca beamed. 'Good for you, dear. Well done!'

'I bet it was really posh,' Sadie said. 'They'd be dressed up to the nines, were they? Tell us what they had on.'

Jenny went into some detail about Rory's dress, then Lady Russell's elegant silk jersey gown that hung in folds like a romanesque sculpture and Mrs MacFarlane's peach satin creation that showed a daring amount of cleavage.

'What about the gentlemen?' Hazel asked. 'They would be wearing dinner jackets and black bow-ties of course. I always feel men look terribly attractive in dinner suits.'

'This Horlicks is delicious,' Jenny murmured in between appreciative sips. 'I was so busy with everything at Rory's place I didn't take time for a cup of tea.'

Milly shook her head. 'I don't believe I could ever have anything to do with another man, no matter how attractive he looked. I immediately tense up in any man's presence, I feel quite sick.'

'And no wonder, dear, with what you suffered from that monster,' Rebecca told her. Then, to Jenny, 'What was Sir Ian like?'

Jenny struggled to remember. 'Grey hair, grey moustache, a soft cultured voice but his eyes reminded me of Rory's. She's awfully nice and friendly but there's something about her eyes that tells you she's an astute business woman. I can't see Sir Ian parting with money very easily.'

'But he does, dear,' Rebecca cried out, 'he does! I read

273

in the paper not long ago he'd given thousands of pounds to the University. There's to be a Sir Ian Russell Lecture there each year from now on.'

Jenny shrugged. 'I'm just telling you my impression of him.'

'How did Amelia get on?' Rebecca asked. 'I hope she said her piece about the refuge.'

'I'm sorry, I don't know what happened about that. I had to leave before she arrived. But she's promised to come tomorrow and tell you how she got on, hasn't she?'

'Yes, that's true. Oh, wouldn't it be marvellous to be able to accommodate more people here. So many poor women need a roof over their heads in an emergency – when they've nowhere else to turn to for help and comfort.' Rebecca sighed. 'And if I could afford it we could publicize the refuge and the good work that's done here, so that everyone would be aware of it . . . the newspapers, radio, television. . . .'

Jenny could see by the dreamy expression now glazing Rebecca's eyes that she was already enjoying the benefits and the kudos of Sir Ian's financial help and patronage.

She sincerely hoped that Rebecca would not be disappointed. But when Jenny eventually managed to escape upstairs to bed in the dormitory and lay pretending to be asleep, it was Al Gregson she was thinking about, not Sir Ian Russell, or Rebecca Abercrombie.

40

Steve Jackson told Rowan in his husky drawl that if she was determined to accompany Mary Beth on the 'sit-in' she ought to go to the preparatory classes.

'Even those,' he said, 'are not foah the faint of heart. I don't believe you know what you are getting into, Rowan.' He was a professor at the local University, lean and tough looking with thoughtful eyes, and a keen intelligence about his hard-boned face.

'I understand what it's all about, if that's what you mean,' Rowan said. She knew, for instance, that although it was a struggle in which the black people were leading the way, everyone of good will who wanted to support them, was seeking to rid America of the scourge of racial segregation and discrimination, not only at lunch counters but in every aspect of life.

Since her arrival in Nashville she'd met and spoken with both white friends of Mary Beth's mother and black students from the university. She'd heard about the Brown versus Board of Education ruling that said in effect that segregation was unconstitutional.

But this Supreme Court decision against segregation, like most others supposedly upholding the democratic rights of the negro population, had become merely scraps of paper gathering dust and cobwebs. They were not being enforced in the Southern States.

She'd heard of beatings and shootings and lynchings of black people and how the perpetrators of these atrocities were either never brought to justice or, time after time, their cases were dismissed and they'd walked free. It all seemed so incredibly unfair and undemocratic it didn't seem real. She believed what people were telling her. Yet at the same time she couldn't believe it.

She wrote to her mother about cases of Freedom Riders who had been attacked and beaten by mobs in which it was the victims, not the attackers, who'd been arrested. 'As if that wasn't unfair and undemocratic enough, in court while an attorney was trying to defend them one judge literally turned his back on the defence attorney. Then when the attorney had stopped speaking the judge turned to face the court to immediately pronounce the defendants guilty . . . . It makes me so angry, Mother. . . .'

'People here keep asking me,' Abbie said, 'why Northerners – especially white people – take to do with something that doesn't concern them and I tell them that injustice anywhere is everybody's concern.'

Rowan wholeheartedly agreed with this. She wrote her mother, 'If somebody like Abbie is game to take an active part in any kind of demonstration why should I who am so much younger and fitter not join in? I know you would want me to do whatever I could, Mother. . . .'

One of the things Rowan admired about the black people of the Southern movement, especially Dr Martin Luther King's movement, was that people like herself, turning up from no place or every place and expressing a desire to participate and work with them were readily welcomed and given something to do and made to feel they were meaningfully participating. She'd already made several young black friends, Linda Mae Johnson and Essie Jean Lampton among them. Linda Mae's daddy was a Baptist minister and Essie Jean's was a lawyer. Rowan had been impressed by their quiet dignity and impeccable manners. She'd been to visit at Essie Jean's house and had been given tea by her momma who was a pretty and gracious woman in a gauzy cream-coloured dress. The men fulfilled Rowan's concept of perfect Southern gentlemen. She wrote indignantly to Hazel:

Can you credit it, Mother? People like the Johnsons and Lamptons are not allowed to sit at lunch

276

counters or restaurants, have to use different toilets and wash basins from whites, aren't allowed to use water fountains reserved for whites, have to sit at the back of buses or give up their seats to white people, have to submit to being called apes and niggers by white bus drivers. Often when they pay their fares to the driver at the front entrance he drives off and leaves them before they've time to get in at the back. I keep asking myself – is this really America, the land of freedom I was taught about in school?

The next day Rowan, Mary Beth, their black girl friends and a black male student called Thomas were delegated to sit in at Woolworth's lunch counter. They were to go early and after making one or two small purchases at other counters as planned they then approached the lunch counter and each hitched themselves on to one of the high stools.

Immediately the waitress came up and said to Linda Mae, 'I'm sorry, we don't serve coloured here.'

Ignoring this, Linda Mae said, 'I would like a slice of pecan pie and a cup of coffee please.'

The waitress repeated that she couldn't serve coloured. Then Essie Jean ordered cherry pie and Thomas asked for apple. They were also refused. Then, as they had practised at the workshop, they asked to see the manager, engaged him in conversation and brought up the fact that it was immoral to discriminate against people because of the colour of their skin. Then they quietly left. Next day they remained sitting at the counter without being served for hours, until in fact, it was time for the store to shut. It was planned that if at any time anyone was arrested, other young protestors would take their place, and so on, and so on. Rowan had been sitting in for four days before she met Jackson again. She'd bumped into him in the street. He said he'd already phoned Willard's place but of course she hadn't been in. He asked if he could take her out to dinner that night. She said 'Yes' and felt far more nervous about going to meet him than she'd been at the sit-ins. He had such a penetrating, intelligent stare.

Later, after they'd ordered their meal he asked how the sit-ins were going.

She shrugged. 'No problem. It's been almost funny in a way. The waitresses are as nervous as us. They keep dropping dishes.'

'I'm told that period is called testing the lunch countahs,' Jackson said.

'That's right. Tomorrow everyone, about 200 of us, white and black together are marching through the town. It'll be our first concentrated effort. We'll tackle all the main city stores at once.'

He smiled at her enthusiasm. 'I hope all goes well.'

'Oh, I'm sure it will. There's such dedication – such total commitment.'

It was then he put his hand over hers. She felt at once surprised and confused by the thrill that his touch immediately triggered off.

'Take cahah, honey,' he said gently.

She gave a careless toss of her pony-tail and withdrew her hand.

'You're quite a Jeremiah, aren't you?'

His eyes acquired a film of hardness.

'I've lived in the South longah than you.'

She hated herself for creating the small distance between them just as they were beginning to get close. She had no idea why she'd acted in such a cutting, almost impertinent manner. She had always felt at ease and behaved perfectly naturally with men before. Then it occurred to her that she hadn't actually been out with any mature men before. It had only been boys she'd known in the past.

'I didn't mean to sound a know-all,' she said miserably.

He had the most wonderful slow smile that reflected deeply and tenderly in his eyes. 'I didn't mean to sound a

278

Jeremiah. But I guess I did. I'm concerned about you, that's all.'

It was all right after that. She asked him about his background and he asked her about Scotland and the evening flew by. She felt perfectly relaxed and happy. Except that when she got into his car and sat close beside him in the darkness she became aware of the racing of her heart. He stopped under some trees in the drive of Willard and Bessie's house.

He turned and looked at her and said softly, 'You're quite a girl Rowan Saundahs.'

'Oh?' she smiled cheekily up at him. 'Why?'

'You have a rich mamma ovah there in Scotland and I guess everything you could want for a real easy lifestyle. But you come ovah heah determined to stick your neck out no mattah what folks say.' His eyes smiled down at her through the shadows. 'I don't know whethah to shake you or kiss you.'

'Don't you dare shake me,' she said.

His kiss was gentle at first and gradually became deeper and more exploratory. Nothing she had ever experienced gave her such a sensation not only of powerful sexual awakening but of joy and peace. She wanted to remain resting against him with eyes closed, savouring every wonderful moment. But too soon he disentangled her arms from around his neck and said, 'You'd bettah go in now, honey. I'll call you.'

It felt an agony to leave him like that. She wanted to know exactly when she'd see him again. She wanted him to take her right now to his flat or wherever he lived, take her to his bed, make love to her. But she knew instinctively he wasn't a man to be rushed or dictated to. Even his voice, although softened with his husky Southern drawl, had a resonance and authority about it. She could imagine him being a good teacher, the type that could control a classroom of students without needing to raise his voice.

Mary Beth was asleep when she reached the bedroom

they shared. Rowan was glad. She wasn't prepared for the eager questions she knew Mary Beth would ask about her date. She didn't want to share Steve Jackson with anyone. She never even mentioned his name in her long detailed letter to her mother. She crept quietly into bed and lay, eyes wide open, dreaming about him. Sometimes her heart missed a beat with apprehension at the thought that she might never have met him. She closed her eyes then and thanked God that her instincts had led her here and to him.

She lay in the heat of the night with only a sheet covering her and sweat running down her face and naked body. Inside the house there was the monotonous whir of the ceiling fans. From outside the blare and wail of police cars drifted in. Another deep hollow echoing sound, too; it had puzzled her when she'd first arrived in America. Now she knew it was the sound of freight trains. The feeling came over her again that she was in a strange detached place, in a different galaxy. But if this strange place was Steve Jackson's country, if he called this America 'home', then from now on America was her country, her home too.

41

'She's left the phone off the hook again.' Rebecca closed
her eyes for a few seconds, her hand still on the phone
she'd lifted over to the table. 'Amelia can be very
annoying at times.'

'She does work in the mornings,' Jenny reminded her.
She was also working. Her weekly batch of scones and
biscuits had been mixed and rolled out on the floury
table top. Now she was taking a tray from the oven with
glove-protected hands. Deftly she transferred the piping
hot scones on to a wire tray, then pushed back a stray
curl that clung damply to her forehead. Her cheeks were
rosy with the heat. 'And she did say she'd pop over this
afternoon.'

'We all have to work, dear, but we don't all feel we
must take our phones off the hook.' Rebecca stretched
her arms and body like a cat. 'Let's go across to the park
and relax with some T'ai Chi.'

'I've still to clear up all this mess,' Jenny said,
indicating the dirty baking tins, bowls and spoons
cluttering the sink and draining board.

Rebecca airily waved her words aside. 'They'll still be
there when we get back, or Hazel and Milly or Sadie can
do them. I feel so unsettled, Jenny, and you know that's
not like me.'

'Oh, all right,' Jenny peeled off her apron. The last
thing she felt like was cavorting about in the park. It
wasn't even a nice day. Gusts of wind were shaking
bronze-coloured leaves from trees, hustling them up
around the monument. She would rather have had peace
to think, to try to make sense of her feelings, work out
how best to cope with them. She kept trying to tell herself
that just because Joe had abused her it surely didn't

mean that every other man she met would be the same. Gregson had been kind. He had helped her.

'You look miles away,' Rebecca said. 'Are you still thinking about that Gregson man?'

'I can't help finding him attractive,' Jenny admitted.

'No doubt you once thought about Joe in the same way,' Rebecca said. 'It's all an illusion, dear. The fact is, in the face of weakness man's aggressive instinct takes over. Some men choose to and are able to control this instinct to varying degrees at different times. But it's always there – waiting for a victim like you.'

'I can't believe all men are like you say,' Jenny protested although the fear that had long since taken root inside her told her it was true. 'Not all men are aggressive.'

'Aren't they, dear?' Rebecca went over to the mirror and rippled her fingers through the luxurious thickness of her hair, the scarlet hoop earrings she was wearing making a vivid contrast to its blackness. 'I believe even children have this characteristic. Have you never looked at children's playgrounds? Even those of very young children. Girls will be playing with skipping ropes or joining hands in some singing game or sitting around exchanging scraps or nursing dollies. Boys will be fighting. They'll be struggling about in the playground bawling and shouting and trying to hurt one another. You must have noticed.'

Jenny sighed as she followed Rebecca from the house. 'You're not cheering me up, Rebecca.'

'I'm sorry dear. But you've got to learn to face facts – for your own protection.'

In the park the trees swayed and shivered and rustled as they passed and Jenny was glad of her thick sweater, although trying to keep up with Rebecca made sure the blood pumped warmly through her veins. The sight of Rebecca in her dazzling scarlet sweater and matching earrings glowed like a flame through the misty air.

'The grass is damp,' Jenny said after she slipped off

her canvas mules, 'we'll probably catch our death of cold.'

'Don't look now,' Rebecca suddenly hissed at her, 'keep perfectly calm. Your husband is coming towards us.' Tension had quickened her normally slow, calm voice.

'Damn,' Jenny said. 'I knew I shouldn't have come out today!'

'Don't be silly. Why should you hide yourself away?'

Despite Rebecca's warning, Jenny turned and watched Joe's tall figure approach. He was hunched into a khaki bomber jacket with the collar up and his hands pushed deep into the pockets. A lock of hair was ruffling across his brow. He looked gaunt and miserable.

'Jenny, we must talk,' he said when he reached her.

'We have talked,' Jenny said.

'I don't mean a few snatched words in a crowded shop or in a houseful of women. I mean in our own home, by ourselves.'

Rebecca put a protective arm around Jenny's shoulders. 'It's high time you accepted the fact, Mr Thornton, you are not ever getting the chance to abuse this woman again. She's finished with you for good and the sooner you realize that the better.'

Joe's eyes narrowed but his voice remained calm. 'It's high time you allowed my wife to speak for herself.'

'I'm sorry, Joe,' Jenny said, 'but it's finished. I could never trust you again.'

'Jenny, I promise –'

'It's no use, Joe. You promised too many times in the past.'

'I know. I know.' The anguish in his eyes when he looked at her was unmistakable and Jenny suffered along with him. 'But this time I'll get help, Jenny. I realize now that I need help. I'll go to a doctor . . . to anybody you say.'

'Joe, I'm sorry,' Jenny said miserably. 'I really am. But it's too late.'

'Jenny, we've known each other all our lives. We belong together. Nothing can ever change that. Not even this monstrous woman.'

'Joe! Rebecca has been good to me. She gave me comfort and shelter when I desperately needed it.'

'It's all right, Jenny,' Rebecca said. 'His insults don't worry me in the slightest. I think however we'd be better to abandon our T'ai Chi for today. I hadn't noticed it was so cold and windy. We would be better just doing a little yoga in the house.'

'Jenny, please!' Joe pleaded. 'I can't live without you. The children need you too – with me working shifts and such long hours I can't see to them properly.'

Rebecca tightened her grip on Jenny. 'Nor could Jenny in the state you got her into. Come on, dear. He's just upsetting you. We'll go back and have a nice cup of camomile tea and one of your delicious biscuits.'

Jenny allowed herself to be led away. She tried not to listen to Joe's cry of, 'Jenny! You're my wife!'

'The sooner you put an end to that the better,' Rebecca told Jenny. 'You'd have no trouble getting a divorce you know.'

'Poor Joe.'

'Will you stop saying that, Jenny? All you're doing when you talk like that is proving you're still a victim. You've just forgotten what it felt like when he hit you.'

Jenny shook her head. 'No, I haven't forgotten.'

Rebecca gave her a reassuring hug. 'Well, then . . .'

Jenny kept silent until they reached Battlefield House. She had developed a tension headache and could hardly think, far less talk. Even Rebecca giving her a scalp massage didn't soothe the wretched confusion of her thoughts or the guilt that tormented her. But whereas before her depression had completely drained away her energy now she could force herself to keep trying in the fight to banish her thoughts. Milly and Hazel still had not returned. Nor had Sadie. Jenny attacked the dirty dishes herself and then began preparing lunch. By the time lunch was ready Milly and Hazel had arrived warmly cocooned in fur coats; Hazel looked like a film star in her mink while bespectacled Milly was more prosaic and less expensive looking in her musquash that smelled faintly of moth-balls. Both of them wore good leather gloves. Hazel always said, 'A lady should never be seen out of doors unless she's wearing her gloves.' Not long after them came a gloveless Sadie in a headsquare and the coat she'd had made out of an RAF blanket during the war.

'I was up at the house showing Milly around,' Hazel said.

'Your house, dear?' Rebecca asked.

'Yes. Milly liked it, didn't you, Milly?'

'I was most impressed, a very superior residence. Very superior.'

'And I suddenly had a splendid idea,' Hazel's china doll face was glowing with pleasure. 'I'm going to return home and Milly is coming with me as my housekeeper companion. Her daily cleaning woman is going to come to my place for a few hours a couple of times a week to help out too. The one who used to 'do' for her bungalow in Bearsden. Milly phoned her from my place and Mrs McFarlane agreed right away. Isn't that wonderful?'

There was a stunned silence for a few seconds. Then Jenny said, 'Of course it is. I do wish you luck, Hazel – and you too, Milly.'

Rebecca seemed to have become strangely withdrawn. She said with great dignity, 'I hope you'll be all right, Hazel. Remember, your problem hasn't gone away. And what happens if your husband finds out where you are, Milly? Who will protect you against him if he comes to Hazel's door?'

Milly visibly stiffened and a shaft of fear showed in her eyes but she said, 'He surely wouldn't dare to come to a big house like that. Anyway, how could he find out where I am? Unless one of you told him.'

'Och,' Sadie said, 'why would any of us do a thing like that? You'll be all right, hen.'

Rebecca rose from the table. 'I'm going through to meditate.'

'You haven't finished your lunch.' The happy excitement in Hazel's eyes was replaced with uncertainty. 'Are you all right?'

'I'm surprised you care,' Rebecca said before sweeping from the room leaving it in tense silence.

'Oh dear,' Hazel said eventually. 'Haven't I done the right thing? Perhaps I have been a tiny bit selfish. I should have waited and discussed it with Rebecca, shouldn't I? It's just that when I saw my home again I must confess it suddenly made this place seem very cramped and uncomfortable. I'm not used to living in these sort of conditions.'

'Nor am I,' Milly agreed, 'my bungalow in Bearsden wasn't large but it was roomy enough and certainly quiet. Not having any family, you see.'

'We'll miss you,' Sadie said. 'I bet that's what's upset Rebecca. She's fond of you as well.'

Hazel patted Sadie's hand. 'How sweet! You must all come to afternoon tea one day. We'll keep in touch, don't worry. I should have said that to Rebecca. I confess I can be a teeny bit thoughtless and selfish at times. Not as bad as I used to be though. I've learned a lot being here. I must speak to Rebecca.'

She made to rise but Jenny said, 'You can't disturb her just now, she'll be trying to compose herself. She's obviously upset.'

'Oh dear,' Hazel sank down again. 'I never thought, I was so excited. Now I'm beginning to feel dreadfully guilty. For the first time for absolutely ages, I feel like a drink.'

'Hazel!' the others cried out in horrified unison.

'I won't take one. I won't, I promise,' Hazel hastily assured them. 'It's just I always have the urge to escape that way from myself when I get upset.'

286

'You'll be all right, hen,' Sadie said. 'You go home and just think yourself lucky you've a home to go to.'

'Yes, I've come to realize how lucky I am,' Hazel said. 'It's just . . . well, Rebecca's the last person in the world I'd want to hurt.'

'I think part of the problem is –' Jenny got up to make a pot of coffee – 'Rebecca was all excited herself. You know how she's been going on about this idea for extending the refuge. She's suddenly thinking in terms of money and all the exciting things she could do with it. You've been giving her very large sums of money, Hazel. She's going to miss that as well as you. I hope to goodness Amelia's able to give her good news when she comes, but I doubt it.'

'Oh, dear.' Hazel gazed helplessly around the table. 'I would like to go on contributing but my house is such an expensive place to run and if I have wages to pay. . . . I'll even have to find a gardener again. The back of the house is like an absolute jungle. But I could postpone moving for a week or two to give Rebecca time to make financial adjustments. Do you think that would help?'

'Here, drink your coffee. And you too, Milly,' Jenny said, noticing how Milly had stiffened up and was staring bleakly into space. 'Rebecca will work everything out for the best.'

She was secretly far from confident however. Rebecca's reaction had surprised her as much as it had Hazel and Milly. It was a further complication in life she had neither expected nor felt prepared for.

42

They marched along Eighth Avenue, Union Street, downtown to the department stores, Harveys, Cain-Sloanes, Caster Knotts, Woolworths and all the five and dime stores. In each place several of the marchers went into the lunch counters and asked for service and were told they couldn't be served. As pre-arranged they sat on and said they weren't going to move until they were served. Rowan was sitting on one of the stools talking in quiet tones to Essie Jean, Linda Mae and Mary Beth. Thomas was sitting further along talking to three black friends, Dave, Sonny and Charlie. Sonny looked about 15 with tight curls and big saucer eyes. All of them were trying to look natural and hide any nervousness. Somebody came in and told them that a large crowd of students from a nearby white school were approaching the store. Rowan could see through the window a mass of policemen gathered round outside – there must have been about ninety of them. It made her feel safer. If the high school students were coming to cause trouble, the police were there in plenty to apply law and order.

The students came in and crowded around chanting anti-Negro slogans and insults. Rowan and the others at the lunch counter sat staring straight ahead and tried to ignore the jeering and the obscenities.

Rowan however felt her cheeks grow hot and her heart pattered quietly beneath her loose sweater. The students jostled closer and starting blowing cigarette smoke in their faces. Then to her surprise and horror one of them ground out his cigarette on Essie Jean's back. She could smell the burning. There was much sniggering then. She could see in the large mirror above the counter the handsome 'clean-cut' faces becoming ugly with hatred.

Essie Jean neither moved nor cried out. Then some-body knocked Charlie off his stool. Charlie struggled to sit up on the stool again. Then Thomas and Dave and Sonny were all yanked off and smashed to the floor. They too struggled back up and without a word regained their seats. The workshop classes had taught them well.

The crowd was chanting, 'Communists, Communists, Communists,' now.

An old man in the crowd yelled at the students to 'Git one o' the Commie gals!'

A big lusty boy yelled back, 'Which one should I get first?'

'One o' them white niggahs,' the man said.

Rowan was frightened. She stole a quick glance towards the window to see if the police were on their way to protect them. The police were still there. They were looking in. Some of them were grinning as if they were enjoying a show. That was when anger as well as terror set in.

Mary Beth was dragged off her stool and was lost sight of in a crowd of male backs. Then suddenly Rowan felt hands clutch at her. She was jerked roughly off her seat then punched in the chest. The unexpected agony in the tender flesh of her breasts caused her to drop down onto her knees choking for breath. Before she could recover she was kicked in the stomach. At the same time someone else grabbed her pony-tail, jerked back her head and crashed a fist into her face.

Somehow, although only half conscious, she remem-bered what she'd been taught at the workshop and rolled up into a ball with her arms over her head. She was vaguely aware of other black people struggling and forcing themselves up on to the stools to take the place of those who were being beaten. And as they were dragged off others again took their place. She could see lying on the floor beside her, Mary Beth, with blood running from the corners of her mouth.

Then they were both dragged by their hair about

thirty feet towards the door. There were policemen in the doorway watching. Rowan's anger kept her conscious – that, and sheer stubborn determination made her struggle up from where she had been thrown and somehow return to the lunch counter. She remembered her mother telling her how glad everyone was when the war was over. But the war was not over. Not here. What was this if not war? Sonny was lying up against the counter with blood gushing from his head. As he tried to protect his face a man kept kicking his head against the counter. Before she could get to him, several other Negro boys and girls had flung themselves down in front of Sonny to protect him with their bodies.

Rowan climbed back up on to her stool. The young white man sitting next to her had 'nigger' in red paint sprayed on to the back of his white shirt. Somebody was emptying a jar of mustard over his head. Somebody else began squirting her with brown ketchup. It mixed with the salty blood dripping down her face. Somebody else started drumming fists in her back. Then they began grabbing other things from the nearby counters and pitching them at everyone sitting on the stools.

She could hear above all the insane screeches of laughter the store manager starting to shout that they couldn't do that unless they paid for the goods. If they didn't pay for the goods he'd ask the police to come in. He wasn't going to stand by and see his goods being stolen. No matter for what good reason.

Gradually his threats got through to the mob and they began, giggling and sniggering and swaggering, to drift off.

Then in through the crowd crushed more Negro and white friends.

'The store's shut,' the manager bawled. 'Y'all clear outah heah. You heah me, niggah?' he said to a distraught Reverend Johnson who'd come looking for Linda Mae. 'Ah'm closin' the doors. Look at all this mess,' he called to the policemen outside. 'All this damage these goddam niggahs have caused.'

290

Rowan could see, as if through a mist, Aunt Abbie hobbling rapidly towards them and crying out to the manager, 'What do you mean, you stupid fellah? It wasn't them that caused the damage. Look at them – it's them that's been damaged. Look what they've done to my Mary Beth.'

Mary Beth had warned Abbie not to come near the sit-in but there was obviously no holding Abbie back from anything.

'Out! Out!' the manager insisted. 'Officahs,' he called to the police, 'this scum is refusin' to leave!'

The police moved in and before Rowan's unbelieving eyes all the Negroes and their white soul brothers and sisters, as they were called who'd shared the sit-in, were arrested for disturbing the peace. The mob who had attacked them were now standing outside waiting to jeer at them as police dragged them into vans, paddy wagons and garbage trucks that were sent to take them to jail.

Aunt Abbie did her best to stop them taking her and Mary Beth. She cracked at least one policeman over the head with her stick as he bent down to get hold of Mary Beth who was still lying on the floor. It took two policemen to drag the old lady off and throw her bodily on to the pavement outside.

They all had to appear in Court and were given a hefty fine. Both she and Mary Beth had to stay in bed for several days after having treatment, including several stitches, in a hospital emergency department. They were the lucky ones, however. Some of the others had broken limbs and fractured skulls. Sonny died of his head wounds a few days later. No one was arrested or charged for his murder.

Mary Beth said his death was only another in the many like it every month in the South. Black women were raped. Black men were blasted with pellets. One man's body had recently been found headless and with his testicles cut off. Black men, women and even children were lynched.

Recently a girl had been flogged for allegedly 'crowding white people' in a store. A 14-year-old boy had been tortured and killed. His body had been found in the river – barbed wire round his neck had been attached to a cotton-gin fan, one of his eyes had been gouged out, his forehead was crushed on one side and there was a bullet in his skull.

A rage burned inside her not only against the segregationists but the society in which such crimes against humanity could happen. She believed the segregationists were evil people who were willing to kill to hang on to their power and privileges over their fellow citizens who happened to have a different skin colour. But what was she supposed to think of a society in which such people were allowed freedom to flourish?

The Reverend Martin Luther King had said:

> . . . One of the great glories of democracy is the right to protest for right . . . if you will protest courageously and with dignity and Christian love, when the history books are written in future generations the historians will pause and say, 'There lived a great people – a black people – who injected new meaning and dignity into the veins of civilization.' That is our challenge and our overwhelming responsibility.

Some challenge! Some democracy! She couldn't see anything glorious about what had happened at today's protest. 'We shall overcome,' he'd said. But how could anyone overcome the apathy, ignorance, the blind prejudice, the cruelty and the hatred she'd witnessed here?

And it wasn't only that. Willard, Mary Beth's daddy, said he was ashamed to be a white southern man, not only because of the violence but the way the black man was cheated by insurance companies and automobile dealers.

Bessie, his wife, said to Rowan, 'There's no use hatin' them though. Because they're sick. There's a sickness

292

here. And it goes deeper than race. It's all part of the exploitation of human beings by other human beings. It's a case of the haves exploiting the have-nots, whether it concerns privilege or power or money. Whites exploit blacks, that's true, and men exploit women that's true. But it's also true that rich Negroes exploit poor Negroes and rich women exploit poor women. I believe what Martin Luther King says: "Every man must decide whether he will walk in the light of creative altruism or the darkness of destructive selfishness. . . ." It all comes down to human nature and the struggle between good and evil in all of us.'

Even Steve Jackson didn't share Rowan's passionate rage; at least, not against the society. He, like all the Americans she'd met was intensely patriotic. It seemed to her a case of 'my country right or wrong.' They argued a lot about that but not at first, not while she was still sick and in agony after the beating she'd suffered. While she was sick she kept thinking, the men who'd beaten and kicked her were patriotic Americans too. And their patriotism stank as far as she was concerned. Steve Jackson at this time spoke only of his anger and disgust at what these men had done to her. He only nursed her in his arms and kissed away her tears and did everything he possibly could to help and comfort her.

She remembered with bitterness what was written on the Statue of Liberty.

Give me your tired, your poor, your huddled masses
    yearning to breathe free,
The wretched refuse of your teeming shore,
Send these, the homeless, tempest-tossed, to me:
I lift my lamp beside the golden door.

What a beautiful sentiment. A pity it wasn't lived up to. Inside the so-called golden door she'd seen what happened to huddled masses yearning to breathe free!

43

Rebecca could not hide the fact from herself that she felt wounded. Sitting in the lotus position on her prayer mat, chin up, eyes closed and nostrils quivering with determined breathing, she was deeply distressed. She had willingly sacrificed her time, her energies, her love and devotion on Hazel and Milly. She had spared them nothing. She had taken them into her home and her heart and helped them in every way humanly possible. No other therapist, indeed, no other human being would have given them such loyal and continual support. When she thought of the struggle she'd had with Hazel in particular at the beginning! And to think that now she could blithely stab her in the back! Hazel had not given a thought to all she'd done for her. Hazel could toss her and their friendship aside as if it had never existed, as if she meant nothing. Rebecca had a terrible premonition that this was like the dangerous crack in the dam and at any moment everything she'd worked for and believed in would drain away and she would be left empty and alone.

For a few desperate minutes she floundered and struggled as if for the very breath of life – until she gratefully remembered that Jesus Christ had been tormented like this. His friends and followers had let Him down and deserted Him. God had tested Him and He had emerged victorious despite what the world did to Him. God was testing her now. She knew it. It was like a revelation, a vision. She actually saw a dazzle of light under her closed lids and a certainty soothed away all her terrors. She was able to breathe slowly and smoothly. A serene smile hovered on her handsome face and when she heard the knock on the sitting room door she was able to call 'Enter' in a perfectly calm and pleasant voice.

'Amelia's through in the kitchen,' Jenny said.

Rebecca opened her eyes. 'Thank you, dear. I'll be right through. Make me a cup of camomile tea, will you?'

She gave one of her catlike stretches then rose from her prayer mat with suppleness and grace. Before leaving the room she gazed at herself in the wall mirror. There was pride in her bearing and no wonder; the spirit of the Lord had touched her. She had been singled out. She was one of the chosen. She had always sensed this of course but today she knew beyond all doubt. It had never been more obvious to her that she even looked different from ordinary people. Her dignified bearing, her strikingly vivid thatch of hair, her noble features, and most unusual of all, her large glowing eyes.

But she must not succumb to vanity, she told herself firmly, she must try to retain true Christian humility. She must also remember forgiveness. God would show the way in this as in everything else. After taking one more deep breath she went through to the kitchen. Jenny had the cup of tea ready at her place. She sat down straight-backed and head held high.

Hazel said, 'I'm sorry if I upset you, Rebecca. I didn't mean to. You've been so good to me. . . .'

'I forgive you, Hazel. It's up to your own conscience what you do. All I care about is that my conscience is clear. I have not spared myself in my loyal and loving devotion to you and your every need. If you do not choose to think about that or to care about me, or the refuge, or the other people in need here, then that is up to your conscience. That is something you will have to live with – all I hope is that you will be able to. As I reminded you earlier your problem has not gone away, you know. You're an alcoholic, and you'll be an alcoholic for the rest of your life.'

'But I thought . . .' Hazel said miserably, 'I thought with Milly, you see –'

295

'Oh yes, Milly. . . .' Rebecca smiled round at the rigidly apprehensive Milly. 'Your husband is a very clever and much respected lawyer, isn't he? I'm not a bit surprised that you found it so difficult to get free of him. He was quite a challenge to me. It took all my courage and quick thinking to deal with him. But I was only too glad to rescue you, Milly. I could see you were totally incapable of dealing with that man on your own. That man is a monster, isn't he? I do hope and pray that now that you have decided to put yourself in such a vulnerable position he doesn't find you.'

Milly seemed incapable of saying anything, but Hazel repeated, 'I'm sorry, Rebecca. It's not that we don't appreciate –'

'No need to say any more, Hazel. Not another word! I told you, I forgive you. Now Amelia, tell me how you got on last night with Sir Ian.'

Amelia was sitting, eyes downcast, looking even more wretched than Hazel. 'I'm not good at that sort of thing, Rebecca. I hate asking people for favours. I hate being dependent on people's so-called generosity. I've always found that –'

'If you could just drag your mind from yourself for a few minutes, dear, and tell me about Sir Ian?'

Amelia flushed a dark crimson. 'He looked all right. I mean, pleasant and friendly. Although I shouldn't have been surprised, he had sharp eyes.'

'Surprised at what, Amelia?'

'At how abrupt he could be. We were chatting away perfectly all right about this and that until I brought up the subject of the refuge and he suddenly changed. "Doing your bit for good works?" he said in a sarcastic voice, then immediately turned off, lost interest, shut me out. He turned away and began talking to Rory. He never spoke to me again for the rest of the night except to say goodbye. I suppose he gets pestered with so many people he's had to develop a way of protecting himself.'

'It wasn't a case of pestering him, it was a case of

interesting him in what I am doing here. If you had handled the situation properly you would have succeeded in doing this. If you had been sincerely interested and enthusiastic and confident he would have caught these vibes and reacted accordingly. But you weren't, were you, Amelia?'

'I admit I couldn't see how he was likely to even *think* of parting with a large sum of money in such unofficial, casual kind of circumstances. I mean . . .,' Amelia coloured miserably under Rebecca's pitying stare, 'it didn't strike me as being very business like, it seemed to me just the kind of thing that dreams were made of. Things never work out that easy in real life – at least they never have for me,' she ended lamely.

'I'm not in the least surprised,' Rebecca said. 'Oh well, if you have so little faith, Amelia, if you stubbornly refuse to help I must simply deal with this myself.'

'How do you mean?'

'I'll go and see Sir Ian at his office in town.'

'You can't just walk into the office and say you want to see him,' Amelia told her. 'His secretary won't let you. The secretary has to know your name or your business before she'll give you an appointment. Rory has a secretary like that.'

'Where there's a will there's a way,' Rebecca said. 'I know! You'll come with me, Amelia. We'll make the appointment in your name. She'll know the name of Donovan all right. And to make sure she thinks it's the right Donovan you can say something like "Mrs Donovan – Sir Ian knows who I am", or "I'm a friend of Sir Ian's".'

Amelia looked taken aback. 'You mean, pretend I'm Rory?'

'He obviously wouldn't give us an appointment if he thought it was you, would he? Or just any old Donovan.'

'No, but . . .' Amelia's face creased with discomfort. 'It's not honest.'

'We won't be telling any lies,' Rebecca gave an

297

impatient flick of her hand. 'You *are* Mrs Donovan.'

'Yes, I know but –'

'Even if you have to tell lies to get an interview with this man, even if you have to resort to any subterfuge to persuade him to finance us, you should. The end justifies the means, Amelia.'

'Oh, I'm not convinced about that.' Amelia shook her head. 'Oh, no.'

Rebecca rolled her eyes. 'You're never convinced about anything. "Oh ye of little faith . . ." ' she quoted, 'Faith, Amelia, can move mountains.'

Hazel said, 'If I could help financially, Rebecca, I would. But as you know, my capital is tied up.'

Rebecca gave her a cool, pitying smile before turning her attention to Amelia again. 'You are surely forgetting, Amelia, that you have already used Rory Donovan. You used her in a most selfish and indeed ruthless way to suit your own purpose.'

'I never did!' Amelia came to life with indignation. 'How can you say such a thing?'

'You didn't like the housekeeper's job you had, you wanted a comfortable home to call your own. You not only used Rory, you used her son. You didn't like her, you didn't love him. But for years you've taken everything you could get from both of them.'

Tears spurted into Amelia's eyes. 'That's a terrible thing to say.'

'But true.'

'No, it wasn't like that.'

'Guilt is a very difficult thing to cope with, Amelia. But before we can deal with problems we have to face them. I think you are the last person, the very last person who should make moral judgements or have the temerity to criticize anyone else.'

Amelia seemed to have shrunk. She sat hunched into herself, hands clutched on lap, eyes down.

'Now, here's the phone,' Rebecca said, lifting the

phone onto the table and placing it in front of her. 'I'll look up the number and you'll make the call.'

Rebecca felt elated after this task had been successfully completed. Her mind soared once more into the realms of what could and should be accomplished. She saw in her mind's eye Sir Ian officially opening the refuge once the spacious extension had been built and the whole place refurbished. She imagined newspaper reporters and radio and television people there to give the occasion as much well-deserved publicity as possible. She would become so widely known for her specialist work with abused women that women would flock gratefully to her from every part of the country. She struggled valiantly to remind herself that she must retain a sense of humility. She too must feel grateful – grateful to her Maker who had chosen her for His work and blessed her with the gift to enable her to carry it out.

The appointment was for the following afternoon and she spent the intervening time in gathering up the case histories of all her 'friends' and tidying them into clean new folders. She was sure this would impress Sir Ian. It would not only prove to him the amount of work she had already accomplished and was continuing to struggle with at the refuge but how efficient she was as an organizer, how businesslike.

She dressed very carefully next day; men were always impressed by outward appearances. Normally she never wore make-up, with such striking features she didn't need to. Today, however, she decided on a touch of glossy lipstick and a dab of powder on her nose. She gave her hair an extra good brush then rubbed it with a silk scarf to heighten its gloss. It was a cold winter's day so she wore her black wool dress with the scarlet and emerald green braid round its high neck and generous hemline. Then she swung on her matching black cape. Surveying herself in her full-length bedroom mirror she felt a surge of satisfaction and pride. She looked absolutely stunning.

Everyone said so when she went through to the kitchen to collect Amelia. Hazel was especially effusive but Rebecca kept her at emotional arm's length, barely favouring her with a distant smile. She had forgiven her of course; she wished her no ill-will. But Hazel had chosen to desert her in favour of Milly so let her find comfort in Milly now. She would not find it very easily, Milly was so pale and stiff and withdrawn. It must already be obvious to Hazel that, in fact, she was on her own.

Rebecca experienced a tiny puff of pleasure. It was only a matter of time now before Hazel would realize what a terrible mistake she had made.

Well, the weak and foolish woman couldn't say she hadn't been warned.

44

Douglas had gone to do preliminary sketches for a portrait in someone's house and Amelia took advantage of the few hours of peace and freedom by inviting Jenny for lunch.

They sat in the Art Deco dining room at a table with U-shaped supports of tubular steel which had been chromium plated. The table top was a slab of cellulose-enamelled wood. The chair supports were curved in a similar way to the table and had uncomfortable wooden arms.

'How did she get on?' Jenny asked. 'I didn't like to say anything to Rebecca, none of us did. She looked so cool and dignified and . . . far away somehow.'

Amelia dished soup from a honey-coloured tureen. 'It was awful. I knew it would be. He was coldly furious the moment he set eyes on us. "I was expecting *Rory* Donovan," he said. "Were you?" Rebecca asked, all innocence but he knew we'd done it purposely to get into his office. Rebecca talks about facing facts but she doesn't seem able to face facts herself.'

'She didn't talk him into anything then?'

'I felt sorry for her. He was so curt and dismissive. Was she registered as a charity? he asked. Didn't she know the proper procedure? He suggested it was time she found out. Then he rang the bell for his secretary to show us the door.'

'Poor Rebecca!'

'I know. She tried her best to say her piece and she did manage to say something. I felt embarrassed for her as well as sorry for her, though.'

'How do you mean?' Jenny asked.

'Well, somehow it seems quite normal in Battlefield

House, talking about all Rebecca's psychic theories. You know how she goes on about knowing our Orishas and massaging our auras. That sort of thing. But in that office in front of that man it all sounded terribly eccentric. I suddenly saw her through his eyes and she seemed odd to the point of being crazy. She went on too much about the spiritual side of things. I was really surprised, Jenny. She didn't put her case at all well.' Amelia shook her head. 'She ought to have known that a hard-headed businessman would have been more impressed with facts and figures.'

'Knowing Rebecca, I don't think she'll give up, do you?'

'That's what worries me. I think she would be better to stick to her routine hypnotherapy and relaxation sessions. She's good at that and everything was fine until she got these big ideas.'

'While she was out,' Jenny said, 'that man phoned.'

'What man?'

'The one I told you about, Al Gregson. He was at Rory's dinner party, remember?'

'Oh, yes,' Amelia said. 'Here, I see what you mean!'

'About what?'

'Gregson, being a pusher, a get-ahead type. He's attractive though, I understand how you feel now. Rory must have told him where you were by the way – I didn't.'

Jenny took a few spoonfuls of soup. 'He wants us to meet and talk.'

'Very attractive,' Amelia murmured absently.

'I've agreed to see him. But ... I don't know. ... Physically I'm so much better. Even my nerves have improved. Remember how I used to jump at every sound? But still ...'

'You're afraid of men, that's the nub of it. And it's quite logical after what you've been through. At least I've known one man who was loving and gentle. It gives you something to cling on to.'

Jenny looked intrigued. 'You can't mean Douglas?'

'No! It was years ago. While I was working in Bearsden. Another writer. He gave me a glimpse of what love between a man and a woman could be like. I've never forgotten it. I don't think I ever will.'

'What happened?'

Amelia shrugged. 'I expect it was my fault. I was far too timid and shy. But another woman wasn't and she married him.'

'Poor Amelia!'

'As long as I've got my writing I'm all right. Tell me about you and Gregson. When are you meeting him?'

'This evening. He's calling for me at Battlefield House about seven and taking me to dinner. In a way I'm really looking forward to it. I'm all sort of fizzy inside with excitement but at the same time I'm collapsing inside. There's still Joe, after all. We talked about Rebecca not giving up. Well, I don't believe Joe will either. And I can't just dismiss him from my mind as if he never existed. When you've known someone for so long they become part of you.'

'Oh Jenny . . . I don't want to influence you. It's your life. But I can't help hoping you never go back to Joe, he frightens me. It's something about his eyes. I think he's a little mad.'

'My mother used to say the war had a lot to answer for. She was probably right. Joe never used to be like that. He brought a sword and a gun back, you know – that used to worry me a lot. And frighten me. Especially the gun. He always kept it in a locker beside where he slept.'

'My God!'

'Oh, don't get me wrong,' Jenny said hastily. 'He never threatened me with it. Not ever. No, I think it was to do with some secret fear of his own.'

Amelia shivered. 'All the same . . .'

'You're right about me being afraid of men though. I must try to fight it. Fear's such a self-destructive thing, isn't it?'

'Don't I know it?' Amelia fervently agreed.

303

'Do you not feel the hypnotherapy is helping you any more?' Jenny asked.

'It worked wonders when I was on radio and television on those book programmes. Douglas said I looked ridiculous. But there I sat feeling quite calm and relaxed. I've seen the day I couldn't have done that, so I suppose it must be helping me. I still feel pretty much the same most of the time though.'

'I've noticed you haven't been having such regular sessions recently.'

A deep sigh rose up from Amelia's chest. 'Maybe it's me. But I'm beginning to feel a bit disillusioned with Rebecca – with everything. I think it must be me. I've done this sort of thing before. I feel that someone is absolutely fantastic, I go overboard for them. Then. . . .' She shrugged. 'Oh, I don't know.'

'For goodness sake, Amelia, don't you get all depressed now.'

'No, I'll be all right. As long as I have my writing. The thing is, Rebecca keeps phoning me and expecting me to be able to talk about her business all the time. Or drop what I'm doing and go over to the refuge to make up her numbers at whatever class or course she's doing or to help in this way or that.' Her face creased with anxiety. 'It's not that I don't want to help – and I like being at the refuge – but I can't write if I keep being interrupted. Even answering the phone spoils my concentration. The trouble is, Rebecca has no interest in fiction. She regards it, if she bothers to think about it at all, as a self-indulgence and a complete waste of time. Certainly not work. If I wrote about some of her psychic theories or about the refuge it might be different, though.'

'Her work means so much to her, Amelia.'

'What do you think my work means to me?' Amelia suddenly snapped and Jenny was taken aback by the passion smouldering in her friend's eyes and the stubborn hardness of the normally soft mouth.

'I'm sorry, I'm not saying what you do isn't important, Amelia.'

'I don't care what you or anybody else says about my work. As long as I can continue doing it. I haven't struggled all my life to be a writer just to let someone like Rebecca Abercrombie stop me.' She was trembling now and Jenny put a hand on her arm.

'Amelia, nobody's trying to stop you writing.'

'They'd better not. I won't have it!'

She suddenly got up, noisily gathered the dirty soup plates together and hurried through to the kitchen. Jenny could imagine her standing there struggling to control her emotions by trying to take deep breaths. When she returned with plates of stewed beef and potatoes she looked pale and subdued.

'What are you going to wear tonight, Jenny?' she asked.

'My black suit I think. It's too cold for a dress. It'll be a thought to take off my boots.'

'You won't be walking through the snow. He'll have his car, won't he?'

Jenny nodded. Excitement was beginning to catch her breath again. Less than half her mind managed to cling to the rest of the conversation with Amelia. All she was really interested in was thinking about her meeting with Gregson. She was impatient to be away and getting ready. At least it would be easier to have a bath in the afternoon. In the morning at Battlefield House or in the evening it was difficult to get into the bathroom; there always seemed to be someone else using it – and taking far too long! It wasn't a very comfortable bathroom either. There was no heated radiator and the plumbing wasn't reliable. Sometimes there was no hot water even if you did manage to get in before anyone else.

She hadn't said anything to Rebecca about going out with Gregson. There hadn't been much chance even if she'd wanted to – which she hadn't. She knew only too well what Rebecca would say. Fortunately Rebecca had been busy in the sitting room with hypnotherapy, relaxation and aura healing appointments.

When Jenny returned from Amelia's house Rebecca was once more shut in the sitting room with a 'friend'. Hazel and Milly were sitting glumly in the kitchen staring silently into empty coffee cups.

'Okay if I have a bath?' Jenny asked. 'Sadie's not in there, is she?'

Hazel shook her head.

'Cheer up, you two!' Jenny said. 'You're about to start a new life. You should be all happy and excited.'

'At first glance,' Milly said stiffly, 'one might think so. But one must think these things through.'

'I thought it was all settled.'

'As Rebecca said – what would happen for instance if my husband came to Hazel's door?' She tightly squeezed her eyes shut. 'It doesn't bear thinking about.'

Hazel gazed appealingly at her. 'I wouldn't let him in, Milly. It's my house. He couldn't come in without my permission.'

'You don't know him, Hazel. Rebecca has been the only person who has been able to stop him. I'd be mad to risk being on my own.'

'But you wouldn't be on your own dear,' Hazel said.

'With respect, Hazel,' Milly said, tight-lipped, 'I hardly think you, of all people would prove much protection against someone like Henry. All your life you've been cherished and protected. Your husband sounds as if he was a saint. You've absolutely no idea what somebody like Henry can be like. I can't risk it, Hazel. I'm sorry, I just can't.'

'Oh Milly, you're just working yourself into a state and I'm sure there's no need. After all, the chances are your husband would never even know you've moved from here, far less where you've gone.'

Milly remained rigidly silent.

'Oh, well.' Jenny had been searching cupboards for a clean towel. 'I think going with Hazel sounds an excellent idea to me, Milly. You and Hazel get on so well together. By the way,' she added before leaving the kitchen, 'if Rebecca is still engaged when I'm ready will you tell her I've gone out to dinner with a friend?'

The bath water ran disappointingly cold after a few minutes and she couldn't linger. She was still shivering as she dressed in her clean underwear and black wool suit. She nevertheless took time to apply make-up carefully and to brush her short curls until they gleamed.

'You look lovely,' Hazel said, when she reappeared in the kitchen. 'And so happy!'

'Happy?' Jenny felt surprised and intrigued. 'Do I?'

'But perhaps another little piece of jewellery dear?'

'I haven't got anything except this string of pearls, they belonged to my grandma.'

Hazel's hands went up to her ears. She carefully removed her pearl studs and held them out to Jenny.

'These will go very nicely with your necklace. You may borrow them for this evening.'

'Oh, thank you, Hazel. They're beautiful!' Clipping them on to her ears she admired herself in the mirror. It was while she was doing this that she thought she heard the doorbell. Immediately every nerve alerted with excitement. 'Was that the door?'

They listened. 'Rebecca's talking to someone,' Hazel said. 'Maybe it's your friend.'

'Oh, God!' Jenny's hand flew to her mouth, then she hurried from the room.

Rebecca's back was a ramrod of disapproval. She was trying to close the door. 'You are blocking my doorway,' she said icily.

Gregson was smiling. His foot was on the doorstep and his big frame leaning in a relaxed, good-humoured manner against the door lintel.

'It's all right, Rebecca,' Jenny called out. 'He's a friend of mine.' Then, breathlessly to Gregson, 'I've just to put on my coat. I won't be a minute.'

307

Rebecca followed her through to the kitchen where she'd left her coat. 'Will you never learn?'

'He's just a friend taking me out to dinner, Rebecca.'

Rebecca gazed pityingly at her as she struggled into her coat. 'I've tried to protect and advise you. Yet still you rush lemming-like to your fate. What else must I do to save you from yourself? What else must I do?'

45

Hazel stayed on at Rebecca's for a few weeks, hoping that it would give Rebecca time to make other arrangements. She prayed too that during those few weeks Milly's nerve would return and they would be able to start their brave new life together as they'd originally planned. Milly had been so enthusiastic when she'd seen round the house in Pollokshields and the housekeeper, lady companion idea had been put to her.

'If a couple of other women took my place,' Hazel suggested to Rebecca, 'that would alleviate any financial suffering.'

Whether or not Rebecca had the opportunity to take anyone else into the refuge, Hazel didn't know. All she became aware of was a subtle distancing, a coolness in Rebecca's attitude.

Even worse, a fence of icicles had grown round Milly. Now instead of Hazel and Milly going to the shops or Miss Buik's restaurant or the hairdresser's together, Milly went with Rebecca. It was as if Hazel had developed some sort of contagious disease that both Milly and Rebecca were afraid of catching. Hazel felt deeply distressed. She was flung back into the empty desert that her life had been before being rescued by Rebecca. She began to miss Derek again – she'd seldom thought of him during her stay at the refuge – or perhaps it was only being loved that she missed now.

'That's how it should be,' Rebecca had told her. 'You must put Derek behind you and build a life and a personality of your own.'

She had believed she was succeeding in doing this and her success had brought a growing sense of achievement and joy. Her move to her own home was meant to be a happy culmination of her achievements. She'd thought Rebecca would be as pleased and proud as she was herself. Now she felt confused – unsure what to think.

There were times when she longed for the balm of alcohol to soothe her troubled spirits. Now, however, she believed she had the strength to fight it. She clung to this belief. But all the time she longed for the warm affection, the emotional support that she'd once so generously received from Rebecca. No one else seemed to notice. Of course on the surface everything seemed much the same. Rebecca still spoke to her, still called her 'dear', still acted in a kindly and forgiving manner. Yet Hazel knew that, no doubt because Rebecca felt hurt, she had completely withdrawn from her. No doubt poor Milly had just lost her nerve and had tightened up with embarrassment. For whatever the reason, Hazel knew both women had shut her out. It was as if she had already gone back to the house in Pollokshields and had no longer any part in the refuge. It made her feel sad. Yet she could not remain there forever; for one thing she had a duty to Rowan. She had to have a home ready for her daughter's return from America. Rowan was bound to come back home in the not too distant future. It was only thoughts of Rowan's return that kept Hazel from breaking down, so keen was her unhappiness and disappointment. She kept reading and re-reading her daughter's letters to give her comfort and strength. Her daughter and her young friends in America were showing such courage in support of what they believed to be right that they were an example to her. Pride in her daughter gave Hazel strength. And oh, how wonderful it would be when they would be together again and able for the first time really to appreciate each other and their newfound relationship.

'You must have those letters off by heart now, hen,' Sadie said.

'My daughter's a wonderful girl,' Hazel sighed. Then with a shake of her head she added, 'When I think of the

310

silly nonsense my friends and I got up to when we were young, it makes me feel ashamed. Young people now are so much more *caring*.'

She'd tried to keep her spirits up by reading Rowan's letters. She wasn't alone in the world as long as she had Rowan. She had a lot to be thankful for. Not many daughters, she felt sure, could speak to their mothers (writing was just like speaking) with such unself-conscious frankness as Rowan did. Not many mothers could accept the very different world of the younger generation and their very different attitudes as Hazel had learned to do. She could read any of Rowan's letters now with hardly a tremor. The discipline of avoiding any hasty reply had become a firmly established habit and it had proved a wonderful success. Indeed Rowan had once used the word 'wonderful'; Hazel had that particular letter off by heart. 'It's so wonderful to be able to talk to you like this, Mother,' Rowan had written, 'It's just as if you've become my best friend.'

'My daughter and I have such a close and loving relationship,' she told Sadie proudly.

On the day she eventually left the refuge nobody was in except Sadie. Hazel felt hurt to the point of tears. She had been such good friends with Milly and yet even she had not returned in time to say au revoir and wish her luck. Jenny could be forgiven because she was out on a catering job and anyway Jenny had wished her luck before she'd left earlier in the day.

Neither Milly nor Rebecca had said anything. Or rather they'd just said the normal, 'See you later,' before going out. Milly, Hazel guessed, felt guilty and upset. In a way she could understand her need to escape having to say goodbye. She wasn't angry at poor Milly. She was far from being angry at Rebecca either. But she couldn't help feeling sad and hurt.

Sadie tried to make up for the absence of the others and Hazel was most touched. It occurred to her with considerable shame, that at one time Sadie would have

been the type of person that she would not have thought
worth a second glance. She would have dismissed Sadie,
her wrap-around overall, her coarse hairnet, her false
teeth, her broad Glasgow accent as frightfully common.
She would not have touched her with the proverbial
barge pole.

Now tears of gratitude sprang to her eyes when Sadie
said, 'I'll miss you, hen. You're a real nice, wee, soul. I
hope everything works out well for you. Remember now,
keep off the bottle and you'll be fine.'

'I'll miss you too, Sadie.' She gave the older woman a
hug and Sadie kissed her cheek and repeated, 'You'll be
fine, hen.'

'You'll always be welcome, Sadie.' Hearing the taxi
honking impatiently outside Hazel picked up her case.
'Any time you want to come to see me at Pollokshields.
Don't forget now.'

'Thanks, hen.'

Hazel was so upset she nearly forgot to put on her
gloves before leaving the house. She sat in the taxi,
gloved hands clasped tightly on fur-coated lap,
struggling not to weep.

It took only ten or fifteen minutes to reach her house in
Pollokshields and as the taxi swept up the steep curving
driveway she thought the house had never looked so big
or bleak. Fighting down the panic of entering the place
and being on her own she fumbled for a long time with
her purse. Then she asked the driver if he would carry
her luggage inside. The door clicked shut after he'd gone
and she was left standing alone beside her case, a small
figure in a lofty ceilinged hall.

Loneliness hit her. She bent forward nursing herself,
trying to protect herself against the agony of it. After a
few minutes she forced herself to carry her case up
to the bedroom. Everything was so still and quiet.
Corridors stretched long and dark and empty. Room
after empty room lay open like menacing black mouths
waiting to swallow her. She had never felt so

alone. She developed a fever of aloneness. She began running about and banging doors shut and switching on lights. She suddenly knew it had been a crazy idea to come here. She wasn't strong at all. She couldn't bear to be alone, she couldn't stand it. She needed a drink. She struggled desperately with the temptation to go to the drinks cabinet and find the vodka bottle. Or any kind of bottle. She tried not to think of the warmth, the comfort, the good cheer and finally the blessed oblivion alcohol would give her. Weeping in distress she shut herself in her bedroom and lay curled in tight foetal position on top of the bed. She daren't even risk going downstairs to make herself a cup of tea.

She clung desperately to thoughts of Rowan and how proud she was of her and how she wanted her daughter to be proud of her too.

It was a long night.

She awoke shivering in the morning, still in the dress she'd been wearing the day before and still without any covering of bedclothes.

A faint mist of light was drifting in through the closed curtains and giving the room a ghostly unreality. It was as if she'd never been away. There was no Rebecca, no Jenny, no Milly, no Sadie. And there was no Derek and no Rowan.

She was alone in the ghostly high-ceilinged room, in a house full of corridors leading nowhere. With an enormous effort she swung her legs from the bed and went over to draw the curtains. She stood gazing helplessly at the jungle of neglected back garden. It all but overwhelmed her. She turned away, talking firmly to herself in her mind: This is breakfast time. You must go downstairs, make a cup of tea and eat something.

In the kitchen she made a slice of toast, spread it with butter and sat automatically eating it without tasting a thing. She discovered by the kitchen clock that it was only seven o'clock in the morning.

It was a long day.

She had a bath, put on fresh make-up, changed her clothes and wondered what she could do next. She avoided the drawing room and the drinks cabinet, hardly daring to allow her eyes to stray in that direction when she crossed the hall.

She decided to go out for the *Herald* and perhaps do a little shopping – although weeks ago she and Milly had stocked up the deep freeze. What fun it had seemed then. What exciting plans they'd had. Oh, how disappointing it was that Milly had not come. Tears came so rapidly and so profusely she had to hurry back to the house in case anyone would see them.

Back in the house she tried to settle to read a book but her mind kept vaguely wandering. Thinking of what everyone would be doing at the refuge made tears blind her again. She felt a panic of loss and confusion. What had she done? Why had everything gone wrong? Why was she sitting here alone? Foolish woman that she was – what had made her think she could cope with anything on her own.

It was still morning. She made herself a cup of coffee. It was a day without end.

46

'We've plenty for a taxi,' Dode said. 'I'm too whacked to walk home.' He and Rose and Harry had been performing at a gig in Ayr, a seaside town some miles from Glasgow. Dode and Rose had nodded off to sleep in the train coming back, Dode with his head bouncing and rolling against the window, Rose with her head drooping on to Harry's chest. He had to put an arm around her to support her otherwise she would have crumpled down on to his knees. The trouble was that neither Dode nor Rose were fit. They were thin, pale and under-nourished and they obviously didn't get enough sleep. Rose's mouth was hanging slightly open and he could feel the moist warmth of her breath through his shirt. The feel of Rose's body cuddled against him was making him suffer all sorts of urgent twitchings and throbbings. But there was tenderness too. He could have gladly sat holding Rose in his arms the whole night through.

He never wanted to do that with anyone else. Nurse Milligan for instance. He still couldn't get over his astonishment at what Nurse Milligan had done.

He'd fallen in the gym at school during PT and got a skelf in his bum. He'd been horribly embarrassed at being sent along to the school nurse. Milligan was nearly as old as his mother. She must be at least 30. He wouldn't bare his bum to his mother for any reason, far less to a stranger – even though she was a medical person.

'Take off your trousers and your underpants,' Nurse Milligan had said and even the husky quaver in her voice hadn't given him a clue.

Trying not to shame himself by blushing he'd stripped off. Then she'd told him to bend over. She'd taken out

315

the skelf all right but before he'd had the chance to straighten up her hand had been between his legs, massaging him. He'd never felt anything so exciting in his life. Despite his astonishment and embarrassment, he'd moaned and writhed with the pleasure of it. The next thing he knew she'd been on the floor underneath him with her blue uniform skirt hitched up. She hadn't a stitch on underneath it. It'd been the first time he'd ever seen a woman's private parts. He'd stared fascinated as she'd widened her legs to give him a better look. Then she'd guided his hand against her and rubbed it back and forwards until she'd begun to moan. Soon he'd been thudding against her and inside her like a piston going at full steam.

It had been a fantastic experience that they'd repeated regularly at lunch time several times a week. Until she'd started to question him about where he went at night and who he went around with. She'd started in fact to sound like his mother. That was when he'd definitely lost interest.

The thing was, with him being so big and muscly he looked so much older than his age. He'd even been in a pub with an older guy he knew and had been served with an alcoholic drink without question. The barman wasn't purposefully breaking the law by serving someone under age, he just hadn't twigged. And no wonder. Harry's determined efforts at being tough physically and in every other way were paying off and he was proud of it. Only the other day – the happiest day so far in his whole life – he had won his Black Belt in Karate. He had discovered he had a real talent for this martial art; he was even fascinated by the whole Eastern philosophy behind it. Every spare minute when he wasn't actually doing Karate he was reading books about it and about Japanese history and culture. Dode was more than a little bitter about this obsession he'd acquired.

'You wouldn't think the Japs were so clever if they tormented you like they did my dad.'

'It's not a case of them being clever,' Harry tried to explain. 'It's just they're so different from us.'

'You can say that again.' Dode's face was tight with misery. 'They're mad.'

'No, it's just they have a different culture, a different philosophy, different traditions.'

'They tortured my dad. Tortured him for years. A man told my Mum.' Tears came into his voice. 'I hate them!'

'But you see,' Harry struggled to explain, 'their culture doesn't recognize surrender. If people gave up, in the Japs' eyes they were giving up any right to manhood. In their eyes too it was even worse if the British guy tried to stand up for himself or make things awkward. I bet your dad was like that because he'd believe, you see, it was the right thing, the manly thing to do. But the Japs were incensed by this attitude because to them he had given up all rights to being treated like a warrior and a man.'

'I don't care what you say,' Dode insisted. 'Nothing excuses them for torturing human beings. They're mad, that's what I say.'

'If anyone was mad during the last war it was the Germans,' Harry said. 'The Japanese were acting strictly within their ancient traditions and culture. The Germans were acting absolutely against their basic cultural beliefs. Germany is supposed to be a Western, twentieth century civilized Christian country. How could people like that do what they did to other human beings – especially to the Jews? It defies belief! Talk abut mad? Talk about tormenting people? Huh!' Harry always became lost for words when thinking about the Germans. They were beyond him. There was no hope in the world if so-called Christian people could do the things that they had. If that was how a white Aryan Christian race could behave – give him a black Jew or a yellow Buddhist every time!

He and Dode and Rose emerged from the main

317

entrance of Glasgow Central and joined the queue of people waiting for a taxi in the dark drizzle of Gordon Street. Crowds of winos, a grey-haired, toothless hag among them, milled around the gratings through which hot air puffed up. A bottle was being passed round from mouth to mouth accompanied by impatient snarls and bursts of garbled antagonism. Another drunk appeared at the beginning of the taxi queue making a farcical show of playing a mouth organ. Between every few sucks and blows he loudly pestered each person in turn for money, sometimes staggering and cursing among the queue, making women cry out in apprehension.

Harry watched and listened with only half his attention. He was too intent on staring round to see if there was any sign of another taxi. Then, noticing a paper boy at the corner selling the next morning's *Daily Record*, he legged it along the few yards to buy one. When he came back two youths who were obviously intent on shoving into the front of the queue were jostling Rose and laughing at her white tired face. Dode was ineffectually trying to stop them with plaintive cries of 'Leave her alone, aw go on . . . We've been waiting for ages here.'

As Harry reached them his hand suddenly exploded forward. His fingers caught one of the youths, boring into the soft flesh on either side of the jaw bone. Squeezing his neck in a vice-like grip Harry leaned forward and hissed venomously, 'Piss off!' With a heave of his arm he rattled the youth's head off the lamp-post. Much subdued the two youths moved off.

'Thanks, Harry,' Rose said.

Rain had sharpened into bullets of hail now and Harry huddled into the turned-up collar of his duffel-jacket, hands plunged deep into pockets, feet stamping to keep circulation going strong.

Rose was violently shivering. 'I'm so tired I could die,' she said.

'I wish you'd give this up, Rosie,' Harry said. 'It's not good for your health having so many late nights and

318

being so often and for so long in stuffy, smoky atmospheres.'

Rose sighed. 'It gets me out of the house. I have to get out somewhere with dad being the way he is.'

Suddenly, without thinking, Harry said, 'Why don't you come out with me sometimes, Rosie? We could go to the pictures or for walks. You might even fancy coming to Karate with me.'

Rose's face shone up at him through the darkness. He wasn't sure if it was rain or tears wetting her cheeks.

'Oh, Harry,' she said, 'that would be wonderful! Oh Harry, I'd love to.'

And he felt the tenderness again.

47

'It's a mattah,' Jackson's deep husky voice insisted, 'of testing, of confronting every Supreme Court ruling, every law down heah.'

'Oh?' Rowan raised a brow as he continued.

'Of putting these laws into practice. Of making sure they're applied.'

'Like the one that says segregation is unconstitutional? We tested it at the downtown lunch counters and it didn't apply.'

'Nothing worthwhile has ever been achieved anywhayah without a struggle,' Jackson said. 'The ball's rolling now. Nothing's going to stop it. But it's not just desegregation of buses and lunch countahs. There's vote registration, that's the area I'm working in. That's where I think the real powah is, the real freedom lies.'

'Freedom to do what?' Rowan scoffed. 'You talk about vote registration but Willard's told me about all the legal technicalities used to discourage and prevent blacks from registering to vote. Educated blacks are even told they've failed the literacy test. And there's the poll tax in Alabama, Mississippi, Texas and Virginia.'

'The Negro cannot be denied a basic constitutional right to vote. These things have got to be overcome. And it's not just the things you've mentioned. There's also ignorance, illiteracy and apathy among the blacks. We've got to educate the Southern white man too. You said to me once that this was war. Well, I believe that. Since war begins in the minds of men it is in the minds of men that peace must begin.'

Rowan looked at his serious, caring face and suddenly wondered why she was arguing with him. She sighed, 'I don't know why we keep arguing. We're both on the

320

same side, aren't we? Despite what I've been saying I'm going on the Freedom Ride.'

'Of course we're on the same side, honey,' he said gently. 'That's one of the reasons I'm going with you.'

'But what about your work?' she asked in surprise.

'I've work to do in Alabama and Mississippi in connection with the Vote Registration. But even without that – I couldn't let you go down theah on your own. I remembah the violence on the last Freedom Ride.'

Her heart was warmed by his concern but she said, 'I'm tougher than I thought I was. Or maybe it's just stubbornness. No ignorant Southern bigot is going to intimidate me.'

'You realize I suppose that this means not only a sit-in at a lunch countah. It's to test the anti-segregation ruling on interstate transport, including station restrooms, waiting-rooms all along the route.'

'I know. But I'll be with friends. . . .' She smiled at him. 'I'm glad you'll be with us too. That makes thirteen, seven blacks and six whites.'

'I hope you're not superstitious.'

She shrugged. 'If our bus doesn't succeed other buses will follow. And of course we'll be joined by local black people at each place we stop. I admit I'm not in the least optimistic about changing Southern whites with minds so full of hate. Nevertheless I see that something has to be done and has to keep being done. I'm not an American but I'm damned if they're going to get away with what happened to me and my friends.' Her voice betrayed a crack of distress and he immediately drew her into his arms and nursed her close to his body.

The warmth and the strength of him comforted her and she clung to him gratefully. In the privacy of his small book-cluttered apartment, for the moment at least, she enjoyed an illusion of safety. As his lips found hers she opened herself to him in a surge of need and he responded with a passion that surprised and over-whelmed her. As they made love over and over again and he kept plunging deep inside her she knew that she would never feel alone again as long as she had him. Home was where he was.

Afterwards she lay in his arms tired but content, until he gently roused her.

'I'd bettah take you back befohah your friends put out a search party.'

She gave a mock groan. 'I don't think I can move. You've exhausted me.'

'I'm sorry, honey.' He looked concerned. 'It was too soon aftah your beating, I should have been mohah careful.'

'I'm all right,' she laughed. 'I told you! I'm tougher than I thought. Now I'm happier than I ever realized I could be as well.'

They went out to his car arm-in-arm. And while he was driving she kept looking round at his face. He had high cheek bones, a straight nose and firm chin. His hair, cropped and straight, was a nut-brown colour. His skin had a healthy tan.

'You look very fit for an academic,' she said.

'Shouldn't an academic be fit?'

'Well, the ones I've seen in Britain have all looked pale and kind of dusty as if they seldom came up for air from their books.'

He laughed. 'There's that sort here too, I suppose. But I enjoy having regular work-outs in the gym. I find I function better that way.'

'You certainly do!' She grinned round at him.

She couldn't sleep for a long time that night but only because she felt so happy. When she did drift away it wasn't to be engulfed in the terrifying nightmares of previous nights. The memories of hate and violence had been banished by dreams of love.

She was still in a happy euphoria when she and Jackson boarded the bus that came to take them on their journey through the Deep South. They sat together holding hands, hardly able to take their eyes off one another. Everything went comparatively well. There were a few unpleasant incidents and occasional scuffles as the riders attempted to use bus terminal rest-rooms and lunchrooms. But they didn't frighten her. Not any more.

Until they got to Alabama. At Atlanta, Georgia they had divided into two bus groups to travel to Birmingham, with only one stop on the way. It was at that stop, while pulling into one of the depots, the Greyhound bus carrying the first group of riders was stoned. Its tyres were slashed and a mob of some 200 people attacked it. Rowan was determined not to allow her terror to give way to panic as faces livid with hatred fought to get nearer the bus. The bus managed to race away but had to stop about 6 miles out of town to fix the flat tyres. Here a mob again surrounded the vehicle and someone tossed a firebomb through the rear door.

'Quick!' Jackson grabbed her arm. 'The emergency door!' Before she could recover from the shock of what had happened he had thrown her out and they were both rolling on the grass. Seconds later the bus burst into flames.

At least this incident got national publicity. The burning image of the bus covered the front pages of every American newspaper.

Rowan felt shaken. She realized now the seriousness of the warnings that the black organizers had given before they'd set off on the ride. They had said to be prepared not only for violence but for the possibility of death. Several of the riders had left letters to be delivered to loved ones if they were killed. She wished now that she had left a letter for her mother.

Jackson tried to persuade Rowan not to go on. When persuasion met with no success he became angry. 'This isn't any of your damn business,' he told her. 'This isn't your fight.' But she remembered what Aunt Abbie had said about injustice being everybody's business and he couldn't deny the truth of that.

'Anyway, you can't get rid of me now,' she said. 'Your

fight, no matter what it's about, is my fight. And where you go, I go.'

He closed his eyes. After a minute he said, 'Have I ever told you that I love you?'

'No.'

'Well, I'm telling you now.'

There was a lot of trouble before they managed to get another bus after the first one had been destroyed by fire. There was also a great deal of negotiating by the black organizers and talk at every level, even as high as the President himself, to put pressure on the bus company and also on the governing bodies of Alabama. A representative of the Justice Department was sent down to tell the Governor of Alabama in person and in no uncertain terms that 'These people have got to have access to interstate transportation.' Not only that but they had to be given protection. Eventually a promise was given that this would happen and a week after the bombing incident and with their number now twenty-one the riders set off for Montgomery.

Two Greyhound bus officials were to accompany them. State police said that a private plane would fly over the bus and there would be a state patrol car every 15 or 20 miles along the highway. This is exactly what happened. The relief and calmness this security brought was wonderful. Everyone relaxed. Rowan put her head down on Jackson's shoulder and napped. She thought he did too. As soon as the bus reached the city limits of Montgomery, however, the plane flew away. Then the patrol cars disappeared as the bus pulled into the quiet Montgomery bus terminal.

Suddenly, terrifyingly, there were cries of 'Niggahs! Kill the niggahs!' As if by magic white people were everywhere and all armed with sticks, baseball bats, bricks and chains. There were women among them, their faces twisted with venom.

Somebody in the bus called out, 'If we get out the back we might have a chance.'

324

'Let the women go that way,' Jackson said calmly. 'I'm walking out front the way I came in.'

'Man, you've got a lot of nerve,' one of the black riders said. 'But I'm with you.'

Before she could stop him Jackson was at the door. At first the crowd just gaped. Obviously they couldn't believe there was a white man helping the black cause. Then suddenly a terrible blood-chilling roar rent the air and Jackson was grabbed and pulled into the mob. It gave the others the chance to make a run for it. Rowan ran towards the mob screaming as if her heart was breaking, not for herself but for Jackson. Hands were pulling and punching at her and forgetting all the non-violent training she struggled like a wild thing to try and get to where Jackson was being mauled and brutalized. Dozens of people were all over him. A woman caught her by her pony-tail, twisted it with one hand and jabbed an umbrella handle into her back with the other. At the same time a skinny, teenage girl in a yellow T-shirt was doing a bouncy backwards dance in front of her, punching gleefully at her face.

'Oh, God' Rowan kept thinking dazedly, 'Oh, please God, help Steve!'

48

Hazel went to bed early again. She couldn't get over the feeling of isolation caused by being cut off from friendship, affection and support by Rebecca. At the same time she was struggling valiantly to get over it. Despite her anguish she was thankful for small mercies; at least she was now able to put up a struggle, to try to defeat her own weaknesses. She kept telling herself how lucky she was. She had her health, she was comfortably off, she had her own home and – most of important of all – she had a wonderful, courageous and loving daughter. She fixed her mind on Rowan. She read and re-read her letters. She planned the delicious meals she would have for her when she returned. She would pamper and cosset and spoil Rowan to make up for all the terrible things the poor girl had suffered in America. She acted out little domestic scenes in her mind.

'You have a long lie in bed, darling,' she would say. 'I'll bring you a breakfast tray.'

She saw herself carrying the tray into Rowan's bedroom and placing it across Rowan's knees. Then she was plumping up the pillows at her back and making her as comfortable as possible, just as Rowan used to do for her.

She'd sit by the bedside with a cup of tea and they would talk. Oh, how they'd talk!

Then she'd give Rowan the *Herald* and she'd say, 'Now just you relax for as long as you like, darling. I'm going downstairs to prepare something really delicious for your lunch.' Of course, she couldn't cook really but still, perhaps with a little practice?

She began searching out recipe books in the kitchen and planning the meals she would make for Rowan when

326

she returned. It passed quite a pleasant morning. In the afternoon she would go to the shops and buy some of the ingredients she needed and she would try one of the recipes for her own dinner that evening. That would be her first practice. By the time Rowan came she would have it perfect. She smiled to herself thinking of Rowan's surprise and pleasure at how different she'd become.

'I knew you'd stopping drinking, Mother,' Rowan would say, 'but I didn't realize what a complete transformation you'd managed. The last time I saw you you didn't even know how to switch on the cooker.' And they'd both laugh.

Then she received Rowan's letter. The one in which she told of her love for an American called Steve Jackson. Rowan wrote:

Now, for the first time, I understand how you felt about Derek. Steve means everything to me. I wouldn't want to live without him. I feel I'm part of him and he's part of me. Despite all the awful things going on here, Mother, and how alien the place feels at times, where he is is where my home is from now on. . . .

For a long time Hazel stared at the letter, too stunned to move or think. Then gradually rivulets of emotion and thought came trickling back. She was glad that Rowan had found a good man that she loved and who loved her, truly glad. She would write back and tell Rowan how happy she was for her. Then behind the rivulets came the storm – she was flung into a vast sea of emptiness. She was panicking. She felt frightened. Her mind refused to work. She needed a drink, just one drink to calm her. With grateful haste she went to the drinks cabinet and poured out a glass of vodka. After she'd gulped it down she felt no better and desperately poured herself another. And another. Then she noticed the bottle was empty. Its emptiness brought back panic.

'But I can go out and get more, can't I?' she said out loud, to comfort herself. 'Of course I can!'

There was an off-licence not ten minutes away. Swaying and staggering by this time she reached the front door and was soon wending a tortuous path down the drive and away along the street. The cool evening air made her head unexpectedly whirl and before long she was feeling so dizzy and faint she couldn't go on. She leaned against a wall drowning now in an ocean of despair.

'Are you ill?'

A man lightly touched her arm. He was perhaps in his late forties, a burly figure with a weatherbeaten skin and a receding hairline. He was wearing a shabby tweed coat with the collar turned up. He had kind grey eyes. Just for a second Hazel nearly said she had 'flu or some such lie. Once upon a time she had told many lies to cover up her drinking – but not any more.

'I'm an alcoholic,' she said. 'I'm all right if I never take that first drink. But tonight, weak fool that I am, I did. Then not content with one, of course, I had another and another. That's why I feel ill.'

'We all have our weak moments,' the man said. 'We all feel down at times. Don't hate yourself.'

'Can I trouble you to help me to get back home,' she said.

'No trouble.'

'May I take your arm? I feel so dizzy and faint.'

'Just hold tight on to me.'

'Thank you. You're very kind.'

She had not forgotten her fearful and shameful experience with the last man she'd allowed into her house. But apart from the fact that she had no choice – she needed help to get home – she somehow knew that this was a different type of person. A working man by the look of him and the muscular feel of his arm. But someone she could trust.

'My name is Dan Walker,' the man told her as they made their way slowly and carefully along.

'How do you do,' Hazel said, 'I'm Hazel Saunders.'

Later, in her kitchen, Dan made her a cup of tea and she began to feel better. They sat at the kitchen table drinking tea and talking as if they had known each other for years. He was a widower and so he understood how she felt. He missed Sheila, his late wife, and often experienced the private hell of loneliness. After a while she felt so much better she was able to make a little supper for both of them. She tied on an apron and felt happy fussing about switching eggs and chopping some tinned ham to put in an omelette. Dan set the table.

She could see by the enthusiastic way he tucked into the omelette that he had thoroughly enjoyed it. He made short work of the milk pudding she made as well.

'You're a good cook, Hazel,' he said, gazing at her in obvious admiration.

'Well, perhaps with a bit of practice. . . .' she agreed. She washed the dishes and he dried.

'I can't be bothered cooking for myself,' he admitted. 'As often as not I just eat a jam sandwich, or cakes or biscuits. I've a terrible sweet tooth.'

'That *is* terrible,' Hazel said. 'It's not the kind of food a man needs, especially a big man like you. There's no nourishment in cakes or biscuits.'

'I know,' he said, 'I must stop being so stupid.'

'You're not stupid!' Hazel assured him. 'You just need somebody to look after you.'

He smiled. 'We're a pair, aren't we? You with your drinking and me with my eating.'

She had to laugh. He laughed too, a nice deep manly laugh. It didn't matter that his hair was thinning and he was a bit on the heavy side. Or that he had rough workman's hands. She liked him. She felt comfortable with him.

'Oh, well,' he said, looking at his watch and rising. 'It's getting late. I'd better go and let you get to bed.'

She helped him on with his coat and followed him out to the hall. At the front door he turned and put out his hand.

'It's been a great pleasure meeting you, Hazel, I really appreciated your company.'

'I don't understand,' she said. 'You say that. Yet you're going away without asking to see me again.'

'Oh, my dear,' he said, 'there's nothing I want more, believe me. But . . .' He gazed round the luxurious hall with its crystal chandeliers and expensive antique ornaments. 'I'm afraid I'm not in your class.'

'Class!' Hazel scoffed. 'What does that matter?'

'I thought it might to a lady like yourself. I'm a builder by trade. I'm self-employed now, but it's only a small local business.'

'You're a good, kind man, Dan Walker,' she said. 'That's all that matters to me.'

He looked down at her in silence for a few moments. Then he said, 'Do you want the truth?'

'Yes.'

'I think you are the most beautiful, the most wonderful woman I've ever met. And I don't want to leave you. I want to stay with you tonight and every night from now on.'

Hazel took a deep breath. Then she smiled and said calmly, 'You lock up. I'll go and check that everything's tidy in the kitchen and switch off the lights.'

49

'Come in.' Victoria's voice was a weak quaver. It made Amelia forget her surprise at finding the outside door unlocked in her anxiety to reach her mother.

Victoria was lying on her side in the opened-down bed-settee in the living room with blankets and an old coat pulled up over her shoulders. Only the top of her black head veiled with grey was visible. The fire hadn't been lit. The room was like a tomb. An air of dejection hung over it.

'Mummy, what's wrong?'

'I've been thinking of Matthew. We never knew his heart was bad, did we? I realize now what the poor soul must have suffered.'

'Mummy, what are you talking about?'

'The doctor's not long away, he says it's my heart. He's given me tablets.'

Amelia's own heart struggled painfully in her chest. She didn't know what to say. She felt frightened. Never before had she considered the possibility of anything happening to her mother. Her mother was indefatigable, a proud, infuriating, talented woman, generous to a fault. How many times when she was young had Amelia sat in the audience at a Church Guild or a YWCA Social and watched her mother at the piano, her fingers rippling effortlessly over the keys, her head flung back in an enthusiastic, chest-heaving rendering of 'Bless This House' or '. . . a tree that looks at God all day and lifts its leafy arms to pray.' Many a meeting her mother had spoken at, too. It used to cause Matthew much anguish the way she never prepared for such occasions – never even took notes. He was always so meticulous about everything. 'Och, I always think of something to say when the time comes,' she would airily brush aside his worries and his offers of help.

'Will I make you a cup of tea?' Amelia asked.

'That would be very nice, dear.' Victoria struggled round and into a sitting position. 'Pile these pillows up at my back. I'm supposed to have them high all the time the doctor says.'

Amelia hurried over to the bed. 'Is that better?'

Her mother nodded, lips pressed together and nostrils quivering as if she was willing herself to keep calm and breathe easily.

'Where's your lodgers? Have they been doing anything for you?'

Victoria gave Amelia a small pitying smile. 'Aggie and her man are both in their seventies. They need somebody to look after them. They've got their names down for an old folk's home.'

'I'll go and put the kettle on. Will I make you anything to eat?'

Her mother shook her head. Amelia felt unnerved by the sad, far-away look in her eyes. Through in the narrow strip of kitchenette, while waiting for the kettle to boil, she laid out two cups and saucers and put milk and sugar in her mother's cup and just milk in her own. She couldn't set a tray with the milk jug and sugar bowl alongside the cups because there was no tray. There was not and never had been any convenience or luxury of any kind in her mother's house. (Except her piano.) It was one of the most infuriating things about her mother. It didn't matter how Amelia tried to help her with material things, how many handy trays or comforting quilts or sets of fine bone china or dressing gowns she'd given her, Victoria either lost them, ruined them, broke them, or gave them away. Mostly she gave things away. 'Her need was greater than mine,' she'd say. Her mother's greatest talent was for remaining poor.

Amelia took the tea through. 'What did the doctor

say, Mummy? What instructions did he give you? Maybe I should have a talk with him.'

'He's coming back to see me tomorrow. I've to rest in bed. It's not just that, though. There's always been something wrong with me. . . .' Her eyes flicked downwards and her mouth tightened with embarrassment, '. . . down there. I was never the same after having you.'

Amelia never knew what to say about that. It was a lifetime too late to apologize, although she often felt it was expected of her. They both sat sipping tea for a minute or two.

Then her mother said, 'I've been thinking of your daddy quite a lot recently.'

This made Amelia frightened again. 'Daddy wouldn't want you to get upset.'

Her mother sighed. 'I've had a hard life, Amelia.'

This was terrible. Her mother was the most optimistic and cheerful of women. She never faced reality. Amelia had a sudden memory from her childhood of Victoria striding about the house singing one of her favourite songs: 'I'm forever blowing bubbles, pretty bubbles in the air. . . .' Amelia was lost for words.

'Your daddy wasn't a bad man,' her mother said after a long pause, 'but he was a difficult man.'

'He loved you,' Amelia managed to say.

'Aye,' her mother had the sad, faraway look in her eyes again. 'And I loved him.'

After another pause Amelia said, 'It's terribly cold in here, Mummy. Where's that electric fire I gave you?'

'Och I gave old Mrs McDevlin a wee loan of it. She's a poor soul.'

Amelia took an immediate headache with irritation and frustration. Her mother's generosity always had this effect on her. Sometimes it made her furious as well – like the time her mother gave away a brooch that Amelia had valued beyond price. It was the only present Andrew Summers had ever given her. She'd been staying at her mother's for a few days, on holiday from work, at the time. 'How dare you,' she'd trembled with outrage, 'you knew that brooch was mine.'

'Och, away you go and don't be so selfish,' her mother had said with a dismissive flick of her hand.

The headachy silence was splintered by a call from the outside door. 'Yoo-hoo! Can I come in, Mrs Drummond?'

'Come away through, Mrs Hamilton,' her mother called with sudden breathless cheerfulness.

'Be careful now, Mummy,' Amelia warned. 'You're supposed to rest.'

It would have been typical of her mother, who loved nothing more than having visitors and entertaining them, to have leapt up to fetch more tea and homemade scones for Mrs Hamilton and then rattle out a cheerful tune on the piano. However her mother stayed where she was and Amelia could see a pulse beating at her neck. The normal bright bounce had returned to her voice, though.

'Come away in, come away in! Would you look at me at this time of day? I must be getting lazy in my old age, Mrs Hamilton.'

Mrs Hamilton was Victoria's next door neighbour, a mountain of a woman with muscular arms that she kept almost perpetually folded across her chest.

'I saw the doctor's car, hen. Is there anything I can do for you?'

'That's very kind of you, Mrs Hamilton, but now that my daughter's here I'll be all right.'

Mrs Hamilton turned to Amelia. 'She didn't look right last night. I said to my man, "Mrs Drummond's in for something".'

'It's my heart and a few other things for good measure,' Victoria said. 'At our age we just begin to wear done.'

'You speak for yourself, hen,' Mrs Hamilton laughed. 'There's a lot of life in this old dog yet. And a lot of life in you as well, I'll bet.' Turning to Amelia again she added, 'She's a wonderful woman!'

There was another call from the outside door now. 'Are you there, Mrs Drummond?'

'Through in the living room, Mrs Petrie.' Another of the neighbours appeared.

'Oh my, you're in bed!' Mrs Petrie was less than half the size of Mrs Hamilton in width at least and she was still wearing her curlers. 'I saw the doctor and I just thought it was you.' Then she added to Mrs Hamilton, 'She didn't look right yesterday.'

'Just what I was saying,' agreed Mrs Hamilton.

'Can I get you a message, Mrs Drummond? I'll be going along to the shops in a wee minute.'

'I need my paper and a few biscuits and I think I'm nearly out of tea but Amelia will run along for them. You and Mrs Hamilton sit down and keep me company if you've a minute to spare. Amelia will fetch you a cup of tea before she goes to the shops.'

Another woman had arrived before Amelia had time to pour the tea and she had to lay out yet another cup.

The other visitor was small, beaky Mrs McDade, her mother's oldest friend after Rory Donovan. She was wearing her inevitable hat. She never took off her hat, a cosy felt with a turned-up brim, indoors or out; Amelia often wondered if she wore it in bed.

The three women pulled chairs over and settled close round the bed. Amelia lit the fire to heat the room before hurrying away with a list of messages, as shopping was called in Glasgow. She had a peculiar feeling of 'déja vu'. It was as if she was a child again anxiously facing the ordeal of handing over one of her mother's notes to a long-suffering shopkeeper.

'Could you please give my wee girl a quarter of tea, a quarter stone of potatoes, a tin of corned beef and a packet of biscuits and I'll pay you at the end of the week.'

This had always happened when Victoria couldn't get any more credit on her 'store book' at the Co-op. Her mother was forever getting into desperate financial straits but because she was a proud woman, she could

335

seldom bring herself to ask for credit in person. Even as a very small child it had always been a humiliation to Amelia. The miserable waiting, eyes down as the shopkeeper read the note, the feeling that all the other customers knew her shame, then the grudging tone of the shopkeeper's voice. 'Well, I'll give you them this time but this has got to be the last, remember!' The hurrying back up the road with the shopping bag. The sight of her mother's anxious, waiting face at the window.

It seemed to Amelia that she had always been locked with her mother in a secret world fraught with anxiety. Her mother could, however, step effortlessly, or so it seemed, into another completely different world. In company she could appear bright and bouncy and supremely happy. She could talk such romantic and optimistic nonsense too. She was always 'forever blowing pretty bubbles in the air.'

It occurred to Amelia for the first time that perhaps this could be the only way that her mother was able to cope with the 'hard life' she had mentioned. *The way she herself did with her writing.* It was shattering to discover she and her mother might have something in common. Amelia felt so distracted by this new line of thought she was nearly run down by a bus when crossing the road on the way back from the shops.

The neighbours were laughing hilariously at one of her mother's stories when Amelia returned to the house. Her mother's eyes were shining brightly like polished brown beads and there was a feverish spot of colour on each cheek.

'Mummy, are you all right?' Amelia could feel every muscle in her own face strain with tension. 'Is it not time you had a wee lie down?'

'I told you,' Victoria replied impatiently, 'the doctor advised me to keep propped up. Oh here, I forgot to ask you to phone Rory. Away back down and give her a ring. She'll want to know that I'm not well.' Then, to the neighbours, 'We've been close friends for years, Rory

336

and me. Right from when we were at primary school. It was just perfect when my Amelia married Rory's boy. That was us legally joined you might say. But we've always been like sisters Rory and me.'

Amelia went hurrying back to the shops and the nearest phone box. It was no use phoning her brother Jamie, of course – he and his wife Fiona were somewhere in the Dordogne on holiday. Not that they were ever around when they were needed. They were great at sending cards though. Amelia had a terrible memory for such things but Jamie and Fiona never forgot to send post cards, Christmas cards, birthday cards, Happy Mother's Day cards; her mother had quite a collection of them. They were one of the few things she treasured.

Amelia phoned Rory's business and was put through to her mother-in-law's office. 'Rory, is that you?'

'Is something wrong Amelia?' Rory's voice sounded wary.

'Well, yes. . . .'

'It's not Douglas?'

'No. It's mummy. She must have had a heart attack during the night. I didn't find out until this morning. I don't think it's too serious. She's sitting up in bed chatting away quite the thing at the moment. But I'm going to see the doctor tomorrow to find out exactly. She told me to phone you.'

'Tell her I'll come over straight after work this afternoon. Tell her I'll stay overnight with her.'

'That's awfully kind of you.'

'Your mother has never liked being on her own at the best of times, Amelia.'

'Oh, she wouldn't be on her own. There's her lodgers and if necessary, I'll stay.'

'I mean sleep with her. Everything's always worse when you're alone in the middle of the night. At least it is for Victoria. I know your mother a lot better than you do. Tell her I'll be over as soon as I can.' She hung up.

Worriedly Amelia phoned home. Harry answered.

'Gran's not well, son. Tell your dad I'll maybe have to stay overnight. Will you manage the meals, do you think?'

'I've had to manage them before,' Harry said.

Hurt added to Amelia's distress. She needed someone to turn to for comfort but there was no one. 'So you have, son.'

'Give gran my love.'

'Yes. I will.'

He hung up.

Her hand trembled as she replaced the receiver. She longed to be back in her office room safely cocooned in her current novel. Instead she was being mercilessly propelled along the frightening paths of reality.

She never had any difficulty in creating plenty of positive action in her books and strong decisive characters. Now however in trying to cope with real life she helplessly dithered. Her mind was a turmoil of indecision. Should she phone the doctor? Should she try to contact Jamie and Fiona? Perhaps the travel agency would know the name of their hotel. But what travel agency? Would her mother want her to make such a fuss? Her obsessional anxiety had always irritated Harry beyond endurance; he could become quite snappy with her. She was always struggling to get the better of her anxious feelings but had never remotely succeeded.

She almost spoke out loud to herself as she made her way absently back to the house. Mummy's going to be all right, she told herself, she's going to be all right. This head-screaming anxiety, this nerve knotting apprehension is *your* illness. It's nothing to do with mummy's condition. It's just you. Mummy's all right.

Victoria looked anxiusly at her as soon as she entered the living room. 'What did Rory say?'

'She'll be over as soon as she finishes work this afternoon and she'll stay with you overnight.'

Her mother visibly relaxed. 'She's a good soul. She stayed with me the night of your daddy's funeral.'

'So she did. I couldn't stay, remember, because I'd left Harry with the Robertsons but I could stay with you tonight.'

'No, no, hen,' her mother said, not unkindly. 'I'll be all right if I've got Rory. Come back tomorrow morning and see that the place is tidy for the doctor coming.'

'But I don't mind staying.'

'You've still got Harry to see to and you've got your man now as well.'

'Harry can make the meals. He's used to it.' The words slipped out before she could stop them. Her mother looked around her assembled friends.

'Is that not terrible?'

'What I mean is . . .' Amelia hastily backtracked away from disapproval, 'he likes cooking and I let him make a meal occasionally.'

'It's that writing of hers, you know,' her mother continued. 'Scribble, scribble, scribble. She's always been the same.'

The moment of kindness had gone. Amelia began gathering up the cups and saucers.

'Rory won't have had anything to eat when she arrives,' Victoria continued. 'You'd better peel a potato and open that tin of corned beef. And there should be enough milk to make a wee drop pudding.'

Amelia made corned beef patties and a pudding with a packet of strawberry custard she found in the cupboard.

As soon as Rory arrived she made straight for the living room and warmly embraced Victoria. Victoria clung gratefully round her neck. 'I knew you wouldn't let me down,' she said.

Amelia dished the meal.

'She's got to go and see to her man,' Victoria said nodding in Amelia's direction. 'I told her I didn't want her staying here neglecting her good man.'

Somehow Amelia managed to say, 'I'm just going, Mummy.'

Once ready with her coat on she stood uncertainly

beside her mother's bed, aching to embrace her as Rory had. Eventually she did. At the same time, to her horror she felt tears gush into her eyes and the stiffness of her features began to quiver and weaken.

'For goodness sake,' her mother laughed. 'What a face! Away you go and don't act daft.'

50

Rebecca kept clinging on to the fact that the last time Alice had read her tarot cards she'd said, 'You're definitely going to be working and living in a much bigger building, Rebecca. Many people will come to you for help and guidance. This building will become famous throughout the land. You will become famous. People will come from far and wide to see you and admire the work you do.'

She needed something to cling on to. She was going through a very worrying patch. Not only had Hazel left but Milly had suddenly packed her bags and gone to be Hazel's housekeeper. After all the warnings she'd given both women! She was surprised at Milly especially. It was that man's fault of course – the man Hazel had secretly married in Martha Street Registrar's office. He looked like a big Irish navvy and Hazel hardly knew him. Hazel would regret such a reckless and foolish step she was sure.

Hazel and Daniel Walker had arrived at the refuge while she'd been out and God knows what they'd said to Milly. She could see when she got back from a house visit to a 'friend' that they had been talking to her. Milly looked quite flushed and excited. After they'd gone Rebecca had tried to get Milly to reveal exactly what they'd been saying but all Milly kept repeating was, 'I'm so happy for Hazel, aren't you Rebecca? What a fine, big man Mr Walker is. So strong and dependable looking.'

Rebecca struggled valiantly with herself. She prayed that both Hazel and Milly would be safe and happy, but she feared for them. She feared for herself too.

She hadn't so many appointments at the moment. She had been very upset when Elvira had stopped coming for her once-a-week visit. It had been during these visits that she'd been persuading Elvira of the importance of the refuge and how Elvira could help by becoming an official patron. She'd thought she was succeeding. Then without any warning Elvira stopped coming, only sending a short note informing Rebecca that she would no longer be requiring any other appointments. Rebecca had written to her, got no reply and phoned her, only to be told by a servant that she was not available. Apart from the fact that she was worried about Elvira, it was a blow to lose her as a client. It sounded impressive that someone like Elvira Fortescue-Brown was even just a 'friend of the refuge'. She only wanted to impress people, of course, in order to get their help and support for her work with abused women. Rebecca had long ago resolved that she would do anything that was necessary to make it succeed – anything at all.

Elvira who despite having titled parents, had suffered a very deprived childhood, was being equally deprived of love and understanding by her insensitive hunting, shooting and fishing husband. Killing poor defenceless animals was all he ever thought of or spoke about, apparently. Elvira needed to be loved and cherished and such a man was totally incapable of treating her with tenderness and sensitivity. She'd told Elvira that and Elvira had silently agreed with her. Yet not long afterwards she had written the polite note cancelling her next appointment.

Receiving no satisfaction with her own letter and phone call, Rebecca had decided, after some serious meditation and prayer, to go to see Elvira and discuss face to face what had happened.

It turned out to be a castle of a place on the banks of Loch Lomond; it had taken all Rebecca's courage and faith in her cause not only to rattle the door knocker but insist on pushing past the servant and refusing to leave until she'd seen her friend, Elvira. The servant had disappeared then returned eventually and commanded, 'Follow me!'

Rebecca was somewhat nonplussed to be led into a room which held not only Elvira but her husband. He was dressed in the kilt and his tree trunk-like legs were firmly planted on a fierce looking tiger-skin rug.

'My servant tells me,' Fortescue-Brown's voice exploded like cannon fire, 'that you forced your way into the house. Explain yourself, woman!'

Rebecca said with dignity, 'I came to see Elvira, Mr Fortescue-Brown. May I sit down?'

'No, you may not, madam,' Mr Fortescue-Brown roared. His wife said in an icy voice, 'I cannot imagine why you wish to see me, Rebecca. Surely you must have received my letter.'

'I would prefer to speak to you alone, Elvira.'

'Anything you wish to say to me' – Elvira's expression was aristocratically distant; she was literally looking down her nose at Rebecca – 'can be said in front of my husband.'

Rebecca couldn't help admiring her nerve. After all, she could have embarrassed Elvira, to say the least, if she had chosen to reveal some of the things Elvira had told her under hypnosis. Rebecca silently prayed for and received enough strength to resist the temptation. 'In that case,' Rebecca said, with head held high, 'all I can say is, you know where to find me if you need me, Elvira.' And with that she left. She felt deeply wounded all the same. After all, she had been nothing but good and patient and kind to Elvira. Knowing she'd travelled all that way the least she could have done was offer her a refreshing cup of tea. When Rebecca thought of all the cups of tea Elvira had enjoyed and been welcome to at Battlefield House! Life could be cruelly hard and unfair.

Long periods of being alone in the house stretched before her like a dangerous black pit. She felt apprehensive and insecure. Jenny was hardly ever in nowadays, what with her catering commissions and her gallivanting about with Al Gregson every time he came up from London or wherever he'd been. He was having a very

343

unsettling influence on Jenny. He was a dangerous man, Rebecca felt sure. Oh, he was always extremely charming to her when he called for Jenny. But she could tell. Even while he was smiling and being polite there was a look in his eyes. She knew.

'He's the same as your husband,' she'd told Jenny.

'Please don't say that, Rebecca,' Jenny pleaded. 'It's just not true. He's nothing like Joe. I don't know why you keep saying that.'

'There's a repressed violence about him, that's why.'

'That's energy. He's like a human dynamo. He only needs three or four hours sleep. He's a workaholic. He enjoys challenges. I find him terribly exciting, Rebecca. Exciting and stimulating.'

'I can see that, dear,' Rebecca sighed, 'but I can't help feeling worried and afraid for you. You know how psychic I am and I keep getting these awful vibes from him. There's definitely an aura of violence about him.'

It was true. And Alice, who'd also met him, agreed with her. She decided on the spur of the moment to go and visit Alice. When she was alone like this thoughts of her mother and the Polish soldier and the air raid and terrible things she'd seen kept intruding into the quietness of her meditation. It was all so long ago and yet the whole thing rolled like a film in vivid Technicolor before her unwilling eyes. She had to struggle with the bitterness and hatred against the Pole, against her father, against the men in the German bomber, against men who started wars, against all men everywhere.

She would feel better once she got to Alice's. She left a note for Sadie who was out at her old folk's club and set off for Alice's house in Pollokshaws. The only drawback, of course, was how near Alice's place was to her old home. Or at least all that was left of it.

Because it was dark although still afternoon and the back streets of the tenements not too safe a place to wander through, Rebecca went the direct way which meant passing the derelict bomb site. She regretted her decision immediately she set foot on the street. Not even her deep breathing could quell the panic that seemed to disintegrate her whole life, her very soul. All her good work at the refuge, everything she'd struggled to do with her life suddenly began crumbling under her feet. Everyone was deserting her. She had nothing to cling on to. Protective veils were being cruelly ripped from her eyes. She began to run and didn't stop until she'd reached the sanctuary of Alice's close. There she stopped in sudden shame. How foolish of her to allow herself to panic like that; she was surprised at herself. The trouble was she had been over-stretching herself, worrying far too much about her friends, suffering for them and, alas, getting little or no thanks for all her agonizing. They were all over her and effusive to the point of adoration when they were at their lowest ebb and desperately needed her. Once they imagined they were all right, however, once they thought they were safe, off they went without a backward glance; she could be dying for all they cared. She managed, with God's help, to calm herself before climbing the stairs then knocking at Alice's door. Alice took a long time to answer and when she did open the door she looked darkly furious.

'I'm in the middle of a tarot reading,' she said. 'You've broken my concentration. I told you never to do that. I told you always to phone and ask first.'

'Oh, I see,' Rebecca said bitterly. 'I've to phone and make an appointment to see you now. That's how you treat your friends, is it?'

'I never interrupt you at your hypnotherapy sessions,' Alice said. 'Don't forget I make my living at this.'

'Oh, far be it from me, Alice, to interrupt you while you're making money,' she said, turning away. 'I'll see you at Battlefield House where you will always be welcome.'

She took the stairs rapidly but carefully. She continued at a hurried pace all the way back to Langside but on nearing Battlefield House felt so upset she couldn't face going in. Neither Sadie or Jenny had returned because every window was in darkness. Instead she swerved into the park. Somewhere in here was the ghost of another beleaguered woman, Mary, Queen of Scots. Rebecca's determination to 'contact' her had never been stronger than it was now. She stood on the grassy slopes of the park in the moonlight and closed her eyes in deep concentration and stretched out her arms.

51

Douglas and Harry were eating their breakfasts. Both had the same hard, muscular look; both had rock-like features and cropped heads. Only Harry's hair was darker than Douglas's. Both men were reading with brows lowered and hard daggers of eyes. Douglas's newspaper was propped up in front of his porridge plate. Harry was concentrating intensely on a book about Karate.

Sitting at the table with them Amelia felt she might as well have been alone in a space capsule suspended somewhere outside the world. She felt a terrible need for Rebecca. Or Jenny. Or even Hazel or Sadie. She needed the comfort and sympathy and understanding that it seemed only a woman could give. Men were no use – she wondered why. Was it because for so long their role had been to go out into the world and earn a living to keep a wife and family and for this they had to be tough and competitive? Was it that they believed they couldn't afford to allow any chink in this armour of toughness in case it put them at a disadvantage and made them fail? If this was true then it was only a surface toughness. Women, who had gone through childbirth, then had to survive the emotional ties and vulnerability of mother-hood and the bringing up of children and all that the actual running of a home and looking after a family entailed, had had a long training in sensitivity and unselfishness. This was a deeper kind of strength.

Yet how could she feel that Harry, her own flesh and blood, was like a stranger to her or was in any way less than perfect? She immediately chastised herself for such a disloyal thought even if it had only lasted a mere fraction of a second. Harry wasn't lacking in sensitivity.

Harry was a good, kind boy. Never had a mother had a better son. A shining jewel in her treasure store of memories was the time when he was only about 3 or 4 years of age. She'd had such a fright one Sunday morning when she'd discovered he was not in bed nor anywhere in the house. Sick with fear she'd run outside – still no sign of him. Frantic then she'd returned to the house and was just about to phone the police when suddenly she'd looked down and there was Harry at her side clutching a bunch of daffodils. She'd forgotten it was Mother's Day but he hadn't. The love that had created the miracle of him waking up in time, dressing himself and procuring the flowers for her (probably stolen from someone's garden) nearly brought tears of gratitude to her eyes even yet.

Somewhere, deep down, he was still that same Harry. And till the day she died she would love him and be grateful for his love in return.

'I promised granny I'd be there first thing this morning,' she said. 'I'd better get going.'

'Right,' Harry said without looking up.

'Douglas.' He made no reply and she repeated loudly, 'Douglas!'

'Okay, okay!' He looked up, his eyes reflecting the irritation in his voice. 'You don't need to shout.'

'Can you not give me a lift? I've some things I want to take to mummy's and it's such a hassle on the bus.' Long ago she'd wanted to learn to drive but Douglas had convinced her she was far too absent-minded and stupid.

'Behind the wheel of a car is one place your writing would kill you,' he had insisted, 'and probably other folk as well. You need to have all your wits about you when you're driving. Not away in a dream making up stories.' She'd thought he probably had a valid point.

'Take a taxi,' he said now.

'Oh, thanks very much,' she replied bitterly. 'You're a great help.'

'I've work to do,' Douglas protested.

'So have I.'

'You? he laughed incredulously. 'What work have you got?'

'You know perfectly well I write in the mornings.'

'Call that work!' He lifted his paper again.

Harry groaned. 'Must you two quarrel at breakfast time? Mum, could you not have asked dad last night?'

She had been too tired and upset when she'd arrived home to think about anything except her mother. Now catching the inflection of Harry's bias towards Douglas she felt exhausted again. And so depressed.

'I'd better phone for a taxi then.' Her voice betrayed a tremble. With a sigh Douglas flung down his paper.

'Oh go and get your coat, I'll take you.' It was his usual routine, the one that went 'You don't deserve this, you hopeless, helpless female, but I'll do you the honour of doing you a big favour as long as you remember to show how truly grateful you are.'

'Oh, thanks, Douglas,' she said, hastily rising before he changed his mind. 'That's very kind of you. The thing is, you see, I'm so upset and worried and feel I need a bit of support.'

That was true at least. Douglas packed the things into the car. A quilt, a set of pretty pink pillow-cases and a pink bedjacket (her mother's greying dark hair and brown eyes would be warmed and enhanced by the shade); a hot-water bottle, a bag of fruit, a tin of toffees (her mother enjoyed a good chew at a toffee); a packet of her mother's favourite chocolate biscuits, half a dozen handkerchiefs, a packet of notepaper and envelopes (in case her mother wanted to write to any friends further afield to let them know how she was); a selection of books by Annie S. Swan, Ethel M. Dell and Eleanor Glyn (her mother never read any of Amelia Donovan's books); a pile of women's magazines and the *Christian Herald*.

Amelia felt a lot more relaxed and happy once they were on their way. In her mind's eye she could see her mother looking comfortable and cosy with the hot-water bottle at her feet, pretty as a picture propped up against the frilly pillows in the crocheted bedjacket, the shiny quilt tucked around her and the box of toffees, books and magazines by her side and all her friends sitting around. Her mother of course would keep pressing the toffees on them, down to the very last one.

Pretty wasn't the right word to describe Victoria though. Handsome was more accurate. 'A fine figure of a woman,' her daddy used to say.

The car drew up at the close. She could see Mrs Hamilton's ample figure standing at the window, muscly arms folded as usual over her chest. She was glad at least one of the neighbours had gone in to keep her mother company between her daughter's arrival and Rory leaving for work. Rory had said she wouldn't have gone to work this morning only she had an important business meeting that she couldn't put off. But she'd be back in time to have lunch with Victoria. Amelia had intended to get to Balornock earlier before Rory left, but Douglas had taken such an excruciatingly long time to get ready; she'd never known him take so long to shave for instance – except on other occasions when she was in a hurry. She was sure he did it purposely to torment her.

'I'll run straight in,' she told him. 'Will you bring all the things?'

'If you're not going to do it I suppose I'll have to.'

She ran up the close stairs to the flat. The door was open. Mrs Hamilton was in the dark, windowless lobby.

'Come in to the front room a minute, will you, hen?' she said.

'Right,' Amelia agreed, glancing impatiently back to see if Douglas was coming yet.

In the front room she was taken aback to find it full of people. All the neighbours seemed to have crowded in and Aggie and her man, the lodgers, were there too. It was really going over the score. Her mother would get far too tired talking to so many people. She knew how

350

extremely popular her mother was, and how her mother enjoyed being the centre of attention but still. . . .

'Sit down, hen,' Mrs Hamilton said. 'We've awful bad news. Your mammy's gone.'

Amelia stared at her. 'Gone?'

'Aye, she went to her Maker less than an hour ago. Aggie and her man were along at the shops. Aggie always goes early for the rolls and he goes for his paper and baccy. They like the bit of exercise first thing. When they got back your mammy didn't give them a welcoming shout like she usually did. They thought she'd just dozed off. They made a cup of tea and took it with a nice hot buttered roll into your mammy. But she had gone.'

Vaguely Amelia became aware that Douglas had come into the room.

'I was just telling the poor wee lassie that her mammy's gone. She'll be sorely missed, so she will. She had a heart as big as a bucket, that woman. A true Christian if ever there was one. You'll want to go through and see her now, hen.'

'No!' Amelia gave a sudden cry of panic. Then immediately ashamed of her inexplicable refusal hurried on to try to explain it. 'I want to remember her as I last saw her. I mean, I'm too upset, I can't take it in. Maybe later. . . .'

'I've got the kettle on,' said Mrs McDade. 'I'll bring you a wee cup of tea, hen. That'll put strength into you.'

Everyone was talking in subdued tones, almost whispering. Amelia sat silently staring at nothing while Douglas spoke, also in hushed respectful tones, to everyone. It was he who went to phone Rory, he who eventually, along with Rory, made all the funeral arrangements. Her contribution had been to insist that there should be a really good meal afterwards and it had to be catered for by the Co-op. Her mother used to work for the Co-op and she had been a life-long member.

At the funeral she tried, with every ounce of will power that was in her, to create a party atmosphere – the kind

351

of thing her mother was so good at and would have enjoyed. 'Have you gone off your nut?' Douglas said. 'Have a bit of respect.'

He had been outraged when she had refused to wear black. But her mother had always found black intolerably depressing. Victoria had never even worn black at Matthew's funeral. In bright colours with a bright welcoming face Amelia moved around the black-clad mourners chatting brightly.

'What do you think you're doing? Douglas asked. What she was doing was trying to please her mother in death as she'd always tried to please her in life.

But all the time she was thinking, 'I wasn't there when she needed me. My beautiful, talented mother. All she ever wanted was people around her – and I allowed her to die alone'.

52

Amelia could see that Douglas was searching his mind for something to criticize her about. They were sitting eating lunch at the tubular chrome table. Harry was out; they sat in silence. He's trying to think of something to complain about, Amelia told herself. I'm not going to scream. I'm going to say 'Yes, dear,' and 'No, dear,' and keep perfectly calm. Her life seemed to be disintegrating around her. She missed Jenny more than she could have foreseen. They had become very close friends until Jenny met Gregson. Her catering jobs began to snowball, too, and attending to them took up a great deal of time. She seldom saw her at all now.

It was as if, now that she had no one, Douglas was going for a real killing. Since her mother had died she was sure he'd got worse. She tried to continue calmly swallowing spoonfuls and willing tears not to come. Douglas always said, 'I don't know what you're crying for. Your mother never cared tuppence for you. She cared more about my mother than she did about you.'

But before she died hadn't her mother become, comparatively speaking, more affectionately disposed towards her? The past and particularly Matthew had become the closest link between them.

'Do you remember your daddy used to say . . .'; 'Your daddy was such a clever, good man . . .'; 'We had a wonderful partnership you know, never a cross or angry word passed between us. . . .'

Amelia had listened to her and just nodded in agreement each time her mother spoke like this. What was the use of distressing her with the truth? She believed that her mother and father, in their own way, had loved each other despite the fact they had battled almost continuously for as far back as Amelia could remember. Bitter conflict had raged as a background to the whole of her childhood draining her, destroying her. All her life she'd just managed to survive and no more. Just somehow managing to exist from day to day, just trying to shut her ears, her mind, her heart to everything, just struggling to protect herself had become the automatic pattern of her life.

How strange it was and how tragic that she had ended up with someone with whom she had to continue this pattern of living, with someone who had the same attitude towards her as her mother.

When Amelia had talked this over with her, Rebecca had said it wasn't strange at all. It often happened. People repeated early life patterns all the time. 'But now that you are aware of it,' she'd said, 'you can break the pattern.' Rebecca had swept aside all her excuses about not wanting to upset Harry by leaving. Or not having any money. Or any place to go. Or not being fit enough phsyically or emotionally to survive on her own.

'Harry is a young man. He doesn't need you any more,' Rebecca had said. 'And you have my place to come to. You have me to look after you.' The thought of Harry not needing her was impossible for Amelia to contemplate; to be separated from Harry was unthinkable.

'What good are you to your son or anyone including yourself the way you are now,' Rebecca had persisted. 'That man is destroying you. You can't even concentrate on your writing any more.'

Since her mother had died she hadn't seemed to be able to concentrate on anything. Her mind had kept continually wandering away to the past. Sometimes she would go out to the shops for something she needed and she would suddenly find herself in Pollokshaws Road when it was Victoria Road she'd meant to go to. The intervening time from Mary House to there would be a complete blank. This had confused as well as frightened her. But nothing had been more frightening than not being able to write. She had sat at her desk day after day, week after week, straining her mind, trying to force it to conjure up characters and plots but it had ground to a halt. She couldn't bear it.

'Look at that fruit bowl,' Douglas suddenly burst out.

She had finished her soup without realizing it. She put down her spoon and stared at the fruit bowl in the middle of the table. It contained apples, pears, grapes and bananas. He's thought of something, she told herself. Keep calm. Keep calm.

'Do you realize,' Douglas said, 'there are *eight* bananas there?'

'So?' she murmured quietly. 'We've lots of lovely bananas.'

Douglas had finished his soup so she gathered the dirty plates together and put them on the sideboard. Cold meat and salad had already been dished on to plates there; she carried the plates over to the table.

'There were four bananas in that bowl yesterday,' Douglas's hacksaw voice was splitting open her head. 'Yet you've gone out this morning and bought another four.'

'So?' she said mildly.

'So no wonder you've never any money, you waste so much of it. Spend, spend, spend. . . .'

She began neatly cutting up her slice of roast beef.

'You're always the same. You haven't a clue. You're getting worse. . . .'

She put a piece in her mouth and with difficulty chewed it and swallowed it.

'You've no idea about money,' he said. 'You'll leave me without a penny before you're done. . . .'

'Douglas you're giving me a headache,' she said, 'not to mention acid indigestion.'

'That's another thing. You're a raving hypochondriac. I suppose you've discovered there's some vitamin or other in bananas that's going to give you the

355

elixir of life and we're all going to get nothing else but bananas –'

'Will you stop nagging,' she suddenly yelled, 'about stupid fuckin' bananas!'

Douglas looked shocked. 'That's terrible! Using filthy language like that in my house.'

She felt hysterical. For years, for a lifetime it seemed, she'd been putting up with terrible cruelties and deprivations and now, suddenly, just because of something so ridiculous and trivial as bananas, she'd had enough.

'Stupid, fuckin' bananas,' she repeated.

'You're going off your head,' Douglas accused.

If she'd stayed in the same room with him another minute she *would* have gone off her head. She got up.

'Where do you think you're going?' Douglas asked. 'You haven't finished your lunch.'

'I'm leaving you,' she told him.

'Don't be stupid,' he said.

She went upstairs and lay down on her bed and wondered where she'd go. She would have to find lodgings. The thought of being in lodgings again, of being rootless, at the mercy of the rules, regulations and peculiarities of landladies, of being without a house she could call her own, of being a failure was unbelievable, unendurable. She couldn't bear it. Yet she couldn't bear staying where she was either. Only thoughts of Harry gave her strength and purpose. For him, with him she could survive anything, accomplish anything. For him, with him she had always survived before. It had always been her and Harry against the world.

Ignoring Douglas's nagging tongue, 'What are you doing now? Where do you think you're going?', she went for a newspaper and then surreptitiously searched the Accommodation To Let columns. There didn't seem anything very suitable but she noted down a few names and addresses nevertheless. Something would turn up. It had to. Next day she began trailing around the town searching for the places and viewing them. Every day

356

she bought the paper and made lists and set out in desperate hope that this would be her lucky day. Every night she dreamed about finding not just digs but a flat to let – some place where she and Harry could be on their own and there wouldn't even be a landlady to criticize or nag at her. She had no idea how she would pay the rent of a flat or even digs for that matter. Until she sold another book she had no money other than what Douglas was giving her for housekeeping. She couldn't imagine Douglas voluntarily giving her money to help keep herself if she left him. He never had before.

But something would turn up, somehow she'd manage – she had to, she no longer had any choice. Then one day, there it was, in the paper, before her very eyes. An unfurnished two-bedroomed flat to let and at a very modest rent. There must of course be something wrong with it. There were never any reasonably priced flats to rent nowadays. There were never any unfurnished flats to let at all. Even though it was a rat-infested slum, however, she would take it if she was offered it. Somehow she would make it all right. The advert only gave a factor's name and address. She phoned them immediately and was given an address over in the west end of the city and a time to view that evening. She didn't know the West End and had no idea what Byres Road would be like. She braced herself for a depressing, derelict property. She prayed she would get the flat no matter what it was like. She and Harry could decorate it in nice bright colours. They'd soon make it cheerful and homely. To get a roof over their heads, any kind of roof, that was the main thing. To be able to shut their own door and have peace. To be safe and secure.

She could hardly believe her eyes when she saw the attractive red sandstone building in the bustling Byres Road. It was just opposite a library. It was as if it was meant to be, yet at the same time, too good to be true. There must be something wrong with it inside. There must be. But there was nothing wrong with it inside. It

357

was an absolutely beautiful flat with high carved ceilings and big bright windows in a good-sized sitting room and dining room and a kitchen big enough to eat in and fitted with lots of modern cupboards. The dining room could be her writing room.

She felt so excited she was in a state of collapse. She wouldn't get it. She couldn't be so lucky – but by God, she would make a jolly good try. She smiled and was as charming as she could be to the man who was showing her round. She brought up the fact that she was a writer because this usually interested and impressed people; he did seem very impressed. He explained, however, that a great many people had shown interest in the flat and the owner was insisting on impeccable references to help him decide which applicant would be successful. All the flats in the block were apparently owned by the same person, an elderly gentleman who liked to make sure they were looked after by careful and respectable tenants and at the same time enjoy a modest but regular income from them.

She phoned her publisher the moment she returned to Mary House and explained the circumstances, promising them that as soon as she was in a place of her own she'd be able to come up with another book. If they would just give her a good enough reference. . . . They did.

She could not believe it when she received the letter telling her to come to the factor's office at her earliest convenience to collect the key. The flat was hers. She read the words over and over again. She dropped down on to her knees in the privacy of her bedroom and fervently thanked God. She remained on her knees a long time clutching the letter in her hand, just feeling thankful.

Now she could tell Harry. She went along to Harry's room as if she was walking on air. Harry was dressed in his white Karate suit practising his Karate. Just as she opened the door his leg snapped up in one of his rapid high kicks and missed her face by a mere whisker.

Unperturbed she laughed. Her eyes were shining. She was still holding the letter.

'Harry,' she said, 'I'm leaving. I've got a flat. I've got a place of my own at last. It's wonderful! You'll love it. The room you'll have is much bigger than this. There'll be plenty of space for your weights and all your other equipment and –'

'I'm not leaving here, I'm not going anywhere with you!' Harry burst out indignantly. 'I'm staying with my dad!'

53

Rowan had managed to get to Jackson and throw her body protectively over his. She lay very still pretending she had fainted in the hope that the mob would soon lose interest.

Fortunately someone did get bored and shouted, 'The rest of them niggahs are gettin' away. Let's catch 'em.'

She lay for a few more minutes until the noise of shouting and running feet had died away. Then she scrambled up. Blood was pouring from Jackson's head and making a widening pool on the floor. He was unconscious. Rowan cried out urgently, 'My God, oh my God.'

She ran outside and looked up and down the street. Further along there was a church. She raced to it and babbled out to the preacher inside that she had to phone for an ambulance and the police. She dialled the number and asked for an ambulance to be sent to the bus terminal because her friend had been terribly beaten up. A laid-back voice said, 'Every ambulance is out on anothah emergency.'

'But that's impossible,' Rowan shouted down the phone. 'He might die. You must send medical help.'

'You'll get no help heah.' A hint of malice entered the voice before it repeated, 'Every ambulance is out on anothah emergency.'

Frantic now she phoned the police to plead with them only to receive exactly the same response: 'Every police car is out on anothah emergency.'

They were purposely leaving her love to die. But she was damned if she was going to let them. 'Have you a car or any means of conveyance?' she asked the preacher.

'I was about to suggest it,' he said. 'I've a station

wagon parked outside. I'll take you and your friend to hospital. I only hope we don't cause him furthah injury while movin' him. These things should be done by medics.'

'We've no choice. Oh, quickly. Please!'

They ran to the wagon and within two or three minutes she was at Jackson's side again.

'Dear God!' the preacher gasped.

'I'll try to support his head,' Rowan said.

Somehow, together they lifted the unconscious man and got him into the back of the station wagon. Once in the hospital he was treated with normal care and efficiency, perhaps helped by the fact that Rowan told the medics that Jackson was a Southern man. Also, soon after his admittance, Federal Troops were sent to guard the hospital. She had her own cuts and bruises treated and she was allowed to wait, drinking innumerable cups of coffee until she heard news of Jackson's condition.

He had a fractured skull and was very ill. But in subsequent daily visits she saw him gradually improve. She and Mary Beth had an invitation to stay at her Aunty Lucy and Uncle Dexter's place, a beautiful white-pillared mansion surrounded by trees. Aunt Lucy was Willard's youngest sister. She was a sweet Southern lady, very active socially and also in the Women's Society for Christian Service. Uncle Dexter was a banker and although not a Ku Klux Klansman himself had many customers who were. He tended to be all things to all men. He was devoted to Lucy, however, and very indulgent and tolerant towards her work with the WSCS in integrating black people. She never took part in any sit-ins, demonstrations or marches but in her own gentle ladylike way she did what she could. She organized little soirées for instance in the church hall to which black professional men's wives were invited and graciously treated.

But being an obedient and loyal wife she was equally gracious when her husband invited segregationists and people like the police chief and Klansmen of different professions to her home. Lucy, it had turned out, had actually witnessed most of the mob riot at the bus terminal. She had been in an upstairs office across the road from the terminal where she had an appointment with her lawyer.

'What shocked me most of all,' she confessed to Rowan, 'was that the mob was made up of just ordinary Montgomery people. I knew them. They'd come down-town for their Saturday shopping just like they always did only this Saturday they'd turned into this raving mob.' She shivered, remembering. 'I saw a young white man come staggering out with blood pouring down his face. He staggered up to a black cab and cried out to be taken to hospital. He was obviously a Northerner. He didn't know black cabmen aren't allowed to carry white passengers and white cabmen aren't allowed to carry black passengers.' She put her hand to her eyes. 'What really terrified me though was how ladies, ordinary kind Montgomery ladies that I'd been living among, were holding up their babies and shouting, "See the niggahs run! See the niggahs run!" And everybody was shouting "Go get the niggahs! Go get the niggahs!" It was the most terrifying and to me the most tragic thing I've evah seen. My people, my friends were enjoying the sight of black people and a few white Freedom Ridahs getting beaten up. I suddenly realized they were so full of hatred, bigotry and meanness they were really crazy. I couldn't look any mohah. I had to go and sit down while my lawyah administered a little brandy.'

Being guests in Lucy and Dexter's house, treated with wonderful kindness and Southern hospitality, neither Mary Beth nor Rowan felt it was right to say anything provocative or critical when they were in the company of some of the people who were regular visitors to Lucy and Dexter's home. Mary Beth's Southern breeding seemed to come more easily to her rescue than Rowan's dour and awkward Scottish background. Rowan found it

362

agonizingly difficult to keep her mouth shut, especially when the subject came up about race as it always did. If anything happened to change the Southern system everyone agreed that all the white women would rush to get a black man. They'd have a race of mulattoes. Actually Rowan thought this would be a splendid solution; if in a few generations everybody was the same colour there would be no colour problem. But what amazed her was the way these men and others like them were maniacal on the subject of sex – it always boiled down to the sex thing. They were really crazy about it. Surely, Rowan thought, it was a terrible reflection on Southern white men. Surely they were not so weak or impotent or such poor lovers that Southern white women couldn't wait to get a black man. (Steve Jackson was a very virile lover and he came from the South.)

It was also a terrible reflection on Southern white women. These men who talked so much about how they were protecting white women ranted vilely about how every black man wanted to rape a white woman and how every white woman apparently wanted to be raped; even Senators, *especially* Senators, made disgusting speeches about this.

Rowan had come to the conclusion that their talk showed a sickness, a Freudian sickness. Their fears stemmed from the fact that white men in the South had had so many affairs with black women. They had just turned it around.

Sometimes she looked at Aunt Lucy and her Christian Service lady friends, so lovely in their summer dresses of light voile, and white shoes, white gloves, white beads and white hats with flowers on them. And then she would remember one Senator losing his temper while speaking at one of their church meetings. A big blubber of a man he was, with loose heavy jowls like a turkey. One of the ladies had asked about the poll tax and he'd stuck his face towards the ladies and bawled, 'I know what you women want – black men laying on you!'

363

Rowan had been shocked and furious. Lucy had been embarrassed but tried to apologize for the Senator. 'He comes from hill country you know. They made theah money quite recently.'

Rowan couldn't see what difference that made. His opinions were shared by practically every Southern white man she'd met.

While Jackson was still in hospital, but happily on the mend, Rowan and Mary Beth were most excited by the news that there was going to be a mass meeting in the First Baptist Church to express support of the Freedom Riders. The black minister Ralph Abernethy preached there and, most exciting of all, the Reverend Martin Luther King was coming to give his support and to address the meeting.

Lucy and Dexter tried their best to persuade them not to go but Rowan said, 'We'll be all right in a church, Lucy. It's not as if we'll be out in the street demonstrating or causing an obstruction or disturbing the peace or any of the things they usually accuse us of. Oh, it will be such an honour to meet Dr King.'

Lucy told them that she and some white ladies of the Christian Service used to have prayers in the church every morning with black ladies. They just used to sit and pray together but their prayer meetings were broken up by Klansmen. But Rowan and Mary Beth were so excited they wouldn't listen.

Instead of putting on their usual blue jeans and shirts they both wore dresses. Mary Beth looked like a real Southern Lady in a peach chiffon dress and a fluffy peach hat with chiffon on it and pearls round the neck. Rowan wore a green checked cotton dress and a string of amber beads that had once been a present from her mother. She pinned a white flower in her hair. They both wore white gloves. It felt nice to dress up for a change. They were really looking forward to their visit to the church and couldn't wait to hear Dr King speak. Everyone who'd ever heard him said he was brilliant, absolutely inspired.

They were taken aback on arriving at the church to find an angry mob surrounding the building and a ring of Federal Marshals trying to hold back the crowd. Rowan and Mary Beth walked into the building trying to ignore the shouts of hatred. Rowan suddenly felt sad and depressed. She didn't think she would ever understand people who could behave like this.

Inside, the church was packed with black people and a few whites. The Reverend Ralph Abernethy and the Reverend Martin Luther King, ignoring the screams of hatred and abuse from outside, took turns to preach and to lead the congregation in singing. But the mob outside were going mad and the tension and terror inside was mounting. The marshals had begun to throw tear gas bombs at the crowd to prevent them storming the place and the crowd were throwing the tear bombs at the Church. The two ministers closed all the windows to prevent the tear gas coming in but it made the place as hot as hell.

Rowan had never been so terrified in her life. They were all afraid that the mob was going to set the place on fire and they would be trapped and burned alive. The Reverend Martin Luther King was on the phone with Robert Kennedy, the President's brother, eventually and apparently Kennedy had said he knew how they all felt. There used to be a lot of anti-Catholic feeling in Boston and he remembered his grandfather telling him how mobs used to attack the nunneries and several nunneries were burned.

It was then that Rowan remembered hearing stories about how Nazis locked people in churches and barns during the war and burned them. Kennedy had given an assurance that this would not be allowed to happen to the church. He was sending in the National Guard.

He was as good as his word and they escaped unscathed. It had been a long ordeal however and they didn't get back to Lucy's house until 3 a.m. Rowan wondered what would have happened if they'd not had the safety of Lucy and Dexter's place to go to. They had so many 'kin' (as they called relations) in the town as well as friends and acquaintances among all sections. Even so, Rowan was at the stage that nothing would have surprised her.

She lay in bed in the breathless heat of the Southern night and could feel no comfort or security except in thoughts of Steve Jackson. Even thinking of him brought apprehension. Would he be safe in the hospital tonight? If people weren't safe in a church would any decent person be safe anywhere? Would hate and violence kept at boiling point by the intolerable heat find another outlet?

Outside she could hear the eerie hissing and clicking of insects. In the distance a police car wailed.

54

Without a word Amelia had turned away and gone back to her own room. She was in a state of shock. There was no way she could cope with Harry not loving her. After a few minutes Harry followed her through; she was sitting on the edge of her bed staring into space. She smiled up at him when he entered the room, remembering him as a baby. She remembered the way she'd nursed him in her arms. From side to side . . . from side to side, her body rocking along with him. 'Mummy's wee darling boy,' she'd chanted, over and over again. 'Mummy's wee darling boy!'

'Mum,' he said. 'Are you sure you know what you're doing?'

'Yes, dear.'

'Are you sure you're doing the right thing? You could do a lot worse than dad and you've a good home here.'

'Yes, dear.'

'How will you manage?'

'I'll be all right.'

'Let's face it, Mum, you're not a good manager – you've admitted yourself you're hopeless with money. And you're such a dreamer. And you get worried and anxious about the slightest thing. And you panic. And you get frightened when you don't feel well. You need dad to balance you up. I know he's not perfect but at least he's sensible and down to earth. You need somebody like that to look after you.'

He hadn't the slightest confidence in her. He didn't even respect her. There was nothing about her he liked or admired. A lifetime of tears was gathering and swelling up in her chest, paining her beyond pain.

'I'll be all right.'

'There's no use looking at me like that!' he suddenly shouted. 'I'm not going to allow you to make me feel guilty any more. I have my own life to lead. I refuse to allow you to weaken and undermine me. If you want to ruin your life that's your business. But you're not going to keep me tied to your apron strings and ruin mine.'

Weaken and undermine him? Ruin his life? What was Harry talking about? She had adored her son from the very first moment she'd set eyes on his beautiful, petal-soft face. For hours she used to sit watching him while he slept. Gently she'd trace the contours of his baby face and the tiny pink buds of hands. As he grew into boyhood everything she did, she did for him. She took him for walks, took him to the zoo, took him to the pictures, to the seaside. She read him stories, played with him, talked to him. Then once he went to school she encouraged him to have friends. She welcomed them. For years she had no friends except the imaginary ones in her writing. She would have given up her life for Harry. In a way she had and gladly, gladly.

'I'm sorry if you've thought I've been weakening you and undermining you and your life, son,' she said. 'I didn't mean to. I'm sorry for asking you to –'

'Mum, will you stop saying you're sorry!' He smacked his hand against his brow.

She could see she was irritating him beyond endurance. Everything she said was the wrong thing. She was afraid to open her mouth now. And what did he mean, 'There's no use looking at me like that?' She lowered her eyes and hunched her shoulders and kept very still.

'Oh Mum!' Suddenly Harry came over to her and hugged her against him. 'I'm just worried about you, that's all. You're so hopeless and helpless. You'll regret it if you leave dad, you need him. Och, you don't really mean it, do you?'

She could hear the distress in his voice. How incredible! She was distressing Harry. Suddenly she knew the only thing to do. Often, in the privacy of her writing room she had acted out scenes in her books, taken the part of different characters, spoken their lines out loud to see if they worked. She'd become quite good at it. She had to act a part now, that was all.

'Look, son,' she said in a good strong voice, 'don't give this another thought.' She rose. 'You're right, it's my business. I shouldn't be bothering you with it. Is this your Karate night, son? How are you getting on with it? Still enjoying it, are you? That was a great article in the paper about your local club.'

His face brightened. 'Did you think so? I thought it fab myself. The publicity's bound to do the club a bit of good. We're badly needing to increase our membership.'

'Oh well, that should do the trick.'

They went out of the room arm-in-arm, chatting quite happily and normally. And all the time the well of her tears was slopping about inside her chest.

'I'd better go down and make the tea.' She laughed. 'Yes, I've actually remembered. I bought lovely pork chops when I was out. How about fried eggs and chips with them?'

'Fab, Mum,' Harry said enthusiastically. And he went back along the landing to his room jabbing out his fists and snapping up his legs. He was absolutely dedicated to Karate.

She made the meal. She dished it up. She sat pretending to eat while she listened to Harry and Douglas discuss the Karate championships that were coming to the Kelvin Hall soon. Douglas knew all the technicalities of Karate. She tried not to hate him.

'I'll pay for a couple of tickets,' he said. 'One for you and one for your mate.'

Harry was eager-eyed and on the edge of his chair with excitement. 'That'll be fab! Thanks a million!' Douglas had been too clever.

He'd been too clever all along. He'd stolen Harry from her. She tried to swallow the food down but couldn't, it was choking her. She gave up eventually and placed her fork and knife neatly side by side on her plate.

'What's up with you now?' Douglas asked. 'That's a good pork chop you're wasting.'

She put on the act again. 'Nothing's wasted as long as we've got Prince,' she said cheerfully and the old collie came ambling towards her flapping its bushy tail. 'Come on through to the kitchen and Mummy'll put it in your dish, pet,' she told the dog.

In the kitchen she stared at herself in the mirror, her fair hair caught back in a glossy chignon at the nape of her neck, her expensively made-up face. She got make-up and clothes cost price at Rory's. After she left she would no longer be allowed any. Nor would she be able to take anything from the house. Douglas would allow her nothing, not even a teaspoon. It didn't matter. Nothing mattered except she didn't have Harry any more.

She had meant to tell Douglas about the flat – not that he would put any credence on it. He had obviously not believed her or had forgotten that she'd told him she was leaving. Now any hassle with Douglas was beyond her emotional resources. All she could do was to try to hold herself together until she got safely away. She concentrated on how she could smuggle out her typewriter, her books, a caseful of clothes and other personal belongings. But first she had the ordeal of going to the bank and talking the bank manager into giving her an overdraft so that she could furnish the flat and buy essentials like pots and pans, cutlery and dishes. She had an appointment next day. That night she took a sleeping tablet to give her merciful oblivion for a few hours.

Next day she put on her cheerful, confident act again and secured the necessary loan with the help of royalty statements proving her earnings and a lot of cheerful talk about even bigger earnings to come. Then she kept herself busy choosing and ordering furniture and everything she needed. She didn't tell anyone, not even Rebecca. She began to experience a secret thrill. The heartbroken feelings about Harry that she daren't think about were being held at bay somewhere at the back of her mind. Overlying them was this strange new experience. It was her first journey into freedom, into 'doing her own thing'. Everything she ordered was to her own taste. It occurred to her she'd never really known what that was until now. She liked pretty pastel shades. She loved the calming effect of blue. It took weeks before the flat was ready and everything in its place, but what a deep emotional effect it all had on her. It was as if she was functioning in a dream world.

At the same time different layers of emotion kept welling up. There was the fear of what she was doing. She had spent all the overdraft on furnishings. Certainly she'd already stocked a cupboard with tea and health foods but when these ran out how would she eat? And how would she pay electricity and gas bills, not to mention the rent? There were only three months paid in advance. How could she possibly survive for any length of time on her own? She would be lonely. She was such a weak person she would be suicidal, she wouldn't be able to cope. What if she took ill? If she had been ill and confined to bed in Mary House at least Douglas would bring her a cup of tea or phone for the doctor if necessary. What would happen in any emergencies in the house? She didn't even know how to mend a fuse.

But at the same time as all her fears were flickering about like dark shadows in her mind there was the thrill, the excitement, the voyage of discovery. She left two notes in the end. One for Douglas and one for Harry giving her new address. In Douglas's letter she made it plain that there was no point in coming after her. Their marriage was finished for good this time. To Harry she said that he mustn't worry and that she was perfectly happy and all right. And of course he would be welcome to come and visit her any time and as often as he wanted. And if there was anything he needed he was never to hesitate to let her know. . . .

She hurried out of Mary House into the waiting taxi in a fever of anxiety in case Douglas would suddenly appear and see her. Once the taxi got clear away she could hardly believe it. She was literally shivering with a hysteria of excitement and relief. Arriving at Byres Road she lugged her suitcases into the close and up the stairs and into the flat. She closed the door. Leaving the cases in the hall she began wandering around. It was as if a sun had begun to rise inside her, warming her inwardly with magic rays.

She stroked the beautiful blue velvet curtains in the sitting room. She feasted her eyes on the floral chinz covers of the three piece suite. She revelled in the novelty of making a cup of tea in the kitchen as if she was a new bride and this was the very first cup of tea she had ever made. She gazed in admiration at the feminine styled bedroom appreciating its soft shades of lavender and blue with white furniture and white jars of make-up with pink and gold lids on the dressing table.

In the dining room that she was using as a writing room she had even bought a desk and had shelves made for her books. What a miracle it all was! Round and round the flat she wandered as if in a dream. Then she stopped at one of the sitting room windows. There were two windows facing directly on to Byres Road and also a bay window on the corner from which she could get an even better view right down the busy street. She sat down at the bay window, propped her elbows on the ledge, cupped her chin in her hands and gazed down at the scene below. It seemed all human life was unfolding before her eyes. Soon, another miracle happened. She began to feel that stirring of excitement in the pit of her stomach that meant she was ready to begin writing again. It happened before every book. Then her mind began to function joyously, creatively.

How incredibly lucky she was! With all her heart and soul she thanked God.

55

'Sho is good to see y'all Miss Abbie.' Crystal, Lucy's plump black servant came shuffling into the sitting room with a jug of iced lemonade and some glasses. 'Sho is. Did you have a good flight, honey?' she enquired as she passed glasses of lemonade around.

'Fine. Just fine, Crystal. Well, it did get a bit bumpy but I just said to myself "I won't worry. I'm nearly 80 and I've got to go sometime".'

Crystal gave a screech of hilarity. 'Ain't she somethin'?' She gazed round at the others. 'Ah just adohah that woman!'

Rowan had also been delighted to see the old lady again and was glad that Abbie had arrived before she and Jackson had left Montgomery. Jackson had to meet up with some of his students and fellow teachers in his namesake city of Jackson, Mississippi. The others had already started going round knocking on black people's doors, trying to persuade them to take an interest and agree to being shown how to fill in registration forms and to go and use their votes. The students and teachers had wanted to set up a 'voting registration clinic' as a meeting place where people could meet and learn what to do. But several black preachers they'd approached were too afraid to allow meetings in their Churches, afraid in case of retribution from whites. There was understandably a very strong element of fear behind everybody's actions or lack of action.

Even at the smallest meetings they had managed to organize, police showed up to harass and threaten people. The county Sheriff had sent officers to record names of people who'd attended the meetings and warned them that they risked losing their jobs if employers saw their name on the list. When people were brave enough to go to the county Courthouse where vote registration was held they clashed with law officers and were arrested. Innumerable difficulties were put in the way of any attempt to register; the Registration Office was opened only two days a month, for instance, and on these days the Registrars would arrive late, take long lunch hours and leave early. The few blacks who did manage to see the Registrars usually 'failed' the literacy tests. More often than not the black would-be voters were met by the Sheriff and helmeted deputies armed with guns and clubs.

'I hear you and Steve are going on to Mississippi,' Abbie said to Rowan, after Crystal had left the room. 'Where's Steve just now, by the way?'

'He's got the use of Dexter's study at the moment. He's now trying to catch up with some paperwork.'

Lucy smiled. 'Anyway he wouldn't want to be heah listenin' to so much girl talk.'

'What girl talk?' Abbie asked.

Rowan had felt like smiling from the moment Abbie came stomping into the house, her stubborn energy defying the frailness of her tiny figure. She had a warming and cheering effect on everybody. Just to look at the pixie face with its baby-soft skin and bright alert eyes made Rowan want to hug her.

'We were jes talkin' before you arrived, Miss Abbie,' drawled Cindy, one of the other ladies, 'about what's been happenin' hehah in Montgomery. So many strangers comin' into town and stirrin' up all the black boys. Why, it's jes wicked what's been happenin' hehah. Real shockin' things, Miss Abbie!'

Abbie enjoyed a drink of lemonade before enquiring with interest, 'Like what?'

'With all those marches and demonstrations and such like hehah in town it's jes been rape, rape, rape!'

'Shame on you, Miss Cindy,' Lucy said gently. 'Theah's been no proof of any such thing.'

374

'Why evahbody's talkin' about it,' Miss Cindy protested. 'Ah'm tellin' y'all, one poor lady was raped forty-seven times – *forty-seven times*,' she repeated.

Abbie said, 'Land's sakes, Miss Cindy, if I'd been that lady I'd rather have screamed than counted!'

Rowan nearly choked over a mouthful of lemonade and Mary Beth, eyes twinkling with suppressed laughter said, 'Are you all right?' Rowan nodded.

Later, alone with Abbie for a few minutes, sitting out on the porch enjoying a pre-dinner drink, they discussed the general situation and how Jackson was determined to continue the fight in Mississippi.

Rowan sighed. 'Sometimes I think it's pretty hopeless. I mean what can anyone do with people who are so bigoted they won't even allow their fellow citizens to vote. It's a basic human right.'

'There's a lot of things even more basic than that they're not allowing,' Abbie said. 'But don't go making the mistake that it's only here that there's ignorance and prejudice and hate and people trying to hang on to power. It's human nature, there's people like that everywhere. It doesn't mean though that decent folk everywhere should give up trying to make the critters see sense.'

Both she and Jackson were sorry to leave Abbie and Lucy and Mary Beth. Rowan could hardly hold back her tears she was so upset.

'I won't worry,' Abbie said, 'Steve's only to be in Mississippi for a few months then he'll be back at college in Nashville. You'll come back with him and Mary Beth and I will see you then.'

Rowan nodded, unable to trust herself to speak. Mary Beth would be going down to New Orleans with the new wave of Freedom Riders before journeying home to Nashville. She looked back at her friend's waving figure. She was a pretty girl with her fair hair piled on top of her head and a delicate flower pinned at one side of it. She always managed to look appealingly feminine, even in checked shirts and blue jeans.

'I hope Mary Beth will be all right,' she said to Jackson later. 'I'm afraid for her.'

'She could have come with us, honey. I told her but as she said, it could be just as dangerous – maybe mohah so – in Mississippi.'

Rowan sighed. 'I keep trying to understand all this, Steve. How did it all come about? I mean, I thought black people were supposed to have got their freedom after the Civil War.'

He nodded. 'We went through about ten years after the war, during occupation, when blacks were given equitable treatment. It was a tough time because they'd come from slavery and many of them were not able to adjust. But the laws were obeyed. There were Federal Troops stationed heah. Then Johnson succeeded Lincoln and he was seen as a Southerner.' Steve shook his head. 'He had a terrible time. After his term Southerners gradually reverted back to the old ways. There was a case called "Plessy versus Ferguson". It was a Supreme Court case in which the Supreme Court of the United States held that it was acceptable under the Constitution to treat citizens of different races separately but equal – the term was "separate but equal". '

'Oh, I get it,' Rowan groaned.

'It said if you provide black citizens a mode of transportation separate but equal to that provided fohah whites – that's acceptable. If you provide them with school systems that are separate but equal – if you provide eating facilities that are separate but equal –'

'Very dangerous,' Rowan said.

'Yes. When that law came down Southern legislators began to pass laws forbidding any mixing of the races; in restaurants, in public places, in schools, in Churches, in neighbourhoods, racial restrictive covenants were written into the law. So in effect, after "Plessy versus Ferguson" we had a segregated society. Until "Brown versus Board of Education".'

' "Separate but equal" turned out to be separate but unequal.'

'Very much so. And I hardly need to tell you now discrimination is pervasive, it's as discriminatory as apartheid in South Africa, it is as legally enforced, it is as violent here and maybe more violent than in South Africa and we have lived with that until now.'

'After all these years of living like that do you think the Civil Rights Movement is going to change things permanently?'

'It's got to, honey.'

'What I don't understand is how you, as a Southerner born and bred in the South, have turned out so different – so determined to help put things right. Where did that "sense of right" come from?' She gazed at him in puzzlement.

'I had a muthah and fathah,' Jackson said, 'who didn't want to change the world but who knew the world was wrong. Many of the children with whom I was raised were taught to say niggah. I nevah heard the word in my home.'

'It strikes me,' Rowan said, 'that anyone like that, living in a society like this but going against the grain of it, must have terrific courage.'

'I don't think there was heroism on my muthah's or fathah's part but at least there was a sense of goodness. And while they never lectured to me or to my brothers and sisters about the wrongs it's clear that we always understood. . . .' Her hesitated thoughtfully before going on. 'When you ask where it came from I couldn't point to anything that my muthah or fathah said except they gave us the environment in which our minds were not closed. Our minds were open and we had sense enough to see that there was a problem heah in our society and in small ways there was something we could do about it.'

'I wish I'd met your mother and father. They sound such nice people and so sensible about bringing up a family.'

377

He gave her one of his slow smiles that was reflected mischievously in his eyes before saying, in the husky Southern voice that she found so attractive, 'Don't worry, honey, weah going to bring up our children just like they did.'

56

Harry felt deeply shocked when his mother left home. He hadn't believed she would do it. Although oddly enough he'd often wished *he* could leave home to be free of the dangers of her weakening influences. For her to leave was distressingly different. To have a father and mother together was your home background, your base in life. It was the right and natural thing and the fact that they had faults was also natural. It was all part of the secure base. He knew his mum and dad, their strengths and weaknesses. He knew where he stood with them. For good or bad they belonged, were part of his family. Or so he'd thought. Now he didn't know what to think.

Everything had turned upside down. His father had been upset as well. At first he was angry and derisive. 'She'll be back quick enough,' he kept saying, 'she'll never manage on her own. She'll be absolutely hopeless and helpless.' He'd even written to her to lay out his terms for taking her back, making what he called 'generous concessions'. He'd given Harry the letter to deliver.

His mother had already made it clear that she did not want his dad to come near her flat at any time and for any reason. 'The marriage is over for good, I never want to see you again,' she'd said in the original note she'd left. His dad had let him see it. They had both been shocked. It was a very brutal, straight-from-the-shoulder note, sharp and to the point with no softening apologies or excuses. It didn't seem like his mother at all.

She didn't even bother to answer his dad's letter offering to take her back. His dad was waiting with barely disguised eagerness for a reply. He felt really sorry for him. He looked so taken aback and confused when he didn't get one. It was just as well, Harry thought, that he hadn't repeated what his mother had said after reading his dad's letter – 'Tell him to get lost,' she'd said. He really didn't know what had come over her.

Gradually his dad had become different as well. Instead of working as usual in his attic studio or going out somewhere and enjoying himself, he hung about downstairs in the house looking lost and pathetic. At one point he took the 'flu or something and Harry found himself having to look after him. He told his mother as he knew his dad was hoping he would but even that didn't soften her to make her come back. It was really terrible. Even the house wasn't the same. It had a cold empty, purposeless feel about it. It didn't feel like home any more.

The thing that was most confusing of all was the fact that his mother seemed so happy. Not only that. Far from not managing and being helpless and hopeless, she seemed to be managing extremely well. In a way, she had become a stranger, not the mum he'd always thought she was. It really shook him to the core.

He didn't know what he would have done if it hadn't been for Rose. He could talk to her, she understood – her home had broken up as well. They had been seeing a lot of each other. In fact since she'd joined the Karate club they were hardly ever apart. He had taken her to the Karate Championship demonstration at first and she had been so impressed and excited by it she had wanted to learn. It was unusual for girls to be club members but there was no rule against it and so he'd got her in. Many a laugh they'd had at first about her efforts to learn. She was such a skinny little thing with no strength or stamina at all. She was so eager though, always blowing her fringe up from her eyes and prancing about doing her Katas in ridiculously wrong ways.

Training was difficult for her to do at home because her dad hated everything Eastern and, as Rose said, would have 'ten thousand fits' if he discovered she was taking part in anything Japanese. Harry had to take the Gi she wore for training home with him. Rose daren't keep it in her house in case her father found it. Nor could she risk reading any of the books at home on Karate or Japanese life, customs or philosophy. 'He'd kill me if he found out,' Rose said. She couldn't even train in the park as he often did – at least, not wearing her Gi. The park covered a big area and the chances of her father seeing her were slight but she was too nervous to risk it.

The way things were in Mary House now, with his father always hanging about like a lost soul, he couldn't take her home to his place. To have to cope with the problems – as his dad would see it – of him still 'going' with her, could finish his dad off.

'He's real cracked-up,' he told Rose. 'I'd better not worry him with anything else. You know what parents are like. They all nagged on at us right from the start about being too young.'

Mostly they trained together at the club. Rose stopped playing at the gigs and as a result was beginning to look more fit; at least the dark shadows under her eyes had disappeared. Dode had managed to join up with another group so he didn't miss her too much. He'd tried to persuade Dode to work at getting fitter as well but poor Dode was too far gone.

At the moment Harry was excited because of the distinguished visitor who was coming to the club. Mr Demura was over from Japan on a tour of clubs in Britain. He was going to have a training session with some of the club members. Mr Demura of course wouldn't deign to waste his time with a beginner like Rose but with Harry now being a Black Belt he would certainly be honoured. Mr Demura had expressed a preference for Kumite, or unrestricted fighting.

Harry had never felt so strung up and nervous in his life. Not because he was afraid of getting hurt, that didn't worry him in the slightest. What he had a horror of was making a fool of himself, looking amateurish, not putting on a good show, especially in front of Rose. But also of letting himself down in front of the revered Sensi or Japanese master.

The Dojo had much the same format (so the Scottish instructor assured them) as its Japanese counterparts, wall mirrors, heavy bags, Makiwara punching pads along the walls. At the end of the training area Japanese and Scottish flags hung side by side.

Demura, Harry discovered, was tall for an oriental, nearly 6 feet of olive muscle. His face although broad and chiselled, had an almost Latin look, far removed from the ludicrous, slant-eyed buck toothed image so common in popular myth. He was dressed conservatively but elegantly in immaculate pinstripe but although his clothes were the epitome of taste, something jarred. Harry detected a feeling of the primitive about him, an inner fire and conviction that belied his studied attempts at nonchalance during the initial introductions.

Afterwards, they all changed into their Gis. Normally at this time there would be much noisy talking and laughing. But tonight there was a quiet, subdued atmosphere, a tense expectancy.

Demura slowly pulled on his heavyweight Gi and wrapped his frayed and faded belt around his muscular waist. His silk Black Belt was so worn that it was more white than black. When he was ready he confidently strode to the dojo floor where a group of young Black Belts, Harry included, were desperately trying to loosen off.

The class lined out at the Scottish instructor's command and bowed first to the instructor and then to Demura. They then partnered off. Harry was sweating and breathless before his turn came to be partnered with Demura. He bowed to the older man then began bobbing lightly around the floor feinting the occasional hand or foot attack. Demura hardly moved. His legs were spread out in a deep, strong stance, guard up, staring hypnotically forward.

Then suddenly Harry's long sinewy leg whipped a roundhouse kick at Demura's head. Demura slid back a fraction and the sharp slap of his block resounded across the hall. Harry flung attack after attack, gaining confidence as he went. Until suddenly, in a blur, Demura exploded forward with a scream. He delivered a roundhouse kick to Harry's temple with his left leg, then sweeping Harry's legs with his right, as Harry crashed down, Demura rocketed in with a reverse punch at the moment Harry hit the floor.

Then Demura bowed and spoke in a voice that was a guttural bark, each syllable projected from the depths of his abdomen.

'Always commit your whole mind all the time and be effective.'

Dazed, Harry replied, 'Os Sensie.'

Later, Rose assured him that he had been absolutely marvellous but he shook his head. 'He knew, Rosie.'

'Knew what?'

'I was thinking more of the effect I was having, I was concerned about what other people were thinking – rather than fully concentrating on what I had to do. "Commit your whole mind," he said. He knew I wasn't doing it.'

'But the instructor told you afterwards that Mr Demura had singled you out for praise. I was there, I heard him. Aren't you thrilled about that, Harry? I am.'

'I could have done better though.'

Still it had been an exhilarating experience and he'd learned by it. It had been great talking outside on the street after they'd all shaken hands and bowed to Demura. After Demura had gone they excitedly dissected and verbally repeated every move they'd made, improved on it, discussed it, were enthusiastic in their praise and admiration of Demura.

'Still,' Harry said at last, 'it was a great night, wasn't it?'

'Marvellous!' Rose agreed.

He put his arm round her waist as they walked along and she stretched her arm around his. It was fab that they had so much in common. They went up Victoria Road and cut into the back lane of her house to have a few kisses and cuddles before she went in. They could never stay more than a few furtive minutes, Rose was so paranoic about her father seeing her.

They arranged that he would meet her next day, after her father had gone to work, and have an early morning jog. They had agreed to meet along at the park gates at the corner of Pollokshaws Road and Balvicar Street but he waited and waited and Rose never turned up. Eventually he decided to risk it and cut round to Queens Drive and along to the corner of Victoria Road. He walked boldly to the front door and rang the bell. Mr Thornton was bound to be away to work by now. Eventually the door opened a crack and he caught a glimpse of Rose's face. It was horribly bruised and swollen. She tried to shut the door again but he was too quick for her. He got his foot in it then pushed it open and strode inside.

'Where is the bastard?' he demanded.

'Oh, Harry.' Rose tried to cover her face with her hands. 'I didn't want you to see me looking ugly like this.'

'Where is he?' Harry repeated. 'Let him try doing that to me. I'll kill him, I'll kill the bastard!'

'He's away to work. But oh please, Harry, don't do anything. It'll just make it worse for me.'

'We'll see about that. Why did he do it? He's never touched you before, has he? It's always been Dode. Where is Dode by the way?'

'He's staying the weekend with one of the boys in that new group he's joined. They were doing a late night gig at the other end of town near where the boy lives. Oh Harry, he found out about the Karate. Somebody saw us talking with Mr Demura outside the club. He was going to kill me.' She began to weep and Harry took her into his arms and stroked her head. 'I know he was, Harry, but I managed to get away. I hid outside. I've been behind the bushes at the end of the garden all night. I only slipped back into the house this morning after he went away. Oh Harry, I'm so frightened. What am I going to do?'

'You're coming with me. I'm going to take you to my mum's flat in the West End. He'll never find you there.'

'Will she take me in, Harry?'

Rose gazed up at him through her fringe. Her face was black and blue and swollen. He still thought she was beautiful.

'She'd better!' he said gruffly.

57

'You work far too hard,' Gregson said.

Jenny smiled. 'Talk about the pot calling the kettle black!'

'It's one thing working for yourself and reaping the rewards. Quite another slaving over in this so-called refuge for damn all. I don't like to see you being taken advantage of.'

'I pay very little for my keep. And I did volunteer to help out in the first place.'

'You're not just "helping out" as you put it. You're a full-time cook-housekeeper there as well as doing your outside catering jobs. You can't go on like that, Jenny.'

She silently agreed with him. She felt claustrophobic at Rebecca's now. Rebecca was like a possessive parent or spouse, always wanting to know where she was going, who she was going with and when she would be back. And lecturing her unceasingly on the wicked ways of men.

She'd told Rebecca outright that she didn't want her interfering with her personal freedom.

'Hazel fought against me interfering with her freedom to drink,' Rebecca had said. 'She was glad that I won in the end. The trouble is, Jenny, that people like you and Hazel don't understand what's good for you.'

'But you do?'

'Of course I do. It's part of the cross I have to bear that the people I'm committed to help cannot see what is best for them.'

For the sake of peace when Gregson came up to Glasgow on one of his now frequent visits she had to go to his hotel room. It was the only place where they could make love. Sex was good with Gregson. He was a passionate but considerate lover. He wanted to marry her and was urging her to make a total commitment. As it was, she felt a closeness, an intimacy with him as if they already were man and wife. Often in the hotel bedroom she'd turn towards his naked body and smooth her exploring fingers over the hard contours of his face and sinewy muscles, or she would watch him get dressed. She felt she knew his body as much as she knew her own.

But hadn't she felt the same with Joe? But there had been another aspect to her relationship with Joe. How many times had she nursed his head against her and stroked it to soothe away his nightmares. In the secret silence of the night Joe had clung to her like a frightened child. She'd known then how desperately Joe needed her. And she knew it still.

She didn't tell Gregson but Joe pursued her whenever he could – waylaying her in shops, on the street, in the park, arguing, bullying, pleading. She didn't dare think of what he'd do if he found out that there was another man. In some strange way, the fact that they did have these distressing confrontations made them both continue to feel they belonged to one another, almost as if they were still living together.

For a long time now she had realized if she was to have any chance of being free of Joe she must get right away from the district, make a clean break. Not just for herself but for the sake of the children. They looked underfed, neglected and unhappy. Rose had recently perked up but she'd found out that Rose's shiny eyes and sudden aura of energy was due to the fact that she was 'madly in love' as Rose had put it, with Harry Donovan, Amelia's boy.

Jenny hadn't been able to sleep for worrying ever since she'd found out. It wasn't that she'd anything against the boy. He seemed a nice enough lad, if somewhat aggressive – Rebecca said he was just like his bully of a father which didn't do much for Jenny's peace of mind.

Amelia, of course, thought Harry was wonderful despite the fact he'd elected to stay with Douglas rather than move to the West End with her. She too, however, was worried about him 'going steady' with Rose. He was far too young, she said, and had his whole life before him. She was hoping he'd go to university soon and get a degree and 'make the most of his potential'.

Jenny wanted Rose to make the most of her life too. She mustn't ruin it by rushing into an early commitment and marriage as she had done with Joe.

Desperately she scanned the papers every day, searching for a place for herself and Dode and Rose. If only she could be as lucky as Amelia but so far there had been nothing to let except bed-sits and places that refused to allow children or students. Not that she could afford to furnish any place. Nor could she persuade any bank manager to give her a loan or overdraft as Amelia had. Both Amelia's husband and wealthy mother-in-law had accounts at Amelia's bank and Amelia could also give impressive figures of earnings from her books as security.

Gregson kept trying to persuade her to allow him to buy her a flat. He insisted it was ridiculous that she should worry about anything that money could buy. He could set her up with everything she needed. Yet still she vacillated, drawing back from committing herself to such a degree. She hadn't started divorce proceedings either, although she kept promising she would. She knew her attitude was hurting Gregson and she was sorry. But she couldn't help it.

Nevertheless the fact that Rose was now seriously at risk had started to put extra pressure on her. She'd have to do something. And soon. Eventually she asked Gregson if they could come to some business arrangement about purchasing a flat. She'd tried to get a mortgage from various building societies without success. Could he put up the money and allow her to pay it back to him in instalments, in the same way that she would have done if she had managed to obtain a loan from a building society?

'Darling,' he said, 'I keep telling you, I'll gladly buy you a flat. There's no question of you needing to pay me back.'

'I know but I want to remain independent.'

'Oh, thanks very much,' he said sarcastically, 'for your usual show of love, trust and commitment.'

'I'm sorry, Al. I can't help how I feel.'

It was at times like these that she could see the hurt beneath his tough exterior; it was betrayed by the unhappiness in his eyes and the bitter twist of his mouth. He eventually agreed to her terms however. From that moment she felt a lift of optimism and excitement. She would work hard and be able to pay him back all right. Her reputation for catering for small parties and dinners and other private social occasions was increasing by word of mouth and she was now able to demand comparatively high fees. Quite apart from being able to have the children with her again she was looking forward so much to being in a place of her own, to having it exactly the way she wanted it, to feeling free at last.

She told Rebecca that she was going to buy a flat as soon as the right one turned up. 'I must make sure I get something really nice for the children's sake as well as my own. Oh, Rebecca, it'll be so wonderful for Rose and Dode and me to be together again.'

'That man has done this,' Rebecca said. 'He has succeeded at last. He has tempted you with money.'

'No, it's not like that, Rebecca.'

'You haven't that kind of money. You couldn't buy a flat on your own.'

'I know but –'

'If you did have that kind of money you would surely have been paying for your keep instead of living off me for so long.'

Jenny flushed. 'That's a terrible thing to say and very unfair. After all. . . .'

'Oh, not that I regret it, Jenny. I don't regret anything I've done for you or grudge anything I've given you. Far from it.'

'It was an understanding,' Jenny said, 'that I did all the cooking and baking –'

'You do your share of the work, as we all do, as anyone in any normal home is expected to do. I thought you did it gladly. Because I have never grudged you any help, Jenny it never occurred to me that you could demean yourself in this way.'

'It's not that I grudge doing anything,' Jenny said unhappily.

'Or be so ungrateful.'

'I'm not ungrateful, Rebecca. Please don't think that.'

'You've conveniently forgotten, Jenny, that I took you into my home when you hadn't a penny and were fit for nothing. I didn't count the cost. I simply opened my arms and took you to my heart like a sister.'

Jenny remembered and felt wretchedly guilty that she was contemplating leaving Rebecca in the lurch. There were several day-courses and meetings scheduled to take place in the refuge for which luncheon and teas had been included in the price when they had been advertised. A whole year's programme had been planned, printed and advertised in advance.

'Little did I think then,' Rebecca went on, 'that this is all the thanks I'd get.'

'I don't want to let you down or cause you any problems,' Jenny said miserably.

'You'll never have any luck, you know,' Rebecca said. 'The dagger will one day rebound in your heart. Poor Jenny.' She sighed. 'I have a terrible premonition that something far, far worse than what you're doing to me, will happen to you.'

Fear hollowed the pit of Jenny's stomach. Fear made her thoughts shrink back. She wanted to ask Rebecca to explain what she meant, to plead for reassurance but Rebecca rose with dignity and swept from the room.

She tried to tell herself not to be foolish. She tried to remember that she had lived so long with fear that it had taken deep root inside her – she must keep trying to fight it and eradicate it. She mustn't allow it any foothold or it would overcome her and take possession of her again. She knew if that happened she would be paralysed again, helpless, unable to do anything. It was a black pit, forever waiting for her to fall into.

She was supposed to meet Gregson at his hotel that night. She longed for the comfort of his arms. But was it not incredibly selfish of her to go out and leave Rebecca now when Rebecca, rightly or wrongly, felt so hurt and betrayed? Wringing her hands in wretched indecision, she hung about the shadowy hall wondering if she should just get her coat and slip away. Or should she tell Rebecca she was going out but say she would be back as soon as she could? The least she could do surely, was to be kind, to show a little consideration and understanding. She doubted if poor Rebecca had ever loved or been loved by anyone except her 'friends'. If they deserted her she had nobody, no children, no lover, no husband, good or bad. She hovered uncertainly in the hall near the sitting room door. Then impulsively she went in. Rebecca was sitting straight-backed on her prayer mat, her legs in the lotus position, her eyes closed.

'I'll stay in with you tonight if you want me to,' Jenny said. 'Maybe we could –'

'Far be it from me, Jenny,' Rebecca said, without opening her eyes, 'to spoil your enjoyment with your lover. Nor would I want you to suffer retribution from him if you did not arrive as he's expecting. Go now, with my blessing. Your retribution will come soon enough.'

58

'Well, the decision's up to you, Jenny,' Amelia said. 'I can only tell you what I feel like being on my own in this flat. I certainly haven't regretted the decision. Not for a moment.' She sighed. 'The only thing is – when I think of all those wasted years of my life.' Her voice firmed. 'But I mustn't allow myself to think like that. They say nothing's ever wasted as a novelist. That's the truth I must remember. It's all grist to the mill.'

'I'm still looking at flats right enough. It's just. . . . Poor Rebecca! I don't know what to do about her.'

'You could still be friends even if you left the refuge.'

'I've told her that, it doesn't seem to make any difference. She says it's all right and I must do what I want. But she's so hurt, Amelia.'

'She wanted me to go to the refuge, you know.'

'Why didn't you? I mean even as a stop-gap until you got a place of your own. Instead of suffering all that time.'

'Instinct, perhaps?'

'How do you mean?'

'I think it's true what Rebecca says about people repeating patterns in their lives. I was dominated by my mother. Then I got myself tied up with a man like Douglas. What I began to ask myself was, could I be repeating the pattern yet again with Rebecca?'

Jenny was silent for a minute. Then she murmured, 'It's strange, isn't it. I keep looking for flats and one part of me longs to leave and the other part of me knows it's impossible.'

'Nothing's impossible, Jenny. I used to think it would be impossible for me to be on my own and survive. I thought I was such a weak character. Now I realize that

I've just been brainwashed into thinking that. I've discovered I really enjoy being on my own. Each day now I'm finding out more about myself, getting to know myself. I'm beginning to think that far from being a weak character, I must have an incredibly strong character to have survived all that's happened to me in my life. Oh, Jenny, it's such an adventure!'

Jenny tried to smile. 'You don't feel a bit guilty, do you?'

'About leaving Douglas? Not in the slightest! I thought I would. I thought I would feel a lot of awful things. But no. I didn't suddenly become an entirely different character overnight, of course. It's all to do with a series of discoveries that are still going on and that are so surprising that they take a little time to sink in.'

'How do you mean?'

'Oh, just silly little things mostly,' Amelia said, laughing. 'The other day, for instance, I'd been typing away like mad for hours and I thought how I'd love to relax with a drink and at the same time realized sadly that I couldn't have one. You see any time I'd helped myself to a drink in Mary House, Douglas nagged at me about becoming an alcoholic.'

'That was ridiculous!'

'I know. But then he nagged at me so much about everything. Anyway, there I was thinking I couldn't have a drink. Then suddenly it came to me! Douglas wasn't there any more. I *could* have a drink if I wanted to.' She laughed again. 'I know it's really no big deal but honestly, Jenny, I've never enjoyed anything so much in all my life. I made quite a ceremony of it. Pouring it out . . . sitting with my feet up . . . taking my time . . . sipping it as if it was the nectar of the gods. I didn't want another. I'm not a drinker – another of my discoveries. It was just the principle of the thing, the fact that I could actually have one if I wanted to.'

'I wonder if you'll ever have another man,' Jenny said.

'God forbid!'

'That's what I thought until I met Al.' Jenny's wide frank eyes and short curly hair gave her something of the appearance of a helpless child as she gazed at her friend. 'Oh Amelia, my life's so complicated. What with all the worries about the children and Joe and Al and now Rebecca.'

'At least you're free of Joe.'

'Free of Joe?' Jenny gave a humourless laugh. 'Is that what you think?'

'Is he still pestering you?'

Jenny nodded. 'He followed me the other day to a job I was doing in Bearsden. Got on the bus with me. Sat opposite me all the way. Followed me to the woman's house – he was convinced I was going to meet a lover. I don't know if it was just his fevered imagination or if he's heard any rumours about Al.'

'What happened about the job?'

'I kept telling him, it was a children's birthday party. I'd prepared most of the things and taken them over the day before. I'd just some cakes and jelly decorations to do and some other last minute jobs like setting the table. He didn't believe me until the woman answered the door and her two children started dancing excitedly around me.'

'You'll have to go to Court and get a restraining order or something to stop him.'

'Do you think I'd get anything while he's not hitting me?'

'It's worth a try. I don't see why you should have to suffer him following you and watching you all the time.'

'It's not all the time. It feels like it, though. It's really affecting my nerves.'

'I couldn't stand that,' Amelia shuddered. 'Especially if I knew the man possessed not only a gun but a horrible weapon like a Japanese sword. It doesn't bear thinking about, Jenny.'

'I can't see any way out of the mess my life's in.'

'Just do one thing at a time. But for God's sake do *something*!'

Harry made Rose a cup of hot, sweet tea and then he bathed Rosie's face.

"What's that?' She kept jerking at every sound. 'Oh, Harry what if he comes back?'

'Too bad on him,' Harry said, 'I'll knock the living daylights out of him. Drink up your tea. You'll feel more able to travel across to the West End after you've got that inside you. And calm down. He's never going to hurt you again, take my word for it.'

After he'd bathed her face he awkwardly but gently combed her hair. Then he helped her on with her coat. He'd already helped her to pack her clothes and belongings. Now he carried the suitcase to the door. 'Come on, Rosie. There's no need to be frightened any more.'

She clung to him all the way to his mother's place and she was still clinging to him when his mother opened her door.

'My God!' his mother cried out when she saw them. 'What happened? Come on in, dear.' She put her arm around Rose's shoulders and led her into the bright, chintzy sitting room.

'Her dad found out she'd been at a Karate meeting with me,' Harry said. 'That would have been bad enough. But at this particular meeting there was a Japanese Black Belt. Somebody must have seen us saying our goodbyes to him outside the hall. That's what her dad kept screaming about apparently, Rosie talking to Mr Demura.'

'Harry,' said Amelia unhappily. 'You might have known. You know how Mr Thornton feels about the Japanese and why.'

'I bet it wasn't even Japanese guards at the camp or the jail or whatever it was he was in,' Harry scoffed. 'Most of the Japanese were fighting at the front. The chances are it was Korean guards he had.'

'Harry!' Amelia protested.

Harry held up his hand. 'Don't get me wrong! I'm not trying to excuse or condone brutality.'

'I'm glad to hear it,' Amelia said.

'But you've always said yourself that it's interesting to understand what makes all different kinds of people tick, what makes them act the way they do.'

'The question at the moment,' Amelia said, 'is what are we going to do about Rosie?'

'Could she stay here with you, Mum?' He put his arm around Amelia and gave her a persuasive hug. 'Please, Mum?'

'I'm certainly not going to turn her away, son.'

'Oh thanks, Mum,' Harry cried out in delight. 'That's fab!'

'But wait a minute Harry. Rosie's place is really with *her* mum. I'll have to contact Jenny right away.'

'That's no use,' Harry protested, 'she doesn't care about Rosie.'

'Of course she does. What a thing to say!'

'Why did her mum go and live at that woman's place then, where Rosie and Dode weren't allowed?'

'I don't want to go there, Harry.' Rose sounded anxious.

'I don't blame you,' Harry said. 'That woman's a right nutter.'

'I don't think there'll be any question of Rosie going to Rebecca's. It's just that I'll have to let Jenny know what's happened. I'll go and phone her.'

Harry sat down beside Rose on the settee after his mother had left the room. He put his arm round her shoulders. She was trembling. 'Don't worry, Rosie,' he kept repeating, 'don't worry.'

He could hear his mother's voice blurring in from the hall. He strained his ears to make out exactly what she was saying but could only catch a few disjointed words. He felt anxious. No way would he allow Rosie to go anywhere near the Southside again. Yet if his mother wouldn't keep Rosie here what could he do? He hadn't

396

any money other than the pocket-money his dad gave
him. He'd just managed to scrape together the bus fares
from the Southside for himself and Rosie. If he'd money
he could get Rosie a place and to hell with parents. But
he hadn't, that was the problem. He wondered, if he
should be thinking about getting a job instead of going to
University.

His mother came back into the room. She looked
worried. 'That's strange,' she murmured, half to herself.
'Rebecca says she's not at the refuge and Jenny told me
she was going straight back to Rebecca's from here.'

59

Jenny got off the bus in Pollokshaws Road at the Langside Hall corner and began walking up Langside Avenue towards Battlefield House. She was just passing the Mulberry gates of the park when she was suddenly confronted by Joe's tall, lean figure. He had a wild look about his eyes and the stubble of fair hair on his face showed he'd neglected to shave.

'Let me pass, please,' Jenny said. 'If you don't stop pestering me like this I'm going to apply for a Court Order to restrain you. I'll have you put in jail if necessary.'

'You're my wife,' Joe said.

'In name only now, Joe. Why can't you accept once and for all that our marriage is finished?'

'No.'

'Yes, Joe.'

'It doesn't matter what happens to me or what anyone does to me as long as I have you.'

'You haven't got me, Joe.'

His blue eyes searched her face. 'But I must.'

'There's no use talking to you. Let me pass.'

She went to push him aside but suddenly his arm was around her shoulders like an iron band and he was forcing her into the park. She struggled as hard as she could but it was impossible to break free of him.

Pleading had no effect, elicited no response. There was only his iron grip and his long loping stride. All she could hear was the whispering of the silver birch trees overhead and the rustle of the bamboo as the hollow canes shook their grass-like leaves against her legs.

By the time they'd reached the Victoria Road gate at the other side of the park she had stopped struggling. She was so breathless with being hassled along at such a pace. Crossing the road towards the flat, however, in desperation she renewed her struggles and protests. It made not the slightest difference. In a matter of minutes she was alone with him in the flat with the door shut behind her.

Near to tears now and still gasping for breath, she managed to say, 'What good is this going to do? You can't keep me a prisoner, Joe. Please, please!'

'I kept dreaming of when we'd be together again,' Joe said.

'We're not together, Joe.'

Suddenly he swept her off her feet and carried her towards the bedroom.

'No!'

With every ounce of strength in her she began to fight him. Always before when he'd struck her she'd cowered helpless before him. Afterwards when he'd made love to her she'd accepted him with equal helplessness. Now, having made love with Gregson, it seemed obscene to allow Joe to touch her in this way. She suddenly knew beyond all doubt that it was Gregson that she belonged to and no one else.

She fought Joe like a tiger, kicking, punching, scratching. Even pinned down by his body, even as he forced himself inside her she kept frantically trying to beat him off with her fists.

Afterwards she wept. Joe made her a cup of tea; she ignored it. She ignored him. She kept thinking, Oh, Al, and shaking her head to herself, Oh, Al.

'You'll stay now, won't you?' Joe pleaded. 'For the children's sake if not for mine. I can't help it, Jenny. First it was Dode and now Rose.'

Jenny immediately became dry-eyed and alert. 'What do you mean – first Dode and now Rose? Where are the children? What's happened to them?'

'I've been losing my temper with Dode. Then yesterday I found that Rose had been going with that Donovan boy to Karate – even taking lessons from a Jap.'

She could see him begin to tremble. 'It's all right, Joe,' she soothed him. 'I'll speak to her. Where is she just now?'

'I don't know. With the Donovan boy, I suppose, she's always with him. But she'd better not go near that yellow bastard again –'

'No, she won't. I'll speak to her, Joe. I promise, I promise. I'll find her and speak to her. Just you go back to work, Joe. It'll be all right. I promise.'

He stood very still for a long minute, his blue eyes expressionless. Eventually he nodded and turned away.

She crouched on top of the bed listening to his feet in the hall. Then the outside door opened and shut very quietly.

'Oh my God!' She put her hand over her mouth and rocked herself backwards and forwards. Then she stretched her hand out for the bedside phone. She dialled Mary House first. Douglas replied that neither Harry nor Rose were there. She tried Amelia's flat next.

'Jenny!' Amelia cried out. 'Where on earth have you been? I've been trying to contact you.'

'Is Rose there?'

'Yes.'

'Thank God! Don't let her go home, Amelia, keep her with you.'

'Don't worry. She'll be safe here with me. Harry's brought her things.'

'Thank God!' Jenny repeated. 'Have you any idea where Dode is?'

'Just a minute. I'll ask Harry. Or probably Rose will know. They're through in the front room. Hang on.' In a minute or two she'd returned.

'He's at George Gordon's house. Harry knows him.'

'Tell Harry to get in touch with Dode and warn him not to go home. Tell him to meet me at your place. I'll be right over.' Then she hung up before Amelia could ask any more questions.

Her first urgency now was to get herself out of the flat.

All her old terror had returned to swamp her. She eased herself apprehensively from the bedroom, afraid even that Joe might be lurking in the hall or somewhere in the house. She felt in a state of collapse with fear; every sound made her jerk and moan. She reached the outside door. It resisted her desperately fumbling hands until suddenly she won the battle with it – and she was running outside and away. Victoria Road was too dangerous. She ran the other way to Pollokshaws Road where she caught a bus over to the west end.

Sitting in the bus she tried to think calmly what she was going to do. Where could she and the children go? She couldn't take them to Rebecca's. They wouldn't agree to go there, even if Rebecca would agree to take them in. Anyway Rebecca's was far too dangerously near the park. She had to get the children and herself as far away from the south side of the city as possible.

She wondered if Amelia would allow them to stay at her place but even if she was willing to there wasn't room. She doubted anyway if Amelia would take kindly to the idea of three people crowding in beside her in the flat, just as she had begun to enjoy being on her own. And there was her writing. If there was one thing that Amelia couldn't stand it was anything that threatened to come between her and her writing.

They could spend at least one night in a hotel. She had enough money to cover that because she'd recently been paid for a catering job. After tonight though – where would they go where neither Joe nor Al Gregson could find them? Gregson was due to come up to Glasgow next day to finalize a property deal. He had negotiated a prime site in the centre of the city where he planned to open a meeting place for young people – coffee bar, disco, fashion boutique and record shop all under the same roof. He had been going to help her find a flat too.

Now she couldn't face hin. Not after being raped. She felt too ashamed. She needed to try to cope with the turmoil of her feelings. Somehow everything between her and Gregson had been irrevocably spoiled.

The logical part of her mind told her the rape hadn't been her fault. Every other part of her, however, was withering with shame. She felt dirty. She just wanted to hide.

But she didn't know where to go.

60

It was Amelia who suggested asking Hazel. But first she'd offered to put them up '. . . at least for tonight.'

Poor Amelia, Jenny thought, the agony of offering even that one night had showed on her face. Then suddenly, she'd brightened and said. 'I've just had a brilliant idea! What about asking Hazel for longer term accommodation?'

'Oh no, I don't think so, Amelia.'

'Why not? She's got plenty of room.'

'Well, there's her husband to consider now. . . .'

But already Jenny was turning the suggestion over in her mind. After all, Hazel had become a friend too. There had been a time, before they'd got to know each other at Rebecca's, when nothing or no one would have persuaded her to live either alone or with the children under Hazel's roof. Hazel had been such a snobbish ineffectual woman. But she certainly wasn't snobbish any more. She had in fact become rather fond of Hazel. All the same Hazel was enjoying her new-found peace and happiness with her husband. She wouldn't want to be burdened by anyone else's problems, especially if it meant having them live with her.

Amelia, however, was completely carried away by her 'brilliant idea'. Amelia had always been subject to sudden wild attacks of enthusiasm. 'Phone her now and ask if you can come to see her. It's too late tonight. Say tomorrow. I know you're in a state and don't feel you can cope but don't worry, I'll come with you.'

'I don't think it'll be any use, Amelia. I can't see Hazel agreeing to take me and the children in just like that.'

'I'll phone her,' Amelia said and had swooped on the phone and dialled the number before Jenny could gather her wits together to stop her.

'Hazel? Hallo! Yes, I'm fine. But I've Jenny here and there's something we'd like to talk to you about. Can we pop over to see you tomorrow? . . . Oh, good. Right then, see you tomorrow afternoon. Bye.'

'Oh, Amelia.' Jenny gazed helplessly at her.

'Everything's going to be all right.' Amelia came over and gave her a hug. 'It's just tonight that's going to be hell because I don't think I've enough blankets and sheets and things.'

Jenny couldn't help smiling and was helped by having to concentrate with Amelia on trying to make temporary sleeping arrangements. It ended up that she and Amelia and Rose crushed together in the one bed and Dode slept on the sitting room couch covered with a quilt.

They had discussed the possibility of Joe phoning. He wouldn't have arrived home from work until late and finding her gone would have assumed she'd returned to Rebecca's. But if he went this morning to Rebecca's and found she was not there he might then find out Amelia's number from Douglas.

Jenny had phoned Rebecca last thing the previous night to tell her she had to leave Battlefield House and would come round to collect her things and return her key as soon as she could manage. She was glad in a way that Rebecca had agreed so abruptly – she had hung up with hardly a word. She was sorry if she had caused Rebecca distress but she just couldn't cope with her while still so distressed herself.

She had pleaded with Amelia that if Gregson also managed to find out her number to tell him that she didn't know where Jenny had gone.

'Don't worry,' Amelia had said, trying to soothe her, 'I know you need time to sort yourself out. I'll help all I can.'

She had already said they could stay another night if need be. Jenny's heart warmed towards her.

'I really appreciate all you're trying to do, Amelia. I know how you must feel being kept off your work with all this hassle.'

'Friends come first,' she said firmly and Jenny couldn't help smiling because she could see that Amelia was struggling valiantly to be firm with herself.

'Well, you're certainly being a good friend to me, Amelia.'

'Come on, then. The children are all right listening to the record-player and I've told them we should be back before six.'

They took a taxi straight to Hazel's house and were waiting on the doorstep after ringing the bell.

'I'd almost forgotten how big this place was,' Jenny said.

'I told you there'd be plenty of room.'

'That's not the point though. . . .'

Just then the door opened and Hazel appeared looking so breathtakingly glamorous, such a picture of happiness, that for a few seconds Jenny gazed at her in confused silence.

'My dear friends!' Hazel stretched out her arms in welcome and drew then into the luxurious hall. 'I've been so looking forward to your visit. I meant to have you over before this but so much has been happening. I'll explain later on. Let me take your coats. This is Milly's day off and she's gone to treat herself to lunch in Cranston's and then she's hoping to buy a new hat and coat. She offered to stay this afternoon but I told her not to be silly, I could manage perfectly well on my own. What a pretty dress, Amelia. I'm very fond of pale blue myself. It looks so nice with hair as fair as ours, doesn't it?'

They had reached the drawing room and Hazel indicated seats over by the fire. 'Do make yourselves comfortable. You look very nice, too, Jenny dear – that's a very smart suit. How clever of you to team beige with a bronze blouse.'

Jenny was trying to keep a smile pinned to her face but her heart was sinking fast. Amelia's idea seemed ridicu-

405

lous now. She was sure by the look on Amelia's anxious face that she was beginning to have doubts herself.

'Hazel, can we talk?' Amelia managed to say.

'Of course dear, of course!' Hazel happily agreed. 'Just wait until I fetch the tea trolley. I've done everything myself. I even baked the fairy cakes,' she added proudly before hurrying off to the kitchen.

Amelia and Jenny sat staring at each other in silence until she returned.

'There we are. Isn't this nice? Now I've just to fetch the tea service.' In a few minutes she'd returned again carrying a silver tray on which sat a large silver tea-pot and a silver milk jug and sugar bowl. She placed the tray on a little side table.

'Now, then . . .' She began pouring the tea into the waiting cups. 'Oh, I have been looking forward to you coming. I've so much to tell you.'

61

For some time now, Hazel had been receiving letters from Mississippi. Rowan and Steve Jackson were involved along with black colleagues in an education project. In addition to the registration drive they planned Freedom schools and remedial centres to teach courses in remedial reading, government, humanities and all kinds of scholastic and vocational subjects. About 1000 students from all over the country as well as volunteer ministers, lawyers, and other skilled people, white as well as black, had come to help.

Of course the white Mississippians were preparing for all this. They were busy making laws to outlaw every phase of the project. As well as all the bills being passed the State police force had been doubled and armed to the teeth. Hazel read with some alarm that a protest march had been organized despite an injunction being issued by a local judge prohibiting all marches and demonstrations. Rowan wrote:

The march had not long started when I saw the police set dogs on the students who were up at the front. Jackson ran ahead to help the students fight off the dogs and in a matter of minutes I had lost sight of him in the violent mêlée. I ran towards it but was caught by helmeted police wielding billy clubs and dragged into a truck already packed with other women.

It was over 100° F that day and humid and I was only too glad of the little air that the open window of the wagon let in. The destination turned out to be an old fairground and once we got there the driver rolled the windows shut and turned the heater on. Two hours passed with agonizing suffocating slowness. Two hours, Mother, before the doors were opened and we were allowed out. Some of the girls stumbled and fell and had to be helped up by other stronger ones.

On the fairground were two compounds, large buildings used to auction off cattle during the State Fair. They each had large openings at both ends where the cattle were driven in. The openings had been closed with wire. The building we were all herded into was already full of sweating women wandering about half-dressed. I gazed through the wire at the police guards. They had dogs and they were armed with rifles and looked some of the roughest men I'd ever seen. It suddenly occurred to me, Mother, how easy it was to imagine I was in a concentration camp in Nazi Germany and these policemen Nazi soldiers. Yet this is America. This is supposed to be the land of the free and the home of the brave. There's certainly plenty of brave people. And there's certainly a free press and media. This is, I believe the real saving grace of America and what makes it a basically open society. . . . The press and the media have recorded as many of our protests and demonstrations as they could and made sure the whole of the American people know exactly what is happening. Some of the most courageous and crusading people I know are newspaper and media men. It's as if this vast country is a breeding ground for these two extremes in man.

Americans' neurotic fears about Communism, for instance, are something I find hard to understand. People believed a drunken dishonest politician named Joseph McCarthy, who used people's fears to get fame and power for himself. He accused all kinds of people, government officials, scientists, famous entertainers. He never gave proof but Americans are so fearful of Communism that many still believe him. McCarthy ruined hundreds of innocent lives. People grew afraid to give jobs or even to show friendship to anyone accused. Again it reminds me of Nazi Germany.

408

After thinking about these things, Mother, I feel I'm in a violent and sick society. They talk of 'the American Dream'. So far, to me it has more the appearance of a nightmare. What do people mean when they speak of the American Dream? Is it the freedom to fight to get enough of the mighty dollar to enable them to scramble to the top of the pile, I wonder? Or does it apply to the more moral issues with which Abraham Lincoln was concerned? But look what they did to him – they shot him!

If high moral issues are the things that matter then it's high time they stopped talking about the dream and instead converted it into reality.

Many Americans of course are trying to do this and not only great Americans like President Kennedy and Martin Luther King, but also all the people I've marched shoulder to shoulder with. And the others too like Lucy who in quieter, less dramatic ways, are doing their best.

As I clung to the wire of the compound building, Mother, in the humid heat of the Mississippi night I struggled to prevent myself from sinking down into unconsciousness. For a terrible few minutes I experienced a wave of homesickness. I remembered with longing my own native land. And you, Mother. Thinking of you, Mother, and how you won the fight to overcome your weaknesses gave me renewed strength to hang on. I thought of Steve Jackson too and his courage. The two of you, the ones I love most in the world are an example to me. I cling to you both. And I cling to the knowledge that Steve loves America. He believes in its greatness. He has faith in its future. Through that faith, Mother, my faith must grow too.

Hazel had been so moved by the letter she'd shown it to Dan and they'd discussed what they must do. Something, they both felt, had to be done to show their love and support for Rowan.

409

Dan, of course, hadn't met Rowan, but his love and admiration for her had grown just by reading her letters. 'I'm proud to have a girl like that for a daughter, love. But a wonderful girl like that is no more than I'd expect with a mother like you.'

She had been planning to read bits of the letter to Amelia and Jenny once they'd chatted for a little but as soon as Amelia started to tell of Jenny's present predicament she realized that that must take first priority.

'It would never have occurred to me to ask this . . .' Jenny took over from Amelia in a faltering voice, 'but Amelia thought . . . Amelia wondered if you could perhaps put us up here for a time. Just until I found a flat or some place of my own.'

Hazel took both women aback by immediately crying out, 'What a splendid idea! Daniel and I are off to America in a couple of days to Rowan's wedding. You will be company for Milly. Oh, she will be pleased. You see, Rowan wrote in her last letter that she and Steve were going to get married. They're back in Nashville, thank goodness, and Steve has resumed work at the university.'

'Oh Hazel,' Jenny said, with tears in her eyes, 'I do love you!'

'My dear,' Hazel said, obviously touched and near to tears herself. Then suddenly she brightened again. 'I know what you need right now, lots of hugs, as Rebecca would say.' And laughing both she and Amelia pounced on Jenny and hugged her enthusiastically.

Once back in her seat again Hazel said, 'Give me tomorrow to finish packing and get everything organized here. Then you and the children can move in the day after. I'll arrange everything with Milly before I go.'

'Oh Hazel,' Jenny repeated helplessly.

'I knew Hazel wouldn't let you down,' Amelia said with great thankfulness in her voice. 'I just knew it!'

They sang Hazel's praises all the way back to the west end. Jenny felt quite faint and feverish with excitement.

410

She had to link arms with Amelia and lean heavily on her, especially going up the stairs to Amelia's flat.

The children were relieved that she had managed to fix up a place not too near Queens Drive but still on the south side of the city, close enough to their friends. Harry who had been waiting with Dode and Rose was pleased that she wouldn't have to live too far from him.

'By the way,' Dode said, 'that man phoned.'

The full force of Jenny's distress returned.

'You mean Al Gregson?'

Dode usually referred to him as 'that man'. Neither of the children seemed sure what to think of him. They'd met him a couple of times now. Dode had looked awkward and hadn't said much, either while Gregson was there or afterwards.

'Well?' Jenny had asked them after the first time, 'What do you think of mum's friend? Do you like him?'

'He's very handsome,' Rose admitted.

'He's all right, I suppose,' Dode said. Then, 'Dad used to be all right.'

'What did he say?' Jenny asked now. 'What did you tell him?'

Dode shrugged. 'Nothing. He said he'd phone back.'

When the phone rang some time later Amelia let Jenny answer it, thinking it would be Gregson. But it was Joe. After standing silently holding the phone for a minute Jenny said, 'Did you actually think I'd be waiting for you after . . . after how you behaved?'

Then after another pause while she tried not to listen to what he was saying, 'Joe, how plain must I be? I'm never coming back to you. There's someone else. I'm in love with another man. But even if there wasn't anyone else I still would never consider having any more to do with you. Now, once and for all, goodbye!'

'I'll kill him.' She caught the words before she had the chance to replace the receiver. They were said with chilling quietness. 'If you so much as look at that bastard again I'll find him and I'll kill him.'

411

'What's wrong?' Amelia came over and helped Jenny into a chair.

'It was Joe. He says he's going to kill Al.'

'Oh, Mummy,' Rose said. 'I'm frightened. Is daddy going to kill us too?'

Harry squared his broad shoulders. 'Don't worry, Rosie. He'd better not lay a finger on you again.'

'It's all right, darling,' Jenny managed. 'Look, why don't you and Dode and Harry go across to the Salon. Didn't I hear one of you mention about a good film being on there?'

'Oh, yeah.' Harry was enthusiastic. 'It's supposed to be a right laugh, it'll cheer us up.'

After they had gone Amelia said, 'What are you going to do about Al?'

Jenny took a deep breath in an attempt to keep tears at bay. 'I knew it was too good to be true. Rebecca spoke about retribution. Well, I guess this is it.'

'What do you mean?'

'Al keeps asking about our future together. But we have no future together. Somehow I always knew it.'

'He loves you.'

'I know. And because I love him I must give him up. I wouldn't want to live if anything happened to him because of me.'

'Oh Jenny,' Amelia said, staring in wretched uncertainty at her friend, 'I don't know what to say.'

'Have you any whisky or brandy in the house?'

'Brandy. I'll pour a couple of glasses. I could do with something myself.'

It was while she was pouring it that the phone rang again.

'Oh dear.' Amelia hurried over to Jenny with a glass slopping with the amber liquid. 'That'll be Al now. Here, drink this.' Jenny swallowed down a mouthful. Then took another deep breath before lifting the phone.

'Is there something wrong, honey?' Al asked. 'When I couldn't get you at Rebecca's –'

'I'm moving from Rebecca's.'

'Where to?'

'That needn't concern you.'

'What the hell do you mean by that? I'm going to be in Glasgow tomorrow. I'll come straight to Amelia's and meet you there.'

'No, I won't be at Amelia's. And I don't want to see you again. Anywhere. I've been thinking things over and that's what I've decided. I don't want to see you again! I mean it Al. It's definitely over between us.'

She hung up while he was still stunned into silence.

62

When Jenny had first told Rebecca that she was looking for a flat and intended to move out as soon as she'd found one, Rebecca had been so grimly, so desperately determined to stop Jenny going, that Jenny thought Rebecca was going somehow to physically prevent her from leaving. She had had momentary visions of being forced into the upstairs cupboard of a room in which Hazel had once been incarcerated. As it had turned out, Rebecca had kept emotionally battering her into a corner. Every type of emotional blackmail had been used. She had been made to feel guilty and ungrateful and cruel and selfish after all Rebecca had 'sacrificed' for her. She had been made to feel helpless because Rebecca'd said that she was a victim born and bred. She had been made to feel fear because Rebecca had warned her about what Joe would do to her and the children. Having had to go through all this hadn't helped to quell the nervousness and apprehension that buzzed like a mosquito at the back of Jenny's mind. She wondered if she'd ever be free of anxiety. It had become like a chronic illness, she'd suffered from it for so long now. Even while she had been happy with Gregson, even when she had been lying in his arms, it had still been there preventing her from relaxing completely.

Even now when she'd successfully managed to do everything she had to do to protect Gregson and the children she still felt apprehensive as well as broken-hearted.

'You'll feel better once you're safely settled in at Hazel's,' Amelia soothed. 'You're not able to think straight just now and I don't blame you.'

'I'm not looking forward to going to Rebecca's tomorrow to collect my things.'

'I could go for them,' Amelia offered. Jenny shook her head.

'It's kind of you, Amelia but I really need to do my own packing. Anyway, I feel bad enough about leaving Rebecca without chickening out on saying goodbye. It couldn't have come at a worse time, though. Did you hear that Sadie's husband died? She's gone back to her own room and kitchen flat.'

'Poor Rebecca,' Amelia said. 'She never could bear to be on her own.'

Rebecca would think everyone had deserted her. Thinking of Rebecca helped to keep Jenny's mind off Al Gregson. She couldn't bear the pain of thinking about him. She concentrated desperately on Rebecca. Rebecca could be in a state of nerves now. She could be in a state of collapse. Who was bothering, who had ever bothered about her?

'It's time I acted like a proper friend,' Jenny told herself. 'Time I began to think of Rebecca instead of myself for a change.'

She would try to reassure Rebecca that she still had her love and gratitude and admiration. She would tell her that she'd still help with the cooking for any special events at the refuge whenever she could. She would invite Rebecca to visit her at Hazel's place as often as she liked – Hazel would welcome her too, she felt sure. She would assure Rebecca that there would also be a welcome for her at Amelia's flat.

Next day was Saturday and she set out for the south side early in the afternoon. She got off the bus at the Langside Halls but crossed to the other side of Langside Avenue to keep well away from the park gates.

Battlefield House, blackened with age, looked strange perched at the top of the hill. The sun was reflected by its windows making them glint slyly across at the monument. Jenny still had her key and as she went in she called Rebecca's name. She went around opening doors and saying 'Rebecca, are you there?' But the house was empty. Jenny felt worried. She tried to tell herself that probably Rebecca was finding solace in sunbathing in the park; she was an avid sun-worshipper. Her skin always became nut-brown in summer; her eyes looked darker too. Yes, that's where she'd be. Jenny forced herself to start packing but all the time her worries kept increasing. She couldn't just leave without seeing her. Poor Rebecca, she kept thinking. Poor Rebecca.

She wondered if she dare risk looking for her in the park. The least she could do was try to offer the woman a little comfort. Hadn't Rebecca given her comfort when she'd needed it? She knew Rebecca's favourite sheltered spot – it was quite near the monument end, only a few minutes beyond the railings. She didn't think there would be any chance of Joe seeing her, not at this end of the park and especially for all the time it would take. Anyway, from what she could remember of his shift rota, this was his Saturday off. Reassured by the memory she entered through the gate opposite Battlefield House. In a matter of minutes she was approaching the clearing when to her surprise she saw through the trees, not only Rebecca but three other women in the eccentric-looking poses of T'ai Chi. The women were all pale-faced, tense, and fearful-looking. One had a black and swollen eye. Another had horrific bruises on both arms. The third looked like someone who'd just escaped from Belsen concentration camp.

Rebecca had never looked more regal and dramatic in her scarlet caftan edged with gold braid that glistened in the sun, and her glossy bush of ebony hair and her great lustrous eyes.

All at once Jenny felt lost, cut off from both past and future. She turned helplessly away. The future she'd hoped for with Gregson had been denied her. There seemed suddenly no escape, no safety anywhere. A mixture of deep depression and inevitability dragged at her heels as she slowly made her way back to the west end. But even deeper and beyond her depression was her longing for Gregson. The idea that he would think she had just used him, played him along until she fixed herself up in a comfortable place, burned like a hot poker in her brain, fevering her.

She was so obsessed with the pain of thinking of him it did not register for a few seconds that in fact she was actually seeing Gregson in the flesh. He was standing outside the entrance to Amelia's close in Byres Road. She stopped, alert now with terror. What if Joe had seen her and followed her? What if he, too, was waiting and watching for her? At any moment she could find herself playing the role of a Judas, pointing Gregson out, signing his death warrant. She turned to run but Gregson was too quick for her. Before she had covered a few yards he had grabbed her and jerked her into his arms. For a minute, oblivious of all the people passing around them in the busy road, they clung to each other.

'What the hell do you think you're playing at?' Gregson said. The urgency of Jenny's fear overcame her again.

'We mustn't be seen together, Al. Joe's threatened to kill you.'

The words were hardly out of her mouth when the sound of a gun being fired exploded through the summer air. Almost simultaneously people began screaming. People were running about in panic looking for shelter. Too stunned to move at first Jenny stared at Gregson. He was lying very still at her feet.

She cradled him in her arms in the ambulance on the way to the hospital. He was still alive and before they took him away from her he had regained consciousness and although unable to move and obviously in pain he had managed a ghost of a grin and a reassuring wink. It was so typical of his ebullient, fighting spirit that she thought she would die with the pain of loving him. She smiled in return, however, and even managed to blow him a kiss as they wheeled the trolley away down the corridor of the hospital towards the operating theatre. It was only after it disappeared from sight that her legs gave way and she had to be helped to a chair and given a cup of tea.

'Oh, please God, please, please God,' she kept praying, 'let him live.'

She didn't know how long she sat in the hospital waiting room repeating the words over and over and over in her mind. It must have been hours because she became vaguely aware of darkening windows. Then, at last a doctor and a nurse came towards her. She froze. She couldn't weep. Then the doctor told her that they'd successfully removed the bullet and Gregson was going to be all right. Then the tears came. She sobbed helplessly with relief.

They told her he was sleeping and she ought to go home and get some sleep too. She would be able to see him in the morning. They called a taxi. She leaned back in its dark anonymity and relaxed in sweet relief and thankfulness. But soon other worries began to crowd her mind. How were the children? What had happened to Joe? Had the police found him? She had a vague recollection now of a policeman being at the hospital. She found herself beginning to tremble and by the time she was climbing the stairs towards Amelia's flat she had to cling on to the banister for support. She took an agonizingly long time fumbling for the key Amelia had given her.

'Is that you, Mummy?' Rose cried out immediately the door opened.

'Yes, darling, it's all right.'

Amelia, Rose and Dode all came running to embrace her.

Amelia said, 'Oh, Jenny, I've been so anxious about you.'

'What's happened to dad?' Dode asked and Jenny could hear the anguish in his voice. 'The police were here looking for him. They're outside watching and waiting now. There's others over at Queens Drive.'

'I don't know, son, but he didn't kill Al. Al's going to be all right.'

'But what about dad?'

She shook her head. 'I don't know. We'll just have to hope and pray that he'll be all right too.'

'I'll make some cocoa and bring it through to the sitting room,' Amelia said.

In the sitting room they huddled together round the electric fire sipping the hot drinks. The thought of going to bed to sleep was impossible.

'Dad hasn't been well,' Dode said eventually. 'He hasn't been well for a long time. Nobody helped him.'

'Your mum always did her best,' Amelia said.

But had she? Jenny thought miserably. Maybe she should have tried harder. Maybe she could have persuaded Joe to go to a psychiatrist. She had a sudden heartbreaking vision of Joe when they'd first been married. He was watching her down on her knees lighting the fire. He had such a wistful look in his gaunt young face. 'I've never been so happy,' he'd said, 'as I am at this moment.' What had he suffered before that had made him feel so grateful for that ordinary moment of domesticity with his young wife? Poor Joe.

'He wasn't always like that,' she said. 'The war has a lot to answer for.'

'Somebody should have helped him,' Dode said.

'Son, try not to feel upset. There was certainly nothing you could do.'

'How can I not feel upset?' Dode's voice loudened. 'What a bloody ridiculous thing to say. He's my dad. There's lots of times we got on all right. Lots of times he was good to me.'

'I know, son. I'm sorry.'

'Don't be sorry for me,' Dode said bitterly. 'Be sorry for him.'

She cupped her hand over her eyes. 'I am, Dode, believe me, I've been sorry for him for years. But that doesn't help. I loved your dad very much but that didn't help either. In a way I still love him and always will. But I couldn't go on living with him the way things were. I just couldn't, Dode. None of us could.'

'No,' Amelia said. 'You mustn't blame yourselves.'

They sat without speaking again for a few minutes until the silence was broken by the ringing of the front doorbell. They gazed in wide-eyed apprehension at each other. Nobody moved. The bell once more echoed loudly through the house.

'You stay here,' Amelia said. 'I'll go.' Then reaching the front door she called out, 'Who is it?'

'The police,' a voice answered.

As she opened the door Jenny came running to her side. 'What's happened?' she asked anxiously. 'Have you found my husband?' The policemen followed the two women into the sitting room.

'No. We've been watching this place and the Queens Drive flat but there's no sign of him. We've also alerted police cars cruising all over the city. We thought you might be able to help.'

'In what way?'

'Do you know of any place where he might have gone? You should know how he thinks better than anyone. Try to imagine what he might do, what his feeling might be now. It might give us a clue.'

Miserably she thought of Joe being hounded, having to hide. Then suddenly she knew.

'He'll be in the park,' she said, 'Queens Park.' He would be hiding in the jungle of foliage. He would be lost in time. He would be listening in the darkness for his Japanese tormentors. She experienced an overwhelming compassion for him.

'I'll come with you,' she said.

The policemen exchanged looks and Amelia's face creased with anxiety. 'Oh Jenny, do you think that's wise?'

'I may be able to be of further help,' Jenny insisted.

'I'll fetch my coat. Dode and Rose, you stay here with Amelia until I get back.'

The high wrought-iron gates at the Victoria Road end of the park slowly creaked open.

'I'm still not convinced that it's a good idea for you to come with us, Mrs Thornton,' the police officer said. 'Your husband is armed and dangerous. For all we know you might be the next target he has in mind.'

Jenny shook her head. 'I told you, I don't believe he's thinking of me at all now.'

'I know what you told me, Mrs Thornton. It doesn't follow that you're right.'

'Anyway, I can't see I'm in any danger surrounded by so many policemen and police marksmen. I just want to try and prevent any more shooting. I don't want anyone else to get hurt.'

'My men will have to spread out. This is a very large area to cover. I don't suppose you've any specific ideas of where in the park he might be?'

'It'll be where there's most trees and thick foliage. There's a wooded area on the south side.'

In a matter of minutes they had reached the area and the policemen were fanning out around the perimeter. The police officer held a loudspeaker to his mouth and his voice sounded strangely hollow as he called out.

'We know you're in there, Mr Thornton. The area is surrounded by police marksmen. The most sensible thing for you to do now is give yourself up.'

Jenny put out her hand for the loudspeaker.

'Please, let me try.' Then she called through it. 'Please Joe, for my sake and the children's. We care about you. We don't want you to get into any more trouble. We know you need help. We'll try to help you. I promise!'

She listened intently in the silence that followed. She thought she heard a rustling but it was the police marksmen moving stealthily forward.

'No, wait,' she cried out. But it was too late. Joe had

421

shot at one of them and another had immediately felled Joe. He was dead before she got to him. Kneeling by his side she could see him clearly by the light of the moon. His thin face had a strange luminous quality.

And it had the same look of gratitude and vulnerability that she remembered when they'd first loved and lived together.

'Oh, my poor Joe. My poor love,' she said, and wept for him and all lost loves, and thought, Oh, hasn't war a lot to answer for.